OXFORD WORLD'S CLASSICS

ELIZABETH GASKELL

Cranford

Edited by
ELIZABETH PORGES WATSON

With a new Introduction and Notes by
CHARLOTTE MITCHELL

OXFORD
UNIVERSITY PRESS

OXFORD

UNIVERSITY PRESS

Great Clarendon Street, Oxford OX2 6DP

Oxford University Press is a department of the University of Oxford.
It furthers the University's objective of excellence in research, scholarship,
and education by publishing worldwide in

Oxford New York

Athens Auckland Bangkok Bogotá Buenos Aires Calcutta
Cape Town Chennai Dar es Salaam Delhi Florence Hong Kong Istanbul
Karachi Kuala Lumpur Madrid Melbourne Mexico City Mumbai
Nairobi Paris São Paulo Singapore Taipei Tokyo Toronto Warsaw

with associated companies in Berlin Ibadan

Oxford is a registered trade mark of Oxford University Press
in the UK and in certain other countries

Published in the United States
by Oxford University Press Inc., New York

First published as an Oxford World's Classics paperback 1998
Reissued 2008

British Library Cataloguing in Publication Data

Data available

ISBN 978–0–19–953827–0

1

Printed in Great Britain by
Clays Ltd, St Ives plc

CONTENTS

INTRODUCTION

CRANFORD's status among Elizabeth Gaskell's novels has shifted a good deal in the century and a half since it was published. It is still perhaps the best-known work of its author, who published five other novels, including three 'social problem' novels, controversial in their day, a historical novel, and one, the last, unfinished, a domestic realist social comedy. She also wrote many short stories and a major biography of her friend Charlotte Brontë. But is *Cranford* a novel at all? What relation does it bear to Gaskell's other works? After her death it became by far her most famous and successful book, frequently celebrated for its inimitable feminine charm, sometimes in contrast to other novels by her. More recently, this characteristic has become less appealing to commentators (and the political and social agendas of some of her other novels more so), and those seeking to defend *Cranford* have dwelt on its dark side and emphasized its exploration of sexual politics.

One question which has arisen again and again for those looking at Gaskell's fiction is: how deep is the split between those novels, such as *Mary Barton, North and South,* and *Ruth,* which openly address painful and divisive subjects like industrial relations and social morality, and works such as *Cranford* and *Cousin Phillis,* which apparently do not? Is it possible to admire both kinds of work? Is it appropriate to read *Cranford* in the light of Gaskell's other fiction? The place of *Cranford* in Gaskell's literary career, its relationship to her other books and their themes, and her changing literary reputation in the twentieth century are all relevant to its assessment.[1] A book which has variously been read as an exercise in cloying nostalgia, a satire on frustrated spinsterhood, and a celebration of female separatism defying the patriarchy, has been curiously receptive to contradictory readings for a hundred and fifty years.

The details of *Cranford*'s appearance in the world are important. It was first published in one volume in June 1853, but had earlier appeared irregularly as a series of stories in *Household Words,* a

---

[1] There is an excellent survey of twentieth-century interpretations of Gaskell's work in Patsy Stoneman, *Elizabeth Gaskell* (Brighton: Harvester, 1987), 2–19.

weekly magazine edited by Charles Dickens, between December 1851 and May 1853 (see Note on the Text). The present edition also includes a later story, 'The Cage at Cranford', published in Dickens's second magazine *All the Year Round* in November 1863, and an earlier, non-fictional article, 'The Last Generation in England', published in the American *Sartain's Union Magazine* in July 1849, which is generally recognized as drawing on some of the same material as *Cranford*, and as differing from it in significant ways. When Gaskell published the first story, Chapters 1 and 2 of the present book, she had no intention of continuing to write about Cranford.[2] She did not subscribe to *Household Words*, does not seem to have kept a copy of her manuscript, and could not, late on, remember how many sketches she had written.[3] The irregularity with which the stories appeared is quite marked; there was a gap of eight months between the appearance of the present chapters eight and nine, and it has often been pointed out that the earlier part of the book is rather different in mood.

In some lists of Gaskell's works *Cranford* appears after *Ruth*, not unreasonably since *Ruth* was published in January and *Cranford* in June 1853. But the actual composition of the two books ran in tandem. *Ruth*, the story of an innocent young working-class girl seduced by an upper-class man, seems to have been begun by March 1851, and by November Gaskell had almost finished the first volume.[4] But during October she went to stay in Knutsford with her uncle Dr Peter Holland, which revived memories of her childhood. From the age of 13 months, after her mother's death, she had been brought up by her aunts, Hannah Lumb and Abigail Holland, in this Cheshire town, south of Manchester, with only occasional visits to her father and stepmother in London. She had already drawn on her memories of that all-female household and

[2] 'The beginning of "Cranford" was *one* paper in "Household Words", and I never meant to write more, so killed Capt Brown very much against my will.' (*The Letters of Mrs Gaskell*, ed. J. A. V. Chapple and Arthur Pollard, Manchester: Manchester University Press, 1966, 748.)

[3] 'I seldom see the Household Words, and I do not now remember if I have written six or seven Cranford papers . . . and I do not know how large a vol it would make . . .' (Letter to John Forster, 3 May 1953, quoted in Dorothy W. Collin, 'The Composition and Publication of Elizabeth Gaskell's *Cranford*', *Bulletin of the John Rylands University Library of Manchester*, 69 (Autumn 1986), 64.

[4] Jenny Uglow, *Elizabeth Gaskell: A Habit of Stories* (London and Boston: Faber and Faber, 1993), 278.

the old-fashioned customs of the town in 'The Last Generation in England' and in a story about a young doctor entitled 'Mr Harrison's Confessions', published in early 1851.[5] She returned to Manchester, where she had lived since her marriage in 1832, and sent the first *Cranford* story to Dickens for *Household Words* in December; it was followed by three other stories, now Chapters 3–8. Between April and December 1852 she returned to the difficult and controversial work on *Ruth*. She knew well from having published *Mary Barton* what it was like to be the woman author of a book attacked on political and ethical grounds; she knew from discussing *Ruth* with her friends and relations that she was unlikely to escape criticism for treating the taboo subject of sexual transgression in fiction; in October 1852 she wrote to her daughter Marianne that 'I dislike its being published so much, I sh[oul]d not wonder if I put it off another year.'[6] But it was at the printers' by Christmas, and Gaskell went back to publishing more tales of Cranford, this time wrapping up the plot to provide a suitable close to a collection in volume form.

When *Ruth* came out it was greeted with the expected storm of protest (though there was much praise as well, and sales were good), and many readers agreed with Harriet Martineau in comparing it unfavourably with the tales in *Household Words*: ' "Ruth" ... all strewn with beauties as it is ... is sadly feeble and *wrong*, I think. ... What a beautiful "Cranford" Mrs Gaskell has given us again.'[7] Martineau does not say, though after her other critics did, that Gaskell had overstepped her range in trying to write about society's treatment of sexual sin, and would do better to keep to ladylike material of which she was fully in command.[8] In

---

[5] 'Mr. Harrison's Confessions', *Ladies' Companion and Monthly Magazine*, 3 (1 Feb. 1851), 1–11; (1 Mar. 1851), 49–56; (1 Apr. 1851), 97–106.

[6] *Letters*, 204.

[7] *Harriet Martineau's Letters to Fanny Wedgwood*, ed. Elisabeth Sanders Arbuckle (Stanford, Calif: Stanford University Press, 1983), 125, cited by Uglow, *Elizabeth Gaskell*, 341. The letter is dated 11 Apr. 1853 and probably refers to 'Stopped Payment at Cranford'.

[8] For example David Cecil in *Early Victorian Novelists: Essays in Revaluation* (London: Constable, 1934), 235, argues that she 'dealt with subjects outside her imaginative range...' Sociological subjects for one thing... It would have been impossible for her... to have found a subject less suited to her talents... neither domestic nor pastoral... [giving] scope neither to the humorous, the pathetic nor the charming.'

the late twentieth century, we are still asking whether the composition of *Cranford* should be seen as complementary to that of *Ruth*, or as a retreat from it. Some have disliked it as a submissive and conservative book, which perpetuates an image of single women as muddle-headed, incompetent, quarrelsome, and eccentric. It has also been argued that in fact *Cranford* continues the arguments of Gaskell's other fiction in another form, demanding reconciliation between estranged groups in the community, emphasizing the role of women and the family in that task of restoration.

Thus *Cranford* comes to us possessing several problematic features, which are also connected to its strengths. Its inconsequential structure, its uncontroversial material, and its accumulation of apparently trivial detail create uncertainty about whether it is to be taken seriously. On one level the modern anxiety about *Cranford* is an inverted version of the Victorian anxiety about *Ruth*. No less than Gaskell and her contemporaries, we assume a gendered hierarchy of value. The public world of social reform is still more important than the private female sphere, and a novel like *Cranford* which parades its absorption in the female world, though condemned as marginal instead of celebrated for its feminine decorum, is being judged in terms of the same opposition. Gaskell (unusual among Victorian women novelists in being a happy wife and mother) seeks to explore in *Cranford* some aspects of female life from an unexpected side, through a comic fantasy of conformity, not a tragic fantasy of rebellion, by caricaturing the doctrine of separate spheres. And the very unexpectedness of this approach makes it more challenging to modern feminist reading than the great Victorian novels of female rebellion, such as *Jane Eyre*, *The Mill on the Floss*, or *The Story of an African Farm*. Yet just as the history of women cannot be confined to the history of their emancipation, equally there are areas of feminine experience other than rebellion which are fit subjects for fictional treatment. The pleasantness of *Cranford*, the sense in which the book, like the place, is a safe feminine territory to which the reader may retreat from the disagreeable world, is paradigmatic of its relation to Gaskell's painful, offensive work on *Ruth*. Yet *Cranford* is also explicitly about feminine decorum, and its limits, and the way in which the external world necessarily impinges even on Cranford and its inhabitants. In the character of the narrator, Mary Smith, Gaskell analyses the female predicament as one of multiple loyalties and sympathies. The book's narrative structure ceaselessly emphasizes the issue of interpretation. This is no doubt an additional reason for the wide variety of readings which have been given.

Gaskell refers explicitly in her letters to the difficulty of reconciling her different duties and desires:

one of my 'Mes,' for I have a great number, and that's the plague. One of my mes is, I do believe, a true Christian—(only people call her socialist and communist), another of my mes is a wife and mother . . . Then again I've another self with a full taste for beauty . . . How am I to reconcile all these warring members? I try to drown myself (my *first* self,) by saying it's Wm [her husband, William] who is to decide on all these things, and his feeling it right ought to be my rule. And so it is—only that does not quite do.[9]

She is not talking about her authorship here, but worrying about the ethics of doing up an expensive new house while conscious of the poverty of her working-class neighbours. That tension between public and private life (her socialist self and her housekeeping self) merges with another opposition between her independent judgement and her wifely deference to her husband's opinion. Both the inner voice of her conscience and the outer one of other people's opinion matter deeply to her. It is this struggle between the warring members which is explored in *Cranford* through the figure of Mary Smith, who gives us the town always in perspective, the old through the eyes of the young, the Cranfordians through the eyes of Drumble, Miss Matty as Mary's father would see her. But she is also lovingly defensive of the town and its inhabitants, arguing for a kind of beauty in housekeeping and self-sacrifice. This ambivalence is at the heart of the book.

The opening tale, which is complete in itself and ends with the death of Miss Jenkyns, sets up the comic idea of the exclusively female town. Considerable emphasis is laid on the characteristic faults of women: opinionated ignorance, inquisitiveness, and a snobbish obsession with etiquette. Captain Brown, a man, a war veteran, and a railway worker, symbolically opposes the values of the ladies of *Cranford*. He comes from the world of war and history, and he is bringing the railway (and hence industrialization, change, and the modern world) nearer to Cranford. This opposition is underlined by a literary dispute over the respective merits of Dickens and Dr Johnson, in which the first stands for vitality,

[9] Letter to Eliza Fox (?Apr. 1850), *Letters*, 108.

originality, spontaneity, modernity, humour, and the spirit of carnival, and the latter is used (most unfairly) as a straw man, associated with life-denying rules, formality, and pomposity. Yet
Captain Brown, though he possesses characteristic male virtues,
such as bravery and 'excellent masculine common sense', is also one
of several people in the novel who cross the boundaries of gender:
nurturing his daughter, sound on domestic detail (boot-blacking,
fire-shovels), kind to aged women and babies. He unites male and
female, where the Jenkyns sisters—Deborah, the prophet of the
rigid rules of the dead past, and Matilda, the soft, submissive, and
compassionate—represent, on one level, polarized genders. When
the crisis of his death comes Miss Jenkyns withdraws her opposition to him, takes on his role as masculine protector of his daughters, forgets her attempt to hold back the course of time ('his wet
boots on the new carpet', p. 16), and encourages Major Gordon's
courtship. She may ostensibly hold out against Dickens, but in
playing Cupid to Miss Jessie's fruitful marriage she presides over
the union of male and female, assists the birth of the future generation, and approves the triumph of romance over reason. Thus
the story is underpinned by a series of gendered oppositions, and its
plot is resolved in sexual union, symbolizing the reunion of the
community. Gaskell continues to use this device, with variations,
throughout the book. But the effects are evocative rather than
diagrammatic. Past, for example, is repeatedly opposed to present,
but the past is sometimes male (old Mr Jenkyns versus youth) and
sometimes female (Cranford versus Drumble). In this world of
serious comic fantasy, the dangers lie in fanaticism and rigidity,
which may afflict either sex.

In the second story the shadowy figure of Miss Matty moves to
centre stage, where she remains throughout the book. Now the
autocratic elder sister is dead, Miss Matty has taken on her role of
upholding the rules and values of the past: 'Miss Jenkyns's rules
were made more stringent than ever' (p. 26). Yet, like the first, the
second story hinges on a change of mind: Miss Matty decides after
all to let her maid have a boyfriend. Martha's story frames the
unfolding of Miss Matty's own romance, nipped in the bud because
her lover, although prosperous and attractive, did not rank as a
gentleman. Her father's and sister's respect for empty status is
opposed to Holbrook's contempt for 'every refinement which had
not its root deep down in humanity' (p. 29). In his healthy appetite

for food ('the peas were going wholesale into his capacious mouth', p. 33) we see an image of sexual appetite, unhampered by social shibboleths. The conservatism of his household arrangements is contrasted with Mary Smith's own attempts, for no good reason, to update Miss Matty's dining habits. Mr Holbrook shares something of Captain Brown's healthy blindness to the social minutiae which obsess the ladies of Cranford, and he also shares his openness to imaginative literature. Tennyson, the modern poet, is praised for a literary realism which enables him to teach something about the natural world even to an observant man who has spent his life farming (p. 35), confirming in literary-critical terms the story's assumption that it is better that reality and the sensual world should defeat culture and formality. And Mr Holbrook's journey to Paris, precipitated by his encounter with Miss Matty, symbolizes his freedom to range through the imaginative as through the actual world, while her upbringing has confined her forever, culturally as well as physically, to the world of Cranford. To her the reminder of the lost opportunity of marriage and motherhood, represented by the idyllic, fruitful farm, brings a sense of loss which issues in the decision not to play the same role as her father and sister: ' "God forbid!... that I should grieve any young hearts." ' (p. 40) Yet although the novel makes us feel the poignancy of Miss Matty's life, the sense in which it has been wasted, particularly that it symbolizes the energy of youth and sexual desire being sacrificed to dead social codes, it also asks from the reader some respect (probably especially difficult for the modern reader to give) for the value of such self-sacrifice. Gaskell, and her assumed audience, have more time for the virtues of self-restraint, and less for self-determination, than most modern readers, also for filial duty when weighed against sexual fulfilment. Miss Jenkyns exclaiming to her sister that 'if she had a hundred offers, she never would marry and leave my father' is made faintly ridiculous by Miss Matty's 'It was not very likely she would have so many... but it was not less to her credit to say so' (p. 58). But Miss Jessie Brown's decision in similar circumstances is definitely the right, because the unselfish, one. Gaskell does not neglect to mock, but it would be a misreading to lose altogether the book's sense of self-abnegation as a peculiarly feminine virtue.

Hilary M. Schor remarks that *Cranford* is 'most often praised for its own quality of loving nostalgia; but what it in fact registers is panic about change'.[10] People of Gaskell's generation had lived through a revolution in transport and communications, which is represented in *Cranford* by the railway which runs over Captain Brown and the penny post which has made Miss Jenkyns's carefully composed and elaborately crossed letters redolent of a past age. Both Thackeray and Dickens repeatedly refer in their fiction to the contrast between the stage-coaches lumbering across England in their childhoods, and the railways circulating newspapers and correspondence from the 1830s.[11] Like all improvements in communication, this tended to iron out regional and local differences, and the impulse which motivates *Cranford* is partly derived from the sense that the peculiarities of provincial society will soon evaporate under the scrutiny of the wider world (see, for instance, 'The Last Generation', p. 163). Its small history is being recorded before it is swallowed up in the values and discourse of Drumble. Just as Miss Matty and Mary Smith, in the third episode of the book, read old letters before casting them into the fire, so the book passes on to the next generation small fragmentary pictures of the past, strange and evocative in smell and shape, unimportant except in that they were once part of the texture of everyday life, an everyday life which no longer exists and cannot be recreated. This is not a shallow nostalgia, but a reminder to the ignorant arrogance of the present that it too is transitory. Gaskell spent her childhood among people much older than herself. Her mother had been 40 when the baby Elizabeth was born in 1810, and died the following year; her sisters, Hannah and Abigail, who brought the child up, were themselves already adult at the turn of the eighteenth century; their parents had been married in 1763. (In the first, *Household Words* version, Miss Matty's parents were married in 1764.) Thus Gaskell, brought up by elderly women, writing in her early forties, was in much the situation as Walter Scott (1771–1832) writing about the '45 rebellion in *Waverley, or, 'Tis Sixty Years Since* (1814), which he called an 'attempt of mine to embody some traits of those characters and manners peculiar to Scotland, the last

[10] Hilary M. Schor, *Scheherazade in the Marketplace: Elizabeth Gaskell and the Victorian Novel* (New York and Oxford: Oxford University Press, 1992), 85.

[11] For an account of the analogous contrast between pre- and post-railway worlds in Gaskell's 'A Dark Night's Work' (1863), see John Sutherland, 'Two-timing Novelists', in his *Is Heathcliff a Murderer? Puzzles in Nineteenth-Century Literature* (Oxford: Oxford University Press, World's Classics, 1996), 128–33.

remnants of which vanished during my own youth'.[12] *Cranford* is only one of many nineteenth-century novels which follow *Waverley* in using the past generation to reflect on the present one, reminding the reader that human emotion and human behaviour are invariably conditioned by the particular cultural and historical context in which they arise.

Peter Keating has drawn attention to the cult of the novel at the end of the nineteenth century and the beginning of the twentieth, and argued that it was during this period that many readers had their sense of the novel falsified by pretty illustrated editions, packaging the book as nostalgia for the supposed innocence of the past.[13] (Modern paperback covers have continued this tradition.) In fact, of course, Gaskell's use of time and her analysis of the way the past affects the present, is sophisticated, and is one of the book's main themes. *Cranford* has a complicated time-scheme. It is set in an approximation of the present, the 1840s or early 1850s, but the first chapter, before Miss Jenkyns's death, seems to belong to the late 1830s. Chapters 3 and 4 take us back to Miss Matty's love-affair, in the first decade of the nineteenth century. Her parents' love-letters, read in Chapter 5, take us back still further, to the 1770s. This chronology does not bear particularly close scrutiny, but it does not need to. The narrow skirts and leg-of-mutton sleeves which appear in the second paragraph of the book, comic survivals of older fashions, are developed by Gaskell, as the material evolves, into an analysis of the way fragments of the past survive, in habits of thought and in material debris, challenging the assumptions of the present. One of the most effective devices is her use of different points of view to give sudden shocking images of the passing of time:

it was 'the prettiest little baby that ever was seen. Dear mother, I wish you could see her! Without any parshality, I do think she will grow up a regular bewty!' I thought of Miss Jenkyns, grey, withered, and wrinkled; and I wondered if her mother had known her in the courts of heaven; and then I knew that she had, and that they stood there in angelic guise. (p. 44)

The reader is here made to feel three different sensations in rapid succession: intimacy with the long-dead mother's love for her

---

[12] Quoted in J. G. Lockhart, *Memoirs of the Life of Sir Walter Scott, Bart.*, 7 vols. (Edinburgh: Robert Cadell; London: John Murray, 1837–8), iii. 126.

[13] Introduction to *Cranford* (Harmondsworth: Penguin, 1976).

child, the poignancy of human mortality, and then, a sudden move to a vision *sub specie aeternitatis*, in which passing time is irrelevant. This small movement is one which recurs on a larger scale throughout the book: the trivial concerns of the ladies of Cranford, the sadness and waste of their lives, are found capable of generating love and goodwill, and, seen from a perspective in which all human concerns are trivial and ephemeral, their lives are still valuable.

Another brilliant moment of narrative irony is Miss Matty's comment: 'There were many old ladies living here then; we are principally ladies now, I know; but we are not so old as the ladies used to be when I was a girl' (p. 50). Fiction often opposes the interests of the old to those of the young, and the young normally win: the plot in which sexual desire conquers codes based on money and power is one of the commonest of all. *Cranford* deals with love and desire and money and power, but its approach is startlingly unusual. Though there are marriages, and children are born, and these events are used, in the customary way, to give closure to the narrative and a happy confidence in renewal to the reader, the main focus is on the feelings of the old. Miss Matty, at this point, feeling young and looking old, expresses a sense of the persistent importance of the old; she is not to be ignored because she is old, and old-fashioned, and comical. She is alive, though her clothes are out of date, and therefore not to be dismissed, although she too, when young, dismissed the old ladies of Cranford with the arrogance of youth.

It was in the third *Household Words* tale, now Chapters 5 and 6, originally entitled 'Memory at Cranford', that Gaskell introduced the character of Peter Jenkyns and fleshed out the personalities of the Rector and Mrs Jenkyns in relation to their children. And simultaneously the opposition between men and women in the book, which so far tended towards gentle mockery of the follies of the latter, alters in emphasis, and what one might term satire of the patriarchy emerges for the first time. The practical concerns of Miss Matty's mother and grandmother contrast with the pompous abstractions of the male letters. But, as before, the gender opposition is not straightforward. The Rector's love-letters have vivid humanity, and Miss Jenkyns's letters possess the male qualities of literariness and abstraction, except when she is frightened into direct description (p. 48). This is a recurring opposition in *Cranford*: 'My father's was just a man's letter; I mean it was very dull, and gave no information beyond that he was well, that they had had a good deal of rain, that trade was very stagnant, and there were many disagreeable rumours afloat' (p. 119). Miss Jenkyns writes a man's letter: 'Miss Matty humbly apologised for writing at the same time as her sister...but, in spite of a little bad spelling, Miss Matty's account gave me the best idea of the commotion occasioned by his lordship's visit...' (p. 13). 'Oh dear! how I wanted facts instead of reflections, before those letters were concluded!' (p. 47).

This distinction is one which Gaskell refers to in her own correspondence, demanding that her friend W. J. Fox tell her about his daughter's marriage: 'oh! do be a woman, and give me all possible details...'[14] This idea about the importance of trifles is developed on the one hand into a literary theory—the woman's-eye account gives a better insight into the fullness of things. This implicitly justifies the kind of book *Cranford* is and Gaskell's project in writing it. On the other hand the idea sustains a moral scheme in which loving-kindness and human community are expressed in small actions and attention to detail: 'I had often occasion to notice the use that was made of fragments and small opportunities in Cranford...Things that many would despise, and actions which it seemed scarcely worth while to perform, were all attended to in Cranford' (p. 15). Captain Brown, carrying the old woman's baked mutton (p. 10) and carving Miss Jenkyns a wooden fire-shovel (p. 11), is a true inhabitant of Cranford, and unites feminine and masculine virtues. Despised by the Cranford ladies for his lack of self-consciousness, he is in fact showing them how true virtue reveals itself not only in events which the outside world thinks important (such as saving Lord Mauleverer's life) but in details of that everyday life which is the special concern of women, because the outside world, of wars and history and politics, has no place for them. Soon after Peter Jenkyns is introduced he is explicitly aligned with this quality in Brown: ' "He was like dear Captain Brown in always being ready to help any old person or a child" ' (p. 50). But where Brown metaphorically takes on female characteristics Peter literally wears women's clothes in the attempt to puncture pomposity. After getting away with a practical joke which exposes his father's self-importance to no one but himself and the

---

[14] *Letters*, 540.

faithful Matty, he embarks on the fatal impersonation of Deborah, the sister who has internalized the father's values, and who has been shown as associated by both Peter and Matty with social inhibition and embargoes on the free play of the spirit. She has taken his place: 'Deborah was the favourite of her father, and when Peter disappointed him, she became his pride.' (p. 50) So he takes hers, imputing to her the extreme of womanly weakness; he shows her to the town, having succumbed to male sexual advances, rapt in maternal fondness (p. 52). He shows her, in fact, as Ruth. Although Miss Matty emphasizes his boyish failure to understand the appalling slur he is casting on his sister (' "he never thought of it as affecting Deborah" ' (p. 52)), although her account of the event foregrounds the male violence of the father, the scene is infinitely suggestive of the gendered rivalry of brother and sister. It recalls, in fact, the anecdote of early nineteenth-century Knutsford life in Gaskell's non-fiction account, 'The Last Generation in England':

hanging on the outskirts of society were a set of young men, ready for mischief and brutality, and every now and then dropping off the pit's brink into crime.... They would stop ladies returning from the card-parties... and whip them; literally whip them as you whip a little child; until administering such chastisement to a good, precise old lady of high family, 'my brother, the magistrate,' came forward and put down such proceedings with a high hand. (p. 162)

In *Cranford* the implied class antagonism, issuing in sexual brutality, is domesticated: Peter pillories his bossy sister; the Rector flogs his transvestite son. In *Mary Barton* Gaskell had linked the breakdown of working-class family relationships to the outbreak of class warfare; in *Cranford*, and especially in this pivotal tale, her subject is the middle-class family's capacity to hurt itself by adhering to inflexible social forms. But it is a curiously suggestive incident. One can interpret the scene by focusing on Mr Jenkyns's male violence, flogging his son, and thus, ultimately, killing his wife. But can it be right to see Peter's act as simply an outbreak of carnival spirit, misunderstood in Cranford? It seems, somehow, more sinister than that. And it is striking how the mother's death and Peter's reappearance are used to mark the eclipse of Deborah:

She was such a daughter to my father...she read book after book, and wrote, and copied... She could do many more things than my poor mother could...But he missed my mother sorely...[When Peter came home] he and my father were such friends!...Deborah used to smile...and say she was quite put in a corner. (p. 58–9)

Deborah, having identified herself totally with her father's interests, cannot complement him, can be neither his wife nor his son. On his death her anomalous situation in society is symbolized by her being stranded in the no man's land of Cranford: 'our circumstances were changed; and...we had to come to this small house...Poor Deborah!' (p. 59.) Again, Gaskell ends the tale by contrasting the waste and loss of the past with Martha and Jem Hearn's healthy young love. But the sense of unresolved conflict associated with sexuality among the middle class remains.

The fourth *Household Words* paper, consisting of the accounts of the two tea-parties given by Miss Barker and Mrs Jamieson, is superficially inconsequential in comparison with the earlier stories, but it develops the book's persistent criticism of snobbishness. '"It would be against both propriety and humanity..."' (p. 18) said Miss Jenkyns to Jessie Brown, and Mr Holbrook 'despised every refinement which had not its root deep down in humanity' (p. 29). There is a disjunction between manners and morality. Where does the artificiality of social forms cease to be innocently comic and become cruel, life-denying, and unchristian? The Miss Barkers' hat shop, run on snobbishly uncommercial lines (p. 60), sounds harmless enough, although the reference to Carlyle (see p. 61 n.) carries the implication that Cranford customs reflect those condemned in the wider world. The first reference to Mrs Fitz-Adam, formerly Mary Hoggins, brings in the story of a marriage across class boundaries (see p. 63 n.), and looks forward to the eventual marriage of her brother and Lady Glenmire, as well as back to the Holbrook/Miss Matty affair and to the Cinderella-like marriage of Miss Jessie Brown. Another image of formality conquered by sensuality is the hospitably excessive lavishness of Miss Betty's tea, an image of the goodwill reigning in the community. Soon, however, another incident ruptures the goodwill and expresses the disjunction between refinement and humanity: 'Miss Matty...a true lady herself, could hardly understand the feeling which made Mrs. Jamieson wish to appear to her noble sister-in-law as if she only visited "county" families' (p. 70). As in the case of Miss Betty Barker's tea-party, the ritual honouring of guests involves the ostracism of others. However, Lady Glenmire, 'stirring' where her sister-in-law is inert, triumphs over the deadly formality, and goodwill is restored. These festivities, which look forward to the book's concluding festival, show how oddly intermingled are the cruelty and the charity of the elaborate ceremony of this society.

In *Cranford*, although the triviality of female concerns is often made the occasion of comedy, there is a persistent invitation to the reader to reverse his or her sense of the hierarchy of importance. Is the world of Drumble, railways, commerce, war, government, science, and reason the real world? Or does the world of *Cranford*, which is an extreme, fantasy version of that inhabited by the female half of the human race, have something to teach the other? Virginia Woolf's first novel, *The Voyage Out* (1915), is much preoccupied with the question of the emancipation of women from the home into the masculine world of jobs and education, and, like *Cranford*, foregrounds the difference between the male and female spheres in middle-class society. It is almost free of affection for the past, a far bitterer book. Yet Woolf, too, wants to include in her debate some consideration for the things women do which are overlooked as not worth mentioning:

her father ... was a great dim force in the house, by means of which they held on to the great world which is represented every morning in the *Times*. But the real life of the house was something quite different from this. ... it was her aunts who influenced her really ... it was their world with its four meals, its punctuality, and servants on the stairs at half-past ten, that she examined so closely and wanted so vehemently to smash to atoms. ...

'And there's a sort of beauty in it ... Old spinsters are always doing things. I don't quite know what they do. ... It was very real.'

She reviewed their little journeys to and fro, to Walworth, to charwomen with bad legs, to meetings for this and that, their minute acts of charity and unselfishness which flowered punctually from a definite view of what they ought to do ...[15]

Separated from one another in age, in time, and in political and historical context, Gaskell and Woolf are recognizably evoking the same issue. Women's lives are narrow, their education and opportunities restricted, they are oppressed and disabled by life-denying social codes. Have they all the same constructed out of this predicament something whose destruction would be a loss? Or should young middle-class women abandon their roles as guardians of

---

[15] Virginia Woolf, *The Voyage Out* (London: Duckworth, 1915), 259–60.

domestic life, charity, and social forms, and take the railways and roads to the outside world of higher education, business, and the newspapers? Novels raise but do not answer such questions. *Cranford* does not seem to incite the reader to smash the world of Cranford to atoms, perhaps because it persistently suggests that it is a world anyway hopelessly vulnerable and doomed to disappearance. But it is equally far from being an uncomplicated nostalgic celebration of the female world of the past. In the conclusion of the novel Gaskell solves her technical problem—how, finally, she places Cranford in relation to its nineteenth-century context—by mythologizing it: it becomes a land of redemptive fantasy.

There are several changes noticeable in the novel after the long gap in composition between Chapters 8 and 9. The personality and the actions of the narrator are increasingly prominent. The structure of the narrative is different: instead of a series of discrete, self-contained stories, we have chapters in a novel which moves to a dramatic denouement. And, round the character of Signor Brunoni (one of the novel's several male travellers, who include Captain Brown, Major Gordon, Major Jenkyns, Mr Holbrook, and Peter Jenkyns) she builds up a series of oppositions between magic and the everyday, rationalism and credulity, the exotic and the familiar, which sustain the book to its conclusion.

The figure of Mary Smith, evidently the only child of a widowed Drumble businessman, neither old nor young, neither of Cranford nor apart from it, mediates between the reader and the society she describes. Her ambivalence, her difficulty in comprehending, her mistakes, her anxiety lest the reader should misjudge or despise Cranford, create a shifting perspective, in which the tension between sympathy and judgement (normal in realist fiction) is forced to the reader's attention. Hilary Schor has argued that we should see Mary Smith as an anthropologist, recreating the cultural context of stories.[16] No doubt on some level she represents also Gaskell's own complex feelings about her career as a woman writer, figuring in the public world of literature and social criticism, yet also a mother and a housewife, affectionately affiliated to her Knutsford childhood, and desirous of using the whole of her experience in her fiction. There are many passages in Gaskell's writing which evoke the tension between her vocation as a writer

[16] Schor, *Scheherezade*, 85–7.

and her duties as a wife and mother; and others in which she portrays herself as torn between her sense of appropriately feminine behaviour and her desire to write fiction which challenged established social morality.[17] At the same time she valued 'the refuge of the hidden world of Art'.[18] Art for her was thus both a duty, and a respite from home duties. Gaskell herself wrote of Charlotte Brontë's predicament:

a woman's principal work in life is hardly left to her own choice; nor can she drop the domestic charges devolving on her as an individual, for the exercise of the most splendid talents that were ever bestowed. And yet she must not shrink from the extra responsibility implied by the very fact of her possessing such talents. She must not hide her gift in a napkin; it was meant for the use and service of others.[19]

In the latter part of *Cranford* the dangers and pleasures of the imagination, story-telling, and the irrational, become a central theme. When Mary Smith, at the beginning of Chapter 9, returns to Cranford from her attendance on her invalid father to see the magician, we are, perhaps for the first time, being invited to see Cranford as a land of magic and fantasy which affords a respite from workaday cares, a place to escape to rather than from. The long story with which Gaskell reopened her Cranford series starts with a recurrence of the old theme of female follies: Miss Matty's vanity, Miss Pole's gossip, Mrs Forrester's muddle-headedness. The pattern of the story is determined by the inaccuracy, credulity, and timidity being atoned for by the practical philanthropy called out by the illness of the conjuror. Just as their tea-party snobbishness was actually cruel, so xenophobia blinds Miss Pole to the needs of the starving beggarwoman (p. 91). The great Cranford panic is a nightmare version of the performance of Signor Brunoni: but where that was a harmless journey into the world of the unreal, the panic brings to the surface loss and aggression and fear buried in the past lives of the ladies of Cranford. Miss Pole and Miss Matty spend the evening with Mrs Forrester, and tell ghost stories because 'she would otherwise be left to a solitary retrospect of her not very happy or fortunate life' (p. 97). Mrs Forrester's fears of

---

[17] For a discussion of this point, see Jane Spencer, *Elizabeth Gaskell* (Basingstoke: Macmillan, 1993), 2–6.

[18] *Letters*, 106.

[19] *The Life of Charlotte Brontë*, 2 vols. (London: Smith, Elder, 1857), ii. 50.

French spies (p. 90) and of the dead (p. 99) reflect her own experience as a daughter and widow of army officers. Miss Matty's fears of a man under the bed connect with her tragic childlessness (pp. 98, 107). Miss Pole's pose of self-sufficiency and rationalism is shown to be bravado, and her contempt for men to conceal a desire for male support which is several times imputed to her (pp. 88, 92, 158). But, in the book's recurring pattern, in community of philanthropy and self-forgetfulness there is restoration. The real nightmare, recounted by Signora Brunoni, of the journey through the jungle to save the life of her last child, shows an officer's wife, Indian villagers, and Peter Jenkyns similarly acting with human sympathy: fear of the unknown is sometimes unjustified, instinct is sound.

The engagement of Lady Glenmire to Mr Hoggins, which opens the next episode, connects with the anti-snobbishness theme. Mr Hoggins (a man of science and therefore a rationalist) discredits Miss Pole's burglary story; Lady Glenmire is sensible both in agreeing with him, and in agreeing to marry him; she shows herself willing to ally herself with what is best in men (good sense, reliability), overlooking the insignificant (lack of refinement). She is the opposite of Miss Pole, who entrenches herself in feminine self-sufficiency, in a parody of Miss Jenkyns, whose opinionated ignorance results in her sister's financial ruin: 'she was quite the woman of business, and always judged for herself' (p. 120). Male protection is desirable, male advice is necessary. But although this episode like its predecessor opens with a satire on female muddle-headedness, and unbusinesslike inaccuracy, it too hinges on a reversal of feeling: Miss Matty's action in exchanging her gold for the note becomes an image of Cranfordian heroism; it is an action inconceivable in Drumble (as is her later attitude to setting up shop, pp. 144–5) but all the same admirable. Her generosity to the farmer is explicitly associated with her gentility, her cultural heritage: she has internalized the doctrine of *noblesse oblige*, not the commercial spirit. Once more the positive aspect of Cranfordian culture triumphs over its stupidity. *Cranford*'s underlying theme is a classic one in women's fiction, that men should become more like women, that the passivity society forces on them is Christlike, and a source of positive power, which is not compromised by their human limitations. The ladies of Cranford are weak, they are laughable, *but out of this arises their strength*. This message is scarcely a programme for radical reform, but it has long been a satisfying myth for the female reader.

One of Mary Smith's remarks is often quoted, though seldom in full:

For my own part, I had vibrated all my life between Drumble and Cranford, and I thought it was quite possible that all Mr. Peter's stories might be true although wonderful; but when I found, that if we swallowed an anecdote of tolerable magnitude one week, we had the dose considerably increased the next, I began to have my doubts; especially as I noticed that when his sister was present the accounts of Indian life were comparatively tame; not that she knew more than we did, perhaps less. (p. 154)

The opposition between Drumble and Cranford values, the modern commercial world and the obsolescent genteel past, is especially emphasized in this last movement of the book. Mary Smith's sense of being divided between them is often cited as a parallel to Gaskell's own situation as a writer, torn between home duties and literary work, and also, in that literary work torn between the urge to document social evil and the urge towards fantasy. It is noteworthy that the actual context of this comment is a discussion of story-telling. Here Drumble is the land of the rational and the prosaic, Cranford of credulity and imaginative release, of an innocent belief in goodness which is itself goodness. In her last *Household Words* paper, now Chapters 15 and 16, Gaskell contrives, with a staginess which is utterly appropriate, a fairy-tale conclusion which ties up a number of thematic loose ends. Peter Jenkyns, another oriental magician, returns, and it rains sweets for the children, and fantasy for the ladies of Cranford. The rewards of Miss Matty's humility include surrogate motherhood, surrogate wifehood, and a return to prosperity. His reconciliation of Mrs Jamieson and the Hogginses reunites the community, in a way which is associated with his story-telling. Stories are sustained by appreciative and attentive audiences, by a willingness to believe which is healthily alive at the end of *Cranford*. Miss Matty, by the end, has become a living saint—'we are all of us better when she is near us' (p. 160). The believing reader, though an inhabitant of Drumble, can become, like Mary, a visitor to Cranford, and temporarily uplifted and improved. But the commercial world, in which banks are run insolvently, in which there is much dishonesty and selfishness, is of course still felt as a force surrounding Cranford. All this emphasis on the magical and fantastic nature of the conclusion serves also to remind us as we close the book that, like Captain Brown, we should look out, the railway train is rumbling towards us.

NOTE ON THE TEXT

THE text of this edition is that prepared by Elizabeth Porges Watson for her Oxford English Novels edition of 1972, based on the first volume edition published by Chapman & Hall in June 1853, collated with the earlier version in Dickens's magazine *Household Words* (December 1851–May 1853) and with the editions subsequently printed in Gaskell's lifetime in 1855 and 1864. A few printing errors have been corrected.

The following table indicates the correspondence between the episodes as published in *Household Words* and the chapters in the one-volume edition of 1853.

Chapters	*Original Title*	Household Words
1 and 2	'Our Society at Cranford'	4 (13 Dec. 1851), 265–74
3 and 4	'A Love Affair at Cranford'	4 (3 Jan. 1852), 349–57
5 and 6	'Memory at Cranford'	4 (13 Mar. 1852), 588–97
7 and 8	'Visiting at Cranford'	5 (3 Apr. 1852), 55–64
9 and 10, as far as p. 95 'acceptable' 'The Great Cranford Panic. In Two Chapters. Chapter the First'		6 (8 Jan. 1853), 390–6
10, from 'Miss Pole' on p. 95, and 11 'The Great Cranford Panic. In Two Chapters. Chapter the Second'		6 (15 Jan. 1853), 413–20
12 and 13	'Stopped Payment at Cranford'	7 (2 Apr. 1853), 108–15
14	'Friends in Need, at Cranford'	7 (7 May 1853), 220–7
15 and 16	'A Happy Return to Cranford'	7 (21 May 1853), 277–85.

SELECT BIBLIOGRAPHY

Gaskell's Works

This is a list of her major works, with date of first publication in volume form. The following have been published in Oxford World's Classics editions.

Mary Barton: A Tale of Manchester Life (1848)
Ruth: A Novel (1853)
Cranford (1853)
North and South (1855)
The Life of Charlotte Brontë (1857)
Sylvia's Lovers (1863)
Wives and Daughters: An Every-day Story (1866)

During Gaskell's lifetime five volumes of her shorter stories, which vary a good deal in length, and which were mostly collected from periodicals, also appeared. These were: *Lizzie Leigh and Other Tales* (1855), *Round the Sofa* (1859), *Right at Last and Other Tales* (1860), *Cousin Phillis and Other Tales* (1865), and *The Grey Woman and Other Tales* (1865). As well as these *The Moorland Cottage* (1850) and *A Dark Night's Work* (1863) were separately published.

Collected editions include:
Novels and Tales by Mrs. Gaskell, 7 vols. (London: Smith, Elder, 1872–3).
The Works of Mrs Gaskell: The Knutsford Edition, ed. A. W. Ward, 8 vols. (London: Smith, Elder, 1906).
The Novels and Tales of Mrs. Gaskell, ed. C. K. Shorter, 11 vols. (Oxford: Oxford University Press, 1906–19).

Bibliography

Welch, Jeffrey, *Elizabeth Gaskell: An Annotated Bibliography 1929–1975* (New York and London: Garland, 1977).
Weyant, Nancy S., *Elizabeth Gaskell: An Annotated Bibliography of English-Language Sources 1976–1991* (Methuen, NJ and London: Scarecrow Press, 1994).

Biography and Letters

The Letters of Mrs Gaskell, ed. J. A. V. Chapple and Arthur Pollard (Manchester: Manchester University Press, 1966).

Chapple, John, *Elizabeth Gaskell: The Early Years* (Manchester: Manchester University Press, 1997).

Uglow, Jenny, *Elizabeth Gaskell: A Habit of Stories* (London and Boston: Faber and Faber, 1993).

Criticism

Auerbach, Nina, *Communities of Women: An Idea in Fiction* (London and Cambridge, Mass.: Harvard University Press, 1978).

Bonaparte, Felicia, *The Gypsy-Bachelor of Manchester: The Life of Mrs. Gaskell's Demon* (Charlottesville and London: University Press of Virginia, 1992).

Collin, Dorothy W., 'The Composition and Publication of Elizabeth Gaskell's *Cranford*', *Bulletin of the John Rylands University Library of Manchester*, 69 (Autumn 1986), 59–95.

Dodsworth, Martin, 'Women without Men at Cranford', *Essays in Criticism*, 13 (1963), 132–45.

Easson, Angus, *Elizabeth Gaskell* (London: Routledge, 1979).

——(ed.), *Elizabeth Gaskell: The Critical Heritage* (London: Routledge, 1992).

Flint, Kate, *Elizabeth Gaskell* (Plymouth: Northcote House, 1995).

Nestor, Pauline, *Female Friendships and Communities: Charlotte Brontë, George Eliot, Elizabeth Gaskell* (Oxford: Clarendon Press, 1985).

Quinn, Mary, *Elizabeth Gaskell and Nineteenth Century Literature: Manuscripts from the John Rylands University Library, Manchester. A Listing and Guide to the Research Publications.*

Microfilm Collection (Reading: Research Publications, 1989).

Rubenius, Aina, *The Woman Question in Mrs Gaskell's Life and Works* (Uppsala: Lundequist, 1950).

Schor, Hilary M., *Scheherazade in the Marketplace: Elizabeth Gaskell and the Victorian Novel* (New York and Oxford: Oxford University Press, 1992).

Selig, Robert L., *Elizabeth Gaskell: A Reference Guide* (Boston, Mass.: G. K. Hall, 1977).

Spencer, Jane, *Elizabeth Gaskell* (Basingstoke: Macmillan, 1993).

Stoneman, Patsy, *Elizabeth Gaskell* (Brighton: Harvester, 1987).

A CHRONOLOGY OF ELIZABETH GASKELL

1810 29 September. Elizabeth Cleghorn Stevenson born to William Stevenson and Elizabeth Holland, in Lindsey Row, Chelsea (now Cheyne Walk); she has one brother, John (b. 1798).

1811 29 October. Her mother, Elizabeth Stevenson, dies in Chelsea. Soon afterwards the baby Elizabeth is taken to Knutsford, Cheshire to be cared for by her mother's elder sister, Hannah Lumb.

1814 William Stevenson marries Catherine Thomson.

1821 Elizabeth goes to a boarding-school near Warwick run by the Byerley sisters, relations of her stepmother and of the Wedgwood family.

1822 Her brother John Stevenson joins the Merchant Navy.

1824 The school moves to Stratford–upon–Avon.

1826 Elizabeth leaves school.

1828 John Stevenson disappears either while on his way to India or after his arrival there. Nothing is ever known of his fate.

1829 22 March. Death of William Stevenson.
      Elizabeth is thought to have spent the winter, and that of 1830–1, with relations, the Turners, in Newcastle upon Tyne and to have visited Edinburgh with Ann Turner, probably in 1830 or 1831.

1831 Meets the Revd William Gaskell (1805–84).

1832 30 August. Marries William Gaskell at St John's Parish Church, Knutsford. They live at 1 Dover Street, Manchester, where he is assistant minister at Cross Street Chapel.

1833 10 July. Birth of a stillborn girl.

1834 12 September. Birth of Marianne Gaskell.

1837 January. Publication of the Gaskells' poem 'Sketches among the Poor' in *Blackwood's Magazine*.
      7 February. Birth of Margaret Emily (Meta) Gaskell.
      1 May. Death of Hannah Lumb.

1840 William Howitt, *Visits to Remarkable Places* includes her description of Clopton Hall. Birth and death of a son, name and date unknown, between 1837 and 1841.

1841 July. William and Elizabeth Gaskell visit Heidelberg.

1842 7 October. Birth of Florence Elizabeth Gaskell.
      Move to 121 Upper Rumford Road, Manchester.

1844 23 October. Birth of William Gaskell.

1845 10 August. Death of the baby William Gaskell on holiday in Wales.

1846 3 September. Birth of Julia Bradford Gaskell.

1847 June. 'Libbie Marsh's Three Eras' published in *Howitt's Journal*.
      September. 'The Sexton's Hero', *Howitt's Journal*.

1848 January. 'Christmas Storms and Sunshine', *Howitt's Journal*.
      October. *Mary Barton*, her first novel.

1849 April–May. Visits London and meets Dickens and Carlyle.
      June–August. Visits the Lake District and meets Wordsworth.
      July. 'The Last Generation in England', *Sartain's Union Magazine*;
      'Hand and Heart', *Sunday School Penny Magazine*.

1850 January. Dickens writes to ask her for contributions to the forth-
      coming *Household Words*.
      February. 'Martha Preston', *Sartain's Union Magazine*.
      March–April. 'Lizzie Leigh', *Household Words*.
      June. Moves to 42 Plymouth Grove, Manchester.
      August. Meets Charlotte Brontë while staying with the Kay-Shuttle-
      worth family.
      November. 'The Well of Pen-Morfa', *Household Words*.
      December. *The Moorland Cottage*; 'The Heart of John Middleton',
      Household Words.

1851 February–April. 'Mr Harrison's Confessions', *Ladies Companion and
      Monthly Magazine*.
      June. 'Disappearances', *Household Words*.
      July. Visit to London and the Great Exhibition.
      October. Visits Knutsford.
      December–May 1853. The *Cranford* papers in *Household Words*.

1852 January–April. 'Bessy's Troubles at Home', *Sunday School Penny
      Magazine*.
      June. 'The Shah's English Gardener', *Household Words*.
      December. 'The Old Nurse's Story', *Household Words*.

1853 January. *Ruth*. Reviews and letters about *Ruth* make Gaskell feel like
      'St Sebastian tied to a tree to be shot at with arrows'. 'Cumberland-
      Sheep Shearers', *Household Words*.
      May. Visits Paris.
      June. *Cranford*.
      August. Visits Normandy.
      September. Visits Charlotte Brontë at Haworth.

November. 'Morton Hall', *Household Words.*
December. 'Traits and Stories of the Huguenots', 'My French Master', 'The Squire's Story', all in *Household Words.*

1854 January. Visits Paris.
February. 'Modern Greek Songs', *Household Words.*
May. 'Company Manners', *Household Words.*
September–January 1855, *North and South*, Household Words.

1855 February. Visits Paris.
31 March. Charlotte Brontë dies.
June. Charlotte Brontë's father asks her to write his daughter's biography.
August. 'An Accursed Race', *Household Words.*
September. *Lizzie Leigh and Other Tales.*
October. 'Half a Lifetime Ago', *Household Words.*

1856 May. Visits Brussels to research Charlotte Brontë's schooldays.
December. 'The Poor Clare', *Household Words.*

1857 February–May. Visits Rome.
March. *The Life of Charlotte Brontë.*
May. Libel action threatened by Lady Scott; Gaskell retracts accusation of adultery with Branwell Brontë in *The Life of CB.*
June. Meta engaged to Captain Charles Hill, widowed officer in the Indian Army. News of the Indian Mutiny causes anxiety to the Gaskells, and Hill is recalled to India.

1858 January. 'The Doom of the Griffiths', *Harper's Monthly Magazine.*
June. 'An Incident at Niagara Falls', *Harper's Monthly Magazine.*
June–September. 'My Lady Ludlow', *Household Words.*
Summer. Meta's engagement to Charles Hill is broken off.
September–December. Visit to Heidelberg.
November. 'The Sin of a Father' (collected as 'Right at Last'), *Household Words.*
December. 'The Manchester Marriage', *Household Words.*

1859 March. *Round the Sofa.*
Summer. Visits Scotland.
October. 'Lois the Witch', *All the Year Round.*
November. Visits Whitby, later to be scene of *Sylvia's Lovers.*
December. 'The Ghost in the Garden Room' (collected as 'The Crooked Branch'), *All the Year Round.*

1860 February. 'Curious if True', *Cornhill Magazine.*
May. *Right at Last and Other Tales.*
July–August. Visits Heidelberg.

1861 January. 'The Grey Woman', *All the Year Round*.
     The American Civil War blockade causes famine among the Lancashire cotton workers.

1862 'Six Weeks at Heppenheim', *Cornhill Magazine*.
     April. Worries that her daughter Marianne may be going to convert to Roman Catholicism.
     May. Visits Normandy to gather material for articles on French life.
     Famine in Lancashire worsens in the winter.

1863 January–March. 'A Dark Night's Work', *All the Year Round*.
     February. *Sylvia's Lovers*; 'Shams', *Fraser's Magazine*.
     March. 'An Italian Institution', *All the Year Round*.
     March–August. Visits France and Italy.
     April. *A Dark Night's Work*.
     8 September. Florence Gaskell marries Charles Crompton.
     November. 'The Cage at Cranford', *All the Year Round*.
     November–February 1864. 'Cousin Phillis', *Cornhill Magazine*.
     December. 'How the First Floor Went to Crowley Castle', *All the Year Round*.

1864 April–June. 'French Life', *Fraser's Magazine*.
     August–January 1866. *Wives and Daughters*, *Cornhill Magazine*.
     August. Visits Switzerland.

1865 March–April. Visits Paris.
     March. 'Columns of Gossip from Paris', *Pall Mall Gazette*.
     June. Buys The Lawns, Holybourne, Hampshire, without telling her husband.
     August–September. 'A Parson's Holiday', *Pall Mall Gazette*.
     October. Visits Dieppe.
     12 November. Dies at Holybourne.
     Cousin Phillis and Other Tales
     The Grey Woman and Other Tales

1866 February. *Wives and Daughters: An Every-day Story*, published posthumously and unfinished.

CRANFORD

CHAPTER I

OUR SOCIETY

In the first place, Cranford is in possession of the Amazons;*all the holders of houses, above a certain rent, are women. If a married couple come to settle in the town, somehow the gentleman disappears; he is either fairly frightened to death by being the only man in the Cranford evening parties, or he is accounted for by being with his regiment, his ship, or closely engaged in business all the week in the great neighbouring commercial town of Drumble,* distant only twenty miles on a railroad. In short, whatever does become of the gentlemen, they are not at Cranford. What could they do if they were there? The surgeon has his round of thirty miles, and sleeps at Cranford; but every man cannot be a surgeon. For keeping the trim gardens full of choice flowers without a weed to speck them; for frightening away little boys who look wistfully at the said flowers through the railings; for rushing out at the geese that occasionally venture into the gardens if the gates are left open; for deciding all questions of literature and politics without troubling themselves with unnecessary reasons or arguments; for obtaining clear and correct knowledge of everybody's affairs in the parish; for keeping their neat maidservants in admirable order; for kindness (somewhat dictatorial) to the poor, and real tender good offices to each other whenever they are in distress, the ladies of Cranford are quite sufficient. 'A man,' as one of them observed to me once, 'is *so* in the way in the house!' Although the ladies of Cranford know all each other's proceedings, they are exceedingly indifferent to each other's opinions. Indeed, as each has her own individuality, not to say eccentricity, pretty strongly developed, nothing is so easy as verbal retaliation; but somehow good-will reigns among them to a considerable degree.

The Cranford ladies have only an occasional little quarrel, spirted out in a few peppery words and angry jerks of the head; just enough to prevent the even tenor of their lives from becoming too flat. Their dress is very independent of fashion; as they observe, 'What does it signify how we dress here at Cranford, where everybody knows us?' And if they go from home, their reason is equally cogent: 'What does it signify how we dress here, where nobody knows us?' The materials of their clothes are, in general, good and plain, and most of them are nearly as scrupulous as Miss Tyler, of cleanly memory;* but I will answer for it, the last gigot, the last tight and scanty petticoat* in wear in England, was seen in Cranford—and seen without a smile.

I can testify to a magnificent family red silk umbrella,* under which a gentle little spinster, left alone of many brothers and sisters, used to patter to church on rainy days. Have you any red silk umbrellas in London? We had a tradition of the first that had ever been seen in Cranford; and the little boys mobbed it, and called it 'a stick in petticoats.' It might have been the very red silk one I have described, held by a strong father over a troop of little ones; the poor little lady—the survivor of all—could scarcely carry it.

Then there were rules and regulations for visiting and calls; and they were announced to any young people, who might be staying in the town, with all the solemnity with which the old Manx laws were read once a year on the Tinwald Mount.*

'Our friends have sent to inquire how you are after your journey to-night, my dear,' '(fifteen miles, in a gentleman's carriage);' 'they will give you some rest to-morrow, but the next day, I have no doubt, they will call; so be at liberty after twelve;—from twelve to three are our calling-hours.'

Then, after they had called,

'It is the third day; I dare say your mamma has told you, my dear, never to let more than three days elapse between receiving a call and returning it; and also, that you are never to stay longer than a quarter of an hour.'

'But am I to look at my watch? How am I to find out when a quarter of an hour has passed?'

'You must keep thinking about the time, my dear, and not allow yourself to forget it in conversation.'

As everybody had this rule in their minds, whether they received or paid a call, of course no absorbing subject was ever spoken about. We kept ourselves to short sentences of small talk, and were punctual to our time.

I imagine that a few of the gentlefolks of Cranford were poor, and had some difficulty in making both ends meet; but they were like the Spartans,* and concealed their smart under a smiling face. We none of us spoke of money, because that subject savoured of commerce and trade, and though some might be poor, we were all aristocratic. The Cranfordians had that kindly *esprit de corps* which made them overlook all deficiencies in success when some among them tried to conceal their poverty. When Mrs. Forrester, for instance, gave a party in her baby-house*of a dwelling, and the little maiden disturbed the ladies on the sofa by a request that she might get the tea-tray out from underneath, every one took this novel proceeding as the most natural thing in the world; and talked on about household forms and ceremonies, as if we all believed that our hostess had a regular servants' hall, second table, with house-keeper and steward; instead of the one little charity-school maiden, whose short ruddy arms could never have been strong enough to carry the tray up-stairs, if she had not been assisted in private by her mistress, who now sate in state, pretending not to know what cakes were sent up; though she knew, and we knew, and she knew that we knew, and we knew that she knew that we knew, she had been busy all the morning making tea-bread* and sponge-cakes.

There were one or two consequences arising from this general but unacknowledged poverty, and this very much acknowledged gentility, which were not amiss, and which might be introduced into many circles of society to their great improvement. For instance, the inhabitants of Cranford kept early hours, and clattered home in their pattens,* under the guidance of a lantern-bearer, about nine o'clock at night; and the whole town was abed and asleep by half-past ten. Moreover, it was considered 'vulgar' (a tremendous word in Cranford) to give anything expensive, in the way of eatable or drinkable, at the evening entertainments. Wafer bread-and-butter and sponge-biscuits were all that the Honourable Mrs. Jamieson gave; and she was sister-in-law to the late Earl of Glenmire, although she did practise such 'elegant economy.'*

'Elegant economy!' How naturally one falls back into the phraseology of Cranford! There, economy was always 'elegant,'

and money-spending always 'vulgar and ostentatious;' a sort of
sour-grapeism, which made us very peaceful and satisfied. I never
shall forget the dismay felt when a certain Captain Brown came to
live at Cranford, and openly spoke about his being poor—not in
a whisper to an intimate friend, the doors and windows being
previously closed; but, in the public street! in a loud military voice!
alleging his poverty as a reason for not taking a particular house.
The ladies of Cranford were already rather moaning over the
invasion of their territories by a man and a gentleman. He was
a half-pay Captain, and had obtained some situation on a neighbouring railroad, which had been vehemently petitioned against
by the little town; and if, in addition to his masculine gender, and
his connexion with the obnoxious railroad, he was so brazen as to
talk of being poor—why! then, indeed, he must be sent to Coventry.
Death was as true and as common as poverty; yet people never
spoke about that, loud out in the streets. It was a word not to be
mentioned to ears polite.* We had tacitly agreed to ignore that any
with whom we associated on terms of visiting equality could ever
be prevented by poverty from doing anything that they wished.
If we walked to or from a party, it was because the night was *so*
fine, or the air *so* refreshing; not because sedan-chairs were expensive. If we wore prints, instead of summer silks, it was because we
preferred a washing material; and so on, till we blinded ourselves
to the vulgar fact, that we were, all of us, people of very moderate
means. Of course, then, we did not know what to make of a man
who could speak of poverty as if it was not a disgrace. Yet, somehow Captain Brown made himself respected in Cranford, and was
called upon, in spite of all resolutions to the contrary. I was surprised to hear his opinions quoted as authority, at a visit which
I paid to Cranford, about a year after he had settled in the town.
My own friends had been among the bitterest opponents of any
proposal to visit the Captain and his daughters, only twelve months
before; and now he was even admitted in the tabooed hours before
twelve. True, it was to discover the cause of a smoking chimney,
before the fire was lighted; but still Captain Brown walked upstairs, nothing daunted, spoke in a voice too large for the room,
and joked quite in the way of a tame man, about the house. He
had been blind to all the small slights and omissions of trivial
ceremonies with which he had been received. He had been friendly,
though the Cranford ladies had been cool; he had answered small

sarcastic compliments in good faith; and with his manly frankness had overpowered all the shrinking which met him as a man who was not ashamed to be poor. And, at last, his excellent masculine common sense, and his facility in devising expedients to overcome domestic dilemmas, had gained him an extraordinary place as authority among the Cranford ladies. He, himself, went on in his course, as unaware of his popularity, as he had been of the reverse; and I am sure he was startled one day, when he found his advice so highly esteemed, as to make some counsel which he had given in jest, be taken in sober, serious earnest.

It was on this subject;—an old lady had an Alderney cow, which she looked upon as a daughter. You could not pay the short quarter-of-an-hour call, without being told of the wonderful milk or wonderful intelligence of this animal. The whole town knew and kindly regarded Miss Betty Barker's* Alderney; therefore great was the sympathy and regret when, in an unguarded moment, the poor cow tumbled into a lime-pit. She moaned so loudly that she was soon heard, and rescued; but meanwhile the poor beast had lost most of her hair, and came out looking naked, cold, and miserable, in a bare skin. Everybody pitied the animal, though a few could not restrain their smiles at her droll appearance. Miss Betty Barker absolutely cried with sorrow and dismay; and it was said she thought of trying a bath of oil. This remedy, perhaps, was recommended by some one of the number whose advice she asked; but the proposal, if ever it was made, was knocked on the head by Captain Brown's decided 'Get her a flannel waistcoat and flannel drawers, Ma'am, if you wish to keep her alive. But my advice is, kill the poor creature at once.'

Miss Betty Barker dried her eyes, and thanked the Captain heartily; she set to work, and by-and-by all the town turned out to see the Alderney meekly going to her pasture, clad in dark grey flannel. I have watched her myself many a time. Do you ever see cows dressed in grey flannel in London?

Captain Brown had taken a small house on the outskirts of the town, where he lived with his two daughters. He must have been upwards of sixty at the time of the first visit I paid to Cranford, after I had left it as a residence. But he had a wiry, well-trained, elastic figure; a stiff military throw-back of his head, and a springing step, which made him appear much younger than he was. His eldest daughter looked almost as old as himself, and betrayed the

fact that his real, was more than his apparent, age. Miss Brown
must have been forty; she had a sickly, pained, careworn expression on her face, and looked as if the gaiety of youth had long faded
out of sight. Even when young she must have been plain and hard-
featured. Miss Jessie Brown was ten years younger than her sister,
and twenty shades prettier. Her face was round and dimpled. Miss
Jenkyns once said, in a passion against Captain Brown (the cause
of which I will tell you presently), 'that she thought it was time
for Miss Jessie to leave off her dimples, and not always to be trying to look like a child.' It was true there was something child-like
in her face; and there will be, I think, till she dies, though she
should live to a hundred. Her eyes were large blue wondering eyes,
looking straight at you; her nose was unformed and snub, and her
lips were red and dewy; she wore her hair, too, in little rows of
curls, which heightened this appearance. I do not know whether
she was pretty or not; but I liked her face, and so did everybody,
and I do not think she could help her dimples. She had something
of her father's jauntiness of gait and manner; and any female
observer might detect a slight difference in the attire of the two
sisters—that of Miss Jessie being about two pounds per annum
more expensive than Miss Brown's. Two pounds was a large sum
in Captain Brown's annual disbursements.

Such was the impression made upon me by the Brown family,
when I first saw them altogether in Cranford church. The Captain
I had met before—on the occasion of the smoky chimney, which
he had cured by some simple alteration in the flue. In church, he
held his double eye-glass to his eyes during the Morning Hymn,
and then lifted up his head erect, and sang out loud and joyfully.
He made the responses louder than the clerk—an old man with
a piping feeble voice, who, I think, felt aggrieved at the Captain's
sonorous bass, and quavered higher and higher in consequence.

On coming out of church, the brisk Captain paid the most gallant
attention to his two daughters. He nodded and smiled to his
acquaintances; but he shook hands with none until he had helped
Miss Brown to unfurl her umbrella, had relieved her of her prayer-
book, and had waited patiently till she, with trembling nervous
hands, had taken up her gown to walk through the wet roads.

I wondered what the Cranford ladies did with Captain Brown
at their parties. We had often rejoiced, in former days, that there
was no gentleman to be attended to, and to find conversation for,

at the card-parties. We had congratulated ourselves upon the snugness of the evenings; and, in our love for gentility, and distaste of mankind, we had almost persuaded ourselves that to be a man was to be 'vulgar;' so that when I found my friend and hostess, Miss Jenkyns, was going to have a party in my honour, and that Captain and the Miss Browns were invited, I wondered much what would be the course of the evening. Card-tables, with green-baize tops, were set out by day-light, just as usual; it was the third week in November, so the evenings closed in about four. Candles, and clean packs of cards were arranged on each table. The fire was made up, the neat maid-servant had received her last directions; and, there we stood dressed in our best, each with a candle-lighter in our hands, ready to dart at the candles as soon as the first knock came. Parties in Cranford were solemn festivities, making the ladies feel gravely elated, as they sat together in their best dresses. As soon as three had arrived, we sat down to 'Preference,'* I being the unlucky fourth. The next four comers were put down immediately to another table; and presently the tea-trays, which I had seen set out in the store-room as I passed in the morning, were placed each on the middle of a card-table. The china was delicate egg-shell; the old-fashioned silver glittered with polishing; but the eatables were of the slightest description. While the trays were yet on the tables, Captain and the Miss Browns came in; and I could see, that somehow or other the Captain was a favourite with all the ladies present. Ruffled brows were smoothed, sharp voices lowered at his approach. Miss Brown looked ill, and depressed almost to gloom. Miss Jessie smiled as usual, and seemed nearly as popular as her father. He immediately and quietly assumed the man's place in the room; attended to every one's wants, lessened the pretty maid-servant's labour by waiting on empty cups, and bread-and-butterless ladies; and yet did it all in so easy and dignified a manner, and so much as if it were a matter of course for the strong to attend to the weak, that he was a true man throughout. He played for three-penny points with as grave an interest as if they had been pounds; and yet, in all his attention to strangers he had an eye on his suffering daughter; for suffering I was sure she was, though to many eyes she might only appear to be irritable. Miss Jessie could not play cards; but she talked to the sitters-out, who, before her coming, had been rather inclined to be cross. She sang, too, to an old cracked piano, which I think had been a spinnet in its youth.

Miss Jessie sang 'Jock of Hazeldean'* a little out of tune; but we were none of us musical, though Miss Jenkyns beat time, out of time, by way of appearing to be so.

It was very good of Miss Jenkyns to do this; for I had seen that, a little before, she had been a good deal annoyed by Miss Jessie Brown's unguarded admission (à propos of Shetland wool) that she had an uncle, her mother's brother, who was a shopkeeper in Edinburgh. Miss Jenkyns tried to drown this confession by a terrible cough—for the Honourable Mrs. Jamieson was sitting at the card-table nearest Miss Jessie, and what would she say or think, if she found out she was in the same room with a shop-keeper's niece! But Miss Jessie Brown (who had no tact, as we all agreed, the next morning) *would* repeat the information, and assure Miss Pole she could easily get her the identical Shetland wool required, 'through my uncle, who has the best assortment of Shetland goods of any one in Edinbro'.' It was to take the taste of this out of our mouths, and the sound of this out of our ears, that Miss Jenkyns proposed music; so I say again, it was very good of her to beat time to the song.

When the trays re-appeared with biscuits and wine, punctually at a quarter to nine, there was conversation; comparing of cards, and talking over tricks; but, by-and-by, Captain Brown sported a bit of literature.

'Have you seen any numbers of "The Pickwick Papers?" '* said he. (They were then publishing in parts.) 'Capital thing!'

Now, Miss Jenkyns was daughter of a deceased rector of Cranford; and, on the strength of a number of manuscript sermons, and a pretty good library of divinity, considered herself literary, and looked upon any conversation about books as a challenge to her. So she answered and said, 'Yes, she had seen them; indeed, she might say she had read them.'

'And what do you think of them?' exclaimed Captain Brown. 'Aren't they famously good?'

So urged, Miss Jenkyns could not but speak.

'I must say I don't think they are by any means equal to Dr. Johnson. Still, perhaps, the author is young. Let him persevere, and who knows what he may become if he will take the great Doctor for his model.' This was evidently too much for Captain Brown to take placidly; and I saw the words on the tip of his tongue before Miss Jenkyns had finished her sentence.

'It is quite a different sort of thing, my dear madam,' he began.

'I am quite aware of that,' returned she. 'And I make allowances, Captain Brown.'

'Just allow me to read you a scene out of this month's number,' pleaded he. 'I had it only this morning, and I don't think the company can have read it yet.'

'As you please,' said she, settling herself with an air of resignation. He read the account of the 'swarry' which Sam Weller gave at Bath.* Some of us laughed heartily. *I* did not dare, because I was staying in the house. Miss Jenkyns sat in patient gravity. When it was ended, she turned to me, and said with mild dignity,

'Fetch me "Rasselas,"*my dear, out of the book-room.'

When I brought it to her, she turned to Captain Brown:

'Now allow *me* to read you a scene, and then the present company can judge between your favourite, Mr. Boz*and Dr. Johnson.'

She read one of the conversations between Rasselas and Imlac, in a high-pitched majestic voice; and when she had ended, she said, 'I imagine I am now justified in my preference of Dr. Johnson, as a writer of fiction.' The Captain screwed his lips up, and drummed on the table, but he did not speak. She thought she would give a finishing blow or two.

'I consider it vulgar, and below the dignity of literature, to publish in numbers.'

'How was the "Rambler"* published, Ma'am?' asked Captain Brown, in a low voice; which I think Miss Jenkyns could not have heard.

'Dr. Johnson's style is a model for young beginners. My father recommended it to me when I began to write letters.—I have formed my own style upon it; I recommend it to your favourite.'

'I should be very sorry for him to exchange his style for any such pompous writing,' said Captain Brown.

Miss Jenkyns felt this as a personal affront, in a way of which the Captain had not dreamed. Epistolary writing, she and her friends considered as her *forte*. Many a copy of many a letter have I seen written and corrected on the slate, before she 'seized the half-hour just previous to post-time to assure' her friends of this or of that; and Dr. Johnson was, as she said, her model in these compositions. She drew herself up with dignity, and only replied to Captain Brown's last remark by saying with marked emphasis on every syllable, 'I prefer Dr. Johnson to Mr. Boz.'

It is said—I won't vouch for the fact—that Captain Brown was heard to say, *sotto voce*, 'D—n Dr. Johnson!' If he did, he was penitent afterwards, as he showed by going to stand near Miss Jenkyns's arm-chair, and endeavouring to beguile her into conversation on some more pleasing subject. But she was inexorable. The next day, she made the remark I have mentioned, about Miss Jessie's dimples.

CHAPTER II

THE CAPTAIN

It was impossible to live a month at Cranford, and not know the daily habits of each resident; and long before my visit was ended, I knew much concerning the whole Brown trio. There was nothing new to be discovered respecting their poverty; for they had spoken simply and openly about that from the very first. They made no mystery of the necessity for their being economical. All that remained to be discovered was the Captain's infinite kindness of heart, and the various modes in which, unconsciously to himself, he manifested it. Some little anecdotes were talked about for some time after they occurred. As we did not read much, and as all the ladies were pretty well suited with servants, there was a dearth of subjects for conversation. We therefore discussed the circumstance of the Captain taking a poor old woman's dinner out of her hands, one very slippery Sunday. He had met her returning from the bakehouse* as he came from church, and noticed her precarious footing; and, with the grave dignity with which he did everything, he relieved her of her burden, and steered along the street by her side, carrying her baked mutton and potatoes safely home. This was thought very eccentric; and it was rather expected that he would pay a round of calls, on the Monday morning, to explain and apologise to the Cranford sense of propriety: but he did no such thing; and then it was decided that he was ashamed, and was keeping out of sight. In a kindly pity for him, we began to say—'After all, the Sunday morning's occurrence showed great goodness of heart;' and it was resolved that he should be comforted on his next appearance amongst us; but, lo! he came down upon us, untouched by any sense of shame, speaking loud and bass as ever, his head thrown back, his wig as jaunty and well-curled as usual, and we were obliged to conclude he had forgotten all about Sunday.

Miss Pole and Miss Jessie Brown had set up a kind of intimacy, on the strength of the Shetland wool and the new knitting stitches; so it happened that when I went to visit Miss Pole, I saw more of the Browns than I had done while staying with Miss Jenkyns; who had never got over what she called Captain Brown's disparaging remarks upon Dr. Johnson, as a writer of light and agreeable fiction. I found that Miss Brown was seriously ill of some lingering, incurable complaint, the pain occasioned by which gave the uneasy expression to her face that I had taken for unmitigated crossness. Cross, too, she was at times, when the nervous irritability occasioned by her disease became past endurance. Miss Jessie bore with her at these times even more patiently than she did with the bitter self-upbraidings by which they were invariably succeeded. Miss Brown used to accuse herself, not merely of hasty and irritable temper; but also of being the cause why her father and sister were obliged to pinch, in order to allow her the small luxuries which were necessaries in her condition. She would so fain have made sacrifices for them and have lightened their cares, that the original generosity of her disposition added acerbity to her temper. All this was borne by Miss Jessie and her father with more than placidity—with absolute tenderness. I forgave Miss Jessie her singing out of tune, and her juvenility of dress, when I saw her at home. I came to perceive that Captain Brown's dark Brutus wig* and padded coat (alas! too often threadbare) were remnants of the military smartness of his youth, which he now wore unconsciously. He was a man of infinite resources, gained in his barrack experience. As he confessed, no one could black his boots to please him, except himself; but, indeed, he was not above saving the little maid-servant's labours in every way,—knowing, most likely, that his daughter's illness made the place a hard one.

He endeavoured to make peace with Miss Jenkyns soon after the memorable dispute I have named, by a present of a wooden fire-shovel (his own making), having heard her say how much the grating of an iron one annoyed her. She received the present with cool gratitude, and thanked him formally. When he was gone, she bade me put it away in the lumber-room; feeling, probably, that no present from a man who preferred Mr. Boz to Dr. Johnson could be less jarring than an iron fire-shovel.

Such was the state of things when I left Cranford and went to Drumble. I had, however, several correspondents who kept me *au fait* to the proceedings of the dear little town. There was Miss Pole, who was becoming as much absorbed in crochet as she had been once in knitting; and the burden of whose letter was something like, 'But don't you forget the white worsted at Flint's,' of the old song;*for, at the end of every sentence of news, came a fresh direction as to some crochet commission which I was to execute for her. Miss Matilda Jenkyns (who did not mind being called Miss Matty, when Miss Jenkyns was not by) wrote nice, kind, rambling letters; now and then venturing into an opinion of her own; but suddenly pulling herself up, and either begging me not to name what she had said, as Deborah thought differently, and *she* knew; or else, putting in a postscript to the effect that, since writing the above, she had been talking over the subject with Deborah, and was quite convinced that, &c.;—(here, probably, followed a recantation of every opinion she had given in the letter.) Then came Miss Jenkyns—Debōrah, as she liked Miss Matty to call her; her father having once said that the Hebrew name ought to be so pronounced. I secretly think she took the Hebrew prophetess* for a model in character; and, indeed, she was not unlike the stern prophetess in some ways; making allowance, of course, for modern customs and difference in dress. Miss Jenkyns wore a cravat, and a little bonnet like a jockey-cap,* and altogether had the appearance of a strong-minded woman; although she would have despised the modern idea of women being equal to men.* Equal, indeed! she knew they were superior.—But to return to her letters. Everything in them was stately and grand, like herself. I have been looking them over (dear Miss Jenkyns, how I honoured her!) and I will give an extract, more especially because it relates to our friend Captain Brown:—

'The Honourable Mrs. Jamieson has only just quitted me; and, in the course of conversation, she communicated to me the intelligence, that she had yesterday received a call from her revered husband's quondam friend, Lord Mauleverer. You will not easily conjecture what brought his lordship within the precincts of our little town. It was to see Captain Brown, with whom, it appears, his lordship was acquainted in the "plumed wars,"* and who had the privilege of averting destruction from his lordship's head, when some great peril was impending over it, off the misnomered Cape of Good Hope. You know our friend the Honourable Mrs. Jamieson's deficiency in the spirit of innocent curiosity; and you will therefore not be so much surprised when I tell you she was quite unable to disclose to me the exact nature of the peril in question. I was anxious, I confess, to ascertain in what manner Captain Brown, with his limited establishment, could receive so distinguished a guest; and I discovered that his lordship retired to rest, and, let us hope, to refreshing slumbers, at the Angel Hotel; but shared the Brunonian* meals during the two days that he honoured Cranford with his august presence. Mrs. Johnson, our civil butcher's wife, informs me that Miss Jessie purchased a leg of lamb; but, besides this, I can hear of no preparation whatever to give a suitable reception to so distinguished a visitor. Perhaps they entertained him with "the feast of reason and the flow of soul;"* and to us, who are acquainted with Captain Brown's sad want of relish for "the pure wells of English undefiled,"* it may be matter for congratulation, that he has had the opportunity of improving his taste by holding converse with an elegant and refined member of the British aristocracy. But from some mundane feelings who is altogether free?'

Miss Pole and Miss Matty wrote to me by the same post. Such a piece of news as Lord Mauleverer's visit was not to be lost on the Cranford letter-writers: they made the most of it. Miss Matty humbly apologised for writing at the same time as her sister, who was so much more capable than she to describe the honour done to Cranford; but, in spite of a little bad spelling, Miss Matty's account gave me the best idea of the commotion occasioned by his lordship's visit, after it had occurred; for, except the people at the Angel, the Browns, Mrs. Jamieson, and a little lad his lordship had sworn at for driving a dirty hoop against the aristocratic legs, I could not hear of any one with whom his lordship had held conversation.

My next visit to Cranford was in the summer. There had been neither births, deaths, nor marriages since I was there last. Everybody lived in the same house, and wore pretty nearly the same well-preserved, old-fashioned clothes. The greatest event was, that Miss Jenkynses had purchased a new carpet for the drawing-room. Oh the busy work Miss Matty and I had in chasing the sunbeams, as they fell in an afternoon right down on this carpet through the blindless window! We spread newspapers over the places, and sat down to our book or our work; and, lo! in a quarter of an hour the sun had moved, and was blazing away on a fresh spot; and down again we went on our knees to alter the position of the newspapers. We were very busy, too, one whole morning before Miss Jenkyns gave her party, in following her directions, and in cutting out and stitching together pieces of newspaper, so as to form little paths to every chair, set for the expected visitors, lest their shoes might dirty or defile the purity of the carpet. Do you make paper paths for every guest to walk upon in London?

Captain Brown and Miss Jenkyns were not very cordial to each other. The literary dispute, of which I had seen the beginning, was a 'raw,' the slightest touch on which made them wince. It was the only difference of opinion they had ever had; but that difference was enough. Miss Jenkyns could not refrain from talking *at* Captain Brown; and though he did not reply, he drummed with his fingers; which action she felt and resented as very disparaging to Dr. Johnson. He was rather ostentatious in his preference of the writings of Mr. Boz; would walk through the street so absorbed in them, that he all but ran against Miss Jenkyns; and though his apologies were earnest and sincere, and though he did not, in fact, do more than startle her and himself, she owned to me she had rather he had knocked her down, if he had only been reading a higher style of literature. The poor, brave Captain! he looked older, and more worn, and his clothes were very threadbare. But he seemed as bright and cheerful as ever, unless he was asked about his daughter's health.

'She suffers a great deal, and she must suffer more; we do what we can to alleviate her pain—God's will be done!' He took off his hat at these last words. I found, from Miss Matty,* that everything had been done, in fact. A medical man, of high repute in that country neighbourhood, had been sent for, and every injunction he had given was attended to, regardless of expense. Miss Matty was sure they denied themselves many things in order to make the invalid comfortable; but they never spoke about it; and as for Miss Jessie! 'I really think she's an angel,' said poor Miss Matty, quite overcome. 'To see her way of bearing with Miss Brown's crossness, and the bright face she puts on after she's been sitting up a whole night and scolded above half of it, is quite beautiful. Yet she looks as neat and as ready to welcome the Captain at breakfast-time, as if she had been asleep in the Queen's bed all night. My dear! you could never laugh at her prim little curls or her pink bows again, if you saw her as I have done.' I could only feel very penitent, and greet Miss Jessie with double respect when I met her next. She looked faded and pinched; and her lips began to quiver, as if she was very weak, when she spoke of her sister. But she brightened, and sent back the tears that were glittering in her pretty eyes, as she said:—

'But, to be sure, what a town Cranford is for kindness! I don't suppose any one has a better dinner than usual cooked, but the best part of all comes in a little covered basin for my sister. The poor people will leave their earliest vegetables at our door for her. They speak short and gruff, as if they were ashamed of it; but I am sure it often goes to my heart to see their thoughtfulness.' The tears now came back and overflowed; but after a minute or two, she began to scold herself, and ended by going away, the same cheerful Miss Jessie as ever.

'But why does not this Lord Mauleverer do something for the man who saved his life?' said I.

'Why, you see, unless Captain Brown has some reason for it, he never speaks about being poor; and he walked along by his lord-ship, looking as happy and cheerful as a prince; and as they never called attention to their dinner by apologies, and as Miss Brown was better that day, and all seemed bright, I dare say his lordship never knew how much care there was in the background. He did send game in the winter pretty often, but now he is gone abroad.'

I had often occasion to notice the use that was made of fragments and small opportunities in Cranford; the rose-leaves that were gathered ere they fell, to make into a pot-pourri for some one who had no garden; the little bundles of lavender-flowers sent to strew the drawers of some town-dweller, or to burn in the chamber of some invalid. Things that many would despise, and actions which it seemed scarcely worth while to perform, were all attended to in Cranford. Miss Jenkyns stuck an apple full of cloves, to be heated and smell pleasantly in Miss Brown's room; and as she put in each clove, she uttered a Johnsonian sentence. Indeed, she never could think of the Browns without talking Johnson; and, as they were seldom absent from her thoughts just then, I heard many a rolling three-piled sentence.

Captain Brown called one day to thank Miss Jenkyns for many little kindnesses, which I did not know until then that she had rendered. He had suddenly become like an old man; his deep bass voice had a quavering in it; his eyes looked dim, and the lines on his face were deep. He did not—could not—speak cheerfully of his daughter's state, but he talked with manly pious resignation, and not much. Twice over he said, 'What Jessie has been to us, God only knows!' and after the second time, he got up hastily, shook hands all round without speaking, and left the room.

That afternoon we perceived little groups in the street, all listening with faces aghast to some tale or other. Miss Jenkyns wondered what could be the matter, for some time before she took the undignified step of sending Jenny out to inquire.

Jenny came back with a white face of terror. 'Oh, Ma'am! oh, Miss Jenkyns, Ma'am! Captain Brown is killed by them nasty cruel railroads!' and she burst into tears. She, along with many others, had experienced the poor Captain's kindness.

'How?—where—where? Good God! Jenny, don't waste time in crying, but tell us something.' Miss Matty rushed out into the street at once, and collared the man who was telling the tale.

'Come in—come to my sister at once,—Miss Jenkyns, the rector's daughter. Oh, man, man! say it is not true,'—she cried, as she brought the affrighted carter, sleeking down his hair, into the drawing-room, where he stood with his wet boots on the new carpet, and no one regarded it.

'Please mum, it is true. I seed it myself,' and he shuddered at the recollection. 'The Captain was a-reading some new book as he was deep in, a-waiting for the down train; and there was a little lass as wanted to come to its mammy, and gave its sister the slip, and came toddling across the line. And he looked up sudden at the sound of the train coming, and seed the child, and he darted on the line and cotched it up, and his foot slipped, and the train came over him in no time. Oh Lord, Lord! Mum, it's quite true—and they've come over to tell his daughters. The child's safe, though, with only a bang on its shoulder, as he threw it to its mammy. Poor Captain would be glad of that, mum, would not he? God bless him!' The great rough carter puckered up his manly face, and turned away to hide his tears. I turned to Miss Jenkyns. She looked very ill, as if she were going to faint, and signed to me to open the window.

'Matilda, bring me my bonnet. I must go to those girls. God pardon me if ever I have spoken contemptuously to the Captain!'

Miss Jenkyns arrayed herself to go out, telling Miss Matilda to give the man a glass of wine. While she was away, Miss Matty and I huddled over the fire, talking in a low and awestruck voice. I know we cried quietly all the time.

Miss Jenkyns came home in a silent mood, and we durst not ask her many questions. She told us that Miss Jessie had fainted, and that she and Miss Pole had had some difficulty in bringing her round: but that, as soon as she recovered, she begged one of them to go and sit with her sister.

'Mr. Hoggins says she cannot live many days, and she shall be spared this shock,' said Miss Jessie, shivering with feelings to which she dared not give way.

'But how can you manage, my dear?' asked Miss Jenkyns; 'you cannot bear up, she must see your tears.'

'God will help me—I will not give way—she was asleep when the news came; she may be asleep yet. She would be so utterly miserable, not merely at my father's death, but to think of what would become of me; she is so good to me.' She looked up earnestly in their faces with her soft true eyes, and Miss Pole told Miss Jenkyns afterwards she could hardly bear it, knowing, as she did, how Miss Brown treated her sister.

However, it was settled according to Miss Jessie's wish. Miss Brown was to be told her father had been summoned to take a short journey on railway business. They had managed it in some way—Miss Jenkyns could not exactly say how. Miss Pole was to stop with Miss Jessie. Mrs. Jamieson had sent to inquire. And this was all we heard that night; and a sorrowful night it was. The next day a full account of the fatal accident was in the county paper, which Miss Jenkyns took in. Her eyes were very weak, she said, and she asked me to read it. When I came to the 'gallant gentleman was deeply engaged in the perusal of a number of 'Pickwick', which he had just received,' Miss Jenkyns shook her head long and solemnly, and then sighed out, 'Poor, dear, infatuated man!'

The corpse was to be taken from the station to the parish church, there to be interred. Miss Jessie had set her heart on following it to the grave; and no dissuasives could alter her resolve. Her restraint upon herself made her almost obstinate; she resisted all Miss Pole's entreaties, and Miss Jenkyns's advice. At last

Miss Jenkyns gave up the point; and after a silence, which I feared
portended some deep displeasure against Miss Jessie, Miss
Jenkyns said she should accompany the latter to the funeral.

'It is not fit for you to go alone. It would be against both propriety
and humanity were I to allow it.'

Miss Jessie seemed as if she did not half like this arrangement;
but her obstinacy, if she had any, had been exhausted in her determination to go to the interment. She longed, poor thing! I have
no doubt, to cry alone over the grave of the dear father to whom
she had been all in all; and to give way, for one little half-hour,
uninterrupted by sympathy, and unobserved by friendship. But
it was not to be. That afternoon Miss Jenkyns sent out for a yard
of black crape, and employed herself busily in trimming the little
black silk bonnet I have spoken about. When it was finished she
put it on, and looked at us for approbation—admiration she
despised. I was full of sorrow, but, by one of those whimsical
thoughts which come unbidden into our heads, in times of deepest
grief, I no sooner saw the bonnet than I was reminded of a helmet;
and in that hybrid bonnet, half-helmet, half-jockey cap, did Miss
Jenkyns attend Captain Brown's funeral; and I believe supported
Miss Jessie with a tender indulgent firmness which was invaluable,
allowing her to weep her passionate fill before they left.

Miss Pole, Miss Matty, and I, meanwhile, attended to Miss
Brown: and hard work we found it to relieve her querulous and
never-ending complaints. But if we were so weary and dispirited,
what must Miss Jessie have been! Yet she came back almost calm,
as if she had gained a new strength. She put off her mourning dress,
and came in, looking pale and gentle; thanking us each with a soft
long pressure of the hand. She could even smile—a faint, sweet,
wintry smile, as if to reassure us of her power to endure; but her
look made our eyes fill suddenly with tears, more than if she had
cried outright.

It was settled that Miss Pole was to remain with her all the
watching live-long night; and that Miss Matty and I were
to return in the morning to relieve them, and give Miss Jessie
the opportunity for a few hours of sleep. But when the morning came, Miss Jenkyns appeared at the breakfast table, equipped
in her helmet bonnet, and ordered Miss Matty to stay at
home, as she meant to go and help to nurse. She was evidently
in a state of great friendly excitement, which she showed by

eating her breakfast standing, and scolding the household all round.

No nursing—no energetic strong-minded woman could help Miss Brown now. There was that in the room as we entered, which was stronger than us all, and made us shrink into solemn awe-struck helplessness. Miss Brown was dying. We hardly knew her voice, it was so devoid of the complaining tone we had always associated with it. Miss Jessie told me afterwards that it, and her face too, were just what they had been formerly, when her mother's death left her the young anxious head of the family, of whom only Miss Jessie survived.

She was conscious of her sister's presence, though not, I think, of ours. We stood a little behind the curtain: Miss Jessie knelt with her face near her sister's, in order to catch the last soft awful whispers.

'Oh, Jessie! Jessie! How selfish I have been! God forgive me for letting you sacrifice yourself for me as you did. I have so loved you—and yet I have thought only of myself. God forgive me!'

'Hush, love! hush!' said Miss Jessie, sobbing.

'And my father! my dear, dear father! I will not complain now, if God will give me strength to be patient. But, oh, Jessie! tell my father how I longed and yearned to see him at last, and to ask his forgiveness. He can never know now how I loved him—oh! if I might but tell him, before I die; what a life of sorrow his has been, and I have done so little to cheer him!'

A light came into Miss Jessie's face. 'Would it comfort you, dearest, to think that he does know—would it comfort you, love, to know that his cares, his sorrows—' Her voice quivered, but she steadied it into calmness,—'Mary! he has gone before you to the place where the weary are at rest.* He knows now how you loved him.'

A strange look, which was not distress, came over Miss Brown's face. She did not speak for some time, but then we saw her lips form the words, rather than heard the sound—'Father, mother, Harry, Archy!'—then, as if it was a new idea throwing a filmy shadow over her darkening mind—'But you will be alone—Jessie!'

Miss Jessie had been feeling this all during the silence, I think; for the tears rolled down her cheeks like rain, at these words; and she could not answer at first. Then she put her hands together tight, and lifted them up, and said,—but not to us—

'Though He slay me, yet will I trust in Him.'*

In a few moments more, Miss Brown lay calm and still; never to sorrow or murmur more.

After this second funeral, Miss Jenkyns insisted that Miss Jessie should come to stay with her, rather than go back to the desolate house; which, in fact, we learned from Miss Jessie, must now be given up, as she had not wherewithal to maintain it. She had something about twenty pounds a-year, besides the interest of the money for which the furniture would sell; but she could not live upon that: and so we talked over her qualifications for earning money.

'I can sew neatly,' said she, 'and I like nursing. I think, too, I could manage a house, if any one would try me as housekeeper; or I would go into a shop, as saleswoman, if they would have patience with me at first.'

Miss Jenkyns declared, in an angry voice, that she should do no such thing; and talked to herself about 'some people having no idea of their rank as a Captain's daughter,' nearly an hour afterwards, when she brought Miss Jessie up a basin of delicately-made arrow-root, and stood over her like a dragoon until the last spoon-ful was finished: then she disappeared. Miss Jessie began to tell me some more of the plans which had suggested themselves to her, and insensibly fell into talking of the days that were past and gone, and interested me so much, I neither knew nor heeded how time passed. We were both startled when Miss Jenkyns reappeared, and caught us crying. I was afraid lest she would be displeased, as she often said that crying hindered digestion, and I knew she wanted Miss Jessie to get strong; but, instead, she looked queer and excited, and fidgeted round us without saying anything. At last she spoke—

'I have been so much startled—no, I've not been at all startled—don't mind me, my dear Miss Jessie—I've been very much surprised—in fact, I've had a caller, whom you knew once, my dear Miss Jessie——'

Miss Jessie went very white, then flushed scarlet, and looked eagerly at Miss Jenkyns—

'A gentleman, my dear, who wants to know if you would see him.'

'Is it?—it is not——' stammered out Miss Jessie—and got no farther.

'This is his card,' said Miss Jenkyns, giving it to Miss Jessie; and while her head was bent over it, Miss Jenkyns went through a series of winks and odd faces to me, and formed her lips into a long sentence, of which, of course, I could not understand a word.

'May he come up?' asked Miss Jenkyns at last.

'Oh, yes! certainly!' said Miss Jessie, as much as to say, this is your house, you may show any visitor where you like. She took up some knitting of Miss Matty's and began to be very busy, though I could see how she trembled all over.

Miss Jenkyns rang the bell, and told the servant who answered it to show Major Gordon up-stairs; and, presently, in walked a tall, fine, frank-looking man of forty, or upwards. He shook hands with Miss Jessie; but he could not see her eyes, she kept them so fixed on the ground. Miss Jenkyns asked me if I would come and help her to tie up the preserves in the store-room; and, though Miss Jessie plucked at my gown, and even looked up at me with begging eye, I durst not refuse to go where Miss Jenkyns asked. Instead of tying up preserves in the store-room, however, we went to talk in the dining-room; and there Miss Jenkyns told me what Major Gordon had told her;—how he had served in the same regiment with Captain Brown, and had become acquainted with Miss Jessie, then a sweet-looking, blooming girl of eighteen; how the acquaintance had grown into love, on his part, though it had been some years before he had spoken; how, on becoming possessed, through the will of an uncle, of a good estate in Scotland, he had offered, and been refused, though with so much agitation, and evident distress, that he was sure she was not indifferent to him; and how he had discovered that the obstacle was the fell disease which was, even then, too surely threatening her sister. She had mentioned that the surgeons fore-told intense suffering; and there was no one but herself to nurse her poor Mary, or cheer and comfort her father during the time of ill-ness. They had had long discussions; and, on her refusal to pledge herself to him as his wife, when all should be over, he had grown angry, and broken off entirely, and gone abroad, believing that she was a cold-hearted person, whom he would do well to forget. He had been travelling in the East, and was on his return home when, at Rome, he saw the account of Captain Brown's death in 'Galignani'.*

Just then Miss Matty, who had been out all the morning, and had only lately returned to the house, burst in with a face of dismay and outraged propriety:—

'Oh, goodness me!' she said. 'Deborah, there's a gentleman sitting in the drawing-room, with his arm round Miss Jessie's waist!' Miss Matty's eyes looked large with terror.

Miss Jenkyns snubbed her down in an instant:—

'The most proper place in the world for his arm to be in. Go away, Matilda, and mind your own business.' This from her sister, who had hitherto been a model of feminine decorum, was a blow for poor Miss Matty, and with a double shock she left the room.

The last time I ever saw poor Miss Jenkyns was many years after this. Mrs. Gordon had kept up a warm and affectionate inter- course with all at Cranford. Miss Jenkyns, Miss Matty, and Miss Pole had all been to visit her, and returned with wonderful accounts of her house, her husband, her dress, and her looks. For, with happiness, something of her early bloom returned; she had been a year or two younger than we had taken her for. Her eyes were always lovely, and, as Mrs. Gordon, her dimples were not out of place. At the time to which I have referred, when I last saw Miss Jenkyns, that lady was old and feeble, and had lost something of her strong mind. Little Flora Gordon was staying with the Misses Jenkyns, and when I came in she was reading aloud to Miss Jenkyns, who lay feeble and changed on the sofa. Flora put down the 'Rambler' when I came in.

'Ah!' said Miss Jenkyns, 'you find me changed, my dear. I can't see as I used to do. If Flora were not here to read to me, I hardly know how I should get through the day. Did you ever read the "Rambler?" It's a wonderful book—wonderful! and the most improving reading for Flora'—(which I dare say it would have been, if she could have read half the words without spelling, and could have understood the meaning of a third)—'better than that strange old book, with the queer name, poor Captain Brown was killed for reading—that book by Mr. Boz, you know—"Old Poz;"* when I was a girl, but that's a long time ago,—I acted Lucy in "Old Poz"'—she babbled on long enough for Flora to get a good long spell at the 'Christmas Carol,'* which Miss Matty had left on the table.

CHAPTER III

A LOVE AFFAIR OF LONG AGO

I THOUGHT that probably my connection with Cranford would cease after Miss Jenkyns's death; at least, that it would have to be kept up by correspondence, which bears much the same relation to personal intercourse that the books of dried plants I sometimes see ('Hortus Siccus', I think they call the thing,) do to the living and fresh flowers in the lanes and meadows. I was pleasantly surprised, therefore, by receiving a letter from Miss Pole (who had always come in for a supplementary week after my annual visit to Miss Jenkyns) proposing that I should go and stay with her; and then, in a couple of days after my acceptance, came a note from Miss Matty, in which, in a rather circuitous and very humble manner, she told me how much pleasure I should confer, if I could spend a week or two with her, either before or after I had been at Miss Pole's; 'for,' she said, 'since my dear sister's death, I am well aware I have no attractions to offer; it is only to the kindness of my friends that I can owe their company.'

Of course, I promised to come to dear Miss Matty, as soon as I had ended my visit to Miss Pole; and the day after my arrival at Cranford, I went to see her, much wondering what the house would be like without Miss Jenkyns, and rather dreading the changed aspect of things. Miss Matty began to cry as soon as she saw me. She was evidently nervous from having anticipated my call. I comforted her as well as I could; and I found the best consolation I could give was the honest praise that came from my heart as I spoke of the deceased. Miss Matty slowly shook her head over each virtue as it was named and attributed to her sister; at last she could not restrain the tears which had long been silently flowing, but hid her face behind her handkerchief, and sobbed aloud.

'Dear Miss Matty!' said I, taking her hand—for indeed I did not know in what way to tell her how sorry I was for her, left deserted in the world. She put down her handkerchief, and said—

'My dear, I'd rather you did not call me Matty. *She* did not like it; but I did many a thing she did not like, I'm afraid—and now she's gone! If you please, my love, will you call me Matilda?'

I promised faithfully, and began to practise the new name with

Miss Pole that very day; and, by degrees, Miss Matilda's feeling on the subject was known through Cranford, and we all tried to drop the more familiar name, but with so little success that by and by we gave up the attempt.*

My visit to Miss Pole was very quiet. Miss Jenkyns had so long taken the lead in Cranford, that, now she was gone, they hardly knew how to give a party. The Honourable Mrs. Jamieson, to whom Miss Jenkyns herself had always yielded the post of honour, was fat and inert, and very much at the mercy of her old servants. If they chose that she should give a party, they reminded her of the necessity for so doing; if not, she let it alone. There was all the more time for me to hear old-world stories from Miss Pole, while she sat knitting, and I making my father's shirts. I always took a quantity of plain sewing to Cranford; for, as we did not read much, or walk much, I found it a capital time to get through my work. One of Miss Pole's stories related to a shadow of a love affair that was dimly perceived or suspected long years before.

Presently, the time arrived when I was to remove to Miss Matilda's house. I found her timid and anxious about the arrangements for my comfort. Many a time, while I was unpacking, did she come backwards and forwards to stir the fire, which burned all the worse for being so frequently poked.

'Have you drawers enough, dear?' asked she. 'I don't know exactly how my sister used to arrange them. She had capital methods. I am sure she would have trained a servant in a week to make a better fire than this, and Fanny has been with me four months.'

This subject of servants was a standing grievance, and I could not wonder much at it; for if gentlemen were scarce, and almost unheard of in the 'genteel society' of Cranford, they or their counterparts—handsome young men—abounded in the lower classes. The pretty neat servant-maids had their choice of desirable 'followers;' and their mistresses, without having the sort of mysterious dread of men and matrimony that Miss Matilda had, might well feel a little anxious, lest the heads of their comely maids should be turned by the joiner, or the butcher, or the gardener; who were obliged, by their callings, to come to the house; and who, as ill-luck would have it, were generally handsome and unmarried. Fanny's lovers, if she had any—and Miss Matilda suspected her of so many flirtations, that, if she had not been very pretty, I should

have doubted her having one—were a constant anxiety to her
mistress. She was forbidden, by the articles of her engagement,
to have 'followers;'* and though she had answered innocently
enough, doubling up the hem of her apron as she spoke, 'Please,
ma'am, I never had more than one at a time,' Miss Matty prohibited that one. But a vision of a man seemed to haunt the kitchen.
Fanny assured me that it was all fancy; or else I should have said
myself that I had seen a man's coat-tails whisk into the scullery
once, when I went on an errand into the store-room at night; and
another evening, when, our watches having stopped, I went to look
at the clock, there was a very odd appearance, singularly like
a young man squeezed up between the clock and the back of the
open kitchen-door: and I thought Fanny snatched up the candle
very hastily, so as to throw the shadow on the clock-face, while
she very positively told me the time half-an-hour too early, as we
found out afterwards by the church-clock. But I did not add to
Miss Matty's anxieties by naming my suspicions, especially as
Fanny said to me, the next day, that it was such a queer kitchen
for having odd shadows about it, she really was almost afraid to
stay; 'for you know Miss,' she added, 'I don't see a creature from
six o'clock tea, till Missus rings the bell for prayers at ten.'

However, it so fell out that Fanny had to leave; and Miss Matilda
begged me to stay and 'settle her' with the new maid; to which
I consented, after I had heard from my father that he did not want
me at home. The new servant was a rough, honest-looking country-
girl, who had only lived in a farm place before; but I liked her
looks when she came to be hired; and I promised Miss Matilda to
put her in the ways of the house. The said ways were religiously
such as Miss Matilda thought her sister would approve. Many
a domestic rule and regulation had been a subject of plaintive
whispered murmur to me, during Miss Jenkyns's life; but now
that she was gone, I do not think that even I, who was a favourite,
durst have suggested an alteration. To give an instance: we constantly adhered to the forms which were observed, at meal times,
in 'my father, the Rector's house.' Accordingly, we had always
wine and dessert;* but the decanters were only filled when there
was a party; and what remained was seldom touched, though we
had two wine glasses apiece every day after dinner, until the next
festive occasion arrived; when the state of the remainder wine was
examined into, in a family council. The dregs were often given to

the poor; but occasionally, when a good deal had been left at the last party (five months ago, it might be,) it was added to some of a fresh bottle, brought up from the cellar. I fancy poor Captain Brown did not much like wine; for I noticed he never finished his first glass, and most military men take several. Then, as to our dessert, Miss Jenkyns used to gather currants and gooseberries for it herself, which I sometimes thought would have tasted better fresh from the trees; but then, as Miss Jenkyns observed, there would have been nothing for dessert in summer-time.* As it was, we felt very genteel with our two glasses apiece, and a dish of goose-berries at the top, of currants and biscuits at the sides, and two decanters at the bottom. When oranges came in, a curious proceed-ing was gone through. Miss Jenkyns did not like to cut the fruit; for, as she observed, the juice all ran out nobody knew where; sucking (only I think she used some more recondite word) was in fact the only way of enjoying oranges; but then there was the unpleasant association with a ceremony frequently gone through by little babies; and so, after dessert, in orange season, Miss Jenkyns and Miss Matty used to rise up, possess themselves each of an orange in silence, and withdraw to the privacy of their own rooms, to indulge in sucking oranges.

I had once or twice tried, on such occasions, to prevail on Miss Matty to stay; and had succeeded in her sister's life-time. I held up a screen,* and did not look, and, as she said, she tried not to make the noise very offensive; but now that she was left alone, she seemed quite horrified when I begged her to remain with me in the warm dining-parlour, and enjoy her orange as she liked best. And so it was in everything. Miss Jenkyns's rules were made more stringent than ever, because the framer of them was gone where there could be no appeal. In all things else Miss Matilda was meek and undecided to a fault. I have heard Fanny turn her round twenty times in a morning about dinner, just as the little hussy chose; and I sometimes fancied she worked on Miss Matilda's weakness in order to bewilder her, and to make her feel more in the power of her clever servant. I determined that I would not leave her till I had seen what sort of a person Martha was; and, if I found her trustworthy, I would tell her not to trouble her mistress with every little decision.

Martha was blunt and plain-spoken to a fault; otherwise she was a brisk, well-meaning, but very ignorant girl. She had not been with us a week before Miss Matilda and I were astounded one morning by the receipt of a letter from a cousin of hers, who had been twenty or thirty years in India,* and who had lately, as we had seen by the 'Army List,' returned to England, bringing with him an invalid wife, who had never been introduced to her English relations. Major Jenkyns wrote to propose that he and his wife should spend a night at Cranford, on his way to Scotland—at the inn, if it did not suit Miss Matilda to receive them into her house; in which case they should hope to be with her as much as possible during the day. Of course, it *must* suit her, as she said; for all Cranford knew that she had her sister's bed-room at liberty; but I am sure she wished the Major had stopped in India and forgotten his cousins out and out.

'Oh! how must I manage?' asked she, helplessly. 'If Deborah had been alive, she would have known what to do with a gentleman-visitor. Must I put razors in his dressing-room? Dear! dear! and I've got none. Deborah would have had them. And slippers, and coat-brushes?' I suggested that probably he would bring all these things with him. 'And after dinner, how am I to know when to get up, and leave him to his wine?*Deborah would have done it so well; she would have been quite in her element. Will he want coffee, do you think?' I undertook the management of the coffee, and told her I would instruct Martha in the art of waiting, in which it must be owned she was terribly deficient; and that I had no doubt Major and Mrs. Jenkyns would understand the quiet mode in which a lady lived by herself in a country town. But she was sadly fluttered. I made her empty her decanters, and bring up two fresh bottles of wine. I wished I could have prevented her from being present at my instructions to Martha; for she frequently cut in with some fresh direction, muddling the poor girl's mind, as she stood open-mouthed, listening to us both.

'Hand the vegetables round,'*said I (foolishly, I see now—for it was aiming at more than we could accomplish with quietness and simplicity): and then, seeing her look bewildered, I added, 'Take the vegetables round to people, and let them help themselves.'

'And mind you go first to the ladies,' put in Miss Matilda. 'Always go to the ladies before gentlemen, when you are waiting.'

'I'll do it as you tell me, ma'am,' said Martha; 'but I like lads best.'

We felt very uncomfortable and shocked at this speech of Martha's; yet I don't think she meant any harm; and, on the whole, she attended very well to our directions, except that she 'nudged' the Major, when he did not help himself as soon as she expected, to the potatoes, while she was handing them round.

The Major and his wife were quiet, unpretending people enough when they did come; languid, as all East Indians are, I suppose. We were rather dismayed at their bringing two servants with them, a Hindoo body-servant for the Major, and a steady elderly maid for his wife; but they slept at the inn, and took off a good deal of the responsibility by attending carefully to their master's and mistress's comfort. Martha, to be sure, had never ended her staring at the East Indian's white turban, and brown complexion, and I saw that Miss Matilda shrunk away from him a little as he waited at dinner. Indeed, she asked me, when they were gone, if he did not remind me of Blue Beard?* On the whole, the visit was most satisfactory, and is a subject of conversation even now with Miss Matilda; at the time, it greatly excited Cranford, and even stirred up the apathetic and Honourable Mrs. Jamieson to some expression of interest, when I went to call and thank her for the kind answers she had vouchsafed to Miss Matilda's inquiries as to the arrangement of a gentleman's dressing-room—answers which I must confess she had given in the wearied manner of the Scandinavian prophetess,—

'Leave me, leave me to repose.'*

And *now* I come to the love affair.

It seems that Miss Pole had a cousin, once or twice removed, who had offered to Miss Matty long ago. Now, this cousin lived four or five miles from Cranford on his own estate; but his property was not large enough to entitle him to rank higher than a yeoman; or rather, with something of the 'pride which apes humility,'* he had refused to push himself on, as so many of his class had done, into the ranks of the squires. He would not allow himself to be called Thomas Holbrook, *Esq.*; he even sent back letters with this address, telling the postmistress at Cranford that his name was *Mr*. Thomas Holbrook, yeoman. He rejected all domestic innovations; he would have the house door stand open in summer, and shut in winter, without knocker or bell to summon a servant. The closed fist or the knob of the stick did this office for

him, if he found the door locked. He despised every refinement
which had not its root deep down in humanity. If people were not
ill, he saw no necessity for moderating his voice. He spoke the
dialect of the country in perfection, and constantly used it in conversation; although Miss Pole (who gave me these particulars)
added, that he read aloud more beautifully and with more feeling
than any one she had ever heard, except the late Rector.

'And how came Miss Matilda not to marry him?' asked I.

'Oh, I don't know. She was willing enough, I think; but you
know Cousin Thomas would not have been enough of a gentleman
for the Rector, and Miss Jenkyns.'*

'Well! but they were not to marry him,' said I, impatiently.

'No; but they did not like Miss Matty to marry below her rank.
You know she was the Rector's daughter, and somehow they are
related to Sir Peter Arley: Miss Jenkyns thought a deal of that.'

'Poor Miss Matty!' said I.

'Nay, now, I don't know anything more than that he offered
and was refused. Miss Matty might not like him—and Miss
Jenkyns might never have said a word—it is only a guess of mine.'

'Has she never seen him since?' I inquired.

'No, I think not. You see, Woodley, Cousin Thomas's house,
lies half-way between Cranford and Misselton; and I know he
made Misselton his market-town very soon after he had offered
to Miss Matty; and I don't think he has been into Cranford above
once or twice since—once, when I was walking with Miss Matty,
in High Street; and suddenly she darted from me, and went up
Shire Lane. A few minutes after, I was startled by meeting Cousin
Thomas.'

'How old is he?' I asked, after a pause of castle-building.

'He must be about seventy, I think, my dear,' said Miss Pole,
blowing up my castle, as if by gunpowder, into small fragments.

Very soon after—at least during my long visit to Miss Matilda—
I had the opportunity of seeing Mr. Holbrook; seeing, too, his first
encounter with his former love, after thirty or forty years' separa-
tion. I was helping to decide whether any of the new assortment of
coloured silks which they had just received at the shop, would do
to match a grey and black mousseline-de-laine* that wanted a new
breadth, when a tall, thin, Don Quixote-looking* old man came
into the shop for some woollen gloves. I had never seen the person,
(who was rather striking) before, and I watched him rather

attentively, while Miss Matty listened to the shopman. The stranger wore a blue coat with brass buttons, drab breeches, and gaiters, and drummed with his fingers on the counter until he was attended to. When he answered the shop-boy's question, 'What can I have the pleasure of showing you to-day, Sir?' I saw Miss Matilda start, and then suddenly sit down; and instantly I guessed who it was. She had made some inquiry which had to be carried round to the other shopman.

'Miss Jenkyns wants the black sarsenet* two-and-twopence the yard;' and Mr. Holbrook had caught the name, and was across the shop in two strides.

'Matty—Miss Matilda—Miss Jenkyns! God bless my soul! I should not have known you. How are you? how are you?' He kept shaking her hand in a way which proved the warmth of his friendship; but he repeated so often, as if to himself, 'I should not have known you!' that any sentimental romance which I might be inclined to build, was quite done away with by his manner.

However, he kept talking to us all the time we were in the shop; and then waving the shopman with the unpurchased gloves on one side, with 'Another time, sir! another time!' he walked home with us. I am happy to say my client, Miss Matilda, also left the shop in an equally bewildered state, not having purchased either green or red silk. Mr. Holbrook was evidently full with honest, loud-spoken joy at meeting his old love again; he touched on the changes that had taken place; he even spoke of Miss Jenkyns as 'Your poor sister! Well, well! we have all our faults;' and bade us good-bye with many a hope that he should soon see Miss Matty again. She went straight to her room; and never came back till our early tea-time, when I thought she looked as if she had been crying.

CHAPTER IV

A VISIT TO AN OLD BACHELOR

A FEW days after, a note came from Mr. Holbrook, asking us—impartially asking both of us—in a formal, old-fashioned style, to spend a day at his house—a long June day—for it was June now. He named that he had also invited his cousin, Miss Pole;

so that we might join in a fly, which could be put up at his house.

I expected Miss Matty to jump at this invitation; but, no! Miss Pole and I had the greatest difficulty in persuading her to go. She thought it was improper; and was even half annoyed when we utterly ignored the idea of any impropriety in her going with two other ladies to see her old lover. Then came a more serious difficulty. She did not think Deborah would have liked her to go. This took us half a day's good hard talking to get over; but, at the first sentence of relenting, I seized the opportunity, and wrote and despatched an acceptance in her name—fixing day and hour, that all might be decided and done with.

The next morning she asked me if I would go down to the shop with her; and there, after much hesitation, we chose out three caps to be sent home and tried on, that the most becoming might be selected to take with us on Thursday.

She was in a state of silent agitation all the way to Woodley. She had evidently never been there before; and, although she little dreamt I knew anything of her early story, I could perceive she was in a tremor at the thought of seeing the place which might have been her home, and round which it is probable that many of her innocent girlish imaginations had clustered. It was a long drive there, through paved jolting lanes. Miss Matilda sate bolt upright, and looked wistfully out of the windows, as we drew near the end of our journey. The aspect of the country was quiet and pastoral. Woodley stood among fields; and there was an old-fashioned garden, where roses and currant-bushes touched each other, and where the feathery asparagus formed a pretty back-ground to the pinks and gilly-flowers; there was no drive up to the door: we got out at a little gate, and walked up a straight box-edged path.

'My cousin might make a drive, I think,' said Miss Pole, who was afraid of ear-ache, and had only her cap on.

'I think it is very pretty,' said Miss Matty, with a soft plaintiveness in her voice, and almost in a whisper; for just then Mr. Holbrook appeared at the door, rubbing his hands in very effervescence of hospitality. He looked more like my idea of Don Quixote than ever, and yet the likeness was only external. His respectable housekeeper stood modestly at the door to bid us welcome; and, while she led the elder ladies upstairs to a bed-room, I begged to look about the garden. My request evidently pleased the old gentleman; who took me all round the place, and showed me his six-and-twenty cows, named after the different letters of the alphabet. As we went along, he surprised me occasionally by repeating apt and beautiful quotations from the poets, ranging easily from Shakspeare and George Herbert to those of our own day. He did this as naturally as if he were thinking aloud, and their true and beautiful words were the best expression he could find for what he was thinking or feeling. To be sure, he called Byron 'my lord Bÿrron,' and pronounced the name of Goethe strictly in accordance with the English sound of the letters—'As Goëthe says, "Ye ever-verdant palaces,"'* &c. Altogether, I never met with a man, before or since, who had spent so long a life in a secluded and not impressive country, with ever-increasing delight in the daily and yearly change of season and beauty.

When he and I went in, we found that dinner was nearly ready in the kitchen,—for so I suppose the room ought to be called, as there were oak dressers and cupboards all round, all over by the side of the fire-place, and only a small Turkey carpet in the middle of the flag-floor. The room might have been easily made into a handsome dark-oak dining-parlour, by removing the oven, and a few other appurtenances of a kitchen, which were evidently never used; the real cooking place being at some distance. The room in which we were expected to sit was a stiffly furnished, ugly apartment; but that in which we did sit was what Mr. Holbrook called the counting-house, when he paid his labourers their weekly wages, at a great desk near the door. The rest of the pretty sitting-room—looking into the orchard, and all covered over with dancing tree-shadows—was filled with books. They lay on the ground, they covered the walls, they strewed the table. He was evidently half ashamed and half proud of his extravagance in this respect. They were of all kinds,—poetry, and wild weird tales prevailing. He evidently chose his books in accordance with his own tastes, not because such and such were classical, or established favourites.

'Ah!' he said, 'we farmers ought not to have much time for reading; yet somehow one can't help it.'

'What a pretty room!' said Miss Matty, *sotto voce*.

'What a pleasant place!' said I, aloud, almost simultaneously.

'Nay! if you like it,'—replied he; 'but can you sit on these great black leather three-cornered chairs? I like it better than the best parlour; but I thought ladies would take that for the smarter place.'

It was the smarter place; but, like most smart things, not at all pretty, or pleasant, or home-like; so, while we were at dinner, the servant-girl dusted and scrubbed the counting-house chairs, and we sate there all the rest of the day.

We had pudding before meat; and I thought Mr. Holbrook was going to make some apology for his old-fashioned ways,* for he began,—

'I don't know whether you like new-fangled ways.'

'Oh! not at all!' said Miss Matty.

'No more do I,' said he. 'My housekeeper *will* have things in her new fashion; or else I tell her, that when I was a young man, we used to keep strictly to my father's rule, "No broth, no ball; no ball, no beef;" and always began dinner with broth. Then we had suet puddings, boiled in the broth with the beef; and then the meat itself. If we did not sup our broth, we had no ball, which we liked a deal better; and the beef came last of all, and only those had it who had done justice to the broth and the ball. Now folks begin with sweet things, and turn their dinners topsy-turvy.'

When the ducks and green peas came, we looked at each other in dismay; we had only two-pronged, black-handled forks. It is true, the steel was as bright as silver; but what were we to do? Miss Matty picked up her peas, one by one, on the point of the prongs, much as Aminé* ate her grains of rice after her previous feast with the Ghoul. Miss Pole sighed over her delicate young peas as she left them on one side of her plate untasted; for they *would* drop between the prongs. I looked at my host: the peas were going wholesale into his capacious mouth, shovelled up by his large round-ended knife. I saw, I imitated, I survived! My friends, in spite of my precedent, could not muster up courage enough to do an ungenteel thing; and, if Mr. Holbrook had not been so heartily hungry, he would probably have seen that the good peas went away almost untouched.

After dinner, a clay pipe was brought in, and a spittoon; and, asking us to retire to another room, where he would soon join us if we disliked tobacco-smoke, he presented his pipe to Miss Matty, and requested her to fill the bowl. This was a compliment to a lady in his youth; but it was rather inappropriate to propose it as an honour to Miss Matty, who had been trained by her sister to hold smoking of every kind in utter abhorrence. But if it was a shock to her refinement, it was also a gratification to her feelings to be thus selected; so she daintily stuffed the strong tobacco into the pipe; and then we withdrew.

'It is very pleasant dining with a bachelor,' said Miss Matty, softly, as we settled ourselves in the counting-house. 'I only hope it is not improper; so many pleasant things are!'

'What a number of books he has!' said Miss Pole, looking round the room. 'And how dusty they are!'

'I think it must be like one of the great Dr. Johnson's rooms,' said Miss Matty. 'What a superior man your cousin must be!'

'Yes!' said Miss Pole; 'he's a great reader; but I am afraid he has got into very uncouth habits with living alone.'

'Oh! uncouth is too hard a word. I should call him eccentric; very clever people always are!' replied Miss Matty.

When Mr. Holbrook returned, he proposed a walk in the fields; but the two elder ladies were afraid of damp, and dirt; and had only very unbecoming calashes* to put on over their caps; so they declined; and I was again his companion in a turn which he said he was obliged to take, to see after his men. He strode along, either wholly forgetting my existence, or soothed into silence by his pipe —and yet it was not silence exactly. He walked before me, with a stooping gait, his hands clasped behind him; and, as some tree or cloud, or glimpse of distant upland pastures, struck him, he quoted poetry to himself; saying it out loud in a grand sonorous voice, with just the emphasis that true feeling and appreciation give. We came upon an old cedar-tree, which stood at one end of the house;

> 'The cedar spreads his dark-green layers of shade.'*

'Capital term—"layers!" Wonderful man!' I did not know whether he was speaking to me or not; but I put in an assenting 'wonderful,' although I knew nothing about it; just because I was tired of being forgotten, and of being consequently silent.

He turned sharp round. 'Aye! you may say "wonderful." Why, when I saw the review of his poems in "Blackwood,"* I set off within an hour, and walked seven miles to Misselton (for the horses were not in the way) and ordered them. Now, what colour are ash-buds in March?'

Is the man going mad? thought I. He is very like Don Quixote.

'What colour are they, I say?' repeated he vehemently.

'I am sure I don't know, sir,' said I, with the meekness of ignorance.

'I knew you didn't. No more did I—an old fool that I am! till this young man comes and tells me. Black as ash-buds in March.* And I've lived all my life in the country; more shame for me not to know. Black: they are jet-black, madam.' And he went off again, swinging along to the music of some rhyme he had got hold of.

When we came back, nothing would serve him but he must read us the poems he had been speaking of; and Miss Pole encouraged him in his proposal, I thought, because she wished me to hear his beautiful reading, of which she had boasted; but she afterwards said it was because she had got to a difficult part of her crochet, and wanted to count her stitches without having to talk. Whatever he had proposed would have been right to Miss Matty; although she did fall sound asleep within five minutes after he had begun a long poem, called 'Locksley Hall,'* and had a comfortable nap, unobserved, till he ended; when the cessation of his voice wakened her up, and she said, feeling that something was expected, and that Miss Pole was counting:—

'What a pretty book!'

'Pretty! madam! it's beautiful! Pretty, indeed!'

'Oh yes! I meant beautiful!' said she, fluttered at his disapproval of her word. 'It is so like that beautiful poem of Dr. Johnson's* my sister used to read—I forget the name of it, what was it, my dear?' turning to me.

'Which do you mean, ma'am? What was it about?'

'I don't remember what it was about, and I've quite forgotten what the name of it was; but it was written by Dr. Johnson, and was very beautiful, and very like what Mr. Holbrook has just been reading.'

'I don't remember it,' said he, reflectively. 'But I don't know Dr. Johnson's poems well. I must read them.'

As we were getting into the fly to return, I heard Mr. Holbrook say he should call on the ladies soon, and inquire how they got home; and this evidently pleased and fluttered Miss Matty at the time he said it; but after we had lost sight of the old house among the trees, her sentiments towards the master of it were gradually absorbed into a distressing wonder as to whether Martha had broken her word, and seized on the opportunity of her mistress's absence to have a 'follower.' Martha looked good, and steady, and composed enough, as she came to help us out; she was always careful of Miss Matty, and to-night she made use of this unlucky speech:—

'Eh! dear ma'am, to think of your going out in an evening in such a thin shawl! It is no better than muslin. At your age, ma'am, you should be careful.'

'My age!' said Miss Matty, almost speaking crossly, for her; for she was usually gentle. 'My age! Why, how old do you think I am, that you talk about my age?'

'Well, ma'am! I should say you were not far short of sixty; but folks' looks is often against them—and I'm sure I meant no harm.'

'Martha, I'm not yet fifty-two!' said Miss Matty, with grave emphasis; for probably the remembrance of her youth had come very vividly before her this day, and she was annoyed at finding that golden time so far away in the past.

But she never spoke of any former and more intimate acquaintance with Mr. Holbrook. She had probably met with so little sympathy in her early love, that she had shut it up close in her heart; and it was only by a sort of watching, which I could hardly avoid, since Miss Pole's confidence, that I saw how faithful her poor heart had been in its sorrow and its silence.

She gave me some good reason for wearing her best cap every day, and sate near the window, in spite of her rheumatism, in order to see, without being seen, down into the street.

He came. He put his open palms upon his knees, which were far apart, as he sate with his head bent down, whistling, after we had replied to his inquiries about our safe return. Suddenly, he jumped up.

'Well, madam! have you any commands for Paris? I am going there in a week or two.'

'To Paris!' we both exclaimed.

'Yes, madam! I've never been there, and always had a wish to go; and I think if I don't go soon, I mayn't go at all; so as soon as the hay is got in I shall go, before harvest-time.'

We were so much astonished, that we had no commissions.

Just as he was going out of the room, he turned back, with his favourite exclamation:

'God bless my soul, madam! but I nearly forgot half my errand. Here are the poems for you, you admired so much the other evening at my house.' He tugged away at a parcel in his coat-pocket.

'Good-bye, miss,' said he; 'good-bye, Matty! take care of your-self.' And he was gone. But he had given her a book, and he had called her Matty, just as he used to do thirty years ago.

'I wish he would not go to Paris,' said Miss Matilda, anxiously. 'I don't believe frogs will agree with him; he used to have to be very careful what he ate, which was curious in so strong-looking a young man.'

Soon after this I took my leave, giving many an injunction to Martha to look after her mistress, and to let me know if she thought that Miss Matilda was not so well; in which case I would volunteer a visit to my old friend, without noticing* Martha's intelligence to her.

Accordingly I received a line or two from Martha every now and then; and, about November, I had a note to say her mistress was 'very low and sadly off her food;' and the account made me so uneasy, that, although Martha did not decidedly summon me, I packed up my things and went.

I received a warm welcome, in spite of the little flurry produced by my impromptu visit, for I had only been able to give a day's notice. Miss Matilda looked miserably ill; and I prepared to com-fort and cosset her.

I went down to have a private talk with Martha.

'How long has your mistress been so poorly?' I asked, as I stood by the kitchen fire.

'Well! I think it's better than a fortnight; it is, I know: it was one Tuesday, after Miss Pole had been, that she went into this moping way. I thought she was tired, and it would go off with a night's rest; but, no! she has gone on and on ever since, till I thought it my duty to write to you, ma'am.'

'You did quite right, Martha. It is a comfort to think she has so faithful a servant about her. And I hope you find your place comfortable?'

'Well, ma'am, missus is very kind, and there's plenty to eat and drink, and no more work but what I can do easily,—but'—Martha hesitated.

'But what, Martha?'

'Why, it seems so hard of missus not to let me have any followers; there's such lots of young fellows in the town; and many a one has as much as offered to keep company with me; and I may never be in such a likely place again, and it's like wasting an opportunity.

Many a girl as I know would have 'em unbeknownst to missus; but
I've given my word, and I'll stick to it; or else this is just the house
for missus never to be the wiser if they did come: and it's such
a capable* kitchen—there's such good dark corners in it—I'd be
bound to hide any one. I counted up last Sunday night—for I'll
not deny I was crying because I had to shut the door in Jem
Hearn's face; and he's a steady young man, fit for any girl; only
I had given missus my word.' Martha was all but crying again;
and I had little comfort to give her, for I knew, from old experience,
of the horror with which both the Miss Jenkynses looked upon
'followers;' and in Miss Matty's present nervous state this dread
was not likely to be lessened.

I went to see Miss Pole the next day, and took her completely
by surprise; for she had not been to see Miss Matilda for two days.

'And now I must go back with you, my dear, for I promised to
let her know how Thomas Holbrook went on; and I'm sorry to
say his housekeeper has sent me word to-day that he has'nt long to
live. Poor Thomas! That journey to Paris was quite too much
for him. His housekeeper says he has hardly ever been round his
fields since; but just sits with his hands on his knees in the counting-
house, not reading or anything, but only saying, what a wonderful
city Paris was! Paris has much to answer for, if it's killed my
cousin Thomas, for a better man never lived.'

'Does Miss Matilda know of his illness?' asked I;—a new light
as to the cause of her indisposition dawning upon me.

'Dear! to be sure, yes! Has not she told you? I let her know
a fortnight ago, or more, when first I heard of it. How odd, she
shouldn't have told you!'

Not at all, I thought; but I did not say anything. I felt almost
guilty of having spied too curiously into that tender heart, and I
was not going to speak of its secrets,—hidden, Miss Matty believed,
from all the world. I ushered Miss Pole into Miss Matilda's little
drawing-room; and then left them alone. But I was not surprised
when Martha came to my bed-room door, to ask me to go down to
dinner alone, for that missus had one of her bad headaches. She
came into the drawing-room at tea-time; but it was evidently an
effort to her; and, as if to make up for some reproachful feeling
against her late sister, Miss Jenkyns, which had been troubling her
all the afternoon, and for which she now felt penitent, she kept
telling me how good and how clever Deborah was in her youth;

how she used to settle what gowns they were to wear at all the parties (faint, ghostly ideas of dim parties far away in the distance, when Miss Matty and Miss Pole were young!); and how Deborah and her mother had started the benefit society for the poor, and taught girls cooking and plain sewing; and how Deborah had once danced with a lord; and how she used to visit at Sir Peter Arley's, and try to remodel the quiet rectory establishment on the plans of Arley Hall, where they kept thirty servants; and how she had nursed Miss Matty through a long, long illness, of which I had never heard before, but which I now dated in my own mind as following the dismissal of the suit of Mr. Holbrook. So we talked softly and quietly of old times, through the long November evening.

The next day Miss Pole brought us word that Mr. Holbrook was dead. Miss Matty heard the news in silence; in fact, from the account of the previous day, it was only what we had to expect. Miss Pole kept calling upon us for some expression of regret, by asking if it was not sad that he was gone: and saying,

'To think of that pleasant day last June, when he seemed so well! And he might have lived this dozen years if he had not gone to that wicked Paris, where they are always having Revolutions.'

She paused for some demonstration on our part. I saw Miss Matty could not speak, she was trembling so nervously; so I said what I really felt: and after a call of some duration—all the time of which I have no doubt Miss Pole thought Miss Matty received the news very calmly—our visitor took her leave.

Miss Matty made a strong effort to conceal her feelings—a concealment she practised even with me, for she has never alluded to Mr. Holbrook again, although the book he gave her lies with her Bible on the little table by her bedside; she did not think I heard her when she asked the little milliner of Cranford to make her caps something like the Honourable Mrs. Jamieson's, or that I noticed the reply—

'But she wears widows' caps,* ma'am?'

'Oh! I only meant something in that style; not widows', of course, but rather like Mrs. Jamieson's.'

This effort at concealment was the beginning of the tremulous motion of head and hands which I have seen ever since in Miss Matty.

The evening of the day on which we heard of Mr. Holbrook's

death, Miss Matilda was very silent and thoughtful; after prayers
she called Martha back, and then she stood uncertain what to say.

'Martha!' she said at last; 'you are young,'—and then she made
so long a pause that Martha, to remind her of her half-finished
sentence, dropped a courtesy, and said—

'Yes, please, ma'am; two-and-twenty last third of October,
please, ma'am.'

'And perhaps, Martha, you may some time meet with a young
man you like, and who likes you. I did say you were not to have
followers; but if you meet with such a young man, and tell me, and
I find he is respectable, I have no objection to his coming to see
you once a week. God forbid!' said she, in a low voice, 'that I should
grieve any young hearts.' She spoke as if she were providing for
some distant contingency, and was rather startled when Martha
made her ready eager answer:—

'Please, ma'am, there's Jem Hearn, and he's a joiner, making
three-and-sixpence a-day, and six foot one in his stocking-feet,
please, ma'am; and if you'll ask about him to-morrow morning,
every one will give him a character for steadiness; and he'll be
glad enough to come to-morrow night, I'll be bound.'

Though Miss Matty was startled, she submitted to Fate and
Love.

CHAPTER V

OLD LETTERS

I HAVE often noticed that almost every one has his own individual
small economies—careful habits of saving fractions of pennies in
some one peculiar direction—any disturbance of which annoys
him more than spending shillings or pounds on some real extravagance. An old gentleman of my acquaintance, who took the
intelligence of the failure of a Joint-Stock Bank,* in which some of
his money was invested, with stoical mildness, worried his family
all through a long summer's day, because one of them had torn
(instead of cutting) out the written leaves of his now useless bank-
book; of course, the corresponding pages at the other end came
out as well; and this little unnecessary waste of paper (his private
economy) chafed him more than all the loss of his money. Envelopes

fretted his soul terribly when they first came in; the only way in which he could reconcile himself to such waste of his cherished article was by patiently turning inside out all that were sent to him, and so making them serve again. Even now, though tamed by age, I see him casting wistful glances at his daughters when they send a whole instead of a half sheet of note-paper, with the three lines of acceptance to an invitation, written on only one of the sides. I am not above owning that I have this human weakness myself. String is my foible. My pockets get full of little hanks of it, picked up and twisted together, ready for uses that never come. I am seriously annoyed if any one cuts the string of a parcel, instead of patiently and faithfully undoing it fold by fold. How people can bring themselves to use Indian-rubber rings, which are a sort of deification of string, as lightly as they do, I cannot imagine. To me an Indian-rubber ring is a precious treasure. I have one which is not new; one that I picked up off the floor, nearly six years ago. I have really tried to use it; but my heart failed me, and I could not commit the extravagance.

Small pieces of butter grieve others. They cannot attend to conversation, because of the annoyance occasioned by the habit which some people have of invariably taking more butter than they want. Have you not seen the anxious look (almost mesmeric) which such persons fix on the article? They would feel it a relief if they might bury it out of their sight, by popping it into their own mouths, and swallowing it down; and they are really made happy if the person on whose plate it lies unused, suddenly breaks off a piece of toast (which he does not want at all) and eats up his butter. They think that this is not waste.

Now Miss Matty Jenkyns was chary of candles. We had many devices to use as few as possible. In the winter afternoons she would sit knitting for two or three hours; she could do this in the dark, or by fire-light; and when I asked if I might not ring for candles to finish stitching my wristbands, she told me to 'keep blind-man's holiday.'* They were usually brought in with tea; but we only burnt one at a time. As we lived in constant preparation for a friend who might come in, any evening (but who never did), it required some contrivance to keep our two candles of the same length, ready to be lighted, and to look as if we burnt two always. The candles took it in turns; and, whatever we might be talking about or doing, Miss Matty's eyes were habitually fixed upon the candle, ready to

jump up and extinguish it, and to light the other before they had
become too uneven in length to be restored to equality in the
course of the evening.

One night, I remember that this candle economy particularly
annoyed me. I had been very much tired of my compulsory 'blind-
man's holiday,'—especially as Miss Matty had fallen asleep, and
I did not like to stir the fire, and run the risk of awakening her; so
I could not even sit on the rug, and scorch myself with sewing by
firelight, according to my usual custom. I fancied Miss Matty
must be dreaming of her early life; for she spoke one or two words,
in her uneasy sleep, bearing reference to persons who were dead
long before. When Martha brought in the lighted candle and tea,
Miss Matty started into wakefulness, with a strange bewildered
look around, as if we were not the people she expected to see about
her. There was a little sad expression that shadowed her face as
she recognised me; but immediately afterwards she tried to give
me her usual smile. All through tea-time, her talk ran upon the
days of her childhood and youth. Perhaps this reminded her of the
desirableness of looking over all the old family letters, and destroying such as ought not to be allowed to fall into the hands of strangers;
for she had often spoken of the necessity of this task, but had
always shrunk from it, with a timid dread of something painful.
To-night, however, she rose up after tea, and went for them—in
the dark; for she piqued herself on the precise neatness of all her
chamber arrangements, and used to look uneasily at me, when
I lighted a bed-candle to go to another room for anything. When
she returned, there was a faint pleasant smell of Tonquin beans*
in the room. I had always noticed this scent about any of the things
which had belonged to her mother; and many of the letters were
addressed to her—yellow bundles of love-letters, sixty or seventy
years old.

Miss Matty undid the packet with a sigh; but she stifled it
directly, as if it were hardly right to regret the flight of time, or of
life either. We agreed to look them over separately, each taking
a different letter out of the same bundle, and describing its contents to the other, before destroying it. I never knew what sad work
the reading of old letters was before that evening, though I could
hardly tell why. The letters were as happy as letters could be—at
least those early letters were. There was in them a vivid and
intense sense of the present time, which seemed so strong and full,

as if it could never pass away, and as if the warm, living hearts that so expressed themselves could never die, and be as nothing to the sunny earth. I should have felt less melancholy, I believe, if the letters had been more so. I saw the tears quietly stealing down the well-worn furrows of Miss Matty's cheeks, and her spectacles often wanted wiping. I trusted at last that she would light the other candle, for my own eyes were rather dim, and I wanted more light to see the pale, faded ink; but no—even through her tears, she saw and remembered her little economical ways.

The earliest set of letters were two bundles tied together, and ticketed (in Miss Jenkyns's handwriting), 'Letters interchanged between my ever-honoured father and my dearly-beloved mother, prior to their marriage, in July, 1774.'* I should guess that the Rector of Cranford was about twenty-seven years of age when he wrote those letters; and Miss Matty told me that her mother was just eighteen at the time of her wedding. With my idea of the Rector, derived from a picture in the dining parlour, stiff and stately, in a huge full-bottomed wig, with gown, cassock, and bands,* and his hand upon a copy of the only sermon he ever published,—it was strange to read these letters. They were full of eager, passionate ardour; short homely sentences, right fresh from the heart; (very different from the grand Latinised, Johnsonian style of the printed sermon, preached before some judge at assize time.) His letters were a curious contrast to those of his girl-bride. She was evidently rather annoyed at his demands upon her for expressions of love, and could not quite understand what he meant by repeating the same thing over in so many different ways; but what she was quite clear about was her longing for a white 'Paduasoy,'* —whatever that might be; and six or seven letters were principally occupied in asking her lover to use his influence with her parents (who evidently kept her in good order) to obtain this or that article of dress, more especially the white 'Paduasoy.' He cared nothing how she was dressed; she was always lovely enough for him, as he took pains to assure her, when she begged him to express in his answers a predilection for particular pieces of finery, in order that she might show what he said to her parents. But at length he seemed to find out that she would not be married till she had a 'trousseau' to her mind; and then he sent her a letter, which had evidently accompanied a whole box full of finery, and in which he requested that she might be dressed in everything her heart desired. This was

the first letter, ticketed in a frail, delicate hand, 'From my dearest
John.' Shortly afterwards they were married,—I suppose, from
the intermission in their correspondence.

'We must burn them, I think,' said Miss Matty, looking doubt-
fully at me. 'No one will care for them when I am gone.' And one
by one she dropped them into the middle of the fire; watching each
blaze up, die out, and rise away, in faint, white, ghostly semblance,
up the chimney, before she gave up another to the same fate. The
room was light enough now; but I, like her, was fascinated into
watching the destruction of those letters, into which the honest
warmth of a manly heart had been poured forth.

The next letter, likewise docketed by Miss Jenkyns, was
endorsed, 'Letter of pious congratulation and exhortation from
my venerable grandfather to my mother, on occasion of my own
birth. Also some practical remarks on the desirability of keeping
warm the extremities of infants, from my excellent grandmother.'

The first part was, indeed, a severe and forcible picture of the
responsibilities of mothers, and a warning against the evils that
were in the world, and lying in ghastly wait for the little baby of two
days old. His wife did not write, said the old gentleman, because
he had forbidden it, she being indisposed with a sprained ankle,
which (he said) quite incapacitated her from holding a pen. However, at the foot of the page was a small 'T.O.,' and on turning it
over, sure enough, there was a letter to 'my dear, dearest Molly,'
begging her, when she left her room, whatever she did, to go *up*
stairs before going *down*: and telling her to wrap her baby's feet
up in flannel, and keep it warm by the fire, although it was summer,
for babies were so tender.

It was pretty to see from the letters, which were evidently
exchanged with some frequency, between the young mother and
the grandmother, how the girlish vanity was being weeded out of
her heart by love for her baby. The white 'Paduasoy' figured again
in the letters, with almost as much vigour as before. In one, it was
being made into a christening cloak for the baby. It decked it when
it went with its parents to spend a day or two at Arley Hall. It
added to its charms when it was 'the prettiest little baby that ever
was seen. Dear mother, I wish you could see her! Without any
parshality, I do think she will grow up a regular bewty!'
I thought of Miss Jenkyns, grey, withered, and wrinkled; and
I wondered if her mother had known her in the courts of heaven;

and then I knew that she had, and that they stood there in angelic guise.

There was a great gap before any of the Rector's letters appeared. And then his wife had changed her mode of endorsement. It was no longer from 'My dearest John;' it was from 'My honoured Husband.' The letters were written on occasion of the publication of the same Sermon which was represented in the picture. The preaching before 'My Lord Judge,' and the 'publishing by request,' was evidently the culminating point—the event of his life. It had been necessary for him to go up to London to superintend it through the press. Many friends had to be called upon, and consulted, before he could decide on any printer fit for so onerous a task; and at length it was arranged that J. and J. Rivingtons were to have the honourable responsibility. The worthy Rector seemed to be strung up by the occasion to a high literary pitch, for he could hardly write a letter to his wife without cropping out into Latin. I remember the end of one of his letters ran thus:—'I shall ever hold the virtuous qualities of my Molly in remembrance, *dum memor ipse mei, dum spiritus hos regit artus,*'* which, considering that the English of his correspondent was sometimes at fault in grammar, and often in spelling, might be taken as a proof of how much he 'idealised' his Molly; and, as Miss Jenkyns used to say, 'People talk a great deal about idealising now-a-days, whatever that may mean.' But this was nothing to a fit of writing classical poetry, which soon seized him; in which his Molly figured away as 'Maria.' The letter containing the *carmen* was endorsed by her, 'Hebrew verses*sent me by my honoured husband. I thowt to have had a letter about killing the pig, but must wait. Mem., to send the poetry to Sir Peter Arley, as my husband desires.' And in a post-scriptum note in his handwriting, it was stated that the Ode had appeared in the 'Gentleman's Magazine,'* December, 1782.

Her letters back to her husband (treasured as fondly by him as if they had been M. T. Ciceronis Epistolæ*) were more satisfactory to an absent husband and father, than his could ever have been to her. She told him how Deborah sewed her seam very neatly every day, and read to her in the books he had set her; how she was a very 'forrard,' good child, but *would* ask questions her mother could not answer; but how she did not let herself down by saying she did not know, but took to stirring the fire, or sending the 'forrard' child on an errand. Matty was now the mother's darling, and promised (like her sister at her age) to be a great beauty. I was reading this aloud to Miss Matty, who smiled and sighed a little at the hope, so fondly expressed, that 'little Matty might not be vain, even if she were a bewty.'

'I had very pretty hair, my dear,' said Miss Matilda; 'and not a bad mouth.' And I saw her soon afterwards adjust her cap and draw herself up.

But to return to Mrs. Jenkyns's letters. She told her husband about the poor in the parish; what homely domestic medicines she had administered; what kitchen physic she had sent. She had evidently held his displeasure as a rod in pickle over the heads of all the ne'er-do-wells. She asked for his directions about the cows and pigs; and did not always obtain them, as I have shown before.

The kind old grandmother was dead, when a little boy was born, soon after the publication of the Sermon; but there was another letter of exhortation from the grandfather, more stringent and admonitory than ever, now that there was a boy to be guarded from the snares of the world. He described all the various sins into which men might fall, until I wondered how any man ever came to a natural death. The gallows seemed as if it must have been the termination of the lives of most of the grandfather's friends and acquaintance; and I was not surprised at the way in which he spoke of this life being 'a vale of tears.'*

It seemed curious that I should never have heard of this brother before; but I concluded that he had died young; or else surely his name would have been alluded to by his sisters.

By-and-by we came to packets of Miss Jenkyns's letters. These, Miss Matty did regret to burn. She said all the others had been only interesting to those who loved the writers; and that it seemed as if it would have hurt her to allow them to fall into the hands of strangers, who had not known her dear mother, and how good she was, although she did not always spell quite in the modern fashion; but Deborah's letters were so very superior! Any one might profit by reading them. It was a long time since she had read Mrs. Chapone,* but she knew she used to think that Deborah could have said the same things quite as well; and as for Mrs. Carter!* people thought a deal of her letters, just because she had written Epictetus, but she was quite sure Deborah would never have made use of such a common expression as 'I canna be fashed!'

Miss Matty did grudge burning these letters, it was evident.

She would not let them be carelessly passed over with any quiet reading, and skipping, to myself. She took them from me, and even lighted the second candle in order to read them aloud with a proper emphasis, and without stumbling over the big words. Oh dear! how I wanted facts instead of reflections, before those letters were concluded! They lasted us two nights; and I won't deny that I made use of the time to think of many other things, and yet I was always at my post at the end of each sentence.

The Rector's letters, and those of his wife and mother-in-law, had all been tolerably short and pithy, written in a straight hand, with the lines very close together. Sometimes the whole letter was contained on a mere scrap of paper. The paper was very yellow, and the ink very brown; some of the sheets were (as Miss Matty made me observe) the old original Post,* with the stamp in the corner, representing a post-boy riding for life and twanging his horn. The letters of Mrs. Jenkyns and her mother were fastened with a great round, red wafer; for it was before Miss Edgeworth's 'Patronage'* had banished wafers from polite society. It was evident, from the tenor of what was said, that franks* were in great request, and were even used as a means of paying debts by needy Members of Parliament. The Rector sealed his epistles with an immense coat of arms, and showed by the care with which he had performed this ceremony, that he expected they should be cut open, not broken by any thoughtless or impatient hand. Now, Miss Jenkyns's letters were of a later date in form and writing. She wrote on the square sheet, which we have learned to call old-fashioned. Her hand was admirably calculated, together with her use of many-syllabled words, to fill up a sheet, and then came the pride and delight of crossing.* Poor Miss Matty got sadly puzzled with this, for the words gathered size like snow-balls, and towards the end of her letter, Miss Jenkyns used to become quite sesquipe-dalian. In one to her father, slightly theological and controversial in its tone, she had spoken of Herod, Tetrarch of Idumea.* Miss Matty read it 'Herod Petrarch of Etruria,' and was just as well pleased as if she had been right.

I can't quite remember the date, but I think it was in 1805 that Miss Jenkyns wrote the longest series of letters; on occasion of her absence on a visit to some friends near Newcastle-upon-Tyne. These friends were intimate with the commandant of the garrison there, and heard from him of all the preparations that were being made to repel the invasion of Buonaparte,* which some people imagined might take place at the mouth of the Tyne. Miss Jenkyns was evidently very much alarmed; and the first part of her letters was often written in pretty intelligible English, conveying particulars of the preparations which were made in the family with whom she was residing against the dreaded event; the bundles of clothes that were packed up ready for a flight to Alston Moor (a wild hilly piece of ground between Northumberland and Cumberland); the signal that was to be given for this flight, and for the simultaneous turning out of the volunteers under arms; which said signal was to consist (if I remember rightly) in ringing the church bells in a particular and ominous manner. One day, when Miss Jenkyns and her hosts were at a dinner-party in Newcastle, this warning-summons was actually given (not a very wise proceeding, if there be any truth in the moral attached to the fable of the Boy and the Wolf,* but so it was,) and Miss Jenkyns, hardly recovered from her fright, wrote the next day to describe the sound, the breathless shock, the hurry and alarm; and then, taking breath, she added, 'How trivial, my dear father, do all our apprehensions of the last evening appear, at the present moment, to calm and inquiring minds!' And here Miss Matty broke in with—

'But, indeed, my dear, they were not at all trivial or trifling at the time. I know I used to wake up in the night many a time, and think I heard the tramp of the French entering Cranford.* Many people talked of hiding themselves in the salt-mines;*—and meat would have kept capitally down there, only perhaps we should have been thirsty. And my father preached a whole set of sermons on the occasion; one set in the mornings, all about David and Goliath, to spirit up the people to fighting with spades or bricks, if need were; and the other set in the afternoons, proving that Napoleon (that was another name for Bony, as we used to call him) was all the same as an Apollyon and Abaddon.* I remember, my father rather thought he should be asked to print this last set; but the parish had, perhaps, had enough of them with hearing.'

Peter Marmaduke Arley Jenkyns, ('poor Peter!' as Miss Matty began to call him) was at school at Shrewsbury by this time. The Rector took up his pen, and rubbed up his Latin, once more, to correspond with his boy. It was very clear that the lad's were what are called show-letters. They were of a highly mental description, giving an account of his studies, and his intellectual hopes of various kinds, with an occasional quotation from the classics; but, now and then, the animal nature broke out in such a little sentence as this, evidently written in a trembling hurry, after the letter had been inspected: 'Mother, dear, do send me a cake, and put plenty of citron in.' The 'mother, dear,' probably answered her boy in the form of cakes and 'goody,'*for there were none of her letters among this set; but a whole collection of the Rector's, to whom the Latin in his boy's letters was like a trumpet to the old war-horse. I do not know much about Latin, certainly, and it is, perhaps, an ornamental language; but not very useful, I think—at least to judge from the bits I remember out of the Rector's letters. One was: 'You have not got that town in your map of Ireland; but *Bonus Bernardus non videt omnia*,* as the Proverbia say.' Presently it became very evident that 'poor Peter' got himself into many scrapes. There were letters of stilted penitence to his father, for some wrong-doing; and, among them all, was a badly written, badly-sealed, badly-directed, blotted note—'My dear, dear, dear, dearest mother, I will be a better boy—I will, indeed; but don't, please, be ill for me; I am not worth it; but I will be good, darling mother.'

Miss Matty could not speak for crying, after she had read this note. She gave it to me in silence, and then got up and took it to her sacred recesses in her own room, for fear, by any chance, it might get burnt. 'Poor Peter!' she said; 'he was always in scrapes; he was too easy. They led him wrong, and then left him in the lurch. But he was too fond of mischief. He could never resist a joke. Poor Peter!'

CHAPTER VI

POOR PETER

POOR Peter's career lay before him rather pleasantly mapped out by kind friends, but *Bonus Bernardus non videt omnia*, in this map too. He was to win honours at Shrewsbury School, and carry them thick to Cambridge, and after that, a living awaited him, the gift of his godfather,* Sir Peter Arley. Poor Peter! his lot in life was very different to what his friends had hoped and planned. Miss Matty told me all about it, and I think it was a relief to her when she had done so.

He was the darling of his mother, who seemed to dote on all her children, though she was, perhaps, a little afraid of Deborah's superior acquirements. Deborah was the favourite of her father, and when Peter disappointed him, she became his pride. The sole honour Peter brought away from Shrewsbury, was the reputation of being the best good fellow that ever was, and of being the captain of the school in the art of practical joking. His father was disappointed, but set about remedying the matter in a manly way. He could not afford to send Peter to read with any tutor, but he could read with him himself; and Miss Matty told me much of the awful preparations in the way of dictionaries and lexicons that were made in her father's study the morning Peter began.

'My poor mother!' said she. 'I remember how she used to stand in the hall, just near enough the study-door to catch the tone of my father's voice. I could tell in a moment if all was going right, by her face. And it did go right for a long time.'

'What went wrong at last?' said I. 'That tiresome Latin, I dare say.'

'No! it was not the Latin. Peter was in high favour with my father, for he worked up well for him. But he seemed to think that the Cranford people might be joked about, and made fun of, and they did not like it; nobody does. He was always hoaxing them; "hoaxing" is not a pretty word, my dear, and I hope you won't tell your father I used it, for I should not like him to think that I was not choice in my language, after living with such a woman as Deborah. And be sure you never use it yourself. I don't know how it slipped out of my mouth, except it was that I was thinking of poor Peter, and it was always his expression. But he was a very gentlemanly boy in many things. He was like dear Captain Brown in always being ready to help any old person or a child. Still, he did like joking and making fun; and he seemed to think the old ladies in Cranford would believe anything. There were many old ladies living here then; we are principally ladies now, I know; but we are not so old as the ladies used to be when I was a girl. I could laugh to think of some of Peter's jokes. No! my dear, I won't tell you of them, because they might not shock you as they ought to do; and they were very shocking. He even took in my father once, by dressing himself up as a lady that was passing through the town and wished to see the Rector of Cranford, "who had published that admirable Assize Sermon." Peter said, he was awfully frightened himself when he saw how my father took it all in, and even offered to copy out all his Napoleon Buonaparte sermons for her—him, I mean—no, her, for Peter was a lady then. He told me he was more terrified than he ever was before, all the time my father was speaking. He did not think my father would have believed him; and yet if he had not, it would have been a sad thing for Peter. As it was, he was none so glad of it, for my father kept him hard at work copying out all those twelve Buonaparte sermons for the lady—that was for Peter himself, you know. He was the lady. And once when he wanted to go fishing, Peter said, "Confound the woman!"—very bad language, my dear; but Peter was not always so guarded as he should have been; my father was so angry with him, it nearly frightened me out of my wits: and yet I could hardly keep from laughing at the little curtsies Peter kept making, quite slyly, whenever my father spoke of the lady's excellent taste and sound discrimination.'

'Did Miss Jenkyns know of these tricks?' said I.

'Oh no! Deborah would have been too much shocked. No! no one knew but me. I wish I had always known of Peter's plans; but sometimes he did not tell me. He used to say, the old ladies in the town wanted something to talk about; but I don't think they did. They had the St. James's Chronicle* three times a-week, just as we have now,* and we have plenty to say; and I remember the clacking noise there always was when some of the ladies got together. But, probably, school-boys talk more than ladies. At last there was a terrible sad thing happened.' Miss Matty got up, went to the door, and opened it; no one was there. She rang the bell for Martha; and when Martha came, her mistress told her to go for eggs to a farm at the other end of the town.

'I will lock the door after you, Martha. You are not afraid to go, are you?'

'No, Ma'am, not at all; Jem Hearn will be only too proud to go with me.'

Miss Matty drew herself up, and, as soon as we were alone, she wished that Martha had more maidenly reserve.

'We'll put out the candle, my dear. We can talk just as well by fire-light, you know. There! well! you see, Deborah had gone from home for a fortnight or so; it was a very still, quiet day, I remember, overhead; and the lilacs were all in flower, so I suppose it was spring. My father had gone out to see some sick people in the parish; I recollect seeing him leave the house, with his wig and shovel-hat,* and cane. What possessed our poor Peter I don't know; he had the sweetest temper, and yet he always seemed to like to plague Deborah. She never laughed at his jokes, and thought him ungenteel, and not careful enough about improving his mind; and that vexed him.

'Well! he went to her room, it seems, and dressed himself in her old gown, and shawl, and bonnet; just the things she used to wear in Cranford, and was known by everywhere; and he made the pillow into a little—you are sure you locked the door, my dear, for I should not like any one to hear—into—into—a little baby, with white long clothes. It was only, as he told me afterwards, to make something to talk about in the town: he never thought of it as affecting Deborah. And he went and walked up and down in the Filbert walk—just half hidden by the rails, and half seen; and he cuddled his pillow, just like a baby; and talked to it all the nonsense people do. Oh dear! and my father came stepping stately up the street, as he always did; and what should he see but a little black crowd of people—I dare say as many as twenty—all peeping through his garden rails. So he thought, at first, they were only looking at a new rhododendron* that was in full bloom, and that he was very proud of; and he walked slower, that they might have more time to admire. And he wondered if he could make out a sermon from the occasion, and thought, perhaps, there was some relation between the rhododendrons and the lilies of the field. My poor father! When he came nearer, he began to wonder that they did not see him; but their heads were all so close together, peeping and peeping! My father was amongst them, meaning, he said, to ask them to walk into the garden with him, and admire the beautiful vegetable production, when—oh, my dear! I tremble to think of it—he looked through the rails himself, and saw—I don't know what he thought he saw, but old Clare told me his face went quite grey-white with anger, and his eyes blazed out under his frowning black brows; and he spoke out—oh, so terribly!—and bade them all stop where they were—not one of them to go, not one to stir a step; and, swift as light, he was in at the garden door, and down the Filbert walk, and seized hold of poor Peter, and tore his clothes

off his back—bonnet, shawl, gown, and all—and threw the pillow
among the people over the railings: and then he was very, very
angry indeed; and before all the people he lifted up his cane, and
flogged Peter!

'My dear! that boy's trick, on that sunny day, when all seemed
going straight and well, broke my mother's heart, and changed my
father for life. It did, indeed. Old Clare said, Peter looked as white
as my father; and stood as still as a statue to be flogged; and my
father struck hard! When my father stopped to take breath, Peter
said, "Have you done enough, Sir?" quite hoarsely, and still standing quite quiet. I don't know what my father said—or if he said
anything. But old Clare said, Peter turned to where the people
outside the railing were, and made them a low bow, as grand and
as grave as any gentleman; and then walked slowly into the house.
I was in the store-room helping my mother to make cowslip-wine.
I cannot abide the wine now, nor the scent of the flowers; they turn
me sick and faint, as they did that day, when Peter came in, looking
as haughty as any man—indeed, looking like a man, not like a boy.
"Mother!" he said, "I am come to say, God bless you for ever."
I saw his lips quiver as he spoke; and I think he durst not say anything more loving, for the purpose that was in his heart. She
looked at him rather frightened, and wondering, and asked him
what was to do? He did not smile or speak, but put his arms round
her, and kissed her as if he did not know how to leave off; and
before she could speak again, he was gone. We talked it over, and
could not understand it, and she bade me go and seek my father,
and ask what it was all about. I found him walking up and down,
looking very highly displeased.

'"Tell your mother I have flogged Peter, and that he richly
deserved it."

'I durst not ask any more questions. When I told my mother,
she sat down, quite faint, for a minute. I remember, a few days
after, I saw the poor, withered cowslip-flowers thrown out to the
leaf-heap, to decay and die there. There was no making of cowslip-
wine that year at the Rectory—nor, indeed, ever after.

'Presently, my mother went to my father. I know I thought of
Queen Esther and King Ahasuerus;* for my mother was very
pretty and delicate-looking, and my father looked as terrible as
King Ahasuerus. Some time after, they came out together; and
then my mother told me what had happened, and that she was

going up to Peter's room, at my father's desire—though she was
not to tell Peter this—to talk the matter over with him. But no
Peter was there. We looked over the house; no Peter was there!
Even my father, who had not liked to join in the search at first,
helped us before long. The Rectory was a very old house: steps
up into a room, steps down into a room, all through. At first, my
mother went calling low and soft—as if to reassure the poor boy—
"Peter! Peter, dear! it's only me;" but, by-and-by, as the servants
came back from the errands my father had sent them, in different
directions, to find where Peter was—as we found he was not in the
garden, nor the hayloft, nor anywhere about—my mother's cry
grew louder and wilder—"Peter! Peter, my darling! where are
you?" for then she felt and understood that that long kiss meant
some sad kind of "good-bye." The afternoon went on—my mother
never resting, but seeking again and again in every possible place
that had been looked into twenty times before; nay, that she had
looked into over and over again herself. My father sat with his head
in his hands, not speaking, except when his messengers came in,
bringing no tidings; then he lifted up his face so strong and sad,
and told them to go again in some new direction. My mother kept
passing from room to room, in and out of the house, moving noise-
lessly, but never ceasing. Neither she nor my father durst leave the
house, which was the meeting-place for all the messengers. At last
(and it was nearly dark), my father rose up. He took hold of my
mother's arm, as she came with wild, sad pace, through one door,
and quickly towards another. She started at the touch of his hand,
for she had forgotten all in the world but Peter.

'"Molly!" said he, "I did not think all this would happen."
He looked into her face for comfort—her poor face, all wild and
white; for neither she nor my father had dared to acknowledge
—much less act upon—the terror that was in their hearts, lest
Peter should have made away with himself. My father saw no
conscious look in his wife's hot, dreary eyes, and he missed
the sympathy that she had always been ready to give him—
strong man as he was; and at the dumb despair in her face, his
tears began to flow. But when she saw this, a gentle sorrow came
over her countenance, and she said, "Dearest John! don't cry;
come with me, and we'll find him," almost as cheerfully as if she
knew where he was. And she took my father's great hand in
her little soft one, and led him along, the tears dropping, as he

walked on that same unceasing, weary walk, from room to room, through house and garden.

'Oh! how I wished for Deborah! I had no time for crying, for now all seemed to depend on me. I wrote for Deborah to come home. I sent a message privately to that same Mr. Holbrook's house—poor Mr. Holbrook!—you know who I mean. I don't mean I sent a message to him, but I sent one that I could trust, to know if Peter was at his house. For at one time Mr. Holbrook was an occasional visitor at the Rectory—you know he was Miss Pole's cousin—and he had been very kind to Peter, and taught him how to fish—he was very kind to everybody, and I thought Peter might have gone off there. But Mr. Holbrook was from home, and Peter had never been seen. It was night now; but the doors were all wide open, and my father and mother walked on and on; it was more than an hour since he had joined her, and I don't believe they had ever spoken all that time. I was getting the parlour fire lighted, and one of the servants was preparing tea, for I wanted them to have something to eat and drink and warm them, when old Clare asked to speak to me.

'"I have borrowed the nets from the weir, Miss Matty. Shall we drag the ponds to-night, or wait for the morning?"

'I remember staring in his face to gather his meaning; and when I did, I laughed out loud. The horror of that new thought—our bright, darling Peter, cold, and stark, and dead! I remember the ring of my own laugh now.

'The next day Deborah was at home before I was myself again. She would not have been so weak to give way as I had done; but my screams (my horrible laughter had ended in crying) had roused my sweet dear mother, whose poor wandering wits were called back and collected, as soon as a child needed her care. She and Deborah sat by my bedside; I knew by the looks of each that there had been no news of Peter—no awful, ghastly news, which was what I most had dreaded in my dull state between sleeping and waking.

'The same result of all the searching had brought something of the same relief to my mother, to whom, I am sure, the thought that Peter might even then be hanging dead in some of the familiar home places, had caused that never-ending walk of yesterday. Her soft eyes never were the same again after that; they had always a restless craving look, as if seeking for what they could

not find. Oh! it was an awful time; coming down like a thunder-
bolt on the still sunny day, when the lilacs were all in bloom.'

'Where was Mr. Peter?' said I.

'He had made his way to Liverpool; and there was war then;
and some of the king's ships lay off the mouth of the Mersey; and
they were only too glad to have a fine likely boy such as him (five
foot nine he was) come to offer himself. The captain wrote to my
father, and Peter wrote to my mother. Stay! those letters will be
somewhere here.'

We lighted the candle, and found the captain's letter, and
Peter's too. And we also found a little simple begging letter from
Mrs. Jenkyns to Peter, addressed to him at the house of an old
school-fellow, whither she fancied he might have gone. They had
returned it unopened; and unopened it had remained ever since,
having been inadvertently put by among the other letters of that
time. This is it:—

'My dearest Peter,

'You did not think we should be so sorry as we are, I know, or
you would never have gone away. You are too good. Your father
sits and sighs till my heart aches to hear him. He cannot hold up
his head for grief; and yet he only did what he thought was right.
Perhaps he has been too severe, and perhaps I have not been kind
enough; but God knows how we love you, my dear only boy. Dor*
looks so sorry you are gone. Come back, and make us happy, who
love you so much. I *know* you will come back.'

But Peter did not come back. That spring day was the last time
he ever saw his mother's face.* The writer of the letter—the last—
the only person who had ever seen what was written in it, was dead
long ago—and I, a stranger, not born at the time when this occurrence took place, was the one to open it.

The captain's letter summoned the father and mother to Liverpool instantly, if they wished to see their boy; and by some of the
wild chances of life, the captain's letter had been detained somewhere, somehow.

Miss Matty went on:—'And it was race-time, and all the post-
horses at Cranford were gone to the races; but my father and
mother set off in our own gig,—and, oh! my dear, they were too
late—the ship was gone! And now, read Peter's letter to my
mother!'

It was full of love, and sorrow, and pride in his new profession, and a sore sense of his disgrace in the eyes of the people at Cranford; but ending with a passionate entreaty that she would come and see him before he left the Mersey:—'Mother! we may go into battle. I hope we shall, and lick those French; but I must see you again before that time.'

'And she was too late,' said Miss Matty; 'too late!'

We sat in silence, pondering on the full meaning of those sad, sad words. At length I asked Miss Matty to tell me how her mother bore it.

'Oh!' she said, 'she was patience itself. She had never been strong, and this weakened her terribly. My father used to sit looking at her: far more sad than she was. He seemed as if he could look at nothing else when she was by; and he was so humble,—so very gentle now. He would, perhaps, speak in his old way—laying down the law, as it were—and then, in a minute or two, he would come round and put his hand on our shoulders, and ask us in a low voice if he had said anything to hurt us? I did not wonder at his speaking so to Deborah, for she was so clever; but I could not bear to hear him talking so to me.

'But, you see, he saw what we did not—that it was killing my mother. Yes! killing her—(put out the candle, my dear; I can talk better in the dark)—for she was but a frail woman, and ill fitted to stand the fright and shock she had gone through; and she would smile at him and comfort him, not in words but in her looks and tones, which were always cheerful when he was there. And she would speak of how she thought Peter stood a good chance of being admiral very soon—he was so brave and clever; and how she thought of seeing him in his navy uniform, and what sort of hats admirals wore; and how much more fit he was to be a sailor than a clergyman; and all in that way, just to make my father think she was quite glad of what came of that unlucky morning's work, and the flogging which was always in his mind, as we all knew. But, oh, my dear! the bitter, bitter crying she had when she was alone;—and at last, as she grew weaker, she could not keep her tears in, when Deborah or me was by, and would give us message after message for Peter,—(his ship had gone to the Mediterranean, or somewhere down there, and then he was ordered off to India, and there was no overland route then);—but she still said that no one knew where their death lay in wait, and that we were not to think hers was near. We did not think it, but we knew it, as we saw her fading away.

'Well, my dear, it's very foolish of me, I know, when in all likelihood I am so near seeing her again.*

'And only think, love! the very day after her death—for she did not live quite a twelvemonth after Peter went away—the very day after—came a parcel for her from India—from her poor boy. It was a large, soft, white India shawl,* with just a little narrow border all round; just what my mother would have liked.

'We thought it might rouse my father, for he had sat with her hand in his all night long; so Deborah took it in to him, and Peter's letter to her, and all. At first, he took no notice; and we tried to make a kind of light careless talk about the shawl, opening it out and admiring it. Then, suddenly, he got up, and spoke:—"She shall be buried in it," he said; "Peter shall have that comfort; and she would have liked it."

'Well! perhaps it was not reasonable, but what could we do or say? One gives people in grief their own way. He took it up and felt it—"It is just such a shawl as she wished for when she was married, and her mother did not give it her. I did not know of it till after, or she should have had it—she should; but she shall have it now."

'My mother looked so lovely in her death! She was always pretty, and now she looked fair, and waxen, and young—younger than Deborah, as she stood trembling and shivering by her. We decked her in the long soft folds; she lay, smiling, as if pleased; and people came—all Cranford came—to beg to see her, for they had loved her dearly—as well they might; and the country-women brought posies; old Clare's wife brought some white violets, and begged they might lie on her breast.

'Deborah said to me, the day of my mother's funeral, that if she had a hundred offers, she never would marry and leave my father. It was not very likely she would have so many—I don't know that she had one; but it was not less to her credit to say so. She was such a daughter to my father, as I think there never was before, or since. His eyes failed him, and she read book after book, and wrote, and copied, and was always at his service in any parish business. She could do many more things than my poor mother could; she even once wrote a letter to the bishop for my father. But he missed my mother sorely; the whole parish noticed it. Not that he was less

active; I think he was more so, and more patient in helping every
one. I did all I could to set Deborah at liberty to be with him; for
I knew I was good for little, and that my best work in the world
was to do odd jobs quietly, and set others at liberty. But my father
was a changed man.'

'Did Mr. Peter ever come home?'

'Yes, once. He came home a Lieutenant; he did not get to be
Admiral. And he and my father were such friends! My father took
him into every house in the parish, he was so proud of him. He
never walked out without Peter's arm to lean upon. Deborah used
to smile (I don't think we ever laughed again after my mother's
death), and say she was quite put in a corner. Not but what my
father always wanted her when there was letter-writing, or reading
to be done, or anything to be settled.'

'And then?' said I, after a pause.

'Then Peter went to sea again; and, by-and-by, my father died,
blessing us both, and thanking Deborah for all she had been to
him; and, of course, our circumstances were changed; and, instead
of living at the Rectory, and keeping three maids and a man, we
had to come to this small house, and be content with a servant-
of-all-work; but, as Deborah used to say, we have always lived
genteelly, even if circumstances have compelled us to simplicity. —
Poor Deborah!'

'And Mr. Peter?' asked I.

'Oh, there was some great war in India* — I forget what they call
it—and we have never heard of Peter since then. I believe he is
dead myself; and it sometimes fidgets me that we have never put
on mourning for him. And then, again, when I sit by myself, and
all the house is still, I think I hear his step coming up the street,
and my heart begins to flutter and beat; but the sound always goes
past—and Peter never comes.

'That's Martha back? No! *I*'ll go, my dear; I can always find
my way in the dark, you know. And a blow of fresh air at the door
will do my head good, and it's rather got a trick of aching.'

So she pattered off. I had lighted the candle, to give the room
a cheerful appearance against her return.

'Was it Martha?' asked I.

'Yes. And I am rather uncomfortable, for I heard such a strange
noise just as I was opening the door.'

'When?' I asked, for her eyes were round with affright.

'In the street—just outside—it sounded like—'

'Talking?' I put in, as she hesitated a little.

'No! kissing—'

CHAPTER VII

VISITING

ONE morning, as Miss Matty and I sat at our work—it was before
twelve o'clock, and Miss Matty had not yet changed the cap with
yellow ribbons, that had been Miss Jenkyns's best, and which
Miss Matty was now wearing out in private, putting on the one
made in imitation of Mrs. Jamieson's at all times when she expected
to be seen—Martha came up, and asked if Miss Betty Barker might
speak to her mistress. Miss Matty assented, and quickly disappeared to change the yellow ribbons, while Miss Barker came
up stairs; but, as she had forgotten her spectacles, and was rather
flurried by the unusual time of the visit, I was not surprised to see
her return with one cap on the top of the other. She was quite
unconscious of it herself, and looked at us with bland satisfaction.
Nor do I think Miss Barker perceived it; for, putting aside the
little circumstance that she was not so young as she had been, she
was very much absorbed in her errand; which she delivered herself of, with an oppressive modesty that found vent in endless
apologies.

Miss Betty Barker was the daughter of the old clerk at Cranford,
who had officiated in Mr. Jenkyns's time. She and her sister had
had pretty good situations as ladies' maids, and had saved up
money enough to set up a milliner's shop, which had been
patronised by the ladies in the neighbourhood. Lady Arley, for
instance, would occasionally give Miss Barkers the pattern of an
old cap of hers, which they immediately copied and circulated
among the *élite* of Cranford. I say the *élite*, for Miss Barkers had
caught the trick of the place, and piqued themselves upon their
'aristocratic connection.' They would not sell their caps and
ribbons to any one without a pedigree. Many a farmer's wife or
daughter turned away huffed from Miss Barkers' select millinery,
and went rather to the universal shop, where the profits of brown

soap and moist sugar enabled the proprietor to go straight to (Paris, he said, until he found his customers too patriotic and John Bullish to wear what the Mounseers wore) London; where, as he often told his customers, Queen Adelaide* had appeared, only the very week before, in a cap exactly like the one he showed them, trimmed with yellow and blue ribbons, and had been complimented by King William on the becoming nature of her head-dress.

Miss Barkers, who confined themselves to truth, and did not approve of miscellaneous customers, throve notwithstanding. They were self-denying, good people. Many a time have I seen the eldest of them (she that had been maid to Mrs. Jamieson) carrying out some delicate mess to a poor person. They only aped their betters in having 'nothing to do' with the class immediately below theirs. And when Miss Barker died, their profits and income were found to be such that Miss Betty was justified in shutting up shop, and retiring from business. She also (as I think I have before said) set up her cow; a mark of respectability in Cranford, almost as decided as setting up a gig*is among some people. She dressed finer than any lady in Cranford; and we did not wonder at it; for it was understood that she was wearing out all the bonnets and caps, and outrageous ribbons, which had once formed her stock in trade. It was five or six years since she had given up shop: so in any other place than Cranford her dress might have been considered *passée*.

And now, Miss Betty Barker had called to invite Miss Matty to tea at her house on the following Tuesday. She gave me also an impromptu invitation, as I happened to be a visitor; though I could see she had a little fear lest, since my father had gone to live in Drumble, he might have engaged in that 'horrid cotton trade,' and so dragged his family down out of 'aristocratic society.' She prefaced this invitation with so many apologies, that she quite excited my curiosity. 'Her presumption' was to be excused. What had she been doing? She seemed so overpowered by it, I could only think that she had been writing to Queen Adelaide, to ask for a receipt for washing lace; but the act which she so characterised was only an invitation she had carried to her sister's former mistress, Mrs. Jamieson. 'Her former occupation considered, could Miss Matty excuse the liberty?' Ah! thought I, she has found out that double cap, and is going to rectify Miss Matty's head-dress. No! it was simply to extend her invitation to Miss Matty and to me. Miss Matty bowed acceptance; and I wondered that, in the graceful action, she did not feel the unusual weight and extraordinary height of her head-dress. But I do not think she did; for she recovered her balance, and went on talking to Miss Betty in a kind, condescending manner, very different from the fidgety way she would have had, if she had suspected how singular her appearance was.

'Mrs. Jamieson is coming, I think you said?' asked Miss Matty.

'Yes. Mrs. Jamieson most kindly and condescendingly said she would be happy to come. One little stipulation she made, that she should bring Carlo. I told her that if I had a weakness, it was for dogs.'

'And Miss Pole?' questioned Miss Matty, who was thinking of her pool at Preference, in which Carlo would not be available as a partner.

'I am going to ask Miss Pole. Of course, I could not think of asking her until I had asked you, Madam—the rector's daughter, Madam. Believe me, I do not forget the situation my father held under yours.'

'And Mrs. Forrester, of course?'

'And Mrs. Forrester. I thought, in fact, of going to her before I went to Miss Pole. Although her circumstances are changed, Madam, she was born a Tyrrell, and we can never forget her alliance to the Bigges, of Bigelow Hall.'

Miss Matty cared much more for the little circumstance of her being a very good card-player.

'Mrs. Fitz-Adam—I suppose'—

'No, Madam. I must draw a line somewhere. Mrs. Jamieson would not, I think, like to meet Mrs. Fitz-Adam. I have the greatest respect for Mrs. Fitz-Adam—but I cannot think her fit society for such ladies as Mrs. Jamieson and Miss Matilda Jenkyns.'

Miss Betty Barker bowed low to Miss Matty, and pursed up her mouth. She looked at me with sidelong dignity, as much as to say, although a retired milliner, she was no democrat, and understood the difference of ranks.

'May I beg you to come as near half-past six, to my little dwelling, as possible, Miss Matilda? Mrs. Jamieson dines at five, but has kindly promised not to delay her visit beyond that time—half-past six.' And with a swimming curtsey Miss Betty Barker took her leave.

My prophetic soul foretold a visit that afternoon from Miss Pole, who usually came to call on Miss Matilda after any event— or indeed in sight of any event—to talk it over with her.

'Miss Betty told me it was to be a choice and select few,' said Miss Pole, as she and Miss Matty compared notes.

'Yes, so she said. Not even Mrs. Fitz-Adam.'

Now Mrs. Fitz-Adam was the widowed sister of the Cranford surgeon, whom I have named before. Their parents were respectable farmers, content with their station. The name of these good people was Hoggins. Mr. Hoggins was the Cranford doctor now; we disliked the name, and considered it coarse; but, as Miss Jenkyns said, if he changed it to Piggins it would not be much better. We had hoped to discover a relationship between him and that Marchioness of Exeter whose name was Molly Hoggins;* but the man, careless of his own interests, utterly ignored and denied any such relationship; although, as dear Miss Jenkyns had said, he had a sister called Mary, and the same Christian names were very apt to run in families.

Soon after Miss Mary Hoggins married Mr. Fitz-Adam, she disappeared from the neighbourhood for many years. She did not move in a sphere in Cranford society sufficiently high to make any of us care to know what Mr. Fitz-Adam was. He died and was gathered to his fathers, without our ever having thought about him at all. And then Mrs. Fitz-Adam reappeared in Cranford, 'as bold as a lion,' Miss Pole said, a well-to-do widow, dressed in rustling black silk, so soon after her husband's death, that poor Miss Jenkyns was justified in the remark she made, that 'bombazine* would have shown a deeper sense of her loss.'

I remember the convocation of ladies, who assembled to decide whether or not Mrs. Fitz-Adam should be called upon by the old blue-blooded inhabitants of Cranford. She had taken a large rambling house, which had been usually considered to confer a patent of gentility upon its tenant; because, once upon a time, seventy or eighty years before, the spinster daughter of an earl* had resided in it. I am not sure if the inhabiting this house was not also believed to convey some unusual power of intellect; for the earl's daughter, Lady Jane, had a sister, Lady Anne, who had married a general officer, in the time of the American war; and this general officer had written one or two comedies, which were still acted on the London boards; and which, when we saw them

advertised, made us all draw up, and feel that Drury Lane was paying a very pretty compliment to Cranford. Still, it was not at all
a settled thing that Mrs. Fitz-Adam was to be visited, when dear
Miss Jenkyns died; and, with her, something of the clear knowledge of the strict code of gentility went out too. As Miss Pole
observed, 'As most of the ladies of good family in Cranford were
elderly spinsters, or widows without children, if we did not relax
a little, and become less exclusive, by-and-by we should have no
society at all.'

Mrs. Forrester continued on the same side.

'She had always understood that Fitz meant something aristocratic; there was Fitz-Roy—she thought that some of the King's
children had been called Fitz-Roy: and there was Fitz-Clarence*
now—they were the children of dear good King William the
Fourth. Fitz-Adam!—it was a pretty name; and she thought it
very probably meant "Child of Adam." No one, who had not some
good blood in their veins, would dare to be called Fitz; there was
a deal in a name—she had had a cousin who spelt his name with
two little ffs—ffoulkes,—and he always looked down upon capital
letters, and said they belonged to lately invented families. She had
been afraid he would die a bachelor, he was so very choice. When
he met with a Mrs. ffaringdon, at a watering-place, he took to her
immediately; and a very pretty genteel woman she was—a widow
with a very good fortune; and "my cousin," Mr. ffoulkes, married
her; and it was all owing to her two little ffs.'

Mrs. Fitz-Adam did not stand a chance of meeting with a Mr.
Fitz-anything in Cranford, so that could not have been her motive
for settling there. Miss Matty thought it might have been the hope
of being admitted in the society of the place, which would certainly
be a very agreeable rise for *ci-devant**Miss Hoggins; and if this had
been her hope, it would be cruel to disappoint her.

So everybody called upon Mrs. Fitz-Adam—everybody but
Mrs. Jamieson, who used to show how honourable she was
by never seeing Mrs. Fitz-Adam, when they met at the Cranford parties. There would be only eight or ten ladies in
the room, and Mrs. Fitz-Adam was the largest of all, and she
invariably used to stand up when Mrs. Jamieson came in, and
curtsey very low to her whenever she turned in her direction
—so low, in fact, that I think Mrs. Jamieson must have looked
at the wall above her, for she never moved a muscle of her face,

no more than if she had not seen her. Still Mrs. Fitz-Adam persevered.

The spring evenings were getting bright and long, when three or four ladies in calashes met at Miss Barker's door. Do you know what a calash is? It is a covering worn over caps, not unlike the heads fastened on old-fashioned gigs; but sometimes it is not quite so large. This kind of head-gear always made an awful impression on the children in Cranford; and now two or three left off their play in the quiet sunny little street, and gathered, in wondering silence, round Miss Pole, Miss Matty, and myself. We were silent, too, so that we could hear loud, suppressed whispers, inside Miss Barker's house: 'Wait, Peggy! wait till I've run upstairs, and washed my hands. When I cough, open the door; I'll not be a minute.'

And, true enough, it was not a minute before we heard a noise, between a sneeze and a crow; on which the door flew open. Behind it stood a round-eyed maiden, all aghast at the honourable company of calashes, who marched in without a word. She recovered presence of mind enough to usher us into a small room, which had been the shop, but was now converted into a temporary dressing-room. There we unpinned and shook ourselves, and arranged our features before the glass into a sweet and gracious company-face; and then, bowing backwards with 'After you, ma'am,' we allowed Mrs. Forrester to take precedence up the narrow staircase that led to Miss Barker's drawing-room. There she sat, as stately and composed as though we had never heard that odd-sounding cough, from which her throat must have been even then sore and rough. Kind, gentle, shabbily dressed Mrs. Forrester was immediately conducted to the second place of honour—a seat arranged something like Prince Albert's near the Queen's*—good, but not so good. The place of pre-eminence was, of course, reserved for the Honourable Mrs. Jamieson, who presently came panting up the stairs—Carlo rushing round her on her progress, as if he meant to trip her up.

And now, Miss Betty Barker was a proud and happy woman! She stirred the fire, and shut the door, and sat as near to it as she could, quite on the edge of her chair. When Peggy came in, tottering under the weight of the tea-tray, I noticed that Miss Barker was sadly afraid lest Peggy should not keep her distance sufficiently. She and her mistress were on very familiar terms in their every-day intercourse, and Peggy wanted now to make several little confidences to her, which Miss Barker was on thorns to hear; but which she thought it her duty, as a lady, to repress. So she turned away from all Peggy's asides and signs; but she made one or two very mal-apropos answers to what was said; and at last, seized with a bright idea, she exclaimed, 'Poor sweet Carlo! I'm forgetting him. Come down stairs with me, poor ittie doggie, and it shall have its tea, it shall!'

In a few minutes she returned, bland and benignant as before; but I thought she had forgotten to give the 'poor ittie doggie' anything to eat; judging by the avidity with which he swallowed down chance pieces of cake. The tea-tray was abundantly loaded. I was pleased to see it, I was so hungry; but I was afraid the ladies present might think it vulgarly heaped up. I know they would have done at their own houses; but somehow the heaps disappeared here. I saw Mrs. Jamieson eating seed-cake,* slowly and considerately, as she did everything; and I was rather surprised, for I knew she had told us, on the occasion of her last party, that she never had it in her house, it reminded her so much of scented soap. She always gave us Savoy biscuits.* However, Mrs. Jamieson was kindly indulgent to Miss Barker's want of knowledge of the customs of high life; and, to spare her feelings, ate three large pieces of seed-cake, with a placid, ruminating expression of countenance, not unlike a cow's.

After tea there was some little demur and difficulty. We were six in number; four could play at Preference, and for the other two there was Cribbage. But all, except myself—(I was rather afraid of the Cranford ladies at cards, for it was the most earnest and serious business they ever engaged in)—were anxious to be of the 'pool.' Even Miss Barker, while declaring she did not know Spadille from Manille,* was evidently hankering to take a hand. The dilemma was soon put an end to by a singular kind of noise. If a Baron's daughter-in-law could ever be supposed to snore, I should have said Mrs. Jamieson did so then; for, overcome by the heat of the room, and inclined to doze by nature, the temptation of that very comfortable arm-chair had been too much for her, and Mrs. Jamieson was nodding. Once or twice she opened her eyes with an effort, and calmly but unconsciously smiled upon us; but, by-and-by, even her benevolence was not equal to this exertion, and she was sound asleep.

'It is very gratifying to me,' whispered Miss Barker at the card-table to her three opponents, whom, notwithstanding her ignorance of the game, she was 'basting'* most unmercifully—'very gratifying indeed, to see how completely Mrs. Jamieson feels at home in my poor little dwelling; she could not have paid me a greater compliment.'

Miss Barker provided me with some literature, in the shape of three or four handsomely bound fashion-books ten or twelve years old, observing, as she put a little table and a candle for my especial benefit, that she knew young people liked to look at pictures. Carlo lay, and snorted, and started at his mistress's feet. He, too, was quite at home.

The card-table was an animated scene to watch; four ladies' heads, with niddle-noddling caps, all nearly meeting over the middle of the table, in their eagerness to whisper quick enough and loud enough: and every now and then came Miss Barker's 'Hush, ladies! if you please, hush! Mrs. Jamieson is asleep.'

It was very difficult to steer clear between Mrs. Forrester's deafness and Mrs. Jamieson's sleepiness. But Miss Barker managed her arduous task well. She repeated the whisper to Mrs. Forrester, distorting her face considerably, in order to show, by the motions of her lips, what was said; and then she smiled kindly all round at us, and murmured to herself, 'Very gratifying, indeed; I wish my poor sister had been alive to see this day.'

Presently the door was thrown wide open; Carlo started to his feet, with a loud snapping bark, and Mrs. Jamieson awoke: or, perhaps, she had not been asleep—as she said almost directly, the room had been so light she had been glad to keep her eyes shut, but had been listening with great interest to all our amusing and agreeable conversation. Peggy came in once more, red with importance. Another tray! 'Oh, gentility!' thought I, 'can you endure this last shock?' For Miss Barker had ordered (nay, I doubt not prepared, although she did say, 'Why! Peggy, what have you brought us?' and looked pleasantly surprised at the unexpected pleasure) all sorts of good things for supper—scalloped oysters, potted lobsters, jelly, a dish called 'little Cupids,'* (which was in great favour with the Cranford ladies; although too expensive to be given, except on solemn and state occasions—maccaroons sopped in brandy, I should have called it, if I had not known its more refined and classical name). In short, we were evidently to be feasted with all that was sweetest and best; and we thought it better to submit graciously, even at the cost of our gentility—which never ate suppers in general—but which, like most non-supper-eaters, was particularly hungry on all special occasions.

Miss Barker, in her former sphere, had, I dare say, been made acquainted with the beverage they call cherry-brandy. We none of us had ever seen such a thing, and rather shrunk back when she proffered it us—'just a little, leetle glass, ladies; after the oysters and lobsters, you know. Shellfish are sometimes thought not very wholesome.' We all shook our heads like female mandarins;* but, at last, Mrs. Jamieson suffered herself to be persuaded, and we followed her lead. It was not exactly unpalatable, though so hot and so strong that we thought ourselves bound to give evidence that we were not accustomed to such things, by coughing terribly—almost as strangely as Miss Barker had done, before we were admitted by Peggy.

'It's very strong,' said Miss Pole, as she put down her empty glass; 'I do believe there's spirit in it.'

'Only a little drop—just necessary to make it keep!' said Miss Barker. 'You know we put brandy-paper over preserves to make them keep. I often feel tipsy myself from eating damson tart.'

I question whether damson tart would have opened Mrs. Jamieson's heart as the cherry-brandy did; but she told us of a coming event, respecting which she had been quite silent till that moment.

'My sister-in-law, Lady Glenmire, is coming to stay with me.'

There was a chorus of 'Indeed!' and then a pause. Each one rapidly reviewed her wardrobe, as to its fitness to appear in the presence of a Baron's widow; for, of course, a series of small festivals were always held in Cranford on the arrival of a visitor at any of our friends' houses. We felt very pleasantly excited on the present occasion.

Not long after this, the maids and the lanterns were announced. Mrs. Jamieson had the sedan chair, which had squeezed itself into Miss Barker's narrow lobby with some difficulty; and most literally, stopped the way. It required some skilful manœuvring on the part of the old chairmen (shoemakers by day; but, when summoned to carry the sedan, dressed up in a strange old livery—long great-coats, with small capes, coeval with the sedan, and similar to the dress of the class in Hogarth's pictures)*to edge, and back, and try at it again, and finally to succeed in carrying their burden out of Miss Barker's front-door. Then we heard their quick pit-a-pat along the quiet little street, as we put on our calashes, and pinned up our gowns; Miss Barker hovering about us with offers of help; which, if she had not remembered her former occupation, and wished us to forget it, would have been much more pressing.

CHAPTER VIII

'YOUR LADYSHIP'

EARLY the next morning—directly after twelve—Miss Pole made her appearance at Miss Matty's. Some very trifling piece of business was alleged as a reason for the call; but there was evidently something behind. At last out it came.

'By the way, you'll think I'm strangely ignorant; but, do you really know, I am puzzled how we ought to address Lady Glenmire. Do you say, "Your Ladyship," where you would say "you" to a common person? I have been puzzling all morning; and are we to say "My lady," instead of "Ma'am?" Now, you knew Lady Arley—will you kindly tell me the most correct way of speaking to the Peerage?'

Poor Miss Matty! she took off her spectacles, and she put them on again—but how Lady Arley was addressed, she could not remember.

'It is so long ago!' she said. 'Dear! dear! how stupid I am! I don't think I ever saw her more than twice. I know we used to call Sir Peter, "Sir Peter,"—but he came much oftener to see us than Lady Arley did. Deborah would have known in a minute. My lady—your ladyship. It sounds very strange, and as if it was not natural. I never thought of it before; but, now you have named it, I am all in a puzzle.'

It was very certain Miss Pole would obtain no wise decision from Miss Matty, who got more bewildered every moment, and more perplexed as to etiquettes of address.

'Well, I really think,' said Miss Pole, 'I had better just go and tell Mrs. Forrester about our little difficulty. One sometimes grows nervous; and yet one would not have Lady Glenmire think we were quite ignorant of the etiquettes of high life in Cranford.'

'And will you just step in here, dear Miss Pole, as you come back, please; and tell me what you decide upon. Whatever you and Mrs. Forrester fix upon, will be quite right, I'm sure. "Lady Arley," "Sir Peter,"' said Miss Matty, to herself, trying to recall the old forms of words.

'Who is Lady Glenmire?' asked I.

'Oh! she's the widow of Mr. Jamieson—that's Mrs. Jamieson's late husband, you know—widow of his eldest brother. Mrs. Jamieson was a Miss Walker, daughter of Governor Walker. Your ladyship. My dear, if they fix on that way of speaking, you must just let me practise a little on you first, for I shall feel so foolish and hot, saying it the first time to Lady Glenmire.'

It was really a relief to Miss Matty when Mrs. Jamieson came on a very unpolite errand. I notice that apathetic people have more quiet impertinence than any others; and Mrs. Jamieson came now to insinuate pretty plainly, that she did not particularly wish that the Cranford ladies should call upon her sister-in-law. I can hardly say how she made this clear; for I grew very indignant and warm, while with slow deliberation she was explaining her wishes to Miss Matty, who, a true lady herself, could hardly understand the feeling which made Mrs. Jamieson wish to appear to her noble sister-in-law as if she only visited 'county' families.* Miss Matty remained puzzled and perplexed long after I had found out the object of Mrs. Jamieson's visit.

When she did understand the drift of the honourable lady's call, it was pretty to see with what quiet dignity she received the intimation thus uncourteously given. She was not in the least hurt—she was of too gentle a spirit for that; nor was she exactly conscious of disapproving of Mrs. Jamieson's conduct; but there was something of this feeling in her mind, I am sure, which made her pass from the subject to others, in a less flurried and more composed manner than usual. Mrs. Jamieson was, indeed, the more flurried of the two, and I could see she was glad to take her leave.

A little while afterwards, Miss Pole returned, red and indignant. 'Well! to be sure! You've had Mrs. Jamieson here, I find from Martha; and we are not to call on Lady Glenmire. Yes! I met Mrs. Jamieson, half-way between here and Mrs. Forrester's, and she told me; she took me so by surprise, I had nothing to say. I wish

I had thought of something very sharp and sarcastic; I dare say I shall to-night. And Lady Glenmire is but the widow of a Scotch baron after all! I went on to look at Mrs. Forrester's Peerage,* to see who this lady was, that is to be kept under a glass case: widow of a Scotch peer—never sat in the House of Lords—and as poor as Job I dare say; and she—fifth daughter of some Mr. Campbell or other. You are the daughter of a rector, at any rate, and related to the Arleys; and Sir Peter might have been Viscount Arley, every one says.'

Miss Matty tried to soothe Miss Pole, but in vain. That lady, usually so kind and good-humoured, was now in a full flow of anger.

'And I went and ordered a cap this morning, to be quite ready,' said she, at last,—letting out the secret which gave sting to Mrs. Jamieson's intimation. 'Mrs. Jamieson shall see if it's so easy to get me to make fourth at a pool, when she has none of her fine Scotch relations with her!'

In coming out of church, the first Sunday on which Lady Glenmire appeared in Cranford, we sedulously talked together, and turned our backs on Mrs. Jamieson and her guest. If we might not call on her, we would not even look at her, though we were dying with curiosity to know what she was like. We had the comfort of questioning Martha in the afternoon. Martha did not belong to a sphere of society whose observation could be an implied compliment to Lady Glenmire, and Martha had made good use of her eyes.

'Well, ma'am! is it the little lady with Mrs. Jamieson, you mean? I thought you would like more to know how young Mrs. Smith was dressed, her being a bride.' (Mrs. Smith was the butcher's wife.)

Miss Pole said, 'Good gracious me! as if we cared about a Mrs. Smith;' but was silent, as Martha resumed her speech.

'The little lady in Mrs. Jamieson's pew had on, ma'am, rather an old black silk, and a shepherd's plaid cloak, ma'am, and very bright black eyes she had, ma'am, and a pleasant, sharp face; not over young, ma'am, but yet, I should guess, younger than Mrs. Jamieson herself. She looked up and down the church, like a bird, and nipped up her petticoats, when she came out, as quick and sharp as ever I see. I'll tell you what, ma'am, she's more like Mrs. Deacon, at the "Coach and Horses," nor any one.'

'Hush, Martha!' said Miss Matty, 'that's not respectful.'

'Isn't it, ma'am? I beg pardon, I'm sure; but Jem Hearn said so as well. He said, she was just such a sharp, stirring sort of a body'—

'Lady,' said Miss Pole.

'Lady—as Mrs. Deacon.'

Another Sunday passed away, and we still averted our eyes from Mrs. Jamieson and her guest, and made remarks to ourselves that we thought were very severe—almost too much so. Miss Matty was evidently uneasy at our sarcastic manner of speaking.

Perhaps by this time Lady Glenmire had found out that Mrs. Jamieson's was not the gayest, liveliest house in the world; perhaps Mrs. Jamieson had found out that most of the county families were in London, and that those who remained in the country were not so alive as they might have been to the circumstance of Lady Glenmire being in their neighbourhood. Great events spring out of small causes; so I will not pretend to say what induced Mrs. Jamieson to alter her determination of excluding the Cranford ladies, and send notes of invitation all round for a small party, on the following Tuesday. Mr. Mulliner himself brought them round. He *would* always ignore the fact of there being a back-door to any house, and gave a louder rat-tat than his mistress, Mrs. Jamieson. He had three little notes, which he carried in a large basket, in order to impress his mistress with an idea of their great weight, though they might easily have gone into his waistcoat pocket.

Miss Matty and I quietly decided we would have a previous engagement at home:—it was the evening on which Miss Matty usually made candle-lighters*of all the notes and letters of the week; for on Mondays her accounts were always made straight—not a penny owing from the week before; so, by a natural arrangement, making candle-lighters fell upon a Tuesday evening, and gave us a legitimate excuse for declining Mrs. Jamieson's invitation. But before our answer was written, in came Miss Pole, with an open note in her hand.

'So!' she said. 'Ah! I see you have got your note, too. Better late than never. I could have told my Lady Glenmire she would be glad enough of our society before a fortnight was over.'

'Yes,' said Miss Matty, 'we're asked for Tuesday evening. And perhaps you would just kindly bring your work across and drink tea with us that night. It is my usual regular time for looking over the last week's bills, and notes, and letters, and making candle-lighters of them; but that does not seem quite reason enough for saying I have a previous engagement at home, though I meant to make it do. Now, if you would come, my conscience would be quite at ease, and luckily the note is not written yet.'

I saw Miss Pole's countenance change while Miss Matty was speaking.

'Don't you mean to go then?' asked she.

'Oh no!' said Miss Matty quietly. 'You don't either, I suppose?'

'I don't know,' replied Miss Pole. 'Yes, I think I do,' said she rather briskly; and on seeing Miss Matty look surprised, she added, 'You see one would not like Mrs. Jamieson to think that anything she could do, or say, was of consequence enough to give offence; it would be a kind of letting down of ourselves, that I, for one, should not like. It would be too flattering to Mrs. Jamieson, if we allowed her to suppose that what she had said affected us a week, nay ten days afterwards.'

'Well! I suppose it is wrong to be hurt and annoyed so long about anything; and, perhaps, after all, she did not mean to vex us. But I must say, I could not have brought myself to say the things Mrs. Jamieson did about our not calling. I really don't think I shall go.'

'Oh, come! Miss Matty, you must go; you know our friend Mrs. Jamieson is much more phlegmatic than most people, and does not enter into the little delicacies of feeling which you possess in so remarkable a degree.'

'I thought you possessed them, too, that day Mrs. Jamieson called to tell us not to go,' said Miss Matty innocently.

But Miss Pole, in addition to her delicacies of feeling, possessed a very smart cap, which she was anxious to show to an admiring world; and so she seemed to forget all her angry words uttered not a fortnight before, and to be ready to act on what she called the great Christian principle of 'Forgive and forget;' and she lectured dear Miss Matty so long on this head, that she absolutely ended by assuring her it was her duty, as a deceased rector's daughter, to buy a new cap, and go to the party at Mrs. Jamieson's. So 'we were most happy to accept,' instead of 'regretting that we were obliged to decline.'

The expenditure in dress in Cranford was principally in that one article referred to. If the heads were buried in smart new caps, the ladies were like ostriches, and cared not what became of their bodies. Old gowns, white and venerable collars, any number of brooches, up and down and everywhere (some with dogs' eyes painted in them; some that were like small picture-frames with mausoleums and weeping-willows neatly executed in hair inside; some, again, with miniatures of ladies and gentlemen sweetly smiling out of a nest of stiff muslin)—old brooches for a permanent ornament, and new caps to suit the fashion of the day; the ladies of Cranford always dressed with chaste elegance and propriety, as Miss Barker once prettily expressed it.

And with three new caps, and a greater array of brooches than had ever been seen together at one time, since Cranford was a town, did Mrs. Forrester, and Miss Matty, and Miss Pole appear on that memorable Tuesday evening. I counted seven brooches myself on Miss Pole's dress. Two were fixed negligently in her cap (one was a butterfly made of Scotch pebbles,* which a vivid imagination might believe to be the real insect); one fastened her net neck-kerchief; one her collar; one ornamented the front of her gown, midway between her throat and waist; and another adorned the point of her stomacher.* Where the seventh was I have forgotten, but it was somewhere about her, I am sure.

But I am getting on too fast, in describing the dresses of the company. I should first relate the gathering, on the way to Mrs. Jamieson's. That lady lived in a large house just outside the town. A road, which had known what it was to be a street, ran right before the house, which opened out upon it, without any intervening garden or court. Whatever the sun was about, he never shone on the front of that house. To be sure, the living-rooms were at the back, looking on to a pleasant garden; the front windows only belonged to kitchens and housekeepers' rooms, and pantries; and in one of them Mr. Mulliner was reported to sit. Indeed, looking askance, we often saw the back of a head, covered with hair-powder,* which also extended itself over his coat-collar down to his very waist; and this imposing back was always engaged in reading the 'St. James's Chronicle,' opened wide, which, in some degree, accounted for the length of time the said newspaper was in reaching us—equal subscribers with Mrs. Jamieson, though, in right of her honourableness, she always had the reading of it first. This very Tuesday, the delay in forwarding the last number had been particularly aggravating; just when both Miss Pole and Miss Matty, the former more especially, had been wanting to see it, in order to coach up the court-news, ready for the evening's interview with aristocracy. Miss Pole told us she had absolutely taken time by the fore-lock, and been dressed by five o'clock, in order to be ready, if the 'St. James's Chronicle' should come in at the last moment—the very 'St. James's Chronicle' which the powdered-head was tranquilly and composedly reading as we passed the accustomed window this evening.

'The impudence of the man!' said Miss Pole, in a low indignant whisper. 'I should like to ask him, whether his mistress pays her quarter-share for his exclusive use.'

We looked at her in admiration of the courage of her thought; for Mr. Mulliner was an object of great awe to all of us. He seemed never to have forgotten his condescension in coming to live at Cranford. Miss Jenkyns, at times, had stood forth as the undaunted champion of her sex, and spoken to him on terms of equality; but even Miss Jenkyns could get no higher. In his pleasantest and most gracious moods, he looked like a sulky cockatoo. He did not speak except in gruff monosyllables. He would wait in the hall when we begged him not to wait, and then looked deeply offended because we had kept him there, while, with trembling, hasty hands, we prepared ourselves for appearing in company.

Miss Pole ventured on a small joke as we went up-stairs, intended, though addressed to us, to afford Mr. Mulliner some slight amusement. We all smiled, in order to seem as if we felt at our ease, and timidly looked for Mr. Mulliner's sympathy. Not a muscle of that wooden face had relaxed; and we were grave in an instant.

Mrs. Jamieson's drawing-room was cheerful; the evening sun came streaming into it, and the large square window was clustered round with flowers. The furniture was white and gold; not the later style, Louis Quatorze I think they call it, all shells and twirls; no, Mrs. Jamieson's chairs and tables had not a curve or bend about them. The chair and table legs diminished as they neared the ground, and were straight and square in all their corners. The chairs were all a-row against the walls, with the exception of four or five which stood in a circle round the fire. They were railed with white bars across the back, and knobbed with gold; neither the railings nor the knobs invited to ease. There was a japanned table devoted to literature, on which lay a Bible, a Peerage, and a Prayer-Book. There was another square Pembroke table* dedicated to the Fine Arts, on which there was a kaleidoscope, conversation-cards,

puzzle-cards (tied together to an interminable length with faded
pink satin ribbon), and a box painted in fond imitation of the draw-
ings which decorate tea-chests.* Carlo lay on the worsted-worked
rug, and ungraciously barked at us as we entered. Mrs. Jamieson
stood up, giving us each a torpid smile of welcome, and looking
helplessly beyond us at Mr. Mulliner, as if she hoped he would
place us in chairs, for if he did not, she never could. I suppose he
thought we could find our way to the circle round the fire, which
reminded me of Stonehenge, I don't know why. Lady Glenmire
came to the rescue of our hostess; and somehow or other we found
ourselves for the first time placed agreeably, and not formally, in
Mrs. Jamieson's house. Lady Glenmire, now we had time to look
at her, proved to be a bright little woman of middle age, who had
been very pretty in the days of her youth, and who was even yet
very pleasant-looking. I saw Miss Pole appraising her dress in the
first five minutes; and I take her word, when she said the next day,

'My dear! ten pounds would have purchased every stitch she
had on—lace and all.'

It was pleasant to suspect that a peeress could be poor, and
partly reconciled us to the fact that her husband had never sat in
the House of Lords; which, when we first heard of it, seemed a kind
of swindling us out of our respect on false pretences; a sort of 'A
Lord and No Lord'* business.

We were all very silent at first. We were thinking what we could
talk about, that should be high enough to interest My Lady. There
had been a rise in the price of sugar, which, as preserving-time was
near, was a piece of intelligence to all our housekeeping hearts, and
would have been the natural topic if Lady Glenmire had not been
by. But we were not sure if the Peerage ate preserves—much less
knew how they were made. At last, Miss Pole, who had always
a great deal of courage and *savoir faire*, spoke to Lady Glenmire,
who on her part had seemed just as much puzzled to know how to
break the silence as we were.

'Has your ladyship been to Court, lately?' asked she; and then
gave a little glance round at us, half timid, and half triumphant, as
much as to say, 'See how judiciously I have chosen a subject
befitting the rank of the stranger!'

'I never was there in my life,' said Lady Glenmire, with a broad
Scotch accent, but in a very sweet voice. And then, as if she had
been too abrupt, she added, 'We very seldom went to London;

only twice, in fact, during all my married life; and before I was married, my father had far too large a family'—(fifth daughter of Mr. Campbell, was in all our minds, I am sure)—'to take us often from our home, even to Edinburgh. Ye'll have been in Edinburgh, may be?' said she, suddenly brightening up with the hope of a common interest. We had none of us been there; but Miss Pole had an uncle who once had passed a night there, which was very pleasant.

Mrs. Jamieson, meanwhile, was absorbed in wonder why Mr. Mulliner did not bring the tea; and, at length, the wonder oozed out of her mouth.

'I had better ring the bell, my dear, had not I?' said Lady Glenmire, briskly.

'No—I think not—Mulliner does not like to be hurried.'

We should have liked our tea, for we dined at an earlier hour than Mrs. Jamieson. I suspect Mr. Mulliner had to finish the 'St. James's Chronicle' before he chose to trouble himself about tea. His mistress fidgetted and fidgetted, and kept saying, 'I can't think why Mulliner does not bring tea. I can't think what he can be about.' And Lady Glenmire at last grew quite impatient, but it was a pretty kind of impatience after all; and she rung the bell rather sharply, on receiving a half permission from her sister-in-law to do so. Mr. Mulliner appeared in dignified surprise. 'Oh!' said Mrs. Jamieson, 'Lady Glenmire rang the bell; I believe it was for tea.'

In a few minutes tea was brought. Very delicate was the china, very old the plate, very thin the bread and butter, and very small the lumps of sugar.* Sugar was evidently Mrs. Jamieson's favourite economy. I question if the little filigree sugar-tongs, made something like scissors, could have opened themselves wide enough to take up an honest, vulgar, good-sized piece; and when I tried to seize two little minnikin pieces at once, so as not to be detected in too many returns to the sugar-basin, they absolutely dropped one, with a little sharp clatter, quite in a malicious and unnatural manner. But before this happened, we had had a slight disappointment. In the little silver jug was cream, in the larger one was milk. As soon as Mr. Mulliner came in, Carlo began to beg, which was a thing our manners forbade us to do, though I am sure we were just as hungry; and Mrs. Jamieson said she was certain we would excuse her if she gave her poor dumb Carlo his tea first. She accordingly mixed a saucer-full for him, and put it down for him

to lap; and then she told us how intelligent and sensible the dear
little fellow was; he knew cream quite well, and constantly refused
tea with only milk in it: so the milk was left for us; but we silently
thought we were quite as, intelligent and sensible as Carlo, and
felt as if insult were added to injury, when we were called upon to
admire the gratitude evinced by his wagging his tail for the cream,
which should have been ours.

After tea we thawed down into common-life subjects. We were
thankful to Lady Glenmire for having proposed some more bread
and butter, and this mutual want made us better acquainted with
her than we should ever have been with talking about the Court,
though Miss Pole did say, she had hoped to know how the dear
Queen was from some one who had seen her.

The friendship, begun over bread and butter, extended on to
cards. Lady Glenmire played Preference to admiration, and was
a complete authority as to Ombre and Quadrille. Even Miss Pole
quite forgot to say 'my lady,' and 'your ladyship,' and said 'Basto!
ma'am;' 'you have Spadille,* I believe,' just as quietly as if we had
never held the great Cranford parliament on the subject of the
proper mode of addressing a peeress.

As a proof of how thoroughly we had forgotten that we were in
the presence of one who might have sat down to tea with a coronet,
instead of a cap, on her head, Mrs. Forrester related a curious little
fact to Lady Glenmire—an anecdote known to the circle of her
intimate friends, but of which even Mrs. Jamieson was not aware.
It related to some fine old lace, the sole relic of better days, which
Lady Glenmire was admiring on Mrs. Forrester's collar.

'Yes,' said that lady, 'such lace cannot be got now for either love
or money; made by the nuns abroad they tell me. They say that
they can't make it now, even there. But perhaps they can now
they've passed the Catholic Emancipation Bill.* I should not
wonder. But, in the meantime, I treasure up my lace very much.
I daren't even trust the washing of it to my maid' (the little charity
school-girl I have named before, but who sounded well as 'my
maid.') 'I always wash it myself. And once it had a narrow escape.
Of course, your ladyship knows that such lace must never be
starched or ironed. Some people wash it in sugar and water; and
some in coffee, to make it the right yellow colour; but I myself
have a very good receipt for washing it in milk, which stiffens it
enough, and gives it a very good, creamy colour. Well, ma'am,

I had tacked it together (and the beauty of this fine lace is, that when it is wet, it goes into a very little space), and put it to soak in milk, when, unfortunately, I left the room; on my return, I found pussy on the table, looking very like a thief, but gulping very uncomfortably, as if she was half-choked with something she wanted to swallow, and could not. And, would you believe it? At first, I pitied her, and said, "Poor pussy! poor pussy!" till, all at once, I looked and saw the cup of milk empty—cleaned out! "You naughty cat!" said I; and I believe I was provoked enough to give her a slap, which did no good, but only helped the lace down— just as one slaps a choking child on the back. I could have cried, I was so vexed; but I determined I would not give the lace up without a struggle for it. I hoped the lace might disagree with her, at any rate; but it would have been too much for Job,* if he had seen, as I did, that cat come in, quite placid and purring, not a quarter of an hour after, and almost expecting to be stroked. "No, pussy!" said I; "if you have any conscience, you ought not to expect that!" And then a thought struck me; and I rang the bell for my maid, and sent her to Mr. Hoggins, with my compliments, and would he be kind enough to lend me one of his top-boots* for an hour? I did not think there was anything odd in the message; but Jenny said, the young men in the surgery laughed as if they would be ill, at my wanting a top-boot. When it came, Jenny and I put pussy in, with her fore-feet straight down, so that they were fastened, and could not scratch, and we gave her a tea-spoonful of currant-jelly, in which (your ladyship must excuse me) I had mixed some tartar emetic. I shall never forget how anxious I was for the next half-hour. I took pussy to my own room, and spread a clean towel on the floor. I could have kissed her when she returned the lace to sight, very much as it had gone down. Jenny had boiling water ready, and we soaked it and soaked it, and spread it on a lavender-bush in the sun, before I could touch it again, even to put it in milk. But now, your ladyship would never guess that it had been in pussy's inside.'

We found out, in the course of the evening, that Lady Glenmire was going to pay Mrs. Jamieson a long visit, as she had given up her apartments in Edinburgh, and had no ties to take her back there in a hurry. On the whole, we were rather glad to hear this, for she had made a pleasant impression upon us; and it was also very comfortable to find, from things which dropped out in the course of conversation, that, in addition to many other genteel qualities, she was far removed from the vulgarity of wealth.

'Don't you find it very unpleasant, walking?' asked Mrs. Jamieson, as our respective servants were announced. It was a pretty regular question from Mrs. Jamieson, who had her own carriage in the coach-house, and always went out in a sedan-chair to the very shortest distances. The answers were nearly as much a matter of course.

'Oh dear, no! it is so pleasant and still at night!' 'Such a refreshment after the excitement of a party!' 'The stars are so beautiful!' This last was from Miss Matty.

'Are you fond of astronomy?' Lady Glenmire asked.

'Not very'—replied Miss Matty, rather confused at the moment to remember which was astronomy, and which was astrology—but the answer was true under either circumstance, for she read, and was slightly alarmed at, Francis Moore's astrological predictions;*and, as to astronomy, in a private and confidential conversation, she had told me, she never could believe that the earth was moving constantly, and that she would not believe it if she could, it made her feel so tired and dizzy whenever she thought about it.

In our pattens, we picked our way home with extra care that night; so refined and delicate were our perceptions after drinking tea with 'my lady.'

CHAPTER IX

SIGNOR BRUNONI

SOON after the events of which I gave an account in my last paper, I was summoned home by my father's illness; and for a time I forgot, in anxiety about him, to wonder how my dear friends at Cranford were getting on, or how Lady Glenmire could reconcile herself to the dulness of the long visit which she was still paying to her sister-in-law, Mrs. Jamieson. When my father grew a little stronger I accompanied him to the sea-side, so that altogether I seemed banished from Cranford, and was deprived of the opportunity of hearing any chance intelligence of the dear little town for the greater part of that year.

Late in November—when we had returned home again, and my father was once more in good health—I received a letter from Miss Matty; and a very mysterious letter it was. She began many sentences without ending them, running them one into another, in much the same confused sort of way in which written words run together on blotting-paper. All I could make out was, that if my father was better (which she hoped he was), and would take warning and wear a great coat from Michaelmas to Lady-day,* if turbans were in fashion, could I tell her? such a piece of gaiety was going to happen as had not been seen or known of since Wombwell's lions came,* when one of them ate a little child's arm; and she was, perhaps, too old to care about dress, but a new cap she must have; and, having heard that turbans were worn, and some of the county families likely to come, she would like to look tidy, if I would bring her a cap from the milliner I employed; and oh, dear! how careless of her to forget that she wrote to beg I would come and pay her a visit next Tuesday; when she hoped to have something to offer me in the way of amusement, which she would not now more particularly describe, only sea-green was her favourite colour. So she ended her letter; but in a P.S. she added, she thought she might as well tell me what was the peculiar attraction to Cranford just now; Signor Brunoni was going to exhibit his wonderful magic in the Cranford Assembly Rooms, on Wednesday and Friday evening in the following week.

I was very glad to accept the invitation from my dear Miss Matty, independently of the conjuror; and most particularly anxious to prevent her from disfiguring her small gentle mousey face with a great Saracen's-head turban; and, accordingly I bought her a pretty, neat, middle-aged cap, which, however, was rather a disappointment to her when, on my arrival, she followed me into my bed-room, ostensibly to poke the fire, but in reality, I do believe, to see if the sea-green turban was not inside the cap-box with which I had travelled. It was in vain that I twirled the cap round on my hand to exhibit back and side fronts: her heart had been set upon a turban, and all she could do was to say, with resignation in her look and voice:

'I am sure you did your best, my dear. It is just like the caps all the ladies in Cranford are wearing, and they have had theirs for a year, I dare say. I should have liked something newer, I confess —something more like the turbans Miss Betty Barker tells me

Queen Adelaide wears; but it is very pretty, my dear. And I dare say lavender will wear better than sea-green. Well, after all, what is dress that we should care about it! You'll tell me if you want anything, my dear. Here is the bell. I suppose turbans have not got down to Drumble yet?'

So saying, the dear old lady gently bemoaned herself out of the room, leaving me to dress for the evening, when, as she informed me, she expected Miss Pole and Mrs. Forrester, and she hoped I should not feel myself too much tired to join the party. Of course I should not; and I made some haste to unpack and arrange my dress; but, with all my speed, I heard the arrivals and the buzz of conversation in the next room before I was ready. Just as I opened the door, I caught the words—'I was foolish to expect anything very genteel out of the Drumble shops—poor girl! she did her best, I've no doubt.' But for all that, I had rather that she blamed Drumble and me than disfigured herself with a turban.

Miss Pole was always the person, in the trio of Cranford ladies now assembled, to have had adventures. She was in the habit of spending the morning in rambling from shop to shop; not to purchase anything (except an occasional reel of cotton, or a piece of tape), but to see the new articles and report upon them, and to collect all the stray pieces of intelligence in the town. She had a way, too, of demurely popping hither and thither into all sorts of places to gratify her curiosity on any point; a way which, if she had not looked so very genteel and prim, might have been considered impertinent. And now, by the expressive way in which she cleared her throat, and waited for all minor subjects (such as caps and turbans) to be cleared off the course, we knew she had something very particular to relate, when the due pause came—and I defy any people, possessed of common modesty, to keep up a conversation long, where one among them sits up aloft in silence, looking down upon all the things they chance to say as trivial and contemptible compared to what they could disclose, if properly entreated. Miss Pole began:

'As I was stepping out of Gordon's shop, to-day, I chanced to go into the George (my Betty has a second-cousin who is chamber-maid there, and I thought Betty would like to hear how she was), and, not seeing any one about, I strolled up the staircase, and found myself in the passage leading to the Assembly Room (you and I remember the Assembly Room, I am sure, Miss Matty! and the

menuets de la cour!*) so I went on, not thinking of what I was about,
when, all at once, I perceived that I was in the middle of the preparations for to-morrow night—the room being divided with
great clothes-maids,* over which Crosby's men were tacking red
flannel; very dark and odd it seemed; it quite bewildered me, and
I was going on behind the screens, in my absence of mind, when
a gentleman (quite the gentleman, I can assure you,) stepped
forwards and asked if I had any business he could arrange for me.
He spoke such pretty broken English, I could not help thinking of
Thaddeus of Warsaw and the Hungarian Brothers, and Santo
Sebastiani;* and while I was busy picturing his past life to myself,
he had bowed me out of the room. But wait a minute! You have
not heard half my story yet! I was going downstairs, when who
should I meet but Betty's second cousin. So, of course, I stopped
to speak to her for Betty's sake; and she told me that I had really
seen the conjuror; the gentleman who spoke broken English was
Signor Brunoni himself. Just at this moment he passed us on the
stairs, making such a graceful bow, in reply to which I dropped
a curtsey—all foreigners have such polite manners, one catches
something of it. But when he had gone downstairs, I bethought me
that I had dropped my glove in the Assembly Room (it was safe in
my muff all the time, but I never found it till afterwards); so I went
back, and, just as I was creeping up the passage left on one side of
the great screen that goes nearly across the room, who should I see
but the very same gentleman that had met me before, and passed
me on the stairs, coming now forwards from the inner part of the
room, to which there is no entrance—you remember Miss Matty!
—and just repeating in his pretty broken English, the inquiry if I
had any business there—I don't mean that he put it quite so
bluntly, but he seemed very determined that I should not pass the
screen—so, of course, I explained about my glove, which, curiously
enough, I found at that very moment.'

Miss Pole then had seen the conjuror—the real live conjuror!
and numerous were the questions we all asked her: 'Had he a
beard?' 'Was he young or old?' 'Fair or dark?' 'Did he look'—
(unable to shape my question prudently, I put it in another form)
—'How did he look?' In short, Miss Pole was the heroine of the
evening, owing to her morning's encounter. If she was not the rose
(that is to say the conjuror), she had been near it.*

Conjuration, sleight of hand, magic, witchcraft were the subjects

of the evening. Miss Pole was slightly sceptical, and inclined to
think there might be a scientific solution found for even the proceedings of the Witch of Endor.* Mrs. Forrester believed everything from ghosts to death-watches. Miss Matty ranged between
the two—always convinced by the last speaker. I think she was
naturally more inclined to Mrs. Forrester's side, but a desire of
proving herself a worthy sister to Miss Jenkyns kept her equally
balanced—Miss Jenkyns, who would never allow a servant to call
the little rolls of tallow that formed themselves round candles,
'winding-sheets,' but insisted on their being spoken of as 'roly-
poleys!'*A sister of hers to be superstitious! It would never do.

After tea, I was dispatched downstairs into the dining-parlour
for that volume of the old encyclopædia which contained the
nouns beginning with C, in order that Miss Pole might prime herself with scientific explanations for the tricks of the following
evening. It spoilt the pool at Preference which Miss Matty and
Mrs. Forrester had been looking forward to, for Miss Pole became
so much absorbed in her subject, and the plates by which it was
illustrated, that we felt it would be cruel to disturb her, otherwise
than by one or two well-timed yawns, which I threw in now and
then, for I was really touched by the meek way in which the two
ladies were bearing their disappointment. But Miss Pole only read
the more zealously, imparting to us no more interesting information than this:

'Ah! I see; I comprehend perfectly. A represents the ball. Put
A between B and D—no! between C and F, and turn the second
joint of the third finger of your left hand over the wrist of your
right H. Very clear indeed! My dear Mrs. Forrester, conjuring
and witchcraft is a mere affair of the alphabet. Do let me read you
this one passage?'

Mrs. Forrester implored Miss Pole to spare her, saying, from
a child upwards, she never could understand being read aloud to;
and I dropped the pack of cards, which I had been shuffling very
audibly; and by this discreet movement, I obliged Miss Pole to
perceive that Preference was to have been the order of the evening,
and to propose, rather unwillingly, that the pool should commence.
The pleasant brightness that stole over the other two ladies' faces
on this! Miss Matty had one or two twinges of self-reproach for
having interrupted Miss Pole in her studies: and did not remember
her cards well, or give her full attention to the game, until she had

soothed her conscience by offering to lend the volume of the Encyclopædia to Miss Pole, who accepted it thankfully, and said Betty should take it home when she came with the lantern.

The next evening we were all in a little gentle flutter at the idea of the gaiety before us. Miss Matty went up to dress betimes, and hurried me until I was ready, when we found we had an hour and a half to wait before the 'doors opened at seven precisely.' And we had only twenty yards to go! However, as Miss Matty said, it would not do to get too much absorbed in anything, and forget the time; so, she thought we had better sit quietly, without lighting the candles, till five minutes to seven. So Miss Matty dozed, and I knitted.

At length we set off; and at the door, under the carriage-way at the George, we met Mrs. Forrester and Miss Pole: the latter was discussing the subject of the evening with more vehemence than ever, and throwing A's and B's at our heads like hail-stones. She had even copied one or two of the 'receipts'—as she called them—for the different tricks, on backs of letters, ready to explain and to detect Signor Brunoni's arts.

We went into the cloak-room adjoining the Assembly Room; Miss Matty gave a sigh or two to her departed youth, and the remembrance of the last time she had been there, as she adjusted her pretty new cap before the strange, quaint old mirror in the cloak-room. The Assembly Room had been added to the inn about a hundred years before, by the different county families, who met together there once a month during the winter, to dance and play at cards. Many a county beauty had first swam through the minuet that she afterwards danced before Queen Charlotte,* in this very room. It was said that one of the Gunnings* had graced the apartment with her beauty; it was certain that a rich and beautiful widow, Lady Williams, had here been smitten with the noble figure of a young artist, who was staying with some family in the neighbourhood for professional purposes, and accompanied his patrons to the Cranford Assembly. And a pretty bargain poor Lady Williams had of her handsome husband, if all tales were true! Now, no beauty blushed and dimpled along the sides of the Cranford Assembly Room; no handsome artist won hearts by his bow, *chapeau bras** in hand: the old room was dingy; the salmon-coloured paint had faded into a drab; great pieces of plaster had chipped off from the white wreaths and festoons on its walls; but

still a mouldy odour of aristocracy lingered about the place, and
a dusty recollection of the days that were gone made Miss Matty
and Mrs. Forrester bridle up as they entered, and walk mincingly
up the room, as if there were a number of genteel observers, instead
of two little boys, with a stick of toffy between them with which to
beguile the time.

We stopped short at the second front row; I could hardly
understand why, until I heard Miss Pole ask a stray waiter if any
of the County families were expected; and when he shook his head,
and believed not, Mrs. Forrester and Miss Matty moved forwards,
and our party represented a conversational square. The front row
was soon augmented and enriched by Lady Glenmire and Mrs.
Jamieson. We six occupied the two front rows, and our aristocratic
seclusion was respected by the groups of shopkeepers who strayed
in from time to time, and huddled together on the back benches.
At least I conjectured so, from the noise they made, and the
sonorous bumps they gave in sitting down; but when, in weariness
of the obstinate green curtain, that would not draw up, but would
stare at me with two odd eyes, seen through holes, as in the old
tapestry story,* I would fain have looked round at the merry
chattering people behind me, Miss Pole clutched my arm, and
begged me not to turn, for 'it was not the thing.' What 'the thing'
was, I never could find out, but it must have been something
eminently dull and tiresome. However, we all sat eyes right,
square front, gazing at the tantalising curtain, and hardly speaking
intelligibly, we were so afraid of being caught in the vulgarity of
making any noise in a place of public amusement. Mrs. Jamieson
was the most fortunate, for she fell asleep.

At length the eyes disappeared—the curtain quivered—one
side went up before the other, which stuck fast; it was dropped
again, and, with a fresh effort, and a vigorous pull from some
unseen hand, it flew up, revealing to our sight a magnificent gentleman in the Turkish costume, seated before a little table, gazing at
us (I should have said with the same eyes that I had last seen
through the hole in the curtain) with calm and condescending
dignity, 'like a being of another sphere,' as I heard a sentimental
voice ejaculate behind me.

'That's not Signor Brunoni!' said Miss Pole decidedly, and so
audibly that I am sure he heard, for he glanced down over his
flowing beard at our party with an air of mute reproach. 'Signor

Brunoni had no beard—but perhaps he'll come soon.' So she
lulled herself into patience. Meanwhile, Miss Matty had recon-
noitered through her eye-glass; wiped it, and looked again. Then
she turned round, and said to me, in a kind, mild, sorrowful
tone:—

'You see, my dear, turbans *are* worn.'

But we had no time for more conversation. The Grand Turk,
as Miss Pole chose to call him, arose and announced himself as
Signor Brunoni.

'I don't believe him!' exclaimed Miss Pole, in a defiant manner.
He looked at her again, with the same dignified upbraiding in his
countenance. 'I don't!' she repeated, more positively than ever.
'Signor Brunoni had not got that muffy sort of thing about his
chin, but looked like a close-shaved Christian gentleman.'

Miss Pole's energetic speeches had the good effect of wakening
up Mrs. Jamieson, who opened her eyes wide, in sign of the
deepest attention—a proceeding which silenced Miss Pole, and
encouraged the Grand Turk to proceed, which he did in very
broken English—so broken that there was no cohesion between
the parts of his sentences; a fact which he himself perceived at last,
and so left off speaking and proceeded to action.

Now we *were* astonished. How he did his tricks I could not
imagine; no, not even when Miss Pole pulled out her pieces of
paper and began reading aloud—or at least in a very audible
whisper—the separate 'receipts' for the most common of his tricks.
If ever I saw a man frown, and look enraged, I saw the Grand
Turk frown at Miss Pole; but, as she said, what could be expected
but unchristian looks from a Mussulman? If Miss Pole was
sceptical, and more engrossed with her receipts and diagrams than
with his tricks, Miss Matty and Mrs. Forrester were mystified
and perplexed to the highest degree. Mrs. Jamieson kept taking
her spectacles off and wiping them, as if she thought it was something defective in them which made the legerdemain; and Lady
Glenmire, who had seen many curious sights in Edinburgh, was
very much struck with the tricks, and would not at all agree with
Miss Pole, who declared that anybody could do them with a little
practice—and that she would, herself, undertake to do all he did,
with two hours given to study the Encyclopædia, and make her
third finger flexible.

At last, Miss Matty and Mrs. Forrester became perfectly

awe-struck. They whispered together. I sat just behind them, so
I could not help hearing what they were saying. Miss Matty asked
Mrs. Forrester, 'if she thought it was quite right to have come to
see such things? She could not help fearing they were lending
encouragement to something that was not quite——' a little shake
of the head filled up the blank. Mrs. Forrester replied, that the
same thought had crossed her mind; she, too, was feeling very
uncomfortable; it was so very strange. She was quite certain that
it was her pocket-handkerchief which was in that loaf just now;
and it had been in her own hand not five minutes before. She
wondered who had furnished the bread? She was sure it could not
be Dakin, because he was the churchwarden. Suddenly, Miss
Matty half turned towards me:—

'Will you look, my dear—you are a stranger in the town, and it
won't give rise to unpleasant reports—will you just look round and
see if the rector is here? If he is, I think we may conclude that
this wonderful man is sanctioned by the Church, and that will be
a great relief to my mind.'

I looked, and I saw the tall, thin, dry, dusty rector, sitting sur-
rounded by National School boys,* guarded by troops of his own
sex from any approach of the many Cranford spinsters. His kind
face was all agape with broad smiles, and the boys around him
were in chinks of laughing.* I told Miss Matty that the Church was
smiling approval, which set her mind at ease.

I have never named Mr. Hayter, the rector, because I, as a well-
to-do and happy young woman, never came in contact with him.
He was an old bachelor, but as afraid of matrimonial reports
getting abroad about him as any girl of eighteen: and he would
rush into a shop, or dive down an entry, sooner than encounter
any of the Cranford ladies in the street; and, as for the Preference
parties, I did not wonder at his not accepting invitations to them.
To tell the truth, I always suspected Miss Pole of having given
very vigorous chace to Mr. Hayter when he first came to Cranford; and not the less, because now she appeared to share so
vividly in his dread lest her name should ever be coupled with
his. He found all his interests among the poor and helpless; he
had treated the National School boys this very night to the performance; and virtue was for once its own reward, for they
guarded him right and left, and clung round him as if he had
been the queen bee, and they the swarm. He felt so safe in their

environment, that he could even afford to give our party a bow as we filed out. Miss Pole ignored his presence, and pretended to be absorbed in convincing us that we had been cheated, and had not seen Signor Brunoni after all.

CHAPTER X

THE PANIC

I THINK a series of circumstances dated from Signor Brunoni's visit to Cranford, which seemed at the time connected in our minds with him, though I don't know that he had anything really to do with them. All at once all sorts of uncomfortable rumours got afloat in the town. There were one or two robberies—real *bonâ fide* robberies; men had up before the magistrates and committed for trial; and that seemed to make us all afraid of being robbed; and for a long time at Miss Matty's, I know, we used to make a regular expedition all round the kitchens and cellars every night, Miss Matty leading the way, armed with the poker, I following with the hearth-brush, and Martha carrying the shovel and fire-irons with which to sound the alarm: and by the accidental hitting together of them she often frightened us so much that we bolted ourselves up, all three together, in the back kitchen, or store-room, or wherever we happened to be, till, when our affright was over, we recollected ourselves, and set out afresh with double valiance. By day we heard strange stories from the shopkeepers and cottagers, of carts that went about in the dead of night, drawn by horses shod with felt, and guarded by men in dark clothes, going round the town, no doubt, in search of some unwatched house or some unfastened door.

Miss Pole, who affected great bravery herself, was the principal person to collect and arrange these reports, so as to make them assume their most fearful aspect. But we discovered that she had begged one of Mr. Hoggins's worn-out hats to hang up in her lobby, and we (at least I) had my doubts as to whether she really would enjoy the little adventure of having her house broken into, as she protested she should. Miss Matty made no secret of being an arrant coward; but she went regularly through her housekeeper's

duty of inspection—only the hour for this became earlier and
earlier, till at last we went the rounds at half-past six, and Miss
Matty adjourned to bed soon after seven, 'in order to get the night
over the sooner.'

Cranford had so long piqued itself on being an honest and moral
town, that it had grown to fancy itself too genteel and well-bred to
be otherwise, and felt the stain upon its character at this time
doubly. But we comforted ourselves with the assurance which we
gave to each other, that the robberies could never have been committed by any Cranford person; it must have been a stranger or
strangers, who brought this disgrace upon the town, and occasioned as many precautions as if we were living among the Red
Indians or the French.

This last comparison of our nightly state of defence and fortifica-
tion, was made by Mrs. Forrester, whose father had served under
General Burgoyne in the American war, and whose husband had
fought the French in Spain.* She indeed inclined to the idea that,
in some way, the French were connected with the small thefts,
which were ascertained facts, and the burglaries and highway
robberies, which were rumours. She had been deeply impressed
with the idea of French spies, at some time in her life; and the
notion could never be fairly eradicated, but sprung up again from
time to time. And now her theory was this: the Cranford people
respected themselves too much, and were too grateful to the
aristocracy who were so kind as to live near the town, ever to disgrace their bringing up by being dishonest or immoral; therefore,
we must believe that the robbers were strangers—if strangers,
why not foreigners?—if foreigners, who so likely as the French?
Signor Brunoni spoke broken English like a Frenchman, and,
though he wore a turban like a Turk, Mrs. Forrester had seen a
print of Madame de Staël with a turban on, and another of Mr.
Denon* in just such a dress as that in which the conjuror had made
his appearance; showing clearly that the French, as well as the
Turks, wore turbans: there could be no doubt Signor Brunoni was
a Frenchman—a French spy, come to discover the weak and un-
defended places of England; and, doubtless, he had his accomplices;
for her part, she, Mrs. Forrester, had always had her own opinion
of Miss Pole's adventure at the George Inn—seeing two men
where only one was believed to be: French people had ways and
means, which she was thankful to say the English knew nothing

about; and she had never felt quite easy in her mind about going to see that conjuror; it was rather too much like a forbidden thing, though the Rector was there. In short, Mrs. Forrester grew more excited than we had ever known her before; and, being an officer's daughter and widow, we looked up to her opinion, of course.

Really I do not know how much was true or false in the reports which flew about like wildfire just at this time; but it seemed to me then that there was every reason to believe that at Mardon (a small town about eight miles from Cranford) houses and shops were entered by holes made in the walls, the bricks being silently carried away in the dead of the night, and all done so quietly that no sound was heard either in or out of the house. Miss Matty gave it up in despair when she heard of this. 'What was the use,' said she, 'of locks and bolts, and bells to the windows, and going round the house every night? That last trick was fit for a conjuror. Now she did believe that Signor Brunoni was at the bottom of it.'

One afternoon, about five o'clock, we were startled by a hasty knock at the door. Miss Matty bade me run and tell Martha on no account to open the door till she (Miss Matty) had reconnoitred through the window; and she armed herself with a footstool to drop down on the head of the visitor, in case he should show a face covered with black crape, as he looked up in answer to her inquiry of who was there. But it was nobody but Miss Pole and Betty. The former came upstairs, carrying a little hand-basket, and she was evidently in a state of great agitation.

'Take care of that!' said she to me, as I offered to relieve her of her basket. 'It's my plate. I am sure there is a plan to rob my house to-night. I am come to throw myself on your hospitality, Miss Matty. Betty is going to sleep with her cousin at the George. I can sit up here all night, if you will allow me; but my house is so far from any neighbours; and I don't believe we could be heard if we screamed ever so!'

'But,' said Miss Matty, 'what has alarmed you so much? Have you seen any men lurking about the house?'

'Oh yes!' answered Miss Pole. 'Two very bad-looking men have gone three times past the house, very slowly; and an Irish beggar-woman came not half an hour ago, and all but forced herself in past Betty, saying her children were starving, and she must speak to the mistress. You see, she said "mistress," though there was a hat hanging up in the hall, and it would have been more natural to have said "master." But Betty shut the door in her face, and came up to me, and we got the spoons together, and sat in the parlour-window watching, till we saw Thomas Jones going from his work, when we called to him and asked him to take care of us into the town.'

We might have triumphed over Miss Pole, who had professed such bravery until she was frightened; but we were too glad to perceive that she shared in the weaknesses of humanity to exult over her; and I gave up my room to her very willingly, and shared Miss Matty's bed for the night. But before we retired, the two ladies rummaged up, out of the recesses of their memory, such horrid stories of robbery and murder, that I quite quaked in my shoes. Miss Pole was evidently anxious to prove that such terrible events had occurred within her experience that she was justified in her sudden panic; and Miss Matty did not like to be outdone, and capped every story with one yet more horrible, till it reminded me, oddly enough, of an old story I had read somewhere, of a nightingale and a musician,* who strove one against the other which could produce the most admirable music, till poor Philomel dropped down dead.

One of the stories that haunted me for a long time afterwards, was of a girl, who was left in charge of a great house* in Cumberland, on some particular fair-day, when the other servants all went off to the gaieties. The family were away in London, and a pedlar came by, and asked to leave his large and heavy pack in the kitchen, saying, he would call for it again at night; and the girl (a game-keeper's daughter) roaming about in search of amusement, chanced to hit upon a gun hanging up in the hall, and took it down to look at the chasing; and it went off through the open kitchen door, hit the pack, and a slow dark thread of blood came oozing out. (How Miss Pole enjoyed this part of the story, dwelling on each word as if she loved it!) She rather hurried over the further account of the girl's bravery, and I have but a confused idea that, somehow, she baffled the robbers with Italian irons,* heated red hot, and then restored to blackness by being dipped in grease.

We parted for the night with an awe-struck wonder as to what we should hear of in the morning—and, on my part, with a vehement desire for the night to be over and gone: I was so afraid lest the robbers should have seen, from some dark lurking-place, that Miss Pole had carried off her plate, and thus have a double motive for attacking our house.

But, until Lady Glenmire came to call next day, we heard of nothing unusual. The kitchen fire-irons were in exactly the same position against the back door, as when Martha and I had skilfully piled them up like spillikins, ready to fall with an awful clatter, if only a cat had touched the outside panels. I had wondered what we should all do if thus awakened and alarmed, and had proposed to Miss Matty that we should cover up our faces under the bed-clothes, so that there should be no danger of the robbers thinking that we could identify them; but Miss Matty, who was trembling very much, scouted this idea, and said we owed it to society to apprehend them, and that she should certainly do her best to lay hold of them, and lock them up in the garret till morning.

When Lady Glenmire came, we almost felt jealous of her. Mrs. Jamieson's house had really been attacked; at least there were men's footsteps to be seen on the flower-borders, underneath the kitchen windows, 'where nae men should be;'* and Carlo had barked all through the night as if strangers were abroad. Mrs. Jamieson had been awakened by Lady Glenmire, and they had rung the bell which communicated with Mr. Mulliner's room, in the third story, and when his night-capped head had appeared over the bannisters, in answer to the summons, they had told him of their alarm, and the reasons for it; whereupon he retreated into his bed-room, and locked the door (for fear of draughts, as he informed them in the morning), and opened the window, and called out valiantly to say, if the supposed robbers would come to him he would fight them; but, as Lady Glenmire observed, that was but poor comfort, since they would have to pass by Mrs. Jamieson's room and her own, before they could reach him, and must be of a very pugnacious disposition indeed, if they neglected the opportunities of robbery presented by the unguarded lower stories to go up to a garret, and there force a door in order to get at the champion of the house. Lady Glenmire, after waiting and listening for some time in the drawing-room, had proposed to Mrs. Jamieson that they should go to bed; but that lady said she should not feel comfortable unless she sat up and watched; and, accordingly, she packed herself warmly up on the sofa, where she was found by the housemaid, when she came into the room at six o'clock, fast asleep; but Lady Glenmire went to bed, and kept awake all night.

When Miss Pole heard of this, she nodded her head in great

satisfaction. She had been sure we should hear of something happening in Cranford that night; and we had heard. It was clear enough they had first proposed to attack her house; but when they saw that she and Betty were on their guard, and had carried off the plate, they had changed their tactics and gone to Mrs. Jamieson's, and no one knew what might have happened if Carlo had not barked, like a good dog as he was!

Poor Carlo! his barking days were nearly over. Whether the gang who infested the neighbourhood were afraid of him; or whether they were revengeful enough, for the way in which he had baffled them on the night in question, to poison him; or whether, as some among the more uneducated people thought, he died of apoplexy, brought on by too much feeding and too little exercise; at any rate, it is certain that, two days after this eventful night, Carlo was found dead, with his poor little legs stretched out stiff in the attitude of running, as if by such unusual exertion he could escape the sure pursuer, Death.

We were all sorry for Carlo, the old familiar friend who had snapped at us for so many years; and the mysterious mode of his death made us very uncomfortable. Could Signor Brunoni be at the bottom of this? He had apparently killed a canary with only a word of command; his will seemed of deadly force; who knew but what he might yet be lingering in the neighbourhood willing all sorts of awful things!

We whispered these fancies among ourselves in the evenings; but in the mornings our courage came back with the daylight, and in a week's time we had got over the shock of Carlo's death; all but Mrs. Jamieson. She, poor thing, felt it as she had felt no event since her husband's death; indeed Miss Pole said, that as the Honourable Mr. Jamieson drank a good deal, and occasioned her much uneasiness, it was possible that Carlo's death might be the greater affliction. But there was always a tinge of cynicism in Miss Pole's remarks. However, one thing was clear and certain; it was necessary for Mrs. Jamieson to have some change of scene; and Mr. Mulliner was very impressive on this point, shaking his head whenever we inquired after his mistress, and speaking of her loss of appetite and bad nights very ominously; and with justice too, for if she had two characteristics in her natural state of health, they were a facility of eating and sleeping. If she could neither eat nor sleep, she must be indeed out of spirits and out of health.

Lady Glenmire (who had evidently taken very kindly to Cranford), did not like the idea of Mrs. Jamieson's going to Cheltenham, and more than once insinuated pretty plainly that it was Mr. Mulliner's doing, who had been much alarmed on the occasion of the house being attacked, and since had said, more than once, that he felt it a very responsible charge to have to defend so many women. Be that as it might, Mrs. Jamieson went to Cheltenham, escorted by Mr. Mulliner; and Lady Glenmire remained in possession of the house, her ostensible office being to take care that the maid-servants did not pick up followers. She made a very pleasant-looking dragon: and, as soon as it was arranged for her stay in Cranford, she found out that Mrs. Jamieson's visit to Cheltenham was just the best thing in the world. She had let her house in Edinburgh, and was for the time houseless, so the charge of her sister-in-law's comfortable abode was very convenient and acceptable.

Miss Pole was very much inclined to install herself as a heroine, because of the decided steps she had taken in flying from the two men and one woman, whom she entitled 'that murderous gang.' She described their appearance in glowing colours, and I noticed that every time she went over the story some fresh trait of villany was added to their appearance. One was tall—he grew to be gigantic in height before we had done with him; he of course had black hair—and by and by, it hung in elf-locks over his forehead and down his back. The other was short and broad—and a hump sprouted out on his shoulder before we heard the last of him; he had red hair—which deepened into carrotty; and she was almost sure he had a cast in his eye—a decided squint. As for the woman, her eyes glared, and she was masculine-looking—a perfect virago; most probably a man dressed in woman's clothes: afterwards, we heard of a beard on her chin, and a manly voice and a stride.

If Miss Pole was delighted to recount the events of that afternoon to all inquirers, others were not so proud of their adventures in the robbery line. Mr. Hoggins, the surgeon, had been attacked at his own door by two ruffians, who were concealed in the shadow of the porch, and so effectually silenced him, that he was robbed in the interval between ringing his bell and the servant's answering it. Miss Pole was sure it would turn out that this robbery had been committed by 'her men,' and went the very day she heard of the report to have her teeth examined, and to question Mr. Hoggins.

She came to us afterwards; so we heard what she had heard, straight and direct from the source, while we were yet in the excitement and flutter of the agitation caused by the first intelligence; for the event had only occurred the night before.

'Well!' said Miss Pole, sitting down with the decision of a person who has made up her mind as to the nature of life and the world, (and such people never tread lightly, or seat themselves without a bump)—'Well, Miss Matty! men will be men. Every mother's son of them wishes to be considered Samson and Solomon rolled into one*—too strong ever to be beaten or discomfited—too wise ever to be outwitted. If you will notice, they have always foreseen events, though they never tell one for one's warning before the events happen; my father was a man, and I know the sex pretty well.'

She had talked herself out of breath, and we should have been very glad to fill up the necessary pause as chorus, but we did not exactly know what to say, or which man had suggested this diatribe against the sex; so we only joined in generally, with a grave shake of the head, and a soft murmur of 'They are very incomprehensible, certainly!'

'Now only think,' said she. 'There I have undergone the risk of having one of my remaining teeth drawn (for one is terribly at the mercy of any surgeon-dentist; and I, for one, always speak them fair till I have got my mouth out of their clutches), and after all, Mr. Hoggins is too much of a man to own that he was robbed last night.'

'Not robbed!' exclaimed the chorus.

'Don't tell me!' Miss Pole exclaimed, angry that we could be for a moment imposed upon. 'I believe he was robbed, just as Betty told me, and he is ashamed to own it: and, to be sure, it was very silly of him to be robbed just at his own door; I dare say, he feels that such a thing won't raise him in the eyes of Cranford society, and is anxious to conceal it—but he need not have tried to impose upon me, by saying I must have heard an exaggerated account of some petty theft of a neck of mutton, which, it seems, was stolen out of the safe in his yard last week; he had the impertinence to add, he believed that that was taken by the cat. I have no doubt, if I could get at the bottom of it, it was that Irishman dressed up in woman's clothes, who came spying about my house, with the story about the starving children.'

After we had duly condemned the want of candour which Mr.
Hoggins had evinced, and abused men in general, taking him for
the representative and type, we got round to the subject about
which we had been talking when Miss Pole came in—namely, how
far, in the present disturbed state of the country, we could venture
to accept an invitation which Miss Matty had just received from
Mrs. Forrester, to come as usual and keep the anniversary of her
wedding-day, by drinking tea with her at five o'clock, and playing
a quiet pool afterwards. Mrs. Forrester had said, that she asked us
with some diffidence, because the roads were, she feared, very
unsafe. But she suggested that perhaps one of us would not object
to take the sedan; and that the others, by walking briskly, might
keep up with the long trot of the chairmen, and so we might all
arrive safely at Over Place, a suburb of the town. (No. That is too
large an expression: a small cluster of houses separated from
Cranford by about two hundred yards of a dark and lonely lane.)
There was no doubt but that a similar note was awaiting Miss Pole
at home; so her call was a very fortunate affair, as it enabled us to
consult together. We would all much rather have declined this
invitation; but we felt that it would not be quite kind to Mrs.
Forrester, who would otherwise be left to a solitary retrospect of
her not very happy or fortunate life. Miss Matty and Miss Pole had
been visitors on this occasion for many years; and now they gal-
lantly determined to nail their colours to the mast, and to go
through Darkness Lane rather than fail in loyalty to their friend.

But when the evening came, Miss Matty (for it was she who was
voted into the chair, as she had a cold), before being shut down in
the sedan, like jack-in-a-box, implored the chairmen, whatever
might befall, not to run away and leave her fastened up there, to
be murdered; and even after they had promised, I saw her tighten
her features into the stern determination of a martyr, and she gave
me a melancholy and ominous shake of the head through the glass.
However, we got there safely, only rather out of breath, for it was
who could trot hardest through Darkness Lane, and I am afraid
poor Miss Matty was sadly jolted.

Mrs. Forrester had made extra preparations in acknowledgment
of our exertion in coming to see her through such dangers. The
usual forms of genteel ignorance as to what her servants might
send up were all gone through; and harmony and Preference
seemed likely to be the order of the evening, but for an interesting

conversation that began I don't know how, but which had relation, of course, to the robbers who infested the neighbourhood of Cranford.

Having braved the dangers of Darkness Lane, and thus having a little stock of reputation for courage to fall back upon; and also, I dare say, desirous of proving ourselves superior to men (*videlicet* Mr. Hoggins), in the article of candour, we began to relate our individual fears, and the private precautions we each of us took. I owned that my pet apprehension was eyes—eyes looking at me, and watching me, glittering out from some dull flat wooden surface; and that if I dared to go up to my looking-glass when I was panic-stricken, I should certainly turn it round, with its back towards me, for fear of seeing eyes behind me looking out of the darkness. I saw Miss Matty nerving herself up for a confession; and at last out it came. She owned that, ever since she had been a girl, she had dreaded being caught by her last leg, just as she was getting into bed, by some one concealed under it. She said, when she was younger and more active, she used to take a flying leap from a distance, and so bring both her legs up safely into bed at once; but that this had always annoyed Deborah, who piqued herself upon getting into bed gracefully, and she had given it up in consequence. But now the old terror would often come over her, especially since Miss Pole's house had been attacked (we had got quite to believe in the fact of the attack having taken place), and yet it was very unpleasant to think of looking under a bed, and seeing a man concealed, with a great fierce face staring out at you; so she had bethought herself of something—perhaps I had noticed that she had told Martha to buy her a penny ball, such as children play with—and now she rolled this ball under the bed every night; if it came out on the other side, well and good; if not, she always took care to have her hand on the bell-rope, and meant to call out John and Harry, just as if she expected men-servants to answer her ring.

We all applauded this ingenious contrivance, and Miss Matty sank back into satisfied silence, with a look at Mrs. Forrester as if to ask for *her* private weakness.

Mrs. Forrester looked askance at Miss Pole, and tried to change the subject a little, by telling us that she had borrowed a boy from one of the neighbouring cottages, and promised his parents a hundredweight of coals at Christmas, and his supper every evening, for the loan of him at nights. She had instructed him in his

possible duties when he first came; and, finding him sensible, she
had given him the major's sword (the major was her late husband),
and desired him to put it very carefully behind his pillow at night,
turning the edge towards the head of the pillow. He was a sharp
lad, she was sure; for, spying out the major's cocked hat, he had
said, if he might have that to wear he was sure he could frighten
two Englishmen, or four Frenchmen, any day. But she had
impressed upon him anew that he was to lose no time in putting
on hats or anything else; but, if he heard any noise, he was to run
at it with his drawn sword. On my suggesting that some accident
might occur from such slaughterous and indiscriminate directions,
and that he might rush on Jenny getting up to wash, and have
spitted her before he had discovered that she was not a Frenchman,
Mrs. Forrester said she did not think that that was likely, for he was
a very sound sleeper, and generally had to be well shaken, or cold-
pigged* in a morning before they could rouse him. She sometimes
thought such dead sleep must be owing to the hearty suppers the
poor lad ate, for he was half-starved at home, and she told Jenny to
see that he got a good meal at night.

Still this was no confession of Mrs. Forrester's peculiar timidity,
and we urged her to tell us what she thought would frighten her
more than anything. She paused, and stirred the fire, and snuffed
the candles, and then she said, in a sounding whisper,—

'Ghosts!'

She looked at Miss Pole, as much as to say she had declared it,
and would stand by it. Such a look was a challenge in itself. Miss
Pole came down upon her with indigestion, spectral illusions,
optical delusions, and a great deal out of Dr. Ferrier and Dr.
Hibbert* besides. Miss Matty had rather a leaning to ghosts, as
I have said before, and what little she did say, was all on Mrs.
Forrester's side, who, emboldened by sympathy, protested that
ghosts were a part of her religion; that surely she, the widow of
a major in the army, knew what to be frightened at, and what not;
in short, I never saw Mrs. Forrester so warm either before or since,
for she was a gentle, meek, enduring old lady in most things. Not
all the elder-wine that ever was mulled, could this night wash out
the remembrance of this difference between Miss Pole and her
hostess. Indeed, when the elder-wine was brought in, it gave
rise to a new burst of discussion: for Jenny, the little maiden
who staggered under the tray, had to give evidence of having seen

a ghost with her own eyes, not so many nights ago, in Darkness
Lane—the very lane we were to go through on our way home.

In spite of the uncomfortable feeling which this last consideration gave me, I could not help being amused at Jenny's position,
which was exceedingly like that of a witness being examined and
cross-examined by two counsel who are not at all scrupulous about
asking leading questions. The conclusion I arrived at was, that
Jenny had certainly seen something beyond what a fit of indigestion
would have caused. A lady all in white, and without her head, was
what she deposed and adhered to, supported by a consciousness of
the secret sympathy of her mistress under the withering scorn with
which Miss Pole regarded her. And not only she, but many others,
had seen this headless lady, who sat by the roadside wringing her
hands as in deep grief. Mrs. Forrester looked at us from time to
time, with an air of conscious triumph; but then she had not to pass
through Darkness Lane before she could bury herself beneath her
own familiar bed-clothes.

We preserved a discreet silence as to the headless lady while we
were putting on our things to go home, for there was no knowing
how near the ghostly head and ears might be, or what spiritual connection they might be keeping up with the unhappy body in
Darkness Lane; and therefore, even Miss Pole felt that it was as
well not to speak lightly on such subjects, for fear of vexing or
insulting that woe-begone trunk. At least, so I conjecture; for,
instead of the busy clatter usual in the operation, we tied on our
cloaks as sadly as mutes at a funeral. Miss Matty drew the curtains
round the windows of the chair to shut out disagreeable sights; and
the men (either because they were in spirits that their labours were
so nearly ended, or because they were going down hill) set off at
such a round and merry pace, that it was all Miss Pole and I could
do to keep up with them. She had breath for nothing beyond an
imploring 'Don't leave me!' uttered as she clutched my arm so
tightly that I could not have quitted her, ghost or no ghost. What
a relief it was when the men, weary of their burden and their quick
trot, stopped just where Headingley-causeway branches off from
Darkness Lane! Miss Pole unloosed me and caught at one of
the men.

'Could not you—could not you take Miss Matty round by
Headingley-causeway,—the pavement in Darkness Lane jolts so,
and she is not very strong?'

A smothered voice was heard from the inside of the chair—

'Oh! pray go on! what is the matter? What is the matter? I will give you sixpence more to go on very fast; pray don't stop here.'

'And I'll give you a shilling,' said Miss Pole, with tremulous dignity, 'if you'll go by Headingley-causeway.'

The two men grunted acquiescence and took up the chair and went along the causeway, which certainly answered Miss Pole's kind purpose of saving Miss Matty's bones; for it was covered with soft thick mud, and even a fall there would have been easy, till the getting up came, when there might have been some difficulty in extrication.

CHAPTER XI

SAMUEL BROWN

THE next morning I met Lady Glenmire and Miss Pole, setting out on a long walk to find some old woman who was famous in the neighbourhood for her skill in knitting woollen stockings. Miss Pole said to me, with a smile half kindly and half contemptuous upon her countenance, 'I have been just telling Lady Glenmire of our poor friend Mrs. Forrester, and her terror of ghosts. It comes from living so much alone, and listening to the bug-a-boo stories of that Jenny of hers.' She was so calm and so much above superstitious fears herself, that I was almost ashamed to say how glad I had been of her Headingley-causeway proposition the night before, and turned off the conversation to something else.

In the afternoon Miss Pole called on Miss Matty to tell her of the adventure—the real adventure they had met with on their morning's walk. They had been perplexed about the exact path which they were to take across the fields, in order to find the knitting old woman, and had stopped to inquire at a little way-side public-house, standing on the high road to London, about three miles from Cranford. The good woman had asked them to sit down and rest themselves, while she fetched her husband, who could direct them better than she could; and, while they were sitting in the sanded parlour, a little girl came in. They thought that she belonged to the landlady, and began some trifling conversation with her; but, on

Mrs. Roberts's return, she told them that the little thing was the only child of a couple who were staying in the house. And then she began a long story, out of which Lady Glenmire and Miss Pole could only gather one or two decided facts, which were that, about six weeks ago, a light spring-cart had broken down just before their door, in which there were two men, one woman, and this child. One of the men was seriously hurt—no bones broken, only 'shaken,' the landlady called it; but he had probably sustained some severe internal injury, for he had languished in their house ever since, attended by his wife, the mother of this little girl. Miss Pole had asked what he was, what he looked like. And Mrs. Roberts had made answer that he was not like a gentleman, nor yet like a common person; if it had not been that he and his wife were such decent, quiet people, she could almost have thought he was a mountebank, or something of that kind, for they had a great box in the cart, full of she did not know what. She had helped to unpack it, and take out their linen and clothes, when the other man—his twin brother, she believed he was—had gone off with the horse and cart.

Miss Pole had begun to have her suspicions at this point, and expressed her idea that it was rather strange that the box and cart and horse and all should have disappeared; but good Mrs. Roberts seemed to have become quite indignant at Miss Pole's implied suggestion; in fact, Miss Pole said, she was as angry as if Miss Pole had told her that she herself was a swindler. As the best way of convincing the ladies, she bethought her of begging them to see the wife; and, as Miss Pole said, there was no doubting the honest, worn, bronzed face of the woman, who, at the first tender word from Lady Glenmire, burst into tears, which she was too weak to check, until some word from the landlady made her swallow down her sobs, in order that she might testify to the Christian kindness shown by Mr. and Mrs. Roberts. Miss Pole came round with a swing to as vehement a belief in the sorrowful tale as she had been sceptical before; and, as a proof of this, her energy in the poor sufferer's behalf was nothing daunted when she found out that he, and no other, was our Signor Brunoni, to whom all Cranford had been attributing all manner of evil this six weeks past! Yes! his wife said his proper name was Samuel Brown—'Sam,' she called him—but to the last we preferred calling him 'the Signor;' it sounded so much better.

The end of their conversation with the Signora Brunoni was, that it was agreed that he should be placed under medical advice, and for any expense incurred in procuring this Lady Glenmire promised to hold herself responsible; and had accordingly gone to Mr. Hoggins to beg him to ride over to the Rising Sun that very afternoon, and examine into the Signor's real state; and as Miss Pole said, if it was desirable to remove him to Cranford to be more immediately under Mr. Hoggins's eye, she would undertake to see for lodgings, and arrange about the rent. Mrs. Roberts had been as kind as could be all throughout; but it was evident that their long residence there had been a slight inconvenience.

Before Miss Pole left us, Miss Matty and I were as full of the morning's adventure as she was. We talked about it all the evening, turning it in every possible light, and we went to bed anxious for the morning, when we should surely hear from some one what Mr. Hoggins thought and recommended. For, as Miss Matty observed, though Mr. Hoggins did say 'Jack's up,' 'a fig for his heels,' and call Preference 'Pref,'*she believed he was a very worthy man, and a very clever surgeon. Indeed, we were rather proud of our doctor at Cranford, as a doctor. We often wished, when we heard of Queen Adelaide or the Duke of Wellington being ill, that they would send for Mr. Hoggins; but, on consideration, we were rather glad they did not, for if we were ailing, what should we do if Mr. Hoggins had been appointed physician-in-ordinary to the Royal Family? As a surgeon we were proud of him; but as a man—or rather, I should say, as a gentleman—we could only shake our heads over his name and himself, and wished that he had read Lord Chesterfield's Letters* in the days when his manners were susceptible of improvement. Nevertheless, we all regarded his dictum in the Signor's case as infallible; and when he said, that with care and attention he might rally, we had no more fear for him.

But although we had no more fear, everybody did as much as if there was great cause for anxiety—as indeed there was, until Mr. Hoggins took charge of him. Miss Pole looked out clean and comfortable, if homely, lodgings; Miss Matty sent the sedan-chair for him; and Martha and I aired it well before it left Cranford, by holding a warming-pan full of red-hot coals in it, and then shutting it up close, smoke and all, until the time when he should get into it at the Rising Sun. Lady Glenmire undertook the medical department under Mr. Hoggins's directions; and rummaged up all Mrs. Jamieson's medicine glasses, and spoons, and bed-tables, in a free and easy way, that made Miss Matty feel a little anxious as to what that lady and Mr. Mulliner might say, if they knew. Mrs. Forrester made some of the bread-jelly, for which she was so famous, to have ready as a refreshment in the lodgings when he should arrive. A present of this bread-jelly*was the highest mark of favour dear Mrs. Forrester could confer. Miss Pole had once asked her for the receipt, but she had met with a very decided rebuff; that lady told her that she could not part with it to any one during her life, and that after her death it was bequeathed, as her executors would find, to Miss Matty. What Miss Matty—or, as Mrs. Forrester called her (remembering the clause in her will, and the dignity of the occasion) Miss Matilda Jenkyns—might choose to do with the receipt when it came into her possession—whether to make it public, or to hand it down as an heir-loom*—she did not know, nor would she dictate. And a mould of this admirable, digestible, unique bread-jelly was sent by Mrs. Forrester to our poor sick conjuror. Who says that the aristocracy are proud? Here was a lady, by birth a Tyrrell, and descended from the great Sir Walter that shot King Rufus, and in whose veins ran the blood of him who murdered the little Princes in the Tower,* going every day to see what dainty dishes she could prepare for Samuel Brown, a mountebank! But, indeed, it was wonderful to see what kind feelings were called out by this poor man's coming amongst us. And also wonderful to see how the great Cranford panic, which had been occasioned by his first coming in his Turkish dress, melted away into thin air on his second coming—pale and feeble, and with his heavy filmy eyes, that only brightened a very little when they fell upon the countenance of his faithful wife, or their pale and sorrowful little girl.

Somehow, we all forgot to be afraid. I dare say it was, that finding out that he, who had first excited our love of the marvellous by his unprecedented arts, had not sufficient every-day gifts to manage a shying horse, made us feel as if we were ourselves again. Miss Pole came with her little basket at all hours of the evening, as if her lonely house, and the unfrequented road to it, had never been infested by that 'murderous gang;' Mrs. Forrester said, she thought that neither Jenny nor she need mind the headless lady who wept and wailed in Darkness Lane, for surely the power was never given to such beings to harm those who went about to try to do what little good was in their power; to which Jenny, trembling, assented; but the mistress's theory had little effect on the maid's practice, until she had sewed two pieces of red flannel, in the shape of a cross,* on her inner garment.

I found Miss Matty covering her penny ball—the ball that she used to roll under her bed—with gay-coloured worsted in rainbow stripes.

'My dear,' said she, 'my heart is sad for that little care-worn child. Although her father is a conjuror, she looks as if she had never had a good game of play in her life. I used to make very pretty balls in this way when I was a girl, and I thought I would try if I could not make this one smart and take it to Phœbe this afternoon. I think "the gang" must have left the neighbourhood, for one does not hear any more of their violence and robbery now.'

We were all of us far too full of the Signor's precarious state to talk about either robbers or ghosts. Indeed, Lady Glenmire said, she never had heard of any actual robberies; except that two little boys had stolen some apples from Farmer Benson's orchard, and that some eggs had been missed on a market-day off Widow Hayward's stall. But that was expecting too much of us; we could not acknowledge that we had only had this small foundation for all our panic. Miss Pole drew herself up at this remark of Lady Glenmire's; and said 'that she wished she could agree with her as to the very small reason we had had for alarm; but, with the recollection of a man disguised as a woman, who had endeavoured to force herself into her house, while his confederates waited outside; with the knowledge gained from Lady Glenmire herself, of the foot-prints seen on Mrs. Jamieson's flower-borders; with the fact before her of the audacious robbery committed on Mr. Hoggins at his own door—' But here Lady Glenmire broke in with a very strong expression of doubt as to whether this last story was not an entire fabrication, founded upon the theft of a cat; she grew so red while she was saying all this, that I was not surprised at Miss Pole's manner of bridling up, and I am certain if Lady Glenmire had not been 'her ladyship,' we should have had a more emphatic contradiction than the 'Well, to be sure!' and similar fragmentary ejaculations, which were all that she ventured upon in my lady's presence. But when she was gone, Miss Pole began a long congratulation to Miss Matty that, so far they had escaped marriage, which she noticed always made people credulous to the last degree;

indeed, she thought it argued great natural credulity in a woman
if she could not keep herself from being married; and in what Lady
Glenmire had said about Mr. Hoggins's robbery, we had a speci-
men of what people came to, if they gave way to such a weakness;
evidently, Lady Glenmire would swallow anything, if she could
believe the poor vamped-up story about a neck of mutton and
a pussy, with which he had tried to impose on Miss Pole, only she
had always been on her guard against believing too much of
what men said.

We were thankful, as Miss Pole desired us to be, that we had
never been married; but I think, of the two, we were even more
thankful that the robbers had left Cranford; at least I judge so from
a speech of Miss Matty's that evening, as we sat over the fire, in
which she evidently looked upon a husband as a great protector
against thieves, burglars, and ghosts; and said, that she did not
think that she should dare to be always warning young people of
matrimony, as Miss Pole did continually;—to be sure, marriage
was a risk, as she saw now she had had some experience; but she
remembered the time when she had looked forward to being
married as much as any one.

'Not to any particular person, my dear,' said she, hastily check-
ing herself up as if she were afraid of having admitted too much;
'only the old story, you know, of ladies always saying "*When*
I marry,*" and gentlemen, "*If* I marry."' It was a joke spoken in
rather a sad tone, and I doubt if either of us smiled; but I could
not see Miss Matty's face by the flickering fire-light. In a little
while she continued:

'But after all I have not told you the truth. It is so long ago, and no
one ever knew how much I thought of it at the time, unless, indeed,
my dear mother guessed; but I may say that there was a time when
I did not think I should have been only Miss Matty Jenkyns all my
life; for even if I did meet with any one who wished to marry me
now (and as Miss Pole says, one is never too safe), I could not take
him—I hope he would not take it too much to heart, but I could *not*
take him—or any one but the person I once thought I should be
married to, and he is dead and gone, and he never knew how it all
came about that I said "no," when I had thought many and many
a time—Well, it's no matter what I thought. God ordains it all,
and I am very happy, my dear. No one has such kind friends as
I,' continued she, taking my hand and holding it in hers.

If I had never known of Mr. Holbrook, I could have said something in this pause, but as I had, I could not think of anything that would come in naturally, and so we both kept silence for a little time.

'My father once made us,' she began, 'keep a diary in two columns; on one side we were to put down in the morning what we thought would be the course and events of the coming day, and at night we were to put down on the other side what really had happened. It would be to some people rather a sad way of telling their lives'—(a tear dropped upon my hand at these words)—'I don't mean that mine has been sad, only so very different to what I expected. I remember, one winter's evening, sitting over our bed-room fire with Deborah—I remember it as if it were yesterday—and we were planning our future lives—both of us were planning, though only she talked about it. She said she should like to marry an archdeacon, and write his charges;* and you know, my dear, she never was married, and, for aught I know, she never spoke to an unmarried archdeacon in her life. I never was ambitious, nor could I have written charges, but I thought I could manage a house (my mother used to call me her right hand), and I was always so fond of little children—the shyest babies would stretch out their little arms to come to me; when I was a girl, I was half my leisure time nursing in the neighbouring cottages—but I don't know how it was, when I grew sad and grave—which I did a year or two after this time—the little things drew back from me, and I am afraid I lost the knack, though I am just as fond of children as ever, and have a strange yearning at my heart whenever I see a mother with her baby in her arms. Nay, my dear,'—(and by a sudden blaze which sprang up from a fall of the unstirred coals, I saw that her eyes were full of tears—gazing intently on some vision of what might have been)—'do you know, I dream sometimes that I have a little child—always the same—a little girl of about two years old; she never grows older, though I have dreamt about her for many years. I don't think I ever dream of any words or sound she makes; she is very noiseless and still, but she comes to me when she is very sorry or very glad, and I have wakened with the clasp of her dear little arms round my neck. Only last night—perhaps because I had gone to sleep thinking of this ball for Phœbe—my little darling came in my dream, and put up her mouth to be kissed, just as I have seen real babies do to real mothers before going to bed. But all this is nonsense, dear! only don't be frightened by Miss Pole from being married. I can fancy it may be a very happy state, and a little credulity helps one on through life very smoothly,—better than always doubting and doubting, and seeing difficulties and disagreeables in everything.'

If I had been inclined to be daunted from matrimony, it would not have been Miss Pole to do it; it would have been the lot of poor Signor Brunoni and his wife. And yet again, it was an encouragement to see how, through all their cares and sorrows, they thought of each other and not of themselves; and how keen were their joys, if they only passed through each other, or through the little Phœbe.

The Signora told me, one day, a good deal about their lives up to this period. It began by my asking her whether Miss Pole's story of the twin-brothers was true; it sounded so wonderful a likeness, that I should have had my doubts, if Miss Pole had not been unmarried. But the Signora, or (as we found out she preferred to be called) Mrs. Brown, said it was quite true; that her brother-in-law was by many taken for her husband, which was of great assistance to them in their profession; 'though,' she continued, 'how people can mistake Thomas for the real Signor Brunoni, I can't conceive; but he says they do; so I suppose I must believe him. Not but what he is a very good man; I am sure I don't know how we should have paid our bill at the Rising Sun, but for the money he sends; but people must know very little about art, if they can take him for my husband. Why, Miss, in the ball trick, where my husband spreads his fingers wide, and throws out his little finger with quite an air and a grace, Thomas just clumps up his hand like a fist, and might have ever so many balls hidden in it. Besides, he has never been in India, and knows nothing of the proper sit of a turban.'

'Have you been in India?' said I, rather astonished.

'Oh yes! many a year, ma'am. Sam was a serjeant in the 31st; and when the regiment was ordered to India, I drew a lot to go, and I was more thankful than I can tell; for it seemed as if it would only be a slow death to me to part from my husband. But, indeed, ma'am, if I had known all, I don't know whether I would not rather have died there and then, than gone through what I have done since. To be sure, I've been able to comfort Sam, and to be with him; but, ma'am, I've lost six children,' said she, looking up at me with those strange eyes, that I have never noticed but in mothers of dead children—with a kind of wild look in them, as if seeking for what they never more might find. 'Yes! Six children died off, like little buds nipped untimely, in that cruel India. I thought, as each died, I never could—I never would—love a child again; and when the next came, it had not only its own love, but the deeper love that came from the thoughts of its little dead brothers and sisters. And when Phœbe was coming, I said to my husband, "Sam, when the child is born, and I am strong, I shall leave you; it will cut my heart cruel; but if this baby dies too, I shall go mad; the madness is in me now; but if you let me go down to Calcutta, carrying my baby step by step, it will may-be work itself off; and I will save, and I will hoard, and I will beg,—and I will die, to get a passage home to England, where our baby may live!" God bless him! he said I might go; and he saved up his pay, and I saved every pice* I could get for washing or any way; and when Phœbe came, and I grew strong again, I set off. It was very lonely; through the thick forests, dark again with their heavy trees—along by the river's side—(but I had been brought up near the ¡Avon in Warwickshire, so that flowing noise sounded like home), from station to station, from Indian village to village, I went along, carrying my child. I had seen one of the officer's ladies with a little picture, ma'am— done by a Catholic foreigner, ma'am—of the Virgin and the little Saviour, ma'am. She had him on her arm, and her form was softly curled round him, and their cheeks touched. Well, when I went to bid good-bye to this lady, for whom I had washed, she cried sadly; for she, too, had lost her children, but she had not another to save, like me; and I was bold enough to ask her, would she give me that print? And she cried the more, and said *her* children were with that little blessed Jesus; and gave it me, and told me she had heard it had been painted on the bottom of a cask, which made it have that round shape.* And when my body was very weary, and my heart was sick—(for there were times when I misdoubted if I could ever reach my home, and there were times when I thought of my husband; and one time when I thought my baby was dying)— I took out that picture and looked at it, till I could have thought the mother spoke to me, and comforted me. And the natives were very kind. We could not understand one another; but they saw my baby on my breast, and they came out to me, and brought me rice and milk, and sometimes flowers—I have got some of the flowers dried. Then, the next morning, I was so tired! and they wanted me to stay with them—I could tell that—and tried to frighten me from going into the deep woods, which, indeed, looked very strange and dark; but it seemed to me as if Death was following me to take my baby away from me; and as if I must go on, and on—and I thought how God had cared for mothers ever since the world was made, and would care for me; so I bade them good-bye, and set off afresh. And once when my baby was ill, and both she and I needed rest, He led me to a place where I found a kind Englishman lived, right in the midst of the natives.'

'And you reached Calcutta safely at last?'

'Yes! safely. Oh! when I knew I had only two days' journey more before me, I could not help it, ma'am—it might be idolatry, I cannot tell—but I was near one of the native temples, and I went in it with my baby to thank God for his great mercy; for it seemed to me that where others had prayed before to their God, in their joy or in their agony, was of itself a sacred place. And I got as servant to an invalid lady, who grew quite fond of my baby aboard-ship; and, in two years' time, Sam earned his discharge, and came home to me, and to our child. Then he had to fix on a trade; but he knew of none; and, once, once upon a time, he had learnt some tricks from an Indian juggler; so he set up conjuring, and it answered so well that he took Thomas to help him—as his man, you know, not as another conjuror, though Thomas has set it up now on his own hook. But it has been a great help to us that likeness between the twins, and made a good many tricks go off well that they made up together. And Thomas is a good brother, only he has not the fine carriage of my husband, so that I can't think how he can be taken for Signor Brunoni himself, as he says he is.'

'Poor little Phœbe!' said I, my thoughts going back to the baby she carried all those hundred miles.

'Ah! you may say so! I never thought I should have reared her, though, when she fell ill at Chunderabaddad; but that good, kind Aga Jenkyns* took us in, which I believe was the very saving of her.'

'Jenkyns!' said I.

'Yes! Jenkyns. I shall think all people of that name are kind; for here is that nice old lady who comes every day to take Phœbe a walk!'

But an idea had flashed through my head: could the Aga Jenkyns be the lost Peter? True, he was reported by many to be dead. But, equally true, some had said that he had arrived at the dignity of great Lama of Thibet. Miss Matty thought he was alive. I would make further inquiry.

CHAPTER XII

ENGAGED TO BE MARRIED!

WAS the 'poor Peter' of Cranford the Aga Jenkyns of Chunderabaddad, or was he not? As somebody says, that was the question.

In my own home, whenever people had nothing else to do, they blamed me for want of discretion. Indiscretion was my bugbear fault. Everybody has a bugbear fault; a sort of standing characteristic—a *pièce de résistance* for their friends to cut at; and in general they cut and come again. I was tired of being called indiscreet and incautious; and I determined for once to prove myself a model of prudence and wisdom. I would not even hint my suspicions respecting the Aga. I would collect evidence and carry it home to lay before my father, as the family friend of the two Miss Jenkynses.

In my search after facts, I was often reminded of a description my father had once given of a Ladies' Committee that he had had to preside over. He said he could not help thinking of a passage in Dickens, which spoke of a chorus in which every man took the tune he knew best,* and sang it to his own satisfaction. So, at this charitable committee, every lady took the subject uppermost in her mind, and talked about it to her own great contentment, but not much to the advancement of the subject they had met to discuss. But even that committee could have been nothing to the Cranford ladies when I attempted to gain some clear and definite information as to poor Peter's height, appearance, and when and where he was seen and heard of last. For instance, I remember asking Miss Pole (and I thought the question was very opportune, for I put it when I met her at a call at Mrs. Forrester's, and both the ladies had known Peter, and I imagined that they might refresh each other's memories); I asked Miss Pole what was the very last thing they had ever heard about him; and then she named the absurd report to which I have alluded, about his having been

elected great Lama of Thibet; and this was a signal for each lady
to go off on her separate idea. Mrs. Forrester's start was made on
the Veiled Prophet in Lalla Rookh*—whether I thought he was
meant for the Great Lama, though Peter was not so ugly, indeed
rather handsome if he had not been freckled. I was thankful to
see her double upon Peter; but, in a moment, the delusive lady
was off upon Rowland's Kalydor,* and the merits of cosmetics and
hair oils in general, and holding forth so fluently that I turned to
listen to Miss Pole, who (through the llamas, the beasts of burden)
had got to Peruvian bonds,* and the Share Market, and her poor
opinion of joint-stock banks in general, and of that one in particular
in which Miss Matty's money was invested. In vain I put in,
'When was it—in what year was it, that you heard that Mr. Peter
was the Great Lama?' They only joined issue to dispute whether
llamas were carnivorous animals or not; in which dispute they were
not quite on fair grounds, as Mrs. Forrester (after they had grown
warm and cool again) acknowledged that she always confused
carnivorous and graminivorous together, just as she did horizontal
and perpendicular; but then she apologised for it very prettily, by
saying that in her day the only use people made of four-syllabled
words was to teach how they should be spelt.

The only fact I gained from this conversation was that certainly
Peter had last been heard of in India, 'or that neighbourhood;' and
that this scanty intelligence of his whereabouts had reached
Cranford in the year when Miss Pole had bought her India
muslin gown, long since worn out (we washed it and mended it,
and traced its decline and fall into a window-blind, before we
could go on); and in a year when Wombwell came to Cranford,
because Miss Matty had wanted to see an elephant in order that
she might the better imagine Peter riding on one; and had seen
a boa-constrictor too, which was more than she wished to imagine
in her fancy pictures of Peter's locality;—and in a year when Miss
Jenkyns had learnt some piece of poetry off by heart, and used to
say, at all the Cranford parties, how Peter was 'surveying mankind
from China to Peru,'* which everybody had thought very grand,
and rather appropriate, because India was between China and
Peru, if you took care to turn the globe to the left instead of
the right.

I suppose all these inquiries of mine, and the consequent
curiosity excited in the minds of my friends, made us blind and

deaf to what was going on around us. It seemed to me as if the sun rose and shone, and as if the rain rained on Cranford just as usual, and I did not notice any sign of the times that could be considered as a prognostic of any uncommon event; and, to the best of my belief, not only Miss Matty and Mrs. Forrester, but even Miss Pole herself, whom we looked upon as a kind of prophetess from the knack she had of foreseeing things before they came to pass—although she did not like to disturb her friends by telling them her fore-knowledge—even Miss Pole herself was breathless with astonishment, when she came to tell us of the astounding piece of news. But I must recover myself; the contemplation of it, even at this distance of time, has taken away my breath and my grammar, and unless I subdue my emotion, my spelling will go too.

We were sitting—Miss Matty and I much as usual; she in the blue chintz easy chair, with her back to the light, and her knitting in her hand—I reading aloud the St. James's Chronicle. A few minutes more, and we should have gone to make the little altera-tions in dress usual before calling time (twelve o'clock) in Cranford. I remember the scene and the date well. We had been talking of the Signor's rapid recovery since the warmer weather had set in, and praising Mr. Hoggins's skill, and lamenting his want of refinement and manner—(it seems a curious coincidence that this should have been our subject, but so it was)—when a knock was heard; a caller's knock—three distinct taps—and we were flying (that is to say, Miss Matty could not walk very fast, having had a touch of rheumatism) to our rooms, to change cap and collars, when Miss Pole arrested us by calling out as she came up the stairs, 'Don't go—I can't wait—it is not twelve, I know—but never mind your dress—I must speak to you.' We did our best to look as if it was not we who had made the hurried movement, the sound of which she had heard; for, of course, we did not like to have it sup-posed that we had any old clothes that it was convenient to wear out in the 'sanctuary of home,' as Miss Jenkyns once prettily called the back parlour, where she was tying up preserves. So we threw our gentility with double force into our manners, and very genteel we were for two minutes while Miss Pole recovered breath, and excited our curiosity strongly by lifting up her hands in amaze-ment, and bringing them down in silence, as if what she had to say was too big for words, and could only be expressed by pantomime.

'What do you think, Miss Matty? What *do* you think? Lady

Glenmire is to marry—is to be married, I mean—Lady Glenmire
—Mr. Hoggins—Mr. Hoggins is going to marry Lady Glenmire!'
    'Marry!' said we. 'Marry! Madness!'
    'Marry!' said Miss Pole, with the decision that belonged to her
character. 'I said Marry! as you do; and I also said, "What a fool
my lady is going to make of herself!" I could have said "Madness!"
but I controlled myself, for it was in a public shop that I heard of
it. Where feminine delicacy is gone to, I don't know! You and I,
Miss Matty, would have been ashamed to have known that our
marriage was spoken of in a grocer's shop, in the hearing of
shopmen!'
    'But,' said Miss Matty, sighing as one recovering from a blow,
'perhaps it is not true. Perhaps we are doing her injustice.'
    'No!' said Miss Pole. 'I have taken care to ascertain that. I went
straight to Mrs. Fitz-Adam, to borrow a cookery book which I
knew she had; and I introduced my congratulations *apropos* of
the difficulty gentlemen must have in house-keeping; and Mrs.
Fitz-Adam bridled up, and said, that she believed it was true,
though how and where I could have heard it she did not know.
She said her brother and Lady Glenmire had come to an understanding at last. "Understanding!" such a coarse word! But my
lady will have to come down to many a want of refinement. I have
reason to believe Mr. Hoggins sups on bread-and-cheese and beer
every night.'
    'Marry!' said Miss Matty once again. 'Well! I never thought of
it. Two people that we know going to be married. It's coming
very near!'
    'So near that my heart stopped beating, when I heard of it,
while you might have counted twelve,' said Miss Pole.*
    'One does not know whose turn may come next. Here, in Cran-
ford, poor Lady Glenmire might have thought herself safe,' said
Miss Matty, with a gentle pity in her tones.
    'Bah!' said Miss Pole, with a toss of her head. 'Don't you
remember poor dear Captain Brown's song "Tibbie Fowler,"*
and the line—
            Set her on the Tintock Tap,
            The wind will blaw a man 'till her.'

    'That was because "Tibbie Fowler" was rich I think.'
    'Well! there is a kind of attraction about Lady Glenmire that I,
for one, should be ashamed to have.'

I put in my wonder. 'But how can she have fancied Mr. Hoggins? I am not surprised that Mr. Hoggins has liked her.'

'Oh! I don't know. Mr. Hoggins is rich, and very pleasant-looking,' said Miss Matty, 'and very good-tempered and kind-hearted.'

'She has married for an establishment, that's it. I suppose she takes the surgery with it,' said Miss Pole, with a little dry laugh at her own joke. But, like many people who think they have made a severe and sarcastic speech, which yet is clever of its kind, she began to relax in her grimness from the moment when she made this allusion to the surgery; and we turned to speculate on the way in which Mrs. Jamieson would receive the news. The person whom she had left in charge of her house to keep off followers from her maids, to set up a follower of her own! And that follower a man whom Mrs. Jamieson had tabooed as vulgar, and inadmissible to Cranford society; not merely on account of his name, but because of his voice, his complexion, his boots, smelling of the stable, and himself, smelling of drugs. Had he ever been to see Lady Glenmire at Mrs. Jamieson's? Chloride of lime* would not purify the house in its owner's estimation if he had. Or had their interviews been confined to the occasional meetings in the chamber of the poor sick conjuror, to whom, with all our sense of the *mésalliance*, we could not help allowing that they had both been exceedingly kind? And now it turned out that a servant of Mrs. Jamieson's had been ill, and Mr. Hoggins had been attending her for some weeks. So the wolf had got into the fold, and now he was carrying off the shepherdess. What would Mrs. Jamieson say? We looked into the darkness of futurity as a child gazes after a rocket up in the cloudy sky, full of wondering expectation of the rattle, the discharge, and the brilliant shower of sparks and light. Then we brought our-selves down to earth and the present time, by questioning each other (being all equally ignorant, and all equally without the slightest data to build any conclusions upon) as to when IT would take place? Where? How much a year Mr. Hoggins had? Whether she would drop her title? And how Martha and the other correct servants in Cranford would ever be brought to announce a married couple as Lady Glenmire and Mr. Hoggins? But would they be visited? Would Mrs. Jamieson let us? Or must we choose between the Honourable Mrs. Jamieson and the degraded Lady Glenmire? We all liked Lady Glenmire the best. She was bright, and kind,

and sociable, and agreeable; and Mrs. Jamieson was dull, and
inert, and pompous, and tiresome. But we had acknowledged the
sway of the latter so long, that it seemed like a kind of disloyalty
now even to meditate disobedience to the prohibition we
anticipated.

Mrs. Forrester surprised us in our darned caps and patched
collars; and we forgot all about them in our eagerness to see how
she would bear the information, which we honourably left to Miss
Pole to impart, although, if we had been inclined to take unfair
advantage, we might have rushed in ourselves, for she had a most
out-of-place fit of coughing for five minutes after Mrs. Forrester
entered the room. I shall never forget the imploring expression of
her eyes, as she looked at us over her pocket-handkerchief. They
said, as plain as words could speak, 'Don't let Nature deprive me
of the treasure which is mine, although for a time I can make no
use of it.' And we did not.

Mrs. Forrester's surprise was equal to ours; and her sense of
injury rather greater, because she had to feel for her Order, and
saw more fully than we could do how such conduct brought stains
on the aristocracy.

When she and Miss Pole left us, we endeavoured to subside into
calmness; but Miss Matty was really upset by the intelligence she
had heard. She reckoned it up, and it was more than fifteen years
since she had heard of any of her acquaintance going to be married,
with the one exception of Miss Jessie Brown; and, as she said, it
gave her quite a shock, and made her feel as if she could not think
what would happen next.

I don't know if it is a fancy of mine, or a real fact, but I have
noticed that, just after the announcement of an engagement in any
set, the unmarried ladies in that set flutter out in an unusual gaiety
and newness of dress, as much as to say, in a tacit and unconscious
manner, 'We also are spinsters.' Miss Matty and Miss Pole talked
and thought more about bonnets, gowns, caps, and shawls, during
the fortnight that succeeded this call, than I had known them do for
years before. But it might be the spring weather, for it was a warm
and pleasant March; and merinoes and beavers,* and woollen
materials of all sorts, were but ungracious receptacles of the bright
sun's glancing rays. It had not been Lady Glenmire's dress that
had won Mr. Hoggins's heart, for she went about on her errands
of kindness more shabby than ever. Although in the hurried

glimpses I caught of her at church or elsewhere, she appeared rather to shun meeting any of her friends, her face seemed to have almost something of the flush of youth in it; her lips looked redder, and more trembling full than in their old compressed state, and her eyes dwelt on all things with a lingering light, as if she was learning to love Cranford and its belongings. Mr. Hoggins looked broad and radiant, and creaked up the middle aisle at church in a bran-new pair of top-boots—an audible, as well as visible, sign of his purposed change of state; for the tradition went, that the boots he had worn till now were the identical pair in which he first set out on his rounds in Cranford twenty-five years ago; only they had been new-pieced, high and low, top and bottom, heel and sole, black leather and brown leather, more times than any one could tell.

None of the ladies in Cranford chose to sanction the marriage by congratulating either of the parties. We wished to ignore the whole affair until our liege lady, Mrs. Jamieson, returned. Till she came back to give us our cue, we felt that it would be better to consider the engagement in the same light as the Queen of Spain's legs*—facts which certainly existed, but the less said about the better. This restraint upon our tongues—for you see if we did not speak about it to any of the parties concerned, how could we get answers to the questions that we longed to ask?—was beginning to be irksome, and our idea of the dignity of silence was paling before our curiosity, when another direction was given to our thoughts, by an announcement on the part of the principal shop-keeper of Cranford, who ranged the trades from grocer and cheesemonger to man-milliner, as occasion required, that the Spring Fashions were arrived, and would be exhibited on the following Tuesday, at his rooms in High Street. Now Miss Matty had been only waiting for this before buying herself a new silk gown. I had offered, it is true, to send to Drumble for patterns, but she had rejected my proposal, gently implying that she had not forgotten her disappointment about the sea-green turban. I was thankful that I was on the spot now, to counteract the dazzling fascination of any yellow or scarlet silk.

I must say a word or two here about myself. I have spoken of my father's old friendship for the Jenkyns family; indeed, I am not sure if there was not some distant relationship. He had willingly allowed me to remain all the winter at Cranford, in consideration of a letter which Miss Matty had written to him, about the time of the panic, in which I suspect she had exaggerated my powers and my bravery as a defender of the house. But now that the days were longer and more cheerful, he was beginning to urge the necessity of my return; and I only delayed in a sort of odd forlorn hope that if I could obtain any clear information, I might make the account given by the Signora of the Aga Jenkyns tally with that of 'poor Peter,' his appearance and disappearance, which I had winnowed out of the conversation of Miss Pole and Mrs. Forrester.

CHAPTER XIII

STOPPED PAYMENT

THE very Tuesday morning on which Mr. Johnson was going to show the fashions, the post-woman brought two letters to the house. I say the post-woman, but I should say the postman's wife. He was a lame shoemaker, a very clean, honest man, much respected in the town; but he never brought the letters round except on unusual occasions, such as Christmas Day, or Good Friday; and on those days the letters, which should have been delivered at eight in the morning, did not make their appearance until two or three in the afternoon; for every one liked poor Thomas, and gave him a welcome on these festive occasions. He used to say, 'he was welly stawed* wi' eating, for there were three or four houses where nowt would serve 'em but he must share in their breakfast;' and by the time he had done his last breakfast, he came to some other friend who was beginning dinner; but come what might in the way of temptation, Tom was always sober, civil, and smiling; and, as Miss Jenkyns used to say, it was a lesson in patience, that she doubted not would call out that precious quality in some minds, where, but for Thomas, it might have lain dormant and undiscovered. Patience was certainly very dormant in Miss Jenkyns's mind. She was always expecting letters, and always drumming on the table till the post-woman had called or gone past. On Christmas Day and Good Friday, she drummed from break-fast till church, from church-time till two o'clock—unless when the fire wanted stirring, when she invariably knocked down the

fire-irons, and scolded Miss Matty for it. But equally certain was
the hearty welcome and the good dinner for Thomas; Miss
Jenkyns standing over him like a bold dragoon, questioning him
as to his children—what they were doing—what school they went
to; upbraiding him if another was likely to make its appearance,
but sending even the little babies the shilling and the mince-pie
which was her gift to all the children, with half-a-crown in addition for both father and mother. The Post was not half of so much
consequence to dear Miss Matty; but not for the world would
she have diminished Thomas's welcome, and his dole, though
I could see that she felt rather shy over the ceremony, which had
been regarded by Miss Jenkyns as a glorious opportunity for giving
advice and benefiting her fellow-creatures. Miss Matty would
steal the money all in a lump into his hand, as if she were ashamed
of herself. Miss Jenkyns gave him each individual coin separate,
with a 'There! that's for yourself; that's for Jenny,' &c. Miss
Matty would even beckon Martha out of the kitchen while he ate
his food: and once, to my knowledge, winked at its rapid disappearance into a blue cotton pocket-handkerchief. Miss Jenkyns
almost scolded him if he did not leave a clean plate, however heaped
it might have been, and gave an injunction with every mouthful.

I have wandered a long way from the two letters that awaited us
on the breakfast-table that Tuesday morning. Mine was from my
father. Miss Matty's was printed. My father's was just a man's
letter; I mean it was very dull, and gave no information beyond
that he was well, that they had had a good deal of rain, that trade
was very stagnant, and there were many disagreeable rumours
afloat. He then asked me, if I knew whether Miss Matty still
retained her shares in the Town and County Bank, as there were
very unpleasant reports about it; though nothing more than he
had always foreseen, and had prophesied to Miss Jenkyns years
ago, when she would invest their little property in it—the only
unwise step that clever woman had ever taken, to his knowledge—
(the only time she ever acted against his advice, I knew). However,
if anything had gone wrong, of course I was not to think of leaving
Miss Matty while I could be of any use, &c.

'Who is your letter from, my dear? Mine is a very civil
invitation, signed Edwin Wilson, asking me to attend an
important meeting of the shareholders of the Town and
County Bank, to be held in Drumble, on Thursday the

twenty-first. I am sure, it is very attentive of them to remember me.'

I did not like to hear of this 'important meeting,' for though I did not know much about business, I feared it confirmed what my father said: however, I thought, ill news always came fast enough, so I resolved to say nothing about my alarm, and merely told her that my father was well, and sent his kind regards to her. She kept turning over, and admiring her letter. At last she spoke:

'I remember their sending one to Deborah just like this; but that I did not wonder at, for everybody knew she was so clear-headed. I am afraid I could not help them much; indeed, if they came to accounts, I should be quite in the way, for I never could do sums in my head. Deborah, I know, rather wished to go, and went so far as to order a new bonnet for the occasion; but when the time came, she had a bad cold; so they sent her a very polite account of what they had done. Chosen a Director, I think it was. Do you think they want me to help them to choose a Director? I am sure, I should choose your father at once.'

'My father has no shares in the Bank,' said I.

'Oh, no! I remember! He objected very much to Deborah's buying any, I believe. But she was quite the woman of business, and always judged for herself; and here, you see, they have paid eight per cent. all these years.'

It was a very uncomfortable subject to me, with my half knowledge; so I thought I would change the conversation, and I asked at what time she thought we had better go and see the Fashions. 'Well, my dear,' she said, 'the thing is this; it is not etiquette to go till after twelve, but then, you see, all Cranford will be there, and one does not like to be too curious about dress and trimmings and caps, with all the world looking on. It is never genteel to be over-curious on these occasions. Deborah had the knack of always looking as if the latest fashion was nothing new to her; a manner she had caught from Lady Arley who did see all the new modes in London, you know. So I thought we would just slip down this morning, soon after breakfast; for I do want half a pound of tea; and then we could go up and examine the things at our leisure, and see exactly how my new silk gown must be made; and then, after twelve, we could go with our minds disengaged, and free from thoughts of dress.'

We began to talk of Miss Matty's new silk gown. I discovered that it would be really the first time in her life that she had had to choose anything of consequence for herself; for Miss Jenkyns had always been the more decided character, whatever her taste might have been; and it is astonishing how such people carry the world before them by the mere force of will. Miss Matty anticipated the sight of the glossy folds with as much delight as if the five sovereigns, set apart for the purchase, could buy all the silks in the shop; and (remembering my own loss of two hours in a toy-shop before I could tell on what wonder to spend a silver threepence) I was very glad that we were going early, that dear Miss Matty might have leisure for the delights of perplexity.

If a happy sea-green could be met with, the gown was to be sea-green: if not, she inclined to maize, and I to silver grey; and we discussed the requisite number of breadths until we arrived at the shop-door. We were to buy the tea, select the silk, and then clamber up the iron corkscrew stairs that led into what was once a loft, though now a Fashion show-room.

The young men at Mr. Johnson's had on their best looks, and their best cravats, and pivotted themselves over the counter with surprising activity. They wanted to show us upstairs at once; but on the principle of business first and pleasure afterwards, we stayed to purchase the tea. Here Miss Matty's absence of mind betrayed itself. If she was made aware that she had been drinking green tea* at any time, she always thought it her duty to lie awake half through the night afterward—(I have known her take it in ignorance many a time without such effects)—and consequently green tea was prohibited the house; yet to-day she herself asked for the obnoxious article, under the impression that she was talking about the silk. However, the mistake was soon rectified; and then the silks were unrolled in good truth. By this time the shop was pretty well filled, for it was Cranford market-day, and many of the farmers and country people from the neighbourhood round came in, sleeking down their hair, and glancing shyly about from under their eye-lids, as anxious to take back some notion of the unusual gaiety to the mistress or the lasses at home, and yet feeling that they were out of place among the smart shopmen and gay shawls and summer prints. One honest-looking man, however, made his way up to the counter at which we stood, and boldly asked to look at a shawl or two. The other country folk confined themselves to the grocery side; but our neighbour was evidently too full of some

kind intention towards mistress, wife, or daughter, to be shy; and
it soon became a question with me, whether he or Miss Matty
would keep their shopman the longest time. He thought each shawl
more beautiful than the last; and, as for Miss Matty, she smiled and
sighed over each fresh bale that was brought out; one colour set off
another, and the heap together would, as she said, make even the
rainbow look poor.

'I am afraid,' said she, hesitating, 'whichever I choose I shall
wish I had taken another. Look at this lovely crimson! it would be
so warm in winter. But spring is coming on, you know. I wish
I could have a gown for every season,' said she, dropping her voice
—as we all did in Cranford whenever we talked of anything we
wished for but could not afford. 'However,' she continued in
a louder and more cheerful tone, 'it would give me a great deal of
trouble to take care of them if I had them; so, I think, I'll only take
one. But which must it be, my dear?'

And now she hovered over a lilac with yellow spots, while
I pulled out a quiet sage-green, that had faded into insignificance
under the more brilliant colours, but which was nevertheless
a good silk in its humble way. Our attention was called off to our
neighbour. He had chosen a shawl of about thirty shillings' value;
and his face looked broadly happy, under the anticipation, no
doubt, of the pleasant surprise he should give to some Molly or
Jenny at home; he had tugged a leathern purse out of his breeches
pocket, and had offered a five-pound note in payment for the shawl,
and for some parcels which had been brought round to him from
the grocery counter; and it was just at this point that he attracted
our notice. The shopman was examining the note with a puzzled,
doubtful air:

'Town and County Bank! I am not sure, sir, but I believe we
have received a warning against notes issued by this bank only this
morning. I will just step and ask Mr. Johnson, sir; but I'm afraid,
I must trouble you for payment in cash, or in a note of a different
bank.'

I never saw a man's countenance fall so suddenly into dismay and
bewilderment. It was almost piteous to see the rapid change.

'Dang it!' said he, striking his fist down on the table, as if to try
which was the harder; 'the chap talks as if notes and gold were to
be had for the picking up.'

Miss Matty had forgotten her silk gown in her interest for the man. I don't think she had caught the name of the bank, and in my nervous cowardice, I was anxious that she should not; and so I began admiring the yellow-spotted lilac gown that I had been utterly condemning only a minute before. But it was of no use.

'What bank was it? I mean, what bank did your note belong to?'

'Town and County Bank.'

'Let me see it,' said she quietly to the shopman, gently taking it out of his hand, as he brought it back to return it to the farmer.

Mr. Johnson was very sorry, but, from information he had received, the notes issued by that bank were little better than waste paper.

'I don't understand it,' said Miss Matty to me in a low voice. 'That is our bank, is it not?—the Town and County Bank?'

'Yes,' said I. 'This lilac silk will just match the ribbons in your new cap, I believe,' I continued—holding up the folds so as to catch the light, and wishing that the man would make haste and be gone—and yet having a new wonder, that had only just sprung up, how far it was wise or right in me to allow Miss Matty to make this expensive purchase, if the affairs of the bank were really so bad as the refusal of the note implied.

But Miss Matty put on the soft dignified manner peculiar to her, rarely used, and yet which became her so well, and laying her hand gently on mine, she said,

'Never mind the silks for a few minutes, dear. I don't understand you, sir,' turning now to the shopman, who had been attending to the farmer. 'Is this a forged note?'

'Oh, no, ma'am. It is a true note of its kind; but you see, ma'am, it is a Joint Stock Bank, and there are reports out that it is likely to break. Mr. Johnson is only doing his duty, ma'am, as I am sure Mr. Dobson knows.'

But Mr. Dobson could not respond to the appealing bow by any answering smile. He was turning the note absently over in his fingers, looking gloomily enough at the parcel containing the lately chosen shawl.

'It's hard upon a poor man,' said he, 'as earns every farthing with the sweat of his brow. However, there's no help for it. You must take back your shawl, my man; Lizzie must do on with her cloak for a while. And yon figs for the little ones—I promised them to 'em —I'll take them; but the 'bacco, and the other things—'

'I will give you five sovereigns for your note, my good man,' said Miss Matty. 'I think there is some great mistake about it, for I am one of the shareholders, and I'm sure they would have told me if things had not been going on right.'

The shopman whispered a word or two across the table to Miss Matty. She looked at him with a dubious air.

'Perhaps so,' said she. 'But I don't pretend to understand business; I only know, that if it is going to fail, and if honest people are to lose their money because they have taken our notes—I can't explain myself,' said she, suddenly becoming aware that she had got into a long sentence with four people for audience—'only I would rather exchange my gold for the note, if you please,' turning to the farmer, 'and then you can take your wife the shawl. It is only going without my gown a few days longer,' she continued, speaking to me. 'Then, I have no doubt, everything will be cleared up.'

'But if it is cleared up the wrong way?' said I.

'Why! then it will only have been common honesty in me, as a shareholder, to have given this good man the money. I am quite clear about it in my own mind; but, you know, I can never speak quite as comprehensibly as others can;—only you must give me your note, Mr. Dobson, if you please, and go on with your purchases with these sovereigns.'

The man looked at her with silent gratitude—too awkward to put his thanks into words; but he hung back for a minute or two, fumbling with his note.

'I'm loth to make another one lose instead of me, if it is a loss; but, you see, five pounds is a deal of money to a man with a family; and, as you say, ten to one in a day or two, the note will be as good as gold again.'

'No hope of that, my friend,' said the shopman.

'The more reason why I should take it,' said Miss Matty quietly. She pushed her sovereigns towards the man, who slowly laid his note down in exchange. 'Thank you. I will wait a day or two before I purchase any of these silks; perhaps you will then have a greater choice. My dear! will you come upstairs?'

We inspected the Fashions with as minute and curious an interest as if the gown to be made after them had been bought. I could not see that the little event in the shop below had in the least damped Miss Matty's curiosity as to the make of sleeves, or the sit of skirts. She once or twice exchanged congratulations with me on our private and leisurely view of the bonnets and shawls; but I was, all the time, not so sure that our examination was so utterly private, for I caught glimpses of a figure dodging behind the cloaks and mantles; and, by a dextrous move, I came face to face with Miss Pole, also in morning costume (the principal feature of which was her being without teeth, and wearing a veil to conceal the deficiency), come on the same errand as ourselves. But she quickly took her departure, because, as she said, she had a bad headache and did not feel herself up to conversation.

As we came down through the shop, the civil Mr. Johnson was awaiting us; he had been informed of the exchange of the note for gold, and with much good feeling and real kindness, but with a little want of tact, he wished to condole with Miss Matty, and impress upon her the true state of the case. I could only hope that he had heard an exaggerated rumour, for he said that her shares were worse than nothing, and that the bank could not pay a shilling in the pound. I was glad that Miss Matty seemed still a little incredulous; but I could not tell how much of this was real or assumed, with that self-control which seemed habitual to ladies of Miss Matty's standing in Cranford, who would have thought their dignity compromised by the slightest expression of surprise, dismay, or any similar feeling to an inferior in station, or in a public shop. However, we walked home very silently. I am ashamed to say, I believe I was rather vexed and annoyed at Miss Matty's conduct, in taking the note to herself so decidedly. I had so set my heart upon her having a new silk gown, which she wanted sadly; in general she was so undecided anybody might turn her round; in this case I had felt that it was no use attempting it, but I was not the less put out at the result.

Somehow, after twelve o'clock, we both acknowledged to a sated curiosity about the Fashions; and to a certain fatigue of body (which was, in fact, depression of mind) that indisposed us to go out again. But still we never spoke of the note; till, all at once, something possessed me to ask Miss Matty, if she would think it her duty to offer sovereigns for all the notes of the Town and County Bank she met with? I could have bitten my tongue out the minute I had said it. She looked up rather sadly, and as if I had thrown a new perplexity into her already distressed mind; and for a minute or two, she did not speak. Then she said—my own dear Miss Matty—without a shade of reproach in her voice:

'My dear! I never feel as if my mind was what people call very strong; and it's often hard enough work for me to settle what I ought to do with the case right before me. I was very thankful to —I was very thankful, that I saw my duty this morning, with the poor man standing by me; but it's rather a strain upon me to keep thinking and thinking what I should do if such and such a thing happened; and, I believe, I had rather wait and see what really does come; and I don't doubt I shall be helped then, if I don't fidget myself, and get too anxious beforehand. You know, love, I'm not like Deborah. If Deborah had lived, I've no doubt she would have seen after them, before they had got themselves into this state.'

We had neither of us much appetite for dinner, though we tried to talk cheerfully about indifferent things. When we returned into the drawing-room, Miss Matty unlocked her desk and began to look over her account-books. I was so penitent for what I had said in the morning, that I did not choose to take upon myself the presumption to suppose that I could assist her; I rather left her alone, as, with puzzled brow, her eye followed her pen up and down the ruled page. By-and-by she shut the book, locked her desk, and came and drew a chair to mine, where I sat in moody sorrow over the fire. I stole my hand into hers; she clasped it, but did not speak a word. At last she said, with forced composure in her voice, 'If that bank goes wrong, I shall lose one hundred and forty-nine pounds thirteen shillings and fourpence a year; I shall only have thirteen pounds a year left.' I squeezed her hand hard and tight. I did not know what to say. Presently (it was too dark to see her face) I felt her fingers work convulsively in my grasp; and I knew she was going to speak again. I heard the sobs in her voice as she said, 'I hope it's not wrong—not wicked—but oh! I am so glad poor Deborah is spared this. She could not have borne to come down in the world,—she had such a noble, lofty spirit.'

This was all she said about the sister who had insisted upon investing their little property in that unlucky bank.* We were later in lighting the candle than usual that night, and until that light shamed us into speaking, we sat together very silently and sadly.

However, we took to our work after tea with a kind of forced cheerfulness (which soon became real as far as it went), talking of that never-ending wonder, Lady Glenmire's engagement. Miss Matty was almost coming round to think it a good thing.

'I don't mean to deny that men are troublesome in a house. I don't judge from my own experience, for my father was neatness itself, and wiped his shoes on coming in as carefully as any woman; but still a man has a sort of knowledge of what should be done in difficulties, that it is very pleasant to have one at hand ready to lean upon. Now, Lady Glenmire, instead of being tossed about, and wondering where she is to settle, will be certain of a home among pleasant and kind people, such as our good Miss Pole and Mrs. Forrester. And Mr. Hoggins is really a very personable man; and as for his manners—why, if they are not very polished, I have known people with very good hearts and very clever minds too, who were not what some people reckoned refined, but who were both true and tender.'

She fell off into a soft reverie about Mr. Holbrook, and I did not interrupt her, I was so busy maturing a plan I had had in my mind for some days, but which this threatened failure of the bank had brought to a crisis. That night, after Miss Matty went to bed, I treacherously lighted the candle again, and sat down in the drawing-room to compose a letter to the Aga Jenkyns—a letter which should affect him, if he were Peter, and yet seem a mere statement of dry facts if he were a stranger. The church clock pealed out two before I had done.

The next morning news came, both official and otherwise, that the Town and County Bank had stopped payment. Miss Matty was ruined.

She tried to speak quietly to me; but when she came to the actual fact, that she would have but about five shillings a week to live upon, she could not restrain a few tears.

'I am not crying for myself, dear,' said she, wiping them away; 'I believe I am crying for the very silly thought, of how my mother would grieve if she could know—she always cared for us so much more than for herself. But many a poor person has less; and I am not very extravagant, and, thank God, when the neck of mutton, and Martha's wages, and the rent, are paid, I have not a farthing owing. Poor Martha! I think she'll be sorry to leave me.'

Miss Matty smiled at me through her tears, and she would fain have had me see only the smile, not the tears.

CHAPTER XIV

FRIENDS IN NEED

IT was an example to me, and I fancy it might be to many others, to see how immediately Miss Matty set about the retrenchment which she knew to be right under her altered circumstances. While she went down to speak to Martha, and break the intelligence to her, I stole out with my letter to the Aga Jenkyns, and went to the Signor's lodgings to obtain the exact address. I bound the Signora to secrecy; and indeed, her military manners had a degree of shortness and reserve in them, which made her always say as little as possible, except when under the pressure of strong excitement. Moreover—(which made my secret doubly sure)—the Signor was now so far recovered as to be looking forward to travelling and conjuring again in the space of a few days, when he, his wife, and little Phœbe, would leave Cranford. Indeed I found him looking over a great black and red placard, in which the Signor Brunoni's accomplishments were set forth, and to which only the name of the town where he would next display them was wanting. He and his wife were so much absorbed in deciding where the red letters would come in with most effect (it might have been the Rubric* for that matter), that it was some time before I could get my question asked privately, and not before I had given several decisions, the wisdom of which I questioned afterwards with equal sincerity as soon as the Signor threw in his doubts and reasons on the important subject. At last I got the address, spelt by sound; and very queer it looked! I dropped it in the post on my way home; and then for a minute I stood looking at the wooden pane, with a gaping slit, which divided me from the letter, but a moment ago in my hand. It was gone from me like life—never to be recalled. It would get tossed about on the sea, and stained with sea-waves perhaps; and be carried among palm-trees, and scented with all tropical fragrance;—the little piece of paper, but an hour ago so familiar and commonplace, had set out on its race to the strange wild countries beyond the Ganges! But I could not afford to lose much time on this speculation. I hastened home, that Miss Matty might not miss me. Martha opened the door to me, her face swollen with crying. As soon as she saw me, she burst out afresh, and taking hold of my arm she pulled me in, and banged the door to, in order to ask me if indeed it was all true that Miss Matty had been saying.

'I'll never leave her! No! I won't. I telled her so, and said I could not think how she could find in her heart to give me warning. I could not have had the face to do it, if I'd been her. I might ha' been just as good-for-nothing as Mrs. Fitz-Adam's Rosy, who struck for wages after living seven years and a half in one place. I said I was not one to go and serve Mammon*at that rate; that I knew when I'd got a good Missus, if she didn't know when she'd got a good servant—'

'But Martha;' said I, cutting in while she wiped her eyes.

'Don't "but Martha" me,' she replied to my deprecatory tone. 'Listen to reason—'

'I'll not listen to reason,' she said—now in full possession of her voice, which had been rather choked with sobbing. 'Reason always means what some one else has got to say. Now I think what I've got to say is good enough reason. But, reason or not, I'll say it, and I'll stick to it. I've money in the Savings' Bank, and I've a good stock of clothes, and I'm not going to leave Miss Matty. No! not if she gives me warning every hour in the day!'

She put her arms akimbo, as much as to say she defied me; and, indeed, I could hardly tell how to begin to remonstrate with her, so much did I feel that Miss Matty in her increasing infirmity needed the attendance of this kind and faithful woman.

'Well!' said I at last—

'I'm thankful you begin with "well!" If you'd ha' begun with "but," as you did afore, I'd not ha' listened to you. Now you may go on.'

'I know you would be a great loss to Miss Matty, Martha—'

'I telled her so. A loss she'd never cease to be sorry for,' broke in Martha, triumphantly.

'Still she will have so little—so very little—to live upon, that I don't see just now how she could find you food—she will even be pressed for her own. I tell you this, Martha, because I feel you are like a friend to dear Miss Matty—but you know she might not like to have it spoken about.'

Apparently this was even a blacker view of the subject than Miss Matty had presented to her; for Martha just sat down on the first chair that came to hand, and cried out loud—(we had been standing in the kitchen).

At last she put her apron down, and looking me earnestly in the face, asked, 'Was that the reason Miss Matty wouldn't order a pudding to-day? She said she had no great fancy for sweet things, and you and she would just have a mutton chop. But I'll be up to her. Never you tell, but I'll make her a pudding, and a pudding she'll like, too, and I'll pay for it myself; so mind you see she eats it. Many a one has been comforted in their sorrow by seeing a good dish come upon the table.'

I was rather glad that Martha's energy had taken the immediate and practical direction of pudding-making, for it staved off the quarrelsome discussion as to whether she should or should not leave Miss Matty's service. She began to tie on a clean apron, and otherwise prepare herself for going to the shop for the butter, eggs, and what else she might require; she would not use a scrap of the articles already in the house for her cookery, but went to an old tea-pot in which her private store of money was deposited, and took out what she wanted.

I found Miss Matty very quiet, and not a little sad; but by-and-by she tried to smile for my sake. It was settled that I was to write to my father, and ask him to come over and hold a consultation; and as soon as this letter was despatched, we began to talk over future plans. Miss Matty's idea was to take a single room, and retain as much of her furniture as would be necessary to fit up this, and sell the rest; and there to quietly exist upon what would remain after paying the rent. For my part, I was more ambitious and less contented. I thought of all the things by which a woman, past middle age, and with the education common to ladies fifty years ago, could earn or add to a living, without materially losing caste; but at length I put even this last clause on one side, and wondered what in the world Miss Matty could do.

Teaching was, of course, the first thing that suggested itself. If Miss Matty could teach children anything, it would throw her among the little elves in whom her soul delighted. I ran over her accomplishments. Once upon a time I had heard her say she could play, '*Ah! vous dirai-je, maman?*'* on the piano; but that was long, long ago; that faint shadow of musical acquirement had died out years before. She had also once been able to trace out patterns very nicely for muslin embroidery, by dint of placing a piece of silver-paper over the design to be copied, and holding both against the window-pane, while she marked the scollop and eyelet-holes. But that was her nearest approach to the accomplishment of drawing, and I did not think it would go very far. Then again as to the branches of a solid English education—fancy-work and the use of the globes—such as the mistress of the Ladies' Seminary, to which all the tradespeople in Cranford sent their daughters, professed to teach; Miss Matty's eyes were failing her, and I doubted if she could discover the number of threads in a worsted-work pattern, or rightly appreciate the different shades required for Queen Adelaide's face, in the loyal wool-work* now fashionable in Cranford. As for the use of the globes,* I had never been able to find it out myself, so perhaps I was not a good judge of Miss Matty's capability of instructing in this branch of education; but it struck me that equators and tropics, and such mystical circles, were very imaginary lines indeed to her, and that she looked upon the signs of the Zodiac as so many remnants of the Black Art.*

What she piqued herself upon, as arts, in which she excelled, was making candle-lighters, or 'spills' (as she preferred calling them), of coloured paper, cut so as to resemble feathers, and knitting garters in a variety of dainty stitches. I had once said, on receiving a present of an elaborate pair, that I should feel quite tempted to drop one of them in the street, in order to have it admired; but I found this little joke (and it was a very little one) was such a distress to her sense of propriety, and was taken with such anxious, earnest alarm, lest the temptation might some day prove too strong for me, that I quite regretted having ventured upon it. A present of these delicately-wrought garters, a bunch of gay 'spills,' or a set of cards on which sewing-silk was wound in a mystical manner, were the well-known tokens of Miss Matty's favour. But would any one pay to have their children taught these arts? or indeed would Miss Matty sell, for filthy lucre, the knack and the skill with which she made trifles of value to those who loved her?

I had to come down to reading, writing, and arithmetic; and, in reading the chapter every morning, she always coughed before coming to long words. I doubted her power of getting through a genealogical chapter,* with any number of coughs. Writing she did well and delicately; but spelling! She seemed to think that the more out-of-the-way this was, and the more trouble it cost her, the greater the compliment she paid to her correspondent; and words that she would spell quite correctly in

her letters to me, became perfect enigmas when she wrote to
my father.

No! there was nothing she could teach to the rising generation
of Cranford; unless they had been quick learners and ready
imitators of her patience, her humility, her sweetness, her quiet
contentment with all that she could not do. I pondered and
pondered until dinner was announced by Martha, with a face all
blubbered and swollen with crying.

Miss Matty had a few little peculiarities, which Martha was apt
to regard as whims below her attention, and appeared to consider
as childish fancies, of which an old lady of fifty-eight should try
and cure herself. But to-day everything was attended to with the
most careful regard. The bread was cut to the imaginary pattern
of excellence that existed in Miss Matty's mind, as being the way
which her mother had preferred; the curtain was drawn so as to
exclude the dead-brick wall of a neighbour's stables, and yet left
so as to show every tender leaf of the poplar which was bursting
into spring beauty. Martha's tone to Miss Matty was just such as
that good, rough-spoken servant usually kept sacred for little
children, and which I had never heard her use to any grown-up
person.

I had forgotten to tell Miss Matty about the pudding, and I was
afraid she might not do justice to it; for she had evidently very
little appetite this day; so I seized the opportunity of letting her
into the secret while Martha took away the meat. Miss Matty's
eyes filled with tears, and she could not speak, either to express
surprise or delight, when Martha returned, bearing it aloft, made
in the most wonderful representation of a lion *couchant* that ever
was moulded. Martha's face gleamed with triumph, as she set it
down before Miss Matty with an exultant 'There!' Miss Matty
wanted to speak her thanks, but could not; so she took Martha's
hand and shook it warmly, which set Martha off crying, and I myself could hardly keep up the necessary composure. Martha burst
out of the room; and Miss Matty had to clear her voice once
or twice before she could speak. At last she said, 'I should like
to keep this pudding under a glass shade, my dear!' and the
notion of the lion *couchant* with his currant eyes, being hoisted
up to the place of honour on a mantel-piece, tickled my hysterical
fancy, and I began to laugh, which rather surprised Miss
Matty.

'I am sure, dear, I have seen uglier things under a glass shade before now,' said she.

So had I, many a time and oft; and I accordingly composed my countenance (and now I could hardly keep from crying), and we both fell to upon the pudding, which was indeed excellent—only every morsel seemed to choke us, our hearts were so full.

We had too much to think about to talk much that afternoon. It passed over very tranquilly. But when the tea-urn was brought in, a new thought came into my head. Why should not Miss Matty sell tea—be an agent to the East India Tea Company which then existed? I could see no objections to this plan, while the advantages were many—always supposing that Miss Matty could get over the degradation of condescending to anything like trade. Tea was neither greasy, nor sticky—grease and stickiness being two of the qualities which Miss Matty could not endure. No shop-window would be required. A small genteel notification of her being licensed to sell tea, would, it is true, be necessary; but I hoped that it could be placed where no one could see it. Neither was tea a heavy article, so as to tax Miss Matty's fragile strength. The only thing against my plan was the buying and selling involved.

While I was giving but absent answers to the questions Miss Matty was putting—almost as absently—we heard a clumping sound on the stairs, and a whispering outside the door: which indeed once opened and shut as if by some invisible agency. After a little while, Martha came in, dragging after her a great tall young man, all crimson with shyness, and finding his only relief in perpetually sleeking down his hair.

'Please, ma'am, he's only Jem Hearn,' said Martha, by way of an introduction; and so out of breath was she, that I imagine she had had some bodily struggle before she could overcome his reluctance to be presented on the courtly scene of Miss Matilda Jenkyns's drawing-room.

'And please, ma'am, he wants to marry me off-hand. And please, ma'am, we want to take a lodger—just one quiet lodger, to make our two ends meet; and we'd take any house conformable; and, oh dear Miss Matty, if I may be so bold, would you have any objections to lodging with us? Jem wants it as much I do.' [To Jem:]— 'You great oaf! why can't you back me?—But he does want it, all the same, very bad—don't you, Jem?—only, you see, he's dazed at being called on to speak before quality.'*

'It's not that,' broke in Jem. 'It's that you've taken me all on a sudden, and I didn't think for to get married so soon—and such quick work does flabbergast a man. It's not that I'm against it, ma'am,' (addressing Miss Matty), 'only Martha has such quick ways with her, when once she takes a thing into her head; and marriage, ma'am,—marriage nails a man, as one may say. I dare say I shan't mind it after it's once over.'

'Please, ma'am,' said Martha—who had plucked at his sleeve, and nudged him with her elbow, and otherwise tried to interrupt him all the time he had been speaking—'don't mind him, he'll come to; 'twas only last night he was an-axing me, and an-axing me, and all the more because I said I could not think of it for years to come, and now he's only taken aback with the suddenness of the joy; but you know, Jem, you are just as full as me about wanting a lodger.' (Another great nudge.)

'Ay! if Miss Matty would lodge with us—otherwise I've no mind to be cumbered with strange folk in the house,' said Jem, with a want of tact which I could see enraged Martha, who was trying to represent a lodger as the great object they wished to obtain, and that, in fact, Miss Matty would be smoothing their path, and conferring a favour, if she would only come and live with them.

Miss Matty herself was bewildered by the pair: their, or rather Martha's sudden resolution in favour of matrimony staggered her, and stood between her and the contemplation of the plan which Martha had at heart. Miss Matty began,—

'Marriage is a very solemn thing, Martha.'

'It is indeed, ma'am,' quoth Jem. 'Not that I've no objections to Martha.'

'You've never let me a-be for asking me for to fix when I would be married,' said Martha—her face all a-fire, and ready to cry with vexation—'and now you're shaming me before my missus and all.'

'Nay, now! Martha, don't ee! don't ee! only a man likes to have breathing-time,' said Jem, trying to possess himself of her hand, but in vain. Then seeing that she was more seriously hurt than he had imagined, he seemed to try to rally his scattered faculties, and with more straight-forward dignity than, ten minutes before I should have thought it possible for him to assume, he turned to Miss Matty, and said, 'I hope, ma'am, you know that I am bound to respect every one who has been kind to Martha. I always looked on her as to be my wife—some time; and she has often and often spoken of you as the kindest lady that ever was; and though the plain truth is I would not like to be troubled with lodgers of the common run; yet if, ma'am, you'd honour us by living with us, I am sure Martha would do her best to make you comfortable; and I'd keep out of your way as much as I could, which I reckon would be the best kindness such an awkward chap as me could do.'

Miss Matty had been very busy with taking off her spectacles, wiping them, and replacing them; but all she could say was, 'Don't let any thought of me hurry you into marriage: pray don't! Marriage is such a very solemn thing!'

'But Miss Matilda will think of your plan, Martha,' said I—struck with the advantages that it offered, and unwilling to lose the opportunity of considering about it. 'And I'm sure neither she nor I can ever forget your kindness; nor yours either, Jem.'

'Why, yes, ma'am! I'm sure I mean kindly, though I'm a bit fluttered by being pushed straight a-head into matrimony, as it were, and mayn't express myself conformable. But I'm sure I'm willing enough, and give me time to get accustomed; so, Martha, wench, what's the use of crying so, and slapping me if I come near?'

This last was *sotto voce*, and had the effect of making Martha bounce out of the room, to be followed and soothed by her lover. Whereupon Miss Matty sat down and cried very heartily, and accounted for it by saying that the thought of Martha being married so soon gave her quite a shock, and that she should never forgive herself if she thought she was hurrying the poor creature. I think my pity was more for Jem, of the two: but both Miss Matty and I appreciated to the full the kindness of the honest couple, although we said little about this, and a good deal about the chances and dangers of matrimony.

The next morning, very early, I received a note from Miss Pole, so mysteriously wrapped up, and with so many seals on it to secure secrecy, that I had to tear the paper before I could unfold it. And when I came to the writing I could hardly understand the meaning, it was so involved and oracular. I made out, however, that I was to go to Miss Pole's at eleven o'clock; the number *eleven* being written in full length as well as in numerals, and *A.M.* twice dashed under, as if I were very likely to come at eleven at night, when all Cranford was usually a-bed, and asleep by ten. There was no signature except Miss Pole's initials, reversed, P.E., but as Martha had given me the note, 'with Miss Pole's kind regards,' it needed no wizard to find out who sent it; and if the writer's name was to be kept secret, it was very well that I was alone when Martha delivered it.

I went, as requested, to Miss Pole's. The door was opened to me by her little maid Lizzy, in Sunday trim, as if some grand event was impending over this work-day. And the drawing-room upstairs was arranged in accordance with this idea. The table was set out, with the best green card-cloth, and writing-materials upon it. On the little chiffonier was a tray with a newly-decanted bottle of cowslip wine, and some ladies'-finger biscuits. Miss Pole herself was in solemn array, as if to receive visitors, although it was only eleven o'clock. Mrs. Forrester was there, crying quietly and sadly, and my arrival seemed only to call forth fresh tears. Before we had finished our greetings, performed with lugubrious mystery of demeanour, there was another rat-tat-tat, and Mrs. Fitz-Adam appeared, crimson with walking and excitement. It seemed as if this was all the company expected; for now Miss Pole made several demonstrations of being about to open the business of the meeting, by stirring the fire, opening and shutting the door, and coughing and blowing her nose. Then she arranged us all round the table, taking care to place me opposite to her; and last of all, she inquired of me, if the sad report was true, as she feared it was, that Miss Matty had lost all her fortune?

Of course, I had but one answer to make; and I never saw more unaffected sorrow depicted on any countenances, than I did there on the three before me.

'I wish Mrs. Jamieson was here!' said Mrs. Forrester at last; but to judge from Mrs. Fitz-Adam's face, she could not second the wish.

'But without Mrs. Jamieson,' said Miss Pole, with just a sound of offended merit in her voice, 'we, the ladies of Cranford, in my drawing-room assembled, can resolve upon something. I imagine we are none of us what may be called rich, though we all possess a genteel competency, sufficient for tastes that are elegant and refined, and would not, if they could, be vulgarly ostentatious.' (Here I observed Miss Pole refer to a small card concealed in her hand, on which I imagine she had put down a few notes.)

'Miss Smith,' she continued, addressing me, (familiarly known as 'Mary' to all the company assembled, but this was a state occasion,) 'I have conversed in private—I made it my business to do so yesterday afternoon—with these ladies on the misfortune which has happened to our friend,—and one and all of us have agreed that, while we have a superfluity, it is not only a duty but a pleasure, —a true pleasure, Mary!'—her voice was rather choked just here, and she had to wipe her spectacles before she could go on—'to give what we can to assist her—Miss Matilda Jenkyns. Only, in consideration of the feelings of delicate independence existing in the mind of every refined female,'—I was sure she had got back to the card now—'we wish to contribute our mites in a secret and concealed manner, so as not to hurt the feelings I have referred to. And our object in requesting you to meet us this morning, is, that believing you are the daughter—that your father is, in fact, her confidential adviser in all pecuniary matters, we imagined that, by consulting with him, you might devise some mode in which our contribution could be made to appear the legal due which Miss Matilda Jenkyns ought to receive from——. Probably, your father, knowing her investments, can fill up the blank.'

Miss Pole concluded her address, and looked round for approval and agreement.

'I have expressed your meaning, ladies, have I not? And while Miss Smith considers what reply to make, allow me to offer you some little refreshment.'

I had no great reply to make; I had more thankfulness at my heart for their kind thoughts than I cared to put into words; and so I only mumbled out something to the effect 'that I would name what Miss Pole had said to my father, and that if anything could be arranged for dear Miss Matty,'—and here I broke down utterly, and had to be refreshed with a glass of cowslip wine before I could check the crying which had been repressed for the last two or three days. The worst was, all the ladies cried in concert. Even Miss Pole cried, who had said a hundred times that to betray emotion before any one was a sign of weakness and want of self-control. She recovered herself into a slight degree of impatient anger, directed against me, as having set them all off; and, moreover, I think she was vexed that I could not make a speech back in return for hers; and if I had known beforehand what was to be said, and had had a card on which to express the probable feelings that would rise in my heart, I would have tried to gratify her. As it was,

Mrs. Forrester was the person to speak when we had recovered
our composure.

'I don't mind, among friends, stating that I—no! I'm not poor
exactly, but I don't think I'm what you may call rich; I wish I were,
for dear Miss Matty's sake,—but, if you please, I'll write down, in
a sealed paper, what I can give. I only wish it was more: my dear
Mary, I do indeed.'

Now I saw why paper, pens, and ink, were provided. Every lady
wrote down the sum she could give annually, signed the paper, and
sealed it mysteriously. If their proposal was acceded to, my father
was to be allowed to open the papers, under pledge of secresy. If
not they were to be returned to their writers.

When this ceremony had been gone through, I rose to depart;
but each lady seemed to wish to have a private conference with me.
Miss Pole kept me in the drawing-room to explain why, in Mrs.
Jamieson's absence, she had taken the lead in this 'movement,' as
she was pleased to call it, and also to inform me that she had heard
from good sources that Mrs. Jamieson was coming home directly,
in a state of high displeasure against her sister-in-law, who was
forthwith to leave her house; and was, she believed, to return to
Edinburgh that very afternoon. Of course this piece of intelligence
could not be communicated before Mrs. Fitz-Adam, more especially as Miss Pole was inclined to think that Lady Glenmire's
engagement to Mr. Hoggins could not possibly hold against the
blaze of Mrs. Jamieson's displeasure. A few hearty inquiries after
Miss Matty's health concluded my interview with Miss Pole.

On coming downstairs, I found Mrs. Forrester waiting for me
at the entrance to the dining parlour; she drew me in, and when the
door was shut, she tried two or three times to begin on some
subject, which was so unapproachable apparently, that I began to
despair of our ever getting to a clear understanding. At last out it
came; the poor old lady trembling all the time as if it were a great
crime which she was exposing to daylight, in telling me how very,
very little she had to live upon; a confession which she was brought
to make from a dread lest we should think that the small contribution named in her paper bore any proportion to her love and regard
for Miss Matty. And yet that sum which she so eagerly relinquished
was, in truth, more than a twentieth part of what she had to live
upon, and keep house, and a little serving-maid, all as became one
born a Tyrrell. And when the whole income does not nearly amount

to a hundred pounds, to give up a twentieth of it will necessitate many careful economies, and many pieces of self-denial—small and insignificant in the world's account, but bearing a different value in another account-book that I have heard of. She did so wish she was rich, she said; and this wish she kept repeating, with no thought of herself in it, only with a longing, yearning desire to be able to heap up Miss Matty's measure of comforts.

It was some time before I could console her enough to leave her; and then, on quitting the house, I was waylaid by Mrs. Fitz-Adam, who had also her confidence to make of pretty nearly the opposite description. She had not liked to put down all that she could afford, and was ready to give. She told me she thought she never could look Miss Matty in the face again if she presumed to be giving her so much as she should like to do. 'Miss Matty!' continued she, 'that I thought was such a fine young lady, when I was nothing but a country girl, coming to market with eggs and butter and such like things. For my father, though well to do, would always make me go on as my mother had done before me; and I had to come in to Cranford every Saturday and see after sales and prices, and what not. And one day, I remember, I met Miss Matty in the lane that leads to Combehurst; she was walking on the foot-path which, you know, is raised a good way above the road, and a gentleman rode beside her, and was talking to her, and she was looking down at some primroses she had gathered, and pulling them all to pieces, and I do believe she was crying. But after she had passed, she turned round and ran after me to ask—oh so kindly—after my poor mother, who lay on her death-bed; and when I cried, she took hold of my hand to comfort me; and the gentleman waiting for her all the time; and her poor heart very full of something, I am sure; and I thought it such an honour to be spoken to in that pretty way by the rector's daughter, who visited at Arley Hall. I have loved her ever since, though perhaps I'd no right to do it; but if you can think of any way in which I might be allowed to give a little more without any one knowing it, I should be so much obliged to you, my dear. And my brother would be delighted to doctor her for nothing—medicines, leeches, and all. I know that he and her ladyship—(my dear! I little thought in the days I was telling you of that I should ever come to be sister-in-law to a ladyship!)—would do anything for her. We all would.'

I told her I was quite sure of it, and promised all sorts of things, in my anxiety to get home to Miss Matty, who might well be wondering what had become of me,—absent from her two hours without being able to account for it. She had taken very little note of time, however, as she had been occupied in numberless little arrangements preparatory to the great step of giving up her house. It was evidently a relief to her to be doing something in the way of retrenchment; for, as she said, whenever she paused to think, the recollection of the poor fellow with his bad five-pound note came over her, and she felt quite dishonest; only if it made her so uncomfortable, what must it not be doing to the directors of the Bank, who must know so much more of the misery consequent upon this failure? She almost made me angry by dividing her sympathy between these directors (whom she imagined overwhelmed by self-reproach for the mismanagement of other people's affairs), and those who were suffering like her. Indeed, of the two, she seemed to think poverty a lighter burden than self-reproach; but I privately doubted if the directors would agree with her.

Old hoards were taken out and examined as to their money value, which luckily was small, or else I don't know how Miss Matty would have prevailed upon herself to part with such things as her mother's wedding-ring, the strange uncouth brooch with which her father had disfigured his shirt-frill, &c. However, we arranged things a little in order as to their pecuniary estimation, and were all ready for my father when he came the next morning.

I am not going to weary you with the details of all the business we went through; and one reason for not telling about them is, that I did not understand what we were doing at the time, and cannot recollect it now. Miss Matty and I sat assenting to accounts, and schemes, and reports, and documents, of which I do not believe we either of us understood a word; for my father was clear-headed and decisive, and a capital man of business, and if we made the slightest inquiry, or expressed the slightest want of comprehension, he had a sharp way of saying, 'Eh? eh? it's as clear as daylight. What's your objection?' And as we had not comprehended anything of what he had proposed, we found it rather difficult to shape our objections; in fact, we never were sure if we had any. So, presently Miss Matty got into a nervously acquiescent state, and said 'Yes' and 'Certainly' at every pause, whether required or not: but when I once joined in as chorus to a 'Decidedly,' pronounced by Miss Matty in a tremblingly dubious tone, my father fired round at me and asked me 'What there was to decide?' And I am sure, to this day, I have never known. But, in justice to him, I must say, he had come over from Drumble to help Miss Matty when he could ill spare the time, and when his own affairs were in a very anxious state.

While Miss Matty was out of the room, giving orders for luncheon—and sadly perplexed between her desire of honouring my father by a delicate dainty meal, and her conviction that she had no right now that all her money was gone, to indulge this desire,—I told him of the meeting of Cranford ladies at Miss Pole's the day before. He kept brushing his hand before his eyes as I spoke;—and when I went back to Martha's offer the evening before, of receiving Miss Matty as a lodger, he fairly walked away from me to the window, and began drumming with his fingers upon it. Then he turned abruptly round, and said, 'See, Mary, how a good innocent life makes friends all around. Confound it! I could make a good lesson out of it if I were a parson; but as it is, I can't get a tail to my sentences—only I'm sure you feel what I want to say. You and I will have a walk after lunch, and talk a bit more about these plans.'

The lunch—a hot savoury mutton-chop, and a little of the cold lion sliced and fried—was now brought in. Every morsel of this last dish was finished, to Martha's great gratification. Then my father bluntly told Miss Matty he wanted to talk to me alone, and that he would stroll out and see some of the old places, and then I could tell her what plan we thought desirable. Just before we went out, she called me back and said, 'Remember dear, I'm the only one left—I mean there's no one to be hurt by what I do. I'm willing to do anything that's right and honest; and I don't think, if Deborah knows where she is, she'll care so very much if I'm not genteel; because, you see, she'll know all, dear. Only let me sell what I can,* and pay the poor people as far as I'm able.'

I gave her a hearty kiss, and ran after my father. The result of our conversation was this. If all parties were agreeable, Martha and Jem were to be married with as little delay as possible, and they were to live on in Miss Matty's present abode; the sum which the Cranford ladies had agreed to contribute annually, being sufficient to meet the greater part of the rent, and leaving Martha free to appropriate what Miss Matty should pay for her lodgings to any little extra comforts required. About the sale, my father was dubious at first. He said the old rectory furniture, however care-

fully used, and reverently treated, would fetch very little; and that
little would be but as a drop in the sea of the debts of the Town and
County Bank. But when I represented how Miss Matty's tender
conscience would be soothed by feeling that she had done what she
could, he gave way; especially after I had told him the five-pound-
note adventure, and he had scolded me well for allowing it. I then
alluded to my idea that she might add to her small income by selling
tea; and, to my surprise, (for I had nearly given up the plan,) my
father grasped at it with all the energy of a tradesman. I think he
reckoned his chickens before they were hatched, for he immediately ran up the profits of the sales that she could effect in Cranford to more than twenty pounds a-year. The small dining-parlour
was to be converted into a shop, without any of its degrading
characteristics; a table was to be the counter; one window was to
be retained unaltered, and the other changed into a glass door.
I evidently rose in his estimation, for having made this bright suggestion. I only hoped we should not both fall in Miss Matty's.

But she was patient and content with all our arrangements. She
knew, she said, that we should do the best we could for her; and she
only hoped, only stipulated, that she should pay every farthing that
she could be said to owe for her father's sake, who had been so
respected in Cranford. My father and I had agreed to say as little as
possible about the Bank, indeed never to mention it again, if it could
be helped. Some of the plans were evidently a little perplexing to
her; but she had seen me sufficiently snubbed in the morning for
want of comprehension to venture on too many inquiries now; and
all passed over well, with a hope on her part that no one would be
hurried into marriage on her account. When we came to the proposal
that she should sell tea, I could see it was rather a shock to her; not on
account of any personal loss of gentility involved, but only because
she distrusted her own powers of action in a new line of life, and
would timidly have preferred a little more privation to any exertion
for which she feared she was unfitted. However, when she saw my
father was bent upon it, she sighed, and said she would try; and if she
did not do well, of course she might give it up. One good thing about
it was, she did not think men ever bought tea; and it was of men
particularly she was afraid. They had such sharp loud ways with
them; and did up accounts, and counted their change so quickly!
Now, if she might only sell comfits to children, she was sure she
could please them!

CHAPTER XV

A HAPPY RETURN

BEFORE I left Miss Matty at Cranford everything had been com-
fortably arranged for her. Even Mrs. Jamieson's approval of her
selling tea had been gained. That oracle had taken a few days to
consider whether by so doing Miss Matty would forfeit her right
to the privileges of society in Cranford. I think she had some little
idea of mortifying Lady Glenmire by the decision she gave at last;
which was to this effect: that whereas a married woman takes her
husband's rank by the strict laws of precedence, an unmarried
woman retains the station her father occupied. So Cranford was
allowed to visit Miss Matty; and, whether allowed or not, it
intended to visit Lady Glenmire.

But what was our surprise—our dismay—when we learnt that
Mr. and *Mrs. Hoggins* were returning on the following Tuesday.
Mrs. Hoggins! Had she absolutely dropped her title,* and so, in
a spirit of bravado, cut the aristocracy to become a Hoggins! She,
who might have been called Lady Glenmire to her dying day! Mrs.
Jamieson was pleased. She said it only convinced her of what she
had known from the first, that the creature had a low taste. But
'the creature' looked very happy on Sunday at church; nor did we
see it necessary to keep our veils down on that side of our bonnets
on which Mr. and Mrs. Hoggins sate, as Mrs. Jamieson did; there-
by missing all the smiling glory of his face, and all the becoming
blushes of hers. I am not sure if Martha and Jem looked more
radiant in the afternoon, when they too made their first appearance.
Mrs. Jamieson soothed the turbulence of her soul, by having the
blinds of her windows drawn down, as if for a funeral, on the day
when Mr. and Mrs. Hoggins received callers; and it was with some
difficulty that she was prevailed upon to continue the St. James's
Chronicle—so indignant was she with its having inserted the
announcement of the marriage.

Miss Matty's sale went off famously. She retained the furniture
of her sitting-room, and bedroom; the former of which she was to
occupy till Martha could meet with a lodger who might wish to
take it; and into this sitting-room and bedroom she had to cram
all sorts of things, which were (the auctioneer assured her) bought

in for her at the sale by an unknown friend. I always suspected Mrs.
Fitz-Adam of this; but she must have had an accessory, who knew
what articles were particularly regarded by Miss Matty on account
of their associations with her early days. The rest of the house
looked rather bare, to be sure; all except one tiny bedroom, of
which my father allowed me to purchase the furniture for my occasional use, in case of Miss Matty's illness.

I had expended my own small store in buying all manner of
comfits and lozenges, in order to tempt the little people whom Miss
Matty loved so much, to come about her. Tea in bright green
canisters—and comfits in tumblers—Miss Matty and I felt quite
proud as we looked round us on the evening before the shop was
to be opened. Martha had scoured the boarded floor to a white
cleanness, and it was adorned with a brilliant piece of oil-cloth on
which customers were to stand before the table-counter. The
wholesome smell of plaster and white-wash prevaded the apartment. A very small 'Matilda Jenkyns, licensed to sell tea', was
hidden under the lintel of the new door, and two boxes of tea with
cabalistic inscriptions all over them stood ready to disgorge their
contents into the canisters.

Miss Matty, as I ought to have mentioned before, had had some
scruples of conscience at selling tea when there was already Mr.
Johnson in the town, who included it among his numerous com-
modities; and, before she could quite reconcile herself to the
adoption of her new business, she had trotted down to his shop,
unknown to me, to tell him of the project that was entertained, and
to inquire if it was likely to injure his business. My father called
this idea of hers 'great nonsense,' and 'wondered how tradespeople
were to get on if there was to be a continual consulting of each
others' interests, which would put a stop to all competition
directly.' And, perhaps, it would not have done in Drumble, but
in Cranford it answered very well; for not only did Mr. Johnson
kindly put at rest all Miss Matty's scruples, and fear of injuring
his business, but I have reason to know, he repeatedly sent
customers to her, saying that the teas he kept were of a common
kind, but that Miss Jenkyns had all the choice sorts. And expensive
tea is a very favourite luxury with well-to-do tradespeople, and
rich farmers' wives, who turn up their noses at the·Congou and
Souchong prevalent at many tables of gentility, and will have
nothing else than Gunpowder and Pekoe* for themselves.

But to return to Miss Matty. It was really very pleasant to see how her unselfishness, and simple sense of justice, called out the same good qualities in others. She never seemed to think any one would impose upon her, because she should be so grieved to do it to them. I have heard her put a stop to the asseverations of the man who brought her coals, by quietly saying, 'I am sure you would be sorry to bring me wrong weight;' and if the coals were short measure that time, I don't believe they ever were again. People would have felt as much ashamed of presuming on her good faith as they would have done on that of a child. But my father says, 'such simplicity might be very well in Cranford, but would never do in the world.' And I fancy the world must be very bad, for with all my father's suspicion of every one with whom he has dealings, and in spite of all his many precautions, he lost upwards of a thousand pounds by roguery only last year.

I just stayed long enough to establish Miss Matty in her new mode of life, and to pack up the library, which the Rector had purchased. He had written a very kind letter to Miss Matty, saying, 'how glad he should be take a library so well selected as he knew that the late Mr. Jenkyns's must have been, at any valuation put upon them.' And when she agreed to this, with a touch of sorrowful gladness that they would go back to the Rectory, and be arranged on the accustomed walls once more, he sent word that he feared that he had not room for them all, and perhaps Miss Matty would kindly allow him to leave some volumes on her shelves. But Miss Matty said that she had her Bible, and Johnson's Dictionary, and should not have much time for reading, she was afraid. Still I retained a few books out of consideration for the Rector's kindness.

The money which he had paid, and that produced by the sale, was partly expended in the stock of tea, and part of it was invested against a rainy day; *i.e.* old age or illness. It was but a small sum, it is true; and it occasioned a few evasions of truth and white lies (all of which I think very wrong indeed—in theory—and would rather not put them in practice), for we knew Miss Matty would be perplexed as to her duty if she were aware of any little reserve-fund being made for her while the debts of the Bank remained unpaid. Moreover, she had never been told of the way in which her friends were contributing to pay the rent. I should have liked to tell her this; but the mystery of the affair gave a piquancy to their deed of kindness which the ladies were unwilling to give up; and at first

Martha had to shirk many a perplexed question as to her ways and means of living in such a house; but by and by Miss Matty's prudent uneasiness sank down into acquiescence with the existing arrangement.

I left Miss Matty with a good heart. Her sales of tea during the first two days had surpassed my most sanguine expectations. The whole country round seemed to be all out of tea at once. The only alteration I could have desired in Miss Matty's way of doing business was, that she should not have so plaintively entreated some of her customers not to buy green tea*—running it down as slow poison, sure to destroy the nerves, and produce all manner of evil. Their pertinacity in taking it, in spite of all her warnings, distressed her so much that I really thought she would relinquish the sale of it, and so lose half her custom; and I was driven to my wits' end for instances of longevity entirely attributable to a persevering use of green tea. But the final argument, which settled the question, was a happy reference of mine to the train oil* and tallow candles which the Esquimaux not only enjoy but digest. After that she acknowledged that 'one man's meat might be another man's poison,' and contented herself thenceforward with an occasional remonstrance, when she thought the purchaser was too young and innocent to be acquainted with the evil effects green tea produced on some constitutions; and an habitual sigh when people old enough to choose more wisely would prefer it.

I went over from Drumble once a quarter at least, to settle the accounts, and see after the necessary business letters. And, speaking of letters, I began to be very much ashamed of remembering my letter to the Aga Jenkyns, and very glad I had never named my writing to any one. I only hoped the letter was lost. No answer came. No sign was made.

About a year after Miss Matty set up shop, I received one of Martha's hieroglyphics, begging me to come to Cranford very soon. I was afraid that Miss Matty was ill, and went off that very afternoon, and took Martha by surprise when she saw me on opening the door. We went into the kitchen, as usual, to have our confidential conference; and then Martha told me she was expecting her confinement very soon—in a week or two; and she did not think Miss Matty was aware of it; and she wanted me to break the news to her, 'for indeed Miss!' continued Martha, crying hysterically, 'I'm afraid she won't approve of it; and I'm sure I don't know who is to take care of her as she should be taken care of, when I am laid up.'

I comforted Martha by telling her I would remain till she was about again; and only wished she had told me her reason for this sudden summons, as then I would have brought the requisite stock of clothes. But Martha was so tearful and tender-spirited, and unlike her usual self, that I said as little as possible about myself, and endeavoured rather to comfort Martha under all the probable and possible misfortunes which came crowding upon her imagination.

I then stole out of the house-door, and made my appearance, as if I were a customer in the shop, just to take Miss Matty by surprise, and gain an idea of how she looked in her new situation. It was warm May weather, so only the little half-door was closed; and Miss Matty sate behind her counter, knitting an elaborate pair of garters: elaborate they seemed to me, but the difficult stitch was no weight upon her mind, for she was singing in a low voice to herself as her needles went rapidly in and out. I call it singing, but I dare say a musician would not use that word to the tuneless yet sweet humming of the low worn voice. I found out from the words, far more than from the attempt at the tune, that it was the Old Hundredth* she was crooning to herself: but the quiet continuous sound told of content, and gave me a pleasant feeling, as I stood in the street just outside the door, quite in harmony with that soft May morning. I went in. At first she did not catch who it was, and stood up as if to serve me; but in another minute watchful pussy had clutched her knitting, which was dropped in her eager joy at seeing me. I found, after we had had a little conversation, that it was as Martha said, and that Miss Matty had no idea of the approaching household event. So I thought I would let things take their course, secure that when I went to her with the baby in my arms I should obtain that forgiveness for Martha which she was needlessly frightening herself into believing that Miss Matty would withhold, under some notion that the new claimant would require attentions from its mother that it would be faithless treason to Miss Matty to render.

But I was right. I think that must be an hereditary quality, for my father says he is scarcely ever wrong. One morning, within a week after I arrived, I went to call Miss Matty, with a little bundle of flannel in my arms. She was very much awe-struck when I showed her what it was, and asked for her spectacles off the dressing-table, and looked at it curiously, with a sort of tender wonder at its small perfection of parts. She could not banish the thought of the surprise all day, but went about on tip-toe, and was very silent. But she stole up to see Martha, and they both cried with joy; and she got into a complimentary speech to Jem, and did not know how to get out of it again, and was only extricated from her dilemma by the sound of the shop-bell, which was an equal relief to the shy, proud, honest Jem, who shook my hand so vigorously when I congratulated him that I think I feel the pain of it yet.

I had a busy life while Martha was laid up. I attended on Miss Matty, and prepared her meals; I cast up her accounts, and examined into the state of her cannisters and tumblers. I helped her too, occasionally, in the shop; and it gave me no small amusement, and sometimes a little uneasiness, to watch her ways there. If a little child came in to ask for an ounce of almond-comfits (and four of the large kind which Miss Matty sold weighed that much), she always added one more by 'way of make-weight' as she called it, although the scale was handsomely turned before; and when I remonstrated against this, her reply was, 'The little things like it so much!' There was no use in telling her that the fifth comfit weighed a quarter of an ounce, and made every sale into a loss to her pocket. So I remembered the green tea, and winged my shaft with a feather out of her own plumage. I told her how unwholesome almond-comfits were; and how ill excess in them might make the little children. This argument produced some effect; for, henceforward, instead of the fifth comfit, she always told them to hold out their tiny palms, into which she shook either peppermint or ginger lozenges, as a preventive to the dangers that might arise from the previous sale. Altogether the lozenge trade, conducted on these principles, did not promise to be remunerative; but I was happy to find she had made more than twenty pounds during the last year by her sales of tea; and, moreover, that now she was accustomed to it, she did not dislike the employment, which brought her into kindly intercourse with many of the people round about. If she gave them good weight they, in their turn, brought many a little country present to the 'old rector's daughter;'— a cream cheese, a few new-laid eggs, a little fresh ripe fruit, a bunch of flowers. The counter was quite loaded with these offerings sometimes, as she told me.

As for Cranford in general, it was going on much as usual. The Jamieson and Hoggins feud still raged, if a feud it could be called, when only one side cared much about it. Mr. and Mrs. Hoggins were very happy together; and, like most very happy people, quite ready to be friendly: indeed, Mrs. Hoggins was really desirous to be restored to Mrs. Jamieson's good graces, because of the former intimacy. But Mrs. Jamieson considered their very happiness an insult to the Glenmire family, to which she had still the honour to belong; and she doggedly refused and rejected every advance. Mr. Mulliner, like a faithful clansman, espoused his mistress's side with ardour. If he saw either Mr. or Mrs. Hoggins, he would cross the street, and appear absorbed in the contemplation of life in general, and his own path in particular, until he had passed them by. Miss Pole used to amuse herself with wondering what in the world Mrs. Jamieson would do, if either she or Mr. Mulliner, or any other member of her household, was taken ill; she could hardly have the face to call in Mr. Hoggins after the way she had behaved to them. Miss Pole grew quite impatient for some indisposition or accident to befal Mrs. Jamieson or her dependants, in order that Cranford might see how she would act under the perplexing circumstances.

Martha was beginning to go about again, and I had already fixed a limit, not very far distant, to my visit, when one afternoon, as I was sitting in the shop-parlour with Miss Matty—I remember the weather was colder now than it had been in May, three weeks before, and we had a fire, and kept the door fully closed—we saw a gentleman go slowly past the window, and then stand opposite to the door, as if looking out for the name which we had so carefully hidden. He took out a double eye-glass and peered about for some time before he could discover it. Then he came in. And, all on a sudden, it flashed across me that it was the Aga himself! For his clothes had an out-of-the-way foreign cut about them; and his face was deep brown as if tanned and re-tanned by the sun. His complexion contrasted oddly with his plentiful snow-white hair; his eyes were dark and piercing, and he had an odd way of contracting them, and puckering up his cheeks into innumerable wrinkles when he looked earnestly at objects. He did so to Miss Matty when he first came in. His glance had first caught and lingered a little upon me, but then turned, with the peculiar searching look I have described, to Miss Matty. She was a little fluttered and nervous, but no more so than she always was when any man came into her shop. She thought that he would probably have a note, or a sovereign at least, for which she would have to give change, which was an operation she very much disliked to perform. But the present customer stood opposite to her, without asking for anything, only looking fixedly at her as he drummed upon the table with his fingers, just for all the world as Miss Jenkyns used to do. Miss Matty was on the point of asking him what he wanted (as she told me afterwards), when he turned sharp to me: 'Is your name Mary Smith?'

'Yes!' said I.

All my doubts as to his identity were set at rest; and, I only wondered what he would say or do next, and how Miss Matty would stand the joyful shock of what he had to reveal. Apparently he was at a loss how to announce himself; for he looked round at last in search of something to buy, so as to gain time; and, as it happened, his eye caught on the almond-comfits, and he boldly asked for a pound of 'those things.' I doubt if Miss Matty had a whole pound in the shop; and besides the unusual magnitude of the order, she was distressed with the idea of the indigestion they would produce, taken in such unlimited quantities. She looked up to remonstrate. Something of tender relaxation in his face struck home to her heart. She said, 'It is—oh, sir! can you be Peter?' and trembled from head to foot. In a moment he was round the table, and had her in his arms, sobbing the tearless cries of old age. I brought her a glass of wine; for indeed her colour had changed so as to alarm me, and Mr. Peter, too. He kept saying, 'I have been too sudden for you, Matty,—I have, my little girl.'

I proposed that she should go at once up into the drawing-room and lie down on the sofa there; she looked wistfully at her brother, whose hand she had held tight, even when nearly fainting; but on his assuring her that he would not leave her, she allowed him to carry her upstairs.

I thought that the best I could do, was to run and put the kettle on the fire for early tea, and then to attend to the shop, leaving the brother and sister to exchange some of the many thousand things they must have to say. I had also to break the news to Martha, who received it with a burst of tears, which nearly infected me. She kept recovering herself to ask if I was sure it was indeed Miss Matty's brother; for I had mentioned that he had gray hair and she

had always heard that he was a very handsome young man. Something of the same kind perplexed Miss Matty at tea-time, when she
was installed in the great easy chair opposite to Mr. Jenkyns's, in
order to gaze her fill. She could hardly drink for looking at him;
and as for eating, that was out of the question.

'I suppose hot climates age people very quickly,' said she,
almost to herself. 'When you left Cranford you had not a gray hair
in your head.'

'But how many years ago is that?' said Mr. Peter, smiling.

'Ah! true! yes! I suppose you and I are getting old. But still
I did not think we were so very old! But white hair is very becoming
to you, Peter,' she continued—a little afraid lest she had hurt him
by revealing how his appearance had impressed her.

'I suppose I forgot dates too, Matty, for what do you think
I have brought for you from India? I have an India muslin gown*
and a pearl necklace for you somewhere or other in my chest
at Portsmouth.' He smiled as if amused at the idea of the incon-
gruity of his presents with the appearance of his sister; but this
did not strike her all at once, while the elegance of the articles did.
I could see that for a moment her imagination dwelt complacently
on the idea of herself thus attired; and instinctively she put her
hand up to her throat—that little delicate throat which (as Miss
Pole had told me) had been one of her youthful charms; but the
hand met the touch of folds of soft muslin, in which she was always
swathed up to her chin; and the sensation recalled a sense of the
unsuitableness of a pearl necklace to her age. She said, 'I'm afraid
I'm too old; but it was very kind of you to think of it. They are
just what I should have liked years ago—when I was young!'

'So I thought, my little Matty. I remembered your tastes; they
were so like my dear mother's.' At the mention of that name, the
brother and sister clasped each other's hands yet more fondly; and
although they were perfectly silent, I fancied they might have
something to say if they were unchecked by my presence, and I got
up to arrange my room for Mr. Peter's occupation that night,
intending myself to share Miss Matty's bed. But at my movement
he started up. 'I must go and settle about a room at the George.
My carpet-bag is there too.'

'No!' said Miss Matty in great distress—'you must not go;
please, dear Peter—pray, Mary—oh! you must not go!'

She was so much agitated that we both promised everything she

wished. Peter sat down again, and gave her his hand, which for
better security she held in both of hers, and I left the room to
accomplish my arrangements.

Long, long into the night, far, far into the morning, did Miss
Matty and I talk. She had much to tell me of her brother's life and
adventures which he had communicated to her, as they had sat
alone. She said that all was thoroughly clear to her; but I never
quite understood the whole story; and when in after days I lost
my awe of Mr. Peter enough to question him myself, he laughed
at my curiosity and told me stories that sounded so very much like
Baron Munchausen's* that I was sure he was making fun of me.
What I heard from Miss Matty was, that he had been a volunteer
at the siege of Rangoon;* had been taken prisoner by the Burmese;
had somehow obtained favour and eventual freedom from knowing how to bleed* the chief of the small tribe in some case of
dangerous illness; that on his release from years of captivity he
had had his letters returned from England with the ominous word
'Dead' marked upon them; and believing himself to be the last
of his race, he had settled down as an indigo planter; and had proposed to spend the remainder of his life in the country to whose
inhabitants and modes of life he had become habituated; when my
letter had reached him; and with the odd vehemence which
characterised him in age as it had done in youth, he had sold his
land and all his possessions to the first purchaser, and come home
to the poor old sister, who was more glad and rich than any
princess when she looked at him. She talked me to sleep at last,
and then I was awakened by a slight sound at the door, for which
she begged my pardon as she crept penitently into bed; but it
seems that when I could no longer confirm her belief that the long-
lost was really here—under the same roof—she had begun to fear
lest it was only a waking dream of hers; that there never had been
a Peter sitting by her all that blessed evening—but that the real
Peter lay dead far away beneath some wild sea-wave, or under
some strange Eastern tree. And so strong had this nervous feeling
of hers become that she was fain to get up and go and convince
herself that he was really there by listening through the door to
his even regular breathing —I don't like to call it snoring, but
I heard it myself through two closed doors—and by-and-by it
soothed Miss Matty to sleep.

I don't believe Mr. Peter came home from India as rich as

a Nabob; he even considered himself poor, but neither he nor Miss
Matty cared much about that. At any rate, he had enough to live
upon 'very genteelly' at Cranford; he and Miss Matty together.
And a day or two after his arrival, the shop was closed, while troops
of little urchins gleefully awaited the showers of comfits and
lozenges that came from time to time down upon their faces as
they stood up-gazing at Miss Matty's drawing-room windows.
Occasionally Miss Matty would say to them (half hidden behind
the curtains), 'My dear children, don't make yourselves ill;' but
a strong arm pulled her back, and a more rattling shower than ever
succeeded. A part of the tea was sent in presents to the Cranford
ladies; and some of it was distributed among the old people who
remembered Mr. Peter in the days of his frolicsome youth. The
India muslin gown was reserved for darling Flora Gordon (Miss
Jessie Brown's daughter). The Gordons had been on the Continent
for the last few years, but were now expected to return very soon;
and Miss Matty, in her sisterly pride, anticipated great delight
in the joy of showing them Mr. Peter. The pearl necklace disappeared; and about that time many handsome and useful presents made their appearance in the households of Miss Pole and
Mrs. Forrester; and some rare and delicate Indian ornaments
graced the drawing-rooms of Mrs. Jamieson and Mrs. Fitz-Adam.
I myself was not forgotten. Among other things, I had the hand-
somest bound and best edition of Dr. Johnson's works that could
be procured; and dear Miss Matty, with tears in her eyes, begged
me to consider it as a present from her sister as well as herself. In
short no one was forgotten; and what was more, every one, however insignificant, who had shown kindness to Miss Matty at any
time, was sure of Mr. Peter's cordial regard.

CHAPTER XVI

'PEACE TO CRANFORD'

IT was not surprising that Mr. Peter became such a favourite at
Cranford. The ladies vied with each other who should admire him
most; and no wonder; for their quiet lives were astonishingly
stirred up by the arrival from India—especially as the person

arrived told more wonderful stories than Sindbad the sailor;*and, as Miss Pole said, was quite as good as an Arabian night any evening. For my own part, I had vibrated all my life between Drumble and Cranford, and I thought it was quite possible that all Mr. Peter's stories might be true although wonderful; but when I found, that if we swallowed an anecdote of tolerable magnitude one week, we had the dose considerably increased the next, I began to have my doubts; especially as I noticed that when his sister was present the accounts of Indian life were comparatively tame; not that she knew more than we did, perhaps less. I noticed also that when the Rector came to call, Mr. Peter talked in a different way about the countries he had been in. But I don't think the ladies in Cranford would have considered him such a wonderful traveller if they had only heard him talk in the quiet way he did to him. They liked him the better, indeed, for being what they called 'so very Oriental.'

One day, at a select party in his honour, which Miss Pole gave, and from which, as Mrs. Jamieson honoured it with her presence, and had even offered to send Mr. Mulliner to wait, Mr. and Mrs. Hoggins and Mrs. Fitz-Adam were necessarily excluded—one day at Miss Pole's Mr. Peter said he was tired of sitting upright against the hard-backed uneasy chairs, and asked if he might not indulge himself in sitting cross-legged. Miss Pole's consent was eagerly given, and down he went with the utmost gravity. But when Miss Pole asked me, in an audible whisper, 'if he did not remind me of the Father of the Faithful?'* I could not help thinking of poor Simon Jones the lame tailor; and while Mrs. Jamieson slowly commented on the elegance and convenience of the attitude, I remembered how we had all followed that lady's lead in condemning Mr. Hoggins for vulgarity because he simply crossed his legs as he sate still on his chair. Many of Mr. Peter's ways of eating were a little strange amongst such ladies as Miss Pole, and Miss Matty, and Mrs. Jamieson, especially when I recollected the untasted green peas and two-pronged forks at poor Mr. Holbrook's dinner.

The mention of that gentleman's name recalls to my mind a conversation between Mr. Peter and Miss Matty one evening in the summer after he returned to Cranford. The day had been very hot, and Miss Matty had been much oppressed by the weather; in the heat of which her brother revelled. I remember that she had been unable to nurse Martha's baby; which had become her favourite

employment of late, and which was as much at home in her arms
as in its mother's, as long as it remained a light weight—portable
by one so fragile as Miss Matty. This day to which I refer, Miss
Matty had seemed more than usually feeble and languid, and only
revived when the sun went down, and her sofa was wheeled to the
open window, through which, although it looked into the principal
street of Cranford, the fragrant smell of the neighbouring hay-
fields came in every now and then, borne by the soft breezes that
stirred the dull air of the summer twilight, and then died away.
The silence of the sultry atmosphere was lost in the murmuring
noises which came in from many an open window and door; even
the children were abroad in the street, late as it was (between ten
and eleven), enjoying the game of play for which they had not had
spirits during the heat of the day. It was a source of satisfaction to
Miss Matty to see how few candles were lighted even in the apartments of those houses from which issued the greatest signs of life.
Mr. Peter, Miss Matty and I, had all been quiet, each with a separate
reverie, for some little time, when Mr. Peter broke in—

'Do you know, little Matty, I could have sworn you were on
the high road to matrimony when I left England that last time! If
anybody had told me you would have lived and died an old maid
then, I should have laughed in their faces.'

Miss Matty made no reply; and I tried in vain to think of some
subject which should effectually turn the conversation; but I was
very stupid; and before I spoke, he went on:

'It was Holbrook; that fine manly fellow who lived at Woodley,
that I used to think would carry off my little Matty. You would not
think it now, I dare say, Mary! but this sister of mine was once
a very pretty girl—at least I thought so; and so I've a notion did
poor Holbrook. What business had he to die before I came home
to thank him for all his kindness to a good-for-nothing cub as
I was? It was that that made me first think he cared for you; for
in all our fishing expeditions it was Matty, Matty, we talked about.
Poor Deborah! What a lecture she read me on having asked him
home to lunch one day, when she had seen the Arley carriage in the
town, and thought that my lady might call. Well, that's long years
ago; more than half a lifetime! and yet it seems like yesterday!
I don't know a fellow I should have liked better as a brother-in-
law. You must have played your cards badly, my little Matty,
somehow or another—wanted your brother to be a good go-between,

eh! little one?' said he, putting out his hand to take hold of hers as she lay on the sofa—'Why what's this? you're shivering and shaking, Matty, with that confounded open window. Shut it, Mary, this minute!'

I did so, and then stooped down to kiss Miss Matty, and see if she really were chilled. She caught at my hand, and gave it a hard squeeze—but unconsciously I think—for in a minute or two she spoke to us quite in her usual voice, and smiled our uneasiness away; although she patiently submitted to the prescriptions we enforced of a warmed bed, and a glass of weak negus. I was to leave Cranford the next day, and before I went I saw that all the effects of the open window had quite vanished. I had superintended most of the alterations necessary in the house and household during the latter weeks of my stay. The shop was once more a parlour; the empty resounding rooms again furnished up to the very garrets.

There had been some talk of establishing Martha and Jem in another house; but Miss Matty would not hear of this. Indeed I never saw her so much roused as when Miss Pole had assumed it to be the most desirable arrangement. As long as Martha would remain with Miss Matty, Miss Matty was only too thankful to have her about her; yes, and Jem too, who was a very pleasant man to have in the house, for she never saw him from week's end to week's end. And as for the probable children, if they would all turn out such little darlings as her god-daughter Matilda, she should not mind the number, if Martha didn't. Besides the next was to be called Deborah; a point which Miss Matty had reluctantly yielded to Martha's stubborn determination that her first-born was to be Matilda. So Miss Pole had to lower her colours, and even her voice, as she said to me that as Mr. and Mrs. Hearn were still to go on living in the same house with Miss Matty, we had certainly done a wise thing in hiring Martha's niece as an auxiliary.

I left Miss Matty and Mr. Peter most comfortable and contented; the only subject for regret to the tender heart of the one and the social friendly nature of the other being the unfortunate quarrel between Mrs. Jamieson and the plebeian Hogginses and their following. In joke I prophesied one day that this would only last until Mrs. Jamieson or Mr. Mulliner were ill, in which case they would only be too glad to be friends with Mr. Hoggins; but Miss Matty did not like my looking forward to anything like illness in so light a manner; and, before the year was out, all had come round in a far more satisfactory way.

I received two Cranford letters on one auspicious October morning. Both Miss Pole and Miss Matty wrote to ask me to come over and meet the Gordons, who had returned to England alive and well, with their two children, now almost grown up. Dear Jessie Brown had kept her old kind nature, although she had changed her name and station; and she wrote to say that she and Major Gordon expected to be in Cranford on the fourteenth, and she hoped and begged to be remembered to Mrs. Jamieson (named first, as became her honourable station), Miss Pole, and Miss Matty—could she ever forget their kindness to her poor father and sister?—Mrs. Forrester, Mr. Hoggins (and here again came in an allusion to kindness shown to the dead long ago), his new wife, who as such must allow Mrs. Gordon to desire to make her acquaintance, and who was moreover an old Scotch friend of her husband's. In short, every one was named, from the Rector—who had been appointed to Cranford in the interim between Captain Brown's death and Miss Jessie's marriage, and was now associated with the latter event—down to Miss Betty Barker; all were asked to the luncheon; all except Mrs. Fitz-Adam, who had come to live in Cranford since Miss Jessie Brown's days, and whom I found rather moping on account of the omission. People wondered at Miss Betty Barker's being included in the honourable list; but then, as Miss Pole said, we must remember the disregard of the genteel proprieties of life in which the poor captain had educated his girls; and for his sake we swallowed our pride; indeed Mrs. Jamieson rather took it as a compliment, as putting Miss Betty (formerly *her* maid)* on a level with 'those Hogginses.'

But when I arrived in Cranford, nothing was as yet ascertained of Mrs. Jamieson's own intentions; would the honourable lady go, or would she not? Mr. Peter declared that she should and she would; Miss Pole shook her head and desponded. But Mr. Peter was a man of resources. In the first place, he persuaded Miss Matty to write to Mrs. Gordon, and to tell her of Mrs. Fitz-Adam's existence, and to beg that one so kind, and cordial, and generous, might be included in the pleasant invitation. An answer came back by return of post, with a pretty little note for Mrs. Fitz-Adam, and a request that Miss Matty would deliver it herself and explain the previous omission. Mrs. Fitz-Adam was as pleased as could be, and thanked Miss Matty over and over again. Mr. Peter had said, 'Leave Mrs. Jamieson to me;' so we did; especially as we knew nothing that we could do to alter her determination if once formed.

I did not know, nor did Miss Matty, how things were going on, until Miss Pole asked me, just the day before Mrs. Gordon came, if I thought there was anything between Mr. Peter and Mrs. Jamieson in the matrimonial line, for that Mrs. Jamieson was really going to the lunch at the George. She had sent Mr. Mulliner down to desire that there might be a foot-stool put to the warmest seat in the room, as she meant to come, and knew that their chairs were very high. Miss Pole had picked this piece of news up, and from it she conjectured all sorts of things, and bemoaned yet more. 'If Peter should marry, what would become of poor dear Miss Matty! And Mrs. Jamieson, of all people!' Miss Pole seemed to think there were other ladies in Cranford who would have done more credit to his choice, and I think she must have had some one who was unmarried in her head, for she kept saying, 'It was so wanting in delicacy in a widow to think of such a thing.'

When I got back to Miss Matty's, I really did begin to think that Mr. Peter might be thinking of Mrs. Jamieson for a wife; and I was as unhappy as Miss Pole about it. He had the proof-sheet of a great placard in his hand. 'Signor Brunoni, Magician to the King of Delhi, the Rajah of Oude, and the Great Lama of Thibet, &c. &c.,' was going to 'perform in Cranford for one night only,'— the very next night; and Miss Matty, exultant, showed me a letter from the Gordons, promising to remain over this gaiety, which Miss Matty said was entirely Peter's doing. He had written to ask the Signor to come, and was to be at all the expenses of the affair. Tickets were to be sent gratis to as many as the room would hold. In short, Miss Matty was charmed with the plan, and said that to-morrow Cranford would remind her of the Preston Guild,* to which she had been in her youth—a luncheon at the George, with the dear Gordons, and the Signor in the Assembly-room in the evening. But I—I looked only at the fatal words:—

'*Under the patronage of the* HONOURABLE MRS. JAMIESON.'

She, then, was chosen to preside over this entertainment of Mr. Peter's; she was perhaps going to displace my dear Miss Matty in his heart, and make her life lonely once more! I could not look forward to the morrow with any pleasure; and every innocent anticipation of Miss Matty's only served to add to my annoyance.

So, angry and irritated, and exaggerating every little incident which could add to my irritation, I went on till we were all assembled in the great parlour at the George. Major and Mrs. Gordon and pretty Flora and Mr. Ludovic were all as bright and handsome and friendly as could be; but I could hardly attend to them for watching Mr. Peter, and I saw that Miss Pole was equally busy. I had never seen Mrs. Jamieson so roused and animated before; her face looked full of interest in what Mr. Peter was saying. I drew near to listen. My relief was great when I caught that his words were not words of love, but that, for all his grave face, he was at his old tricks. He was telling her of his travels in India, and describing the wonderful height of the Himalaya mountains: one touch after another added to their size; and each exceeded the former in absurdity; but Mrs. Jamieson really enjoyed all in perfect good faith. I suppose she required strong stimulants to excite her to come out of her apathy. Mr. Peter wound up his account by saying that, of course, at that altitude there were none of the animals to be found that existed in the lower regions; the game—everything was different. Firing one day at some flying creature, he was very much dismayed, when it fell, to find that he had shot a cherubim! Mr. Peter caught my eye at this moment, and gave me such a funny twinkle, that I felt sure he had no thoughts of Mrs. Jamieson as a wife, from that time. She looked uncomfortably amazed:

'But, Mr. Peter—shooting a cherubim—don't you think—I am afraid that was sacrilege!'

Mr. Peter composed his countenance in a moment, and appeared shocked at the idea! which, as he said truly enough, was now presented to him for the first time; but then Mrs. Jamieson must remember that he had been living for a long time among savages— all of whom were heathens—some of them, he was afraid, were downright Dissenters. Then, seeing Miss Matty draw near, he hastily changed the conversation, and after a little while, turning to me, he said, 'Don't be shocked, prim little Mary, at all my wonderful stories; I consider Mrs. Jamieson fair game, and besides, I am bent on propitiating her, and the first step towards it is keeping her well awake. I bribed her here by asking her to let me have her name as patroness for my poor conjuror this evening; and

I don't want to give her time enough to get up her rancour against the Hogginses, who are just coming in. I want everybody to be friends, for it harasses Matty so much to hear of these quarrels. I shall go at it again by-and-by, so you need not look shocked. I intend to enter the Assembly-room to-night with Mrs. Jamieson on one side, and my lady Mrs. Hoggins on the other. You see if I don't.'

Somehow or another he did; and fairly got them into conversation together. Major and Mrs. Gordon helped at the good work with their perfect ignorance of any existing coolness between any of the inhabitants of Cranford.

Ever since that day there has been the old friendly sociability in Cranford society; which I am thankful for, because of my dear Miss Matty's love of peace and kindliness. We all love Miss Matty, and I somehow think we are all of us better when she is near us.

THE END

APPENDICES

APPENDIX I

The Last Generation in England

This essay first appeared in America, in *Sartain's Union Magazine*, 5 (July 1849), and was not reprinted until 1972. Gaskell was asked for a contribution by Mary Howitt, who herself wrote for *Sartain's*, and whose husband William Howitt, editor of *Howitt's Journal*, published several of Gaskell's early works, notably her first story, 'Libbie Marsh's Three Eras'. Slight and inconsequentially told as it is, 'The Last Generation' includes much material from Gaskell's reminiscences of her childhood in Knutsford which she subsequently reworked in fictional form in various of the *Cranford* stories. The connections between this essay and *Cranford* have been indicated in the Explanatory Notes.

THE LAST GENERATION IN ENGLAND

BY THE AUTHOR OF 'MARY BARTON'

Communicated for Sartain's Magazine by Mary Howitt

I HAVE just taken up by chance an old number of the Edinburgh Review (April, 1848), in which it is said that Southey had proposed to himself to write a 'history of English domestic life.' I will not enlarge upon the infinite loss we have had in the non-fulfilment of this plan; every one must in some degree feel its extent who has read those charming glimpses of home scenes contained in the early volumes of the 'Doctor, &c.' This quarter of an hour's chance reading has created a wish in me to put upon record some of the details of country town life, either observed by myself, or handed down to me by older relations; for even in small towns, scarcely removed from villages, the phases of society are rapidly changing; and much will appear strange, which yet occurred only in the generation immediately proceding ours. I must however say before going on, that although I choose to disguise my own identity, and to conceal the name of the town to which I refer, every circumstance and occurrence which I shall relate is strictly and truthfully told without exaggeration. As for classing the details with which I am acquainted under any heads, that will be impossible from their heterogeneous nature; I must write them down as they arise in my memory.

The town in which I once resided is situated in a district inhabited by large landed proprietors of very old family. The daughters of these families, if unmarried, retired to live in——on their annuities, and gave the ton to the society there; stately ladies they were, remembering etiquette and precedence in every occurrence of life, and having their genealogy at their tongue's end. Then there were the widows of the cadets of these same families; also poor, and also proud, but I think more genial and less given to recounting their pedigrees than the former. Then came the professional men and their wives; who were more wealthy than the ladies I have named, but who always treated them with deference and respect, sometimes even amounting to obsequiousness; for was there not 'my brother, Sir John——,' and 'my uncle, Mr.——, of——,' to give employment and patronage to the doctor or the attorney? A grade lower came a class of single or widow ladies; and again it was possible, not to say probable, that their pecuniary circumstances were in better condition than those of the aristocratic dames, who nevertheless refused to meet in general society the *ci-devant* housekeepers, or widows of stewards, who had been employed by their fathers and brothers, they would occasionally condescend to ask 'Mason,' or 'that good Bentley,' to a private tea-drinking, at which I doubt not much gossip relating to former days at the hall would pass; but that was patronage; to associate with them at another person's house, would have been an acknowledgment of equality.

Below again came the shopkeepers, who dared to be original; who gave comfortable suppers after the very early dinners of that day, not checked by the honourable Mr. D—'s precedent of a seven o'clock tea on the most elegant and economical principles, and a supperless turn-out at nine. There were the usual respectable and disrespectable poor; and hanging on the outskirts of society were a set of young men, ready for mischief and brutality, and every now and then dropping off the pit's brink into crime. The habits of this class (about forty years ago) were much such as those of the Mohawks* a century before. They would stop ladies returning from the card-parties, which were the staple gaiety of the place, and who were only attended by a maidservant bearing a lantern, and whip them; literally whip them as you whip a little child; until administering such chastisement to a good, precise old lady of high family, 'my brother, the magistrate,' came forward and put down such proceedings with a high hand.

Certainly there was more individuality of character in those days than now; no one even in a little town of two thousand inhabitants would now be found to drive out with a carriage full of dogs; each dressed in the male or female fashion of the day, as the case might be; each dog provided with a pair of house-shoes, for which his carriage boots were changed on his return. No old lady would be so oblivious of 'Mrs. Grundy's'* existence now as to dare to invest her favourite cow, after its unlucky fall into a lime-pit, in flannel waistcoat and drawers,* in which the said cow paraded the streets of——to the day of its death.

There were many regulations which were strictly attended to in the society of——, and which probably checked more manifestations of eccentricity. Before a certain hour in the morning calls were never paid,* nor yet after a certain hour in the afternoon; the consequence was that everybody was out, calling on everybody at the same time, for it was *de rigueur* that morning calls should be returned within three days; and accordingly, making due allowance for our proportion of rain in England, every fine morning was given up to this employment. A quarter of an hour was the limit of a morning call.

Before the appointed hour of reception, I fancy the employment of many of the ladies was fitting up their laces and muslins (which, for the information of all those whom it may concern, were never ironed, but carefully stretched, and pinned, thread by thread, with most Lilliputian pieces, on a board covered with flannel). Most of these scions of quality had many pounds' worth of valuable laces descended to them from mothers and grandmothers, which must be 'got up' by no hands, as you may guess, but those of Fairly Fair. Indeed when muslin and net were a guinea a yard, this was not to be wondered at. The lace was washed in buttermilk, which gave rise to an odd little circumstance. One lady left her lace, basted up, in some not very sour buttermilk; and unluckily the cat lapped it up,* lace and all (one would have thought the lace would have choked her, but so it was); the lace was too valuable to be lost, so a small dose of tartar emetic was administered to the poor cat; the lace returned to view was carefully darned, and decked the good old lady's best cap for many a year after; and many a time did she tell the story, gracefully bridling up in a prim sort of way, and giving a little cough, as if preliminary to a rather improper story. The first sentence of it was always, I remember, 'I do not think you can guess where the lace on my cap has been;' dropping her voice, 'in pussy's inside, my dear!'

The dinner hour was three o'clock in all houses of any pretension to gentility; and a very late hour it was considered to be. Soon after four one or two inveterate card-players might be seen in calash and pattens, picking their way along the streets to the house where the party of the evening was to be held. As soon as they arrived and had unpacked themselves, an operation of a good half-hour's duration in the dining-parlour, they were ushered into the drawing-room, where, unless in the very height of summer, it was considered a delicate attention to have the shutters closed, the curtains drawn, and the candles lighted. The card-tables were set out, each with two new packs of cards, for which it was customary to pay by each person placing a shilling under one of the candlesticks.

The ladies settled down to Preference, and allowed of no interruption; even the tea-trays were placed on the middle of the cardtables, and tea hastily gulped down with a few remarks on the good or ill fortune of the evening. New arrivals were greeted with nods in the intervals of the game; and as people entered the room, they were pounced upon by the lady of the house to form another table.* Cards were a business in those days, not a recreation. Their very names were to be treated with reverence. Some one came to——from a place where flippancy was in fashion; he called the knave 'Jack,' and everybody looked grave, and voted him vulgar; but when he was overheard calling Preference—the decorous, highly-respectable game of Preference,—Pref.,* why, what course remained for us but to cut him, and cut him we did.

About half-past eight, notices of servants having arrived for their respective mistresses were given: the games were concluded, accounts settled, a few parting squibs and crackers let off at careless or unlucky partners, and the party separated. By ten o'clock all—— was in bed and asleep.* I have made no mention of gentlemen at these parties, because if ever there was an Amazonian town* in England it was——. Eleven widows of respectability at one time kept house there; besides spinsters innumerable. The doctor preferred his arm-chair and slippers to the forms of society, such as I have described, and so did the attorney, who was besides not insensible to the charms of a hot supper. Indeed, I suppose it was because of the small incomes of the more aristocratic portion of our little society not sufficing both for style and luxury, but it was a fact, that as gentility decreased good living increased in proportion. We had the honour and glory of looking at old plate and delicate china at the *comme il faut* tea-parties, but the slices of bread and butter were like wafers, and the sugar for coffee was rather of the brownest, still there was much gracious kindness among our *haute volée*.* In those times, good Mr. Rigmarole, carriage were carriages, and there were not the infinite variety of broughams, droskys, &c., &c., down to a wheelbarrow, which now make locomotion easy; nor yet were there cars and cabs and flys ready for hire in our little town. A post-chaise was the only conveyance besides *the* sedan-chair, of which more anon. So the widow of an earl's son, who possessed a proper old-fashioned coach and pair, would, on rainy nights, send her carriage, the only private carriage of——, round the town, picking up all the dowagers and invalids, and conveying them dry and safe to and from their evening engagement. The various other ladies who, in virtue of their relations holding manors and maintaining game-keepers, had frequent presents, during the season, of partridges, pheasants, &c., &c., would daintily carve off the tidbits, and putting them carefully into a hot basin, bid Betty or Molly cover it up quickly, and carry it to Mrs. or Miss So-and-so, whose appetite was but weakly and who required dainties to tempt it which she could not afford to purchase.*

These poorer ladies had also their parties in turn; they were too proud to accept invitations if they might not return them, although various and amusing were their innocent make-shifts and imitations. To give you only one instance, I remember a card-party at one of these good ladies' lodgings; where, when tea-time arrived, the ladies sitting on the sofa had to be displaced for a minute, in order that the tea-trays, (plates of cake, bread and butter, and all,) might be extricated from their concealment under the valances of the couch.*

You may imagine the subjects of the conversation amongst these ladies; cards, servants, relations, pedigrees, and last and best, much mutual interest about the poor of the town, to whom they were one and all kind and indefatigable benefactresses; cooking, sewing for, advising, doctoring, doing everything but educating them. One or two old ladies dwelt on the glories of former days; when——

boasted of two earl's daughters as residents. Though it must be sixty years since they died, there are traces of their characters yet lingering about the place. Proud, precise, and generous; bitter tories were they. Their sister had married a General,* more distinguished for a successful comedy, than for his mode of conducting the war in America; and, consequently, his sisters-in-law held the name of Washington in deep abhorrence. I can fancy the way in which they must have spoken of him, from the shudder of abomination with which their devoted admirers spoke years afterwards of 'that man Washington.' Lady Jane was moreover a benefactress to——. Before her day, the pavement of the foot-path was composed of loose round stones, placed so far apart that a delicate ankle might receive a severe wrench from slipping between; but she left a sum of money in her will to make and keep in repair a flag pavement, on condition that it should only be broad enough for one to walk abreast, in order 'to put a stop to the indecent custom coming into vogue, of ladies linking with gentlemen;' linking being the old-fashioned word for walking arm-in-arm. Lady Jane also left her sedan and money to pay the bearers for the use of the ladies of——, who were frequently like Adam and Eve in the weather-glass in consequence, the first arrival at a party having to commence the order of returning when the last lady was only just entering upon the gaieties of the evening.

The old ladies were living hoards of family tradition and old custom. One of them, a Shropshire woman, had been to school in London about the middle of the last century. The journey from Shropshire took her a week. At the school to which she was sent, besides fine work of innumerable descriptions, pastry, and the art of confectionary were taught to those whose parents desired it. The dancing-master gave his pupils instructions in the art of using a fan properly. Although an only child, she had never sat down in her parents' presence without leave until she was married; and spoke with infinite disgust of the modern familiarity with which children treated their parents. 'In my days,' said she, 'when we wrote to our fathers and mothers, we began "Honoured Sir," or "Honoured Madam," none of your "Dear Mamas," or "Dear Papas" would have been permitted; and we ruled off our margin before beginning our letters, instead of cramming writing into every corner of the paper; and when we ended our letters we asked our parents' blessing if we were writing to them; and if we wrote to a friend we were content to "remain your affectionate friend," instead of hunting up some new-fangled expression, such as "your attached, your loving," &c. Fanny, my dear! I got a letter to-day signed "Yours cordially," like a dram-shop! what will this world come to?' Then she would tell how a gentleman having asked her to dance in her youth, never thought of such familiarity as offering her his arm to conduct her to her place, but taking up the flap of his silk-lined coat, he placed it over his open palm, and on it the lady daintily rested the tips of her fingers. To be sure, my dear old lady once confessed to a story neither so pretty nor so proper, namely, that one of the amusements of her youth was 'measuring noses' with some gentlemen,—not an uncommon thing in those days; and, as lips lie below noses, such measurements frequently ended in kisses. At her house there was a little silver basket-strainer, and once remarking on this, she showed me a silver saucer pierced through with holes, and told me it was a relic of the times when tea was first introduced into England; after it had been infused and the beverage drank, the leaves were taken out of the teapot and placed on this strainer, and then eaten by those who liked with sugar and butter, 'and very good they were,' she added. Another relic which she possessed was an old receipt-book, dating back to the middle of the sixteenth century. Our grandmothers must have been strong-headed women, for there were numerous receipts for 'ladies' beverages,' &c., generally beginning with 'Take a gallon of brandy, or any other spirit.' The puddings, too, were no light matters: one receipt, which I copied for the curiosity of the thing, begins with, 'Take thirty eggs, two quarts of cream,' &c. These brobdignagian puddings she explained by saying that the afternoon meal, before the introduction of tea, generally consisted of cakes and cold puddings, together with a glass of what we should now call liqueur, but which was then denominated bitters.

The same old lady advocated strongly the manner in which marriages were formerly often brought about. A young man went up to London to study for the bar, to become a merchant, or what not, and arrived at middle age without having thought about matrimony; when, finding himself rich and desirous of being married, he would frequently write to some college friend, or to the clergyman of his native place, asking him to recommend a wife; whereupon the friend would send a list of suitable ladies; the bachelor would make his selection, and empower his friend to wait upon the parents of the chosen one, who accepted or refused without much consultation of their daughter's wishes; often the first intelligence she had of the affair was by being told by her mother to adorn herself in her best, as the gentleman her parents proposed for her husband was expected by the night-coach to supper.

'And very happy marriages they turned out, my dear—very,' my venerable informant would add, sighing. I always suspected that her own had been of this description.

APPENDIX II

The Cage at Cranford

This additional story about the characters in *Cranford* was published by Gaskell in Dickens's magazine *All The Year Round* (which he had started after closing down *Household Words*) in November 1863. The comedy is broader than in the earlier stories. Dorothy M. Collin suggests, in 'The Composition and Publication of Elizabeth Gaskell's *Cranford*', *Bulletin of the John Rylands Library*, 69 (Autumn 1986), 59–95, that its publication may have been related to Gaskell's negotiations over the *Cranford* copyright.

THE CAGE AT CRANFORD

HAVE I told you anything about my friends at Cranford since the year 1856? I think not.

You remember the Gordons, don't you? She that was Jessie Brown, who married her old love, Major Gordon: and from being poor became quite a rich lady: but for all that never forgot any of her old friends in Cranford.

Well! the Gordons were travelling abroad, for they were very fond of travelling; people who have had to spend part of their lives in a regiment always are, I think. They were now at Paris, in May, 1856, and were going to stop there, and in the neighbourhood all summer, but Mr. Ludovic was coming to England soon; so Mrs. Gordon wrote me word. I was glad she told me, for just then I was waiting to make a little present to Miss Pole, with whom I was staying; so I wrote to Mrs. Gordon, and asked her to choose me out something pretty and new and fashionable, that would be acceptable to Miss Pole. Miss Pole had just been talking a great deal about Mrs. FitzAdam's* caps being so unfashionable, which I suppose made me put in that word fashionable; but afterwards I wished I had sent to say my present was not to be too fashionable; for there *is* such a thing, I can assure you! The price of my present was not to be more than twenty shillings, but that is a very handsome sum if you put it in that way, though it may not sound so much if you only call it a sovereign.

Mrs. Gordon wrote back to me, pleased, as she always was, with doing anything for her old friends. She told me she had been out for a day's shopping before going into the country, and had got a cage* for herself of the newest and most elegant description, and had thought that she could not do better than get another like it as my present for Miss Pole, as cages were so much better made in Paris than anywhere else. I was rather dismayed when I read this letter, for, however pretty a cage might be, it was something for Miss Pole's own self, and not for her parrot, that I had intended to get. Here had I been finding ever so many reasons against her buying a new cap at Johnson's fashion-show, because I thought that the present which Mrs. Gordon was to choose for me in Paris might turn out to be an elegant and fashionable head-dress; a kind of cross between a turban and a cap, as I see those from Paris mostly are; and now I had to veer round, and advise her to go as fast as she could, and secure Mr. Johnson's cap before any other purchaser snatched it up. But Miss Pole was too sharp for me.

'Why, Mary,' said she, 'it was only yesterday you were running down that cap like anything. You said, you know, that lilac was too old a colour for me; and green too young; and that the mixture was very unbecoming.'

'Yes, I know,' said I; 'but I have thought better of it. I thought about it a great deal last night, and I think—I thought—they would neutralise each other; and the shadows of any colour are, you know—something I know—complementary colours.' I was not sure of my own meaning, but I had an idea in my head, though I could not express it. She took me up shortly.

'Child, you don't know what you are saying. And besides, I don't want compliments at my time of life. I lay awake, too, thinking of the cap. I only buy one ready-made once a year, and of course it's a matter for consideration; and I came to the conclusion that you were quite right.'

'Oh! dear Miss Pole! I was quite wrong; if you only knew—I did think it a very pretty cap—only——'

'Well! do just finish what you've got to say. You're almost as bad as Miss Matty in your way of talking, without being half as good as she is in other ways; though I'm very fond of you, Mary, I don't mean I am not; but you must see you're very off and on, and very muddle-headed. It's the truth, so you will not mind my saying so.'

It was just because it did seem like the truth at that time that I did mind her saying so; and, in despair, I thought I would tell her all.

'I did not mean what I said; I don't think lilac too old or green too young; and I think the mixture very becoming to you; and I think you will never get such a pretty cap again, at least in Cranford.' It was fully out, so far, at least.

'Then, Mary Smith, will you tell me what you did mean, by speaking as you did, and convincing me against my will, and giving me a bad night?'

'I meant—oh, Miss Pole, I meant to surprise you with a present from Paris; and I thought it would be a cap. Mrs. Gordon was to choose it, and Mr. Ludovic to bring it. I dare say it is in England now; only it's not a cap. And I did not want you to buy Johnson's cap, when I thought I was getting another for you.'

Miss Pole found this speech 'muddle-headed,' I have no doubt, though she did not say so, only making an odd noise of perplexity. I went on: 'I wrote to Mrs. Gordon, and asked her to get you a present—something new and pretty. I meant it to be a dress, but I suppose I did not say so; I thought it would be a cap, for Paris is so famous for caps, and it is——'

'You're a good girl, Mary' (I was past thirty, but did not object to being called a girl; and, indeed, I generally felt like a girl at Cranford, where everybody was so much older than I was), 'but when you want a thing, say what you want; it is the best way in general. And now I suppose Mrs. Gordon has bought something quite different?—a pair of shoes, I dare say, for people talk a deal of Paris shoes. Anyhow, I'm just as much obliged to you, Mary, my dear. Only you should not go and spend your money on me.'

'It was not much money; and it was not a pair of shoes. You'll let me go and get the cap, won't you? It was so pretty—somebody will be sure to snatch it up.'

'I don't like getting a cap that's sure to be unbecoming.'

'But it is not; it was not. I never saw you look so well in anything,' said I.

'Mary, Mary, remember who is the father of lies!'

'But he's not my father,' exclaimed I, in a hurry, for I saw Mrs. FitzAdam go down the street in the direction of Johnson's shop. 'I'll eat my words; they were all false; Only just let me run down and buy you that cap—that pretty cap.'

'Well! run off, child. I liked it myself till you put me out of taste with it.'

I brought it back in triumph from under Mrs. FitzAdam's very nose, as she was hanging in meditation over it; and the more we saw of it, the more we felt pleased with our purchase. We turned it on this side, and we turned it on that; and though we hurried it away into Miss Pole's bedroom at the sound of a double knock at the door, when we found it was only Miss Matty and Mr. Peter, Miss Pole could not resist the opportunity of displaying it, and said in a solemn way to Miss Matty:

'Can I speak to you for a few minutes in private?' And I knew feminine delicacy too well to explain what this grave prelude was to lead to; aware how immediately Miss Matty's anxious tremor would be allayed by the sight of the cap. I had to go on talking to Mr. Peter, however, when I would far rather have been in the bedroom, and heard the observations and comments.

We talked of the new cap all day; what gowns it would suit; whether a certain bow was not rather too coquettish for a woman of Miss Pole's age. 'No longer young,' as she called herself, after a little struggle with the words, though at sixty-five she need not have blushed as if she were telling a falsehood. But at last the cap was put away, and with a wrench we turned our thoughts from the subject. We had been silent for a little while, each at our work with a candle between us, when Miss Pole began:

'It was very kind of you, Mary, to think of giving me a present from Paris.'

'Oh, I was only too glad to be able to get you something! I hope you will like it, though it is not what I expected.'

'I am sure I shall like it. And a surprise is always so pleasant.'

'Yes; but I think Mrs. Gordon has made a very odd choice.'

'I wonder what it is. I don't like to ask, but there's a great deal in anticipation; I remember hearing dear Miss Jenkyns say that "anticipation was the soul of enjoyment," or something like that. Now there is no anticipation in a surprise; that's the worst of it.'

'Shall I tell you what it is?'

'Just as you like, my dear. If it is any pleasure to you, I am quite willing to hear.'

'Perhaps I had better not. It is something quite different to what I expected, and meant to have got; and I'm not sure if I like it as well.'

'Relieve your mind, if you like, Mary. In all disappointments sympathy is a great balm.'

'Well, then, it's something not for you; it's for Polly. It's a cage. Mrs. Gordon says they make such pretty ones in Paris.'

I could see that Miss Pole's first emotion was disappointment. But she was very fond of her cockatoo, and the thought of his smartness in his new habitation made her be reconciled in a moment; besides that she was really grateful to me for having planned a present for her.

'Polly! Well, yes; his old cage is very shabby; he is so continually pecking at it with his sharp bill. I dare say Mrs. Gordon noticed it when she called here last October. I shall always think of you, Mary, when I see him in it. Now we can have him in the drawing-room, for I dare say a French cage will be quite an ornament to the room.'

And so she talked on, till we worked ourselves up into high delight at the idea of Polly in his new abode, presentable in it even to the Honourable Mrs. Jamieson. The next morning Miss Pole said she had been dreaming of Polly with her new cap on his head, while she herself sat on a perch in the new cage and admired him. Then, as if ashamed of having revealed the fact of imagining 'such arrant nonsense' in her sleep, she passed on rapidly to the philosophy of dreams, quoting some book she had lately been reading, which was either too deep in itself, or too confused in her repetition for me to understand it. After breakfast, we had the cap out again; and that in its different aspects occupied us for an hour or so; and then, as it was a fine day, we turned into the garden, where Polly was hung on a nail outside the kitchen window. He clamoured and screamed at the sight of his mistress, who went to look for an almond for him. I examined his cage meanwhile, old discoloured wicker-work, clumsily made by a Cranford basket-maker. I took out Mrs. Gordon's letter; it was dated the fifteenth, and this was the twentieth, for I had kept it secret for two days in my pocket. Mr. Ludovic was on the point of setting out for England when she wrote.

'Poor Polly!' said I, as Miss Pole, returning, fed him with the almond.

'Ah! Polly does not know what a pretty cage he is going to have,' said she, talking to him as she would have done to a child; and then turning to me, she asked when I thought it would come? We reckoned up dates, and made out that it might arrive that very day. So she called to her little stupid servant-maiden Fanny, and bade her go out and buy a great brass-headed nail, very strong, strong enough to bear Polly and the new cage, and we all three weighed the cage in our hands, and on her return she was to come up into the drawing-room with the nail and a hammer.

Fanny was a long time, as she always was, over her errands; but as soon as she came back, we knocked the nail, with solemn earnestness, into the house-wall, just outside the drawing-room window; for, as Miss Pole observed, when I was not there she had no one to talk to, and as in summer-time she generally sat with the window open, she could combine two purposes, the giving air and sun to Polly-Cockatoo, and the having his agreeable companionship in her solitary hours.

'When it rains, my dear, or even in a very hot sun, I shall take the cage in. I would not have your pretty present spoilt for the world. It was very kind of you to think of it; I am quite come round to liking it better than any present of mere dress; and dear Mrs. Gordon has shown all her usual pretty observation in remembering my Polly-Cockatoo.'

'Polly-Cockatoo' was his grand name; I had only once or twice heard him spoken of by Miss Pole in this formal manner, except when she was speaking to the servants; then she always gave him his full designation, just as most people call their daughters Miss, in speaking of them to strangers or servants. But since Polly was to have a new cage, and all the way from Paris too, Miss Pole evidently thought it necessary to treat him with unusual respect.

We were obliged to go out to pay some calls; but we left strict orders with Fanny what to do if the cage arrived in our absence, as (we had calculated) it might. Miss Pole stood ready bonneted and shawled at the kitchen door, I behind her, and cook behind Fanny, each of us listening to the conversation of the other two.

'And Fanny, mind if it comes you coax Polly-Cockatoo nicely into it. He is very particular, and may be attached to his old cage, though it is so shabby. Remember, birds have their feelings as much as we have! Don't hurry him in making up his mind.'

'Please, ma'am, I think an almond would help him to get over his feelings,' said Fanny, dropping a curtsey at every speech, as she had been taught to do at her charity school.

'A very good idea, very. If I have my keys in my pocket I will give you an almond for him. I think he is sure to like the view up the street from the window; he likes seeing people, I think.'

'It's but a dull look-out into the garden; nowt but dumb flowers,' said cook, touched by this allusion to the cheerfulness of the street, as contrasted with the view from her own kitchen window.

'It's a very good look-out for busy people,' said Miss Pole, severely. And then, feeling she was likely to get the worst of it in an encounter with her old servant, she withdrew with meek dignity, being deaf to some sharp reply; and of course I, being bound to keep order, was deaf too. If the truth must be told, we rather hastened our steps, until we had banged the street-door behind us.

We called on Miss Matty, of course; and then on Mrs. Hoggins. It seemed as if ill-luck would have it that we went to the only two households of Cranford where there was the encumbrance of a man, and in both places the man was where he ought not to have been—namely, in his own house, and in the way. Miss Pole—out of civility to me, and because she really was full of the new cage for Polly, and because we all in Cranford relied on the sympathy of our neighbours in the veriest trifle that interested us—told Miss Matty, and Mr. Peter, and Mr. and Mrs. Hoggins; he was standing in the drawing-room, booted and spurred, and eating his hunk of bread-and-cheese in the very presence of his aristocratic wife, my lady that was. As Miss Pole said afterwards, if refinement was not to be found in Cranford, blessed as it was with so many scions of county families, she did not know where to meet with it. Bread-and-cheese in a drawing-room! Onions next.

But for all Mr. Hoggins's vulgarity, Miss Pole told him of the present she was about to receive.

'Only think! a new cage for Polly—Polly—Polly-Cockatoo, you know, Mr. Hoggins. You remember him, and the bite he gave me once because he wanted to be put back in his cage, pretty bird?'

'I only hope the new cage will be strong as well as pretty, for I must say a——' He caught a look from his wife, I think, for he stopped short. 'Well, we're old friends, Polly and I, and he put some practice in my way once. I shall be up the street this afternoon, and perhaps I shall step in and see this smart Parisian cage.'

'Do!' said Miss Pole, eagerly. 'Or, if you are in a hurry, look up at my drawing-room window; if the cage is come, it will be hanging out there, and Polly in it.'

We had passed the omnibus that met the train from London some time ago, so we were not surprised as we returned home to see Fanny half out of the window, and cook evidently either helping or hindering her. Then they both took their heads in; but there was no cage hanging up. We hastened up the steps.

Both Fanny and the cook met us in the passage.

'Please, ma'am,' said Fanny, 'there's no bottom to the cage, and Polly would fly away.'

'And there's no top,' exclaimed cook. 'He might get out at the top quite easy.'

'Let me see,' said Miss Pole, brushing past, thinking no doubt that her superior intelligence was all that was needed to set things to rights. On the ground lay a bundle, or a circle of hoops, neatly covered over with calico, no more like a cage for Polly-Cockatoo than I am like a cage. Cook took something up between her finger and thumb, and lifted the unsightly present from Paris. How I wish it had stayed there!—but foolish ambition has brought people to ruin before now; and my twenty shillings are gone, sure enough, and there must be some use or some ornament intended by the maker of the thing before us.

'Don't you think it's a mousetrap, ma'am?' asked Fanny, dropping her little curtsey.

For reply, the cook lifted up the machine, and showed how easily mice might run out; and Fanny shrank back abashed. Cook was evidently set against the new invention, and muttered about its being all of a piece with French things—French cooks, French plums (nasty dried-up things), French rolls (as had no substance in 'em).

Miss Pole's good manners, and desire of making the best of things in my presence, induced her to try and drown cook's mutterings.

'Indeed, I think it will make a very nice cage for Polly- Cockatoo. How pleased he will be to go from one hoop to another, just like a ladder, and with a board or two at the bottom, and nicely tied up at the top——'

Fanny was struck with a new idea.

'Please, ma'am, my sister-in-law has got an aunt as lives lady's maid with Sir John's daughter—Miss Arley. And they did say as she wore iron petticoats all made of hoops——'

'Nonsense, Fanny!' we all cried; for such a thing had not been heard of in all Drumble, let alone Cranford, and I was rather looked upon in the light of a fast young woman by all the laundresses of Cranford, because I had two corded petticoats.

'Go mind thy business, wench,' said cook, with the utmost contempt; 'I'll warrant we'll manage th' cage without thy help.'

'It is near dinner-time, Fanny, and the cloth not laid,' said Miss Pole, hoping the remark might cut two ways; but cook had no notion of going. She stood on the bottom step of the stairs, holding the Paris perplexity aloft in the air.

'It might do for a meat-safe,' said she. 'Cover it o'er wi' canvas, to keep th' flies out. It is a good framework, I reckon, anyhow!' She held her head on one side, like a connoisseur in meat-safes, as she was.

Miss Pole said, 'Are you sure Mrs. Gordon called it a cage, Mary? Because she is a woman of her word, and would not have called it so if it was not.'

'Look here; I have the letter in my pocket.'

' "I have wondered how I could best fulfil your commission for me to purchase something to the value of"—um, um, never mind—"fashionable and pretty for dear Miss Pole, and at length I have decided upon one of the new kind of 'cages' " (look here, Miss Pole; here is the word, C.A.G.E.), "which are made so much lighter and more elegant in Paris than in England. Indeed, I am not sure if they have ever reached you, for it is not a month since I saw the first of the kind in Paris.'

'Does she say anything about Polly-Cockatoo?' asked Miss Pole. 'That would settle the matter at once, as showing that she had him in her mind.'

'No—nothing.'

Just then Fanny came along the passage with the tray full of dinner-things in her hands. When she had put them down, she stood at the door of the dining-room taking a distant view of the article. 'Please, ma'am, it looks like a petticoat without any stuff in it; indeed it does, if I'm to be whipped for saying it.'

But she only drew down upon herself a fresh objurgation from the cook; and sorry and annoyed, I seized the opportunity of taking the thing out of cook's hand, and carrying it upstairs, for it was full time to get ready for dinner. But we had very little appetite for our meal, and kept constantly making suggestions, one to the other, as to the nature and purpose of this Paris 'cage,' but as constantly snubbing poor little Fanny's reiteration of 'Please, ma'am, I do believe it's a kind of petticoat—indeed I do.' At length Miss Pole turned upon her with almost as much vehemence as cook had done, only in choicer language.

'Don't be so silly, Fanny. Do you think ladies are like children, and must be put in go-carts,* or need wire guards like fires to surround them; or can get warmth out of bits of whalebone and steel; a likely thing indeed! Don't keep talking about what you don't understand.'

So our maiden was mute for the rest of the meal. After dinner we had Polly brought upstairs in her old cage, and I held out the new one, and we turned it about in every way. At length Miss Pole said:

'Put Polly-Cockatoo back, and shut him up in his cage. You hold this French thing up' (alas! that my present should be called a 'thing'), 'and I'll sew a bottom on to it. I'll lay a good deal, they've forgotten to sew in the bottom before sending it off.' So I held and she sewed; and then she held and I sewed, till it was all done. Just as we had put Polly-Cockatoo in, and were closing up the top with a pretty piece of old yellow ribbon—and, indeed, it was not a badlooking cage after all our trouble—Mr. Hoggins came up-stairs, having been seen by Fanny before he had time to knock at the door.

'Hallo!' said he, almost tumbling over us, as we were sitting on the floor at our work. 'What's this?'

'It's this pretty present for Polly-Cockatoo,' said Miss Pole, raising herself up with as much dignity as she could, 'that Mary has had sent from Paris for me.' Miss Pole was in great spirits now we had got Polly in; I can't say that I was.

Mr. Hoggins began to laugh in his boisterous vulgar way.

'For Polly—ha! ha! It's meant for you, Miss Pole—ha! ha! It's a new invention to hold your gowns out—ha! ha!'

'Mr. Hoggins! you may be a surgeon, and a very clever one, but nothing—not even your profession—gives you a right to be indecent.'

Miss Pole was thoroughly roused, and I trembled in my shoes. But Mr. Hoggins only laughed the more. Polly screamed in concert, but Miss Pole stood in stiff rigid propriety, very red in the face.

'I beg your pardon, Miss Pole, I am sure. But I am pretty certain I am right. It's no indecency that I can see; my wife and Mrs. FitzAdam take in a Paris fashion-book between 'em, and I can't help seeing the plates of fashions sometimes—ha! ha! ha! Look, Polly has got out of his queer prison—ha! ha! ha!'

Just then Mr. Peter came in; Miss Matty was so curious to know if the expected present had arrived. Mr. Hoggins took him by the arm, and pointed to the poor thing lying on the ground, but could not explain for laughing. Miss Pole said:

'Although I am not accustomed to give an explanation of my conduct to gentlemen, yet, being insulted in my own house by—by Mr. Hoggins, I must appeal to the brother of my old friend—my very oldest friend. Is this article a lady's petticoat, or a bird's cage?'

She held it up as she made this solemn inquiry. Mr. Hoggins seized the moment to leave the room, in shame, as I supposed, but, in reality, to fetch his wife's fashion-book; and, before I had completed the narration of the story of my unlucky commission, he returned, and, holding the fashion-plate open by the side of the extended article, demonstrated the identity of the two.

But Mr. Peter had always a smooth way of turning off anger, by either his fun or a compliment. 'It is a cage,' said he, bowing to Miss Pole; 'but it is a cage for an angel, instead of a bird! Come along, Hoggins, I want to speak to you!'

And, with an apology, he took the offending and victorious surgeon out of Miss Pole's presence. For a good while we said nothing; and we were now rather shy of little Fanny's superior wisdom when she brought up tea. But towards night our spirits revived, and we were quite ourselves again, when Miss Pole proposed that we should cut up the pieces of steel or whalebone—which, to do them justice, were very elastic—and make ourselves two good comfortable English calashes out of them with the aid of a piece of dyed silk which Miss Pole had by her.

EXPLANATORY NOTES

For these Notes the present editor is much indebted to the earlier annotation of
Elizabeth Porges Watson.

ABBREVIATIONS

HW   The text of the first, serial version of *Cranford* as it appeared in *House-
           hold Words*, 1851–3.

1853   The first volume edition of *Cranford*, Chapman and Hall, June
           1853.

Letters *The Letters of Mrs Gaskell*, ed. J. A. V. Chapple and Arthur Pollard
           (Manchester: Manchester University Press, 1966).

  1 *the Amazons*: in Greek mythology, a race of warrior women living without
men.

    the great neighbouring commercial town of Drumble: Cranford bears the same
relation to Drumble as Knutsford, Cheshire, the town Elizabeth Gaskell
was brought up in, does to Manchester.

  2 *Miss Tyler, of cleanly memory*: the aunt of the poet Robert Southey; he
lived as a child with her, and was 'never allowed to do anything in which
by possibility I might dirt myself' (*The Life and Correspondence of the late
Robert Southey*, ed. C. C. Southey, 6 vols., London: Longman, 1849, i. 34).
Southey's plan of writing a 'history of English domestic life' is mentioned
in the sketch 'The Last Generation in England' (see below, p. 161), which
anticipates *Cranford* in several ways.

    last gigot, the last tight and scanty petticoat: a gigot, or leg-of-mutton, sleeve,
is full at the shoulder and tight on the forearm: it went out of fashion in the
mid-1830s. In her *Life of Charlotte Brontë*, 2 vols. (London: Smith, Elder,
1857), i. 253 Gaskell mentions Emily Brontë's 'wearing them long after
they were "gone out" '. Between the early and the mid-nineteenth century
women's skirts steadily increased in dimensions, and were held out by ever
bulkier petticoats.

    red silk umbrella: cotton umbrellas replaced silk in the 1840s.

    the Tinwald Mount: a hill (now Tynwald) in the Isle of Man where its
traditional laws were read yearly.

  3 *the Spartans*: Sparta was a city-state of ancient Greece; its inhabitants were
famous for their culture of austere self-discipline.

    baby-house: doll's house.

    tea-bread: a spiced and sweetened bread.

pattens: wooden soles which strapped on, used to protect the shoes from wet and muddy streets.

'*elegant economy*': the phrase is used by Eliza Acton in her famous *Modern Cookery* (1845), which has a recipe for 'The Elegant Economist's Pudding'. It seems to have become a joke for Gaskell: see *Letters*, 174.

4 *not to be mentioned to ears polite*: Alexander Pope, *Moral Essays*, iv. 149–50: 'To rest, the Cushion and soft Dean invite, | Who never mentions Hell to ears polite.'

5 *Miss Betty Barker*: in *HW*, *1853*, and later editions this character is here named Miss Betsy Barker. All later references call her Miss Betty Barker; evidently the mistake was overlooked.

7 '*Preference*': a card game, originally for three players; it is clear that a four-handed version is played in Cranford. It evolved from the popular seventeenth-century game ombre, and is related to quadrille, whist, and bridge. Players bid both for trumps and for the number of tricks they will win.

'*Jock of Hazeldean*': a ballad by Sir Walter Scott about a melancholy lady who runs away with her lover, beginning 'Why weep ye by the tide, ladie? | Why weep ye by the tide?'

8 "*The Pickwick Papers*": a comic novel by Charles Dickens, published in parts between April 1836 and November 1837, and in one volume in 1837. As editor of *Household Words*, Dickens altered this and subsequent references (pp. 9, 22, 111) to his books when the *Cranford* papers appeared in the journal. They were restored when the novel was published separately. Hilary M. Schor has argued that *Cranford* is 'a female version of *Pickwick*: in its spirit of "benevolence", its focus on social gatherings and "swarrys," and its preoccupations with "bachelorhood"' (*Scheherazade in the Marketplace* (New York and Oxford; Oxford University Press, 1992), 113).

9 *the account of the 'swarry' which Sam Weller gave at Bath*: in *The Pickwick Papers*, ch. 38.

"*Rasselas*": a novel by Samuel Johnson (1709–84), published in 1759.

Mr. Boz: the pseudonym used by Dickens in *The Pickwick Papers*.

the "Rambler": a series of papers, almost all written by Johnson, published twice a week between 1750 and 1752.

10 *the bakehouse*: it was common for those too poor to have ovens to have their dinners cooked by the baker in the heat remaining from the morning's bread-baking.

11 *Brutus wig*: the 'Brutus' hairstyle was modelled on that in Roman statues; it was fashionable during the French Revolution and afterwards.

12 *the old song*: the refrain of a song called 'Country Commissions to my Cousin in Town' was 'a skein of white worsted from Flint's'. Flint's was a London haberdasher, near the Monument.

the Hebrew prophetess: Judges 4: 4: 'And Deborah, a prophetess, the wife of Lapidoth, she judged Israel at that time.'

a jockey-cap: a peaked cap.

the modern idea of women being equal to men: in the early 1850s Gaskell had become friends with several women interested in campaigning for women's rights and female suffrage. Much contemporary feminist debate centred around the problematic role of the middle-class spinster, although there was also a campaign for legal rights for married women. See Jenny Uglow, *Elizabeth Gaskell: A Habit of Stories* (London: Faber and Faber, 1993), 311–16.

the "plumed wars": *Othello*, III. iii: 'Farewell the plumed troop and the big wars | That make ambition virtue'.

13 *Brunonian*: an adjective rather pompously formed from Brown; 'the meals of the Browns'.

"the feast of reason and the flow of soul": Pope, *Imitations of Horace*, Satire I, Book II, 128: 'There St. John mingles with my friendly bowl | The Feast of Reason and the Flow of soul:'.

"the pure wells of English undefiled": Edmund Spenser, *The Faerie Queene*, IV. ii. 32: 'Dan *Chaucer*, well of English vndefyled, | On Fames eternall beadroll worthie to be fyled.'

14 *from Miss Matty*: this was changed from HW, which has 'Miss Pole'.

19 *where the weary are at rest*: Job 3: 17: 'There the wicked cease from troubling; and there the weary be at rest.'

'*Though He slay me, yet will I trust in Him.*': Job 13: 15: 'Though he slay me, yet will I trust in him: but I will maintain mine own ways before him.'

21 '*Galignani*': Galignani was a firm of publishers in Paris, which published English books and also, from 1814, an English newspaper, *Galignani's Messenger*, which circulated widely on the Continent among English speaking travellers. It carried English news and also details of the movements of the English abroad.

22 *Mr. Boz, you know—"Old Poz"*: see p. 9 n. Miss Jenkyns confuses the word 'Boz' with the name of an old-fashioned children's story, Maria Edgeworth's 'Old Poz', from *The Parent's Assistant* (1795). Lucy is a character in 'Old Poz'.

the 'Christmas Carol': Dickens's Christmas book for 1843. In *HW* the tale ends 'Poor, dear, Miss Jenkyns! Cranford is Man-less now.' Presumably this was dropped when the sketches were collected because of the incorporation of Mr Hoggins and Peter into the community.

24 *gave up the attempt*: this is a shortened version of *HW*, which had '. . . and the appelation of Matey was dropped by all, except a very old woman, who had been nurse in the rector's family, and had persevered, through many long years, in calling the Miss Jenkynses "the girls"; she said "Matey" to the day of her death.' *HW* has Matey for Matty throughout.

25 *'followers'*: admirers,

wine and dessert: at the end of the meal, after both savoury and sweet dishes had been finished, it was the custom to remove the tablecloth and serve nuts, fruit, and sweets with wine: this was called dessert.

26 *in summer-time*: in winter imported and dried fruits would be eaten.

a screen: hand-screens were used by ladies to shield their complexions from the heat of open fires and prevent unbecoming flushes.

27 *twenty or thirty years in India*: it was not uncommon for those who served the British empire in India to do so, since the journey home was long and expensive.

to get up, and leave him to his wine: the ladies would withdraw from the dining-room after the meal proper had ended, leaving the gentlemen at the table to drink more.

'Hand the vegetables round': Mary Smith tries to bring Martha and Miss Matty into line with current fashion. Until the 1840s it was the custom in middle- and upper-class houses for the food to be placed on the table and the host and guests to serve themselves and each other; it gradually became usual for the dishes to be handed round by servants. This was more awkward when, as in this case, the same person was doing both cooking and serving.

28 *Blue Beard*: a sinister bearded wife-murderer in the fairy-tale by Charles Perrault.

'Leave me, leave me to repose': Thomas Gray, 'The Descent of Odin: An Ode', 49–50: 'Unwilling I my lips unclose: | Leave me, leave me to repose.'

a yeoman . . . the 'pride which apes humility': a yeoman was a freeholder who was not a gentleman. The quotation is from S. T. Coleridge and Robert Southey, 'The Devil's Thoughts', 21–4: 'He saw a cottage with a double coach-house, | A cottage of gentility; | And the Devil did grin, for his darling sin | Is pride that apes humility.'

29 *the Rector, and Miss Jenkyns*: *HW* has 'Mrs Jenkyns'.

mousseline-de-laine: a kind of fine wool cloth.

Don Quixote-looking: the hero of Cervantes's novel, published in two parts in 1605 and 1615.

30 *sarsenet*: a thin soft silk.

32 *"Ye ever-verdant palaces"*: see Alan Mehennet, 'A Goethe Reference in *Cranford, Gaskell Society Journal*, 8 (1994), 111–12. The name of the German poet Johann Wolfgang von Göthe (1749–1832) is usually spelt Goethe in English. Gaskell writes Goëthe to indicate that Mr Holbrook pronounced it 'Go–eth' not 'Gerter'.

33 *his old-fashioned ways*: this is another allusion to the changes in dining habits. Mr Holbrook's housekeeper still serves a pudding before meat, but has given up serving the stock from the boiled joint first. Both these customs are old country habits, designed to save on expensive meat by taking the edge off the diners' hunger before serving it.

Aminé: a character in the *Arabian Nights* who has fed on human flesh.

34 *calashes*: folding hoods to cover ladies' caps for outdoor wear.

'The cedar spreads his dark-green layers of shade': Alfred Tennyson, 'The Gardener's Daughter', 115.

"Blackwood": *Blackwood's Edinburgh Magazine* was an important periodical, carrying fiction, poetry, articles, and reviews. A review of Tennyson's *Poems* appeared in the issue of April 1849, but it was not particularly favourable and Gaskell may have been thinking of some other, more enthusiastic review.

35 *Black as ash-buds in March*: Tennyson, 'The Gardener's Daughter', 28: 'more black than ashbuds in the front of March'.

'Locksley Hall': in this poem the hero expresses his anger that the woman he loved and who loved him married someone else for social reasons: 'Cursed be the social wants that sin against the strength of youth! | Cursed be the social lies that warp us from the living truth!'

that beautiful poem of Dr. Johnson's: it is difficult to identify such a poem, which is probably the point: Miss Matty is confused and vague.

37 *noticing*: mentioning.

capable: capacious.

39 *widows' caps*: these completely covered the hair, and had streamers or weepers hanging from them. The distinctive pointed front or 'widow's peak' does not seem to have become fashionable until the 1860s.

40 *Joint-Stock Bank*: a bank owned by a large number of shareholders, who were jointly liable for its debts, as opposed to a private bank owned by a small number of trading partners. Such banks were of recent origin, from 1844, and confined to the provinces. Until the introduction of limited-liability companies from 1856, the investment of capital was fraught with danger. Persons living, like the Jenkyns sisters, on the interest of a small amount of capital, faced a choice between safe but low-yielding government stocks and more attractive returns which might involve them in bankruptcy. However, in *Cranford* the issue of the danger of investing in

joint-stock banks is confused with that of Miss Jenkyns's folly in putting all their eggs in one basket; nor does it seem from pp. 142 and 145 that Miss Matty is pursued by the bank's creditors to the point of bankruptcy.

41 *blind man's holiday*: a proverbial term for night or twilight.

42 *Tonquin beans*: the seeds of *dipterix oderata*, a Brazilian tree, which were used as scent, either powdered or whole, and in snuff.

43 *July, 1774*: *HW* has 1764, which indicates that Gaskell tightened the chronology of the book in revising for volume publication.

full-bottomed wig, with gown, cassock and bands: clergymen and lawyers went on wearing wigs after the early eighteenth century, when they had ceased to be worn by others. A black cassock or long coat, with an academic gown over it and a collar of two starched white linen strips or bands, was the formal costume of an Anglican clergyman in the eighteenth century, but by the 1850s a clergyman would not wear a wig.

Paduasoy: a thick corded silk.

45 *dum memor ipse mei, dum spiritus hos regit artus*: Virgil, *Aeneid*, iv. 336. Gaskell omits the word *hos* from the line, which translates 'while I have memory of myself, and while breath still sways these limbs'.

Hebrew verses: it sounds as if the verses were in Latin not Hebrew; perhaps Mrs Jenkyns did not know the difference.

'Gentleman's Magazine': a periodical devoted to antiquarian and literary subject; *December, 1782*: *HW* has 1772. See above, p. 43 n.

M. T. Ciceronis Epistolæ: Marcus Tullius Cicero (103–43 BC), the famous Roman orator, left several collections of letters, including *Epistulae ad Familiares*, letters to his family.

46 *a vale of tears*: a conventional description of the world, deriving from the translation of Psalm 84, 6 'valley of Baca' as 'vale of tears' in Sternhold and Hopkins's metrical *Psalter* (1562).

Mrs. Chapone: Hester Chapone (1717–1801), friend of Samuel Johnson and author of a popular eighteenth-century advice book, *Letters on the Improvement of the Mind* (1773–4).

Mrs. Carter: Elizabeth Carter (1717–1806), also a friend of Johnson's, translated (rather than wrote) the works of the Greek philosopher Epictetus. Her *Letters* appeared in 1809 and 1817.

47 *the old original Post*: a type of letter paper, watermarked with a postman's horn.

Miss Edgeworth's 'Patronage': in Maria Edgeworth, *Patronage* (1814), i. 248, a character throws aside a letter sealed with a gummed wafer, saying ' "*I wonder how any man can have the impertinence to send me his spittle!*" '

47 *franks*: members of the House of Commons and the House of Lords could send letters carriage-free by writing their names on the envelope. This meant, since postage was expensive, that they were constantly requested for their signature by friends and relations.

crossing: letters were charged by weight, and so at the end of the first page some writers would swivel the page and begin writing over the top, at right angles. Third and even fourth pages were sometimes superimposed diagonally. For this method to be decipherable the handwriting must be exceptionally clear and evenly spaced.

Herod, Tetrarch of Idumea: Herod the Great (d. 4 BC), grandfather of the Herod who condemned Christ. He is said to have ordered the Massacre of the Innocents.

48 *the invasion of Buonaparte*: Napoleon Bonaparte, Emperor of the French, with whom Britain was at war from 1803 to 1814 and in 1815.

the fable of the Boy and the Wolf: the story of the boy who cried 'Wolf, wolf' falsely, and was therefore ignored and killed when a wolf really appeared.

the French entering Cranford: *HW* has at this point an additional sentence: 'My mother has sat by my bed half a night through, holding my hand and comforting me; and ...'.

the salt-mines: there are salt-mines at Northwich, about seven miles from Knutsford.

David and Goliath ... Apollyon and Abaddon: in I Samuel 17 the boy David kills the giant Goliath with a stone in a sling. The second reference is to Revelation 9: 11: 'And they had a king over them, which is the angel of the bottomless pit, whose name in the Hebrew tongue is Abaddon, but in the Greek tongue hath his name Apollyon.'

49 *'goody'*: sweets, tuck.

Bonus Bernardus non videt omnia: 'good Bernard doesn't see everything'; a proverb associated with St Bernard of Clairvaux.

a living awaited him, the gift of his godfather: his godfather would make him clergyman of a parish.

51 *The St. James's Chronicle*: this newspaper circulated widely among the upper class and especially the clergy.

as we have now: *HW* adds 'the very same advantage as we have'.

52 *shovel-hat*: a hat with a broad brim turned up on both sides, particularly associated with clergymen.

new rhododendron: newly introduced to Britain. Actually this is rather an anachronism of Gaskell's; it was in the 1850s that exotic rhododendrons were exciting the horticultural world, although species were known earlier.

53 *Queen Esther and King Ahasuerus*: Esther 8: 3: 'And Esther spake yet again before the king, and fell down at his feet, and besought him with tears to put away the mischief of Haman the Agagite...'.

56 *Dor*: this is the reading in *HW*, and perhaps is a pet form of Deborah. Later editions have 'Don', which makes even less sense.

the last time he ever saw his mother's face: *HW* has 'saw father or mother'.

57 *I am so near seeing her again*: *HW* adds 'But Miss Matey was not foolish, poor dear thing!'

India shawl: the cashmere shawls of north India, warm and often intricately patterned, were immensely prized in Europe from the late eighteenth century.

59 *some great war in India*: when Peter returns he says he has been a 'volunteer at the siege of Rangoon', which was during the First Burmese War (1824–6). For the disappearance of Gaskell's brother John Holland in India, which was swiftly followed by the death of their father, see Uglow, *Elizabeth Gaskell*, 53–5.

61 *Queen Adelaide*: Adelaide of Saxe-Coburg Meiningen (1792–1849) was the wife of William IV, king of England from 1830 to 1837.

a mark of respectability... as decided as setting up a gig: during the murder trial of John Thurtell in 1824 a witness was supposed to have been asked 'What do you mean by "respectable"?', and answered 'He always kept a gig.' This was thought exquisitely funny by the historian Thomas Carlyle (1795–1881), who told the anecdote in his review of Boswell's *Life of Johnson* in *Fraser's Magazine*, 5 (May 1832), 379–413, and who coined the words 'gigman' and 'gigmanity' to refer to a kind of contemptible respectability measured in material terms. The article on Boswell's biography argues that its detailed picture of social life gives a better idea of how men lived in the eighteenth century than conventional histories of the period, an idea which has some relevance to the conception of *Cranford*.

63 *that Marchioness of Exeter whose name was Molly Hoggins*: Sarah Hoggins (1773–97) was a Shropshire girl who was married in 1790 to Henry Cecil (1754–1804), at first under the false name of John Jones and bigamously, since he was not yet divorced from his first wife, and then, again, legally, in 1791. He inherited the Earldom of Exeter in 1793, and was created 1st Marquess of Exeter in 1801, after her death. The romantic story of the girl who does not realize she has married a rich nobleman is supposed to have been the germ of Tennyson's poem 'The Lord of Burleigh'. It is also referred to in the story 'Hannah' in Mary Russell Mitford's *Our Village: Sketches of Rural Character and Scenery* (London: Whittaker, 1824), a collection of sketches of a spinster's life in a quiet country village, which was widely read in the nineteenth century. See below, p. 92 n. for another possible link between *Our Village* and *Cranford*.

63 *bombazine*: a woollen or wool-and-cotton dress fabric, dull in surface. In the days when mourning was worn for the dead not only its colour but its texture was of significance. The gleam of jewellery and shine of silk were especially to be avoided, and a woman recently widowed was meant to wear the most sombre mourning possible.

the spinster daughter of an earl: General John Burgoyne (1722–92) was forced to surrender to the American revolutionary forces at the battle of Saratoga in 1777. He was the author of plays including *The Maid of the Oaks* (1774) and *The Heiress* (1786). He was married to Lady Charlotte Stanley (d. 1776), daughter of the 11th Earl of Derby, who had four spinster sisters, one of whom, Lady Jane, lived in Knutsford. See below, pp. 90 and 166, and for Lady Jane's will, Uglow, *Elizabeth Gaskell*, 48.

64 *Fitz-Roy ... Fitz-Clarence*: these surnames were given to the illegitimate children of English kings.

ci-devant: during the French Revolution titles were abolished, and nobles referred to as the *ci-devant* ('the former') *baron* or *comte*.

65 *Prince Albert's near the Queen's*: Albert (1819–61), husband of Queen Victoria, who ranked below her.

66 *seed-cake*: cake flavoured with caraway seeds.

Savoy biscuits: sponge fingers.

did not know Spadille from Manille: Spadille is the term for the Ace of Spades in the games of Ombre and Quadrille, and Manille is the second best trump.

67 *'basting'*: in ombre and its variants, including preference, a player who makes fewer tricks than he has bid is said to be 'beasted' or 'basted'. Here Gaskell is playing on that sense of the word and its literal meaning 'to thrash or beat' somebody.

a dish called 'little Cupids': this seems to have been a kind of trifle made with macaroons, soaked in alcohol and covered in cream.

68 *female mandarins*: china figurines with heads, fixed on wires, which nodded at a touch.

stopped the way ... Hogarth's pictures: when guests were leaving a party their carriages were summoned, and it was usual for servants to announce that 'So-and-so's carriage stops the way', indicating that its occupants should get in and drive off. A sedan chair with chairmen is depicted in the second print in the series 'The Rake's Progress' by William Hogarth (1697–1764).

70 *'county' families*: the landed gentry of the district.

71 *a Scotch baron ... Mrs. Forrester's Peerage*: after the Act of Union of 1707 Scottish peers had the right to send sixteen of their number, elected among themselves, to sit in the House of Lords. Lord Glenmire is not

one of these representative peers. Mrs Forrester has a copy of one of the reference books on the peerage, in which their titles, descent, dates, and so on, could be discovered.

72 *candle-lighters*: spills or rolls of paper.

74 *Scotch pebbles*: semi-precious stones, a kind of agate found in Scottish rivers.

stomacher: a bodice, pointed at the waist, and already old-fashioned at this date.

hair-powder: footmen in livery still wore powder at this date, though it had gone out of fashion for gentlemen.

75 *square Pembroke table*: a drop-leaf table.

76 *conversation-cards, puzzle-cards . . . tea-chests*: the game of conversation cards involved cards with questions on one side and answers on the other; the joke was the inconsequence or appropriateness with which they matched. Puzzle cards had riddles on. Painting boxes and furniture was a common pastime for early nineteenth-century ladies; the tea-chests would have had Chinese designs on.

'A Lord and No Lord': this may be a reference to the play *A King and No King* (1611) by Beaumont and Fletcher, or to a ballad of *c.*1726 about Lord Bolingbroke, 'A Lord and no Lord and Squire Squot'.

77 *the lumps of sugar*: not modern cubes but irregular chippings. Sugar was at this time sold in solid cone-shaped chunks, from which the customer had to chop portions.

78 *Ombre and Quadrille*: see p. 7 n.; *Basto . . . Spadille*: the ace of clubs and the ace of spades in ombre, and evidently also in the version of preference current in Cranford. These cards are the highest trumps and Miss Pole, playing basto, can force Lady Glenmire to play spadille.

the Catholic Emancipation Bill: the Catholic Emancipation Act (1829) removed most of the remaining disabilities of Roman Catholics, enabling them, for example, to hold public office and stand for parliament.

79 *too much for Job*: in the Bible Job is a type of patient endurance in adversity.

top-boots: a kind of boot with a top of different-coloured leather, coming high up the leg. They were worn with riding- dress, and surgeons had to ride around visiting their patients, which accounts for Mr Hoggins wearing them. There is other reference to Mr Hoggins's top-boots on p. 117.

80 *Francis Moore's astrological predictions*: Francis Moore (1657–1715?), a quack doctor and astrologer, published an annual almanac from 1699 which soon became famous for its prophecies. It continued as *Old Moore's Almanac*.

81 *from Michaelmas to Lady-day*: from 29 September to 25 March.

Wombwell's lions: George Wombwell (1778–1850) was the owner of a travelling circus.

83 *the menuets de la cour*: the minuet was an old-fashioned dance by the Victorian period. Here it serves to date Miss Matty, Miss Pole, and the Assembly Room itself.

clothes-maids: clothes-horses, folding wooden screens.

Thaddeus of Warsaw and the Hungarian Brothers, and Santo Sebastiani: *Thaddeus of Warsaw* (1803) is an historical novel by Jane Porter (1776–1850); *The Hungarian Brothers* (1807) and *Don Sebastian* (1809) are by her sister Anna Maria Porter (1780–1832). Miss Pole or Gaskell may have confused the last with Catherine Cuthbertson's *The Young Protector, or, Santo Sebastiano* (1806), which Gaskell recommended to a friend in October 1851 (see *Letters*, 167).

if she was not the rose... she had been near it: a reference to Francis Gladwin's translation of *The Gulistan of Sady* (1806): 'a worthless piece of clay, but having for a season associated with the rose, the virtue of my companion was communicated to me.'

84 *the Witch of Endor*. In I Samuel 28 Saul causes the witch to conjure up the ghost of the prophet Samuel.

'winding-sheets'... 'roly-poleys': a cluster of drips on the side of a candle, supposed to look like a folded sheet, was held to be an omen of death.

85 *Queen Charlotte*: Charlotte of Mecklenberg-Strelitz (1744–1818), wife of George III.

the Gunnings: two famous eighteenth-century beauties who made brilliant marriages: Maria Gunning (1733–60) married the Earl of Coventry, and her sister Elizabeth Gunning (1734–90) married successively the Dukes of Hamilton and Argyll.

chapeau bras: a three-cornered hat, worn at court, fashionable in the second half of the eighteenth century.

86 *the old tapestry story*: evidently one of the spooky stories which Gaskell delighted in, but untraced.

87 *National School boys*: the National Schools were started in 1816 to give poor children elementary education on Church of England principles.

in chinks of laughing: in fits of laughter.

90 *General Burgoyne... the French in Spain*: see above, p. 63 n. Mrs Forrester's father had fought during the American War of Independence (1775–81), and her husband during the Peninsular War (1803–14).

Madame de Staël... Mr Denon: the portrait by Gérard of Anne-Louise-Germaine de Staël (1766–1817), the famous French writer, in such a turban was engraved by J. Thomson and published in 1819. Baron Dominique-Vivant Denon (1747–1825) was an expert on Egypt.

92 *an old story . . . of a nightingale and a musician*: the story is referred to in John Ford's play *The Lover's Melancholy* (1628), which is quoted in 'The Cowslip Ball', in Mary Russell Mitford's *Our Village: Sketches of Rural Character and Scenery* (London: Whittaker, 1824).

a girl, who was left in charge of a great house: this is a folk-tale from the Scots borders; one version is James Hogg's terrifying *The Long Pack* (1817).

Italian irons: crimping irons, used in fine laundering for pleating frills.

93 *'where nae men should be'*: in the ballad 'Our goodman came home at e'en': 'Ben went our goodman, | And ben went he, | And there he spy'd a sturdy man | Where nae man shou'd be' (David Herd, *Ancient and Modern Scottish Songs*, 2 vols., Glasgow: Kerr & Richardson, 1869, ii. 172).

96 *Samson and Solomon rolled into one*: Samson was the strongest man in the world, Solomon the wisest, see Judges 16: 5 and 1 Kings 3: 12.

99 *cold-pigged*: doused with cold water.

Dr. Ferrier and Dr. Hibbert: Dr John Ferrier (1761–1815) was the author of 'An Essay towards a Theory of Apparitions', and Dr Samuel Hibbert (1782–1848) of *Sketches of the Philosophy of Apparitions* (1824).

103 *say 'Jack's up,' 'a fig for his heels,' and call Preference 'Pref'*: the first two expressions are probably, like the last, vulgarly used in playing card games.

Lord Chesterfield's Letters: a famous book of advice on gentlemanly behaviour, *Letters to his Son* (1774) by Philip Stanhope, 4th Earl of Chesterfield (1694–1773).

104 *bread-jelly*: evidently a dish of invalid cookery.

an heir-loom: in law, something handed down within a family which an individual is not empowered to bequeath to an outsider.

a Tyrrell . . . King Rufus . . . the little Princes in the Tower: Sir James Tyrrell (d. 1502), the murderer of the child Edward V and his brother Richard, Duke of York, came from a Suffolk family which claimed descent from Walter Tyrrell (*fl.* 1100), who is supposed to have murdered William II, known as William Rufus. In giving Mrs Forrester this lineage Gaskell is joking about the absurdity of pride in ancient descent from murderers.

105 *two pieces of red flannel, in the shape of a cross*: a charm against witchcraft.

107 *marry an archdeacon, and write his charges*: in the Church of England, an archdeacon is an official appointed by a bishop to supervise the clergy in an area of his diocese. One of his duties is to write 'charges' or instructions to the clergy in his district.

109 *pice*: the smallest coin in the Indian currency; there were 64 pice in a rupee.

that round shape: the circular *Madonna della Sedia* of Raphael is supposed to have been painted on the bottom of a cask.

110 *Aga Jenkyns*: Aga is a Turkish title which was used to honour Europeans in India.

a passage in Dickens . . . :The Pickwick Papers, ch. 32.

112 *Lalla Rookh*: a poem by Thomas Moore, published in 1817; it consists of four linked narrative poems of which the first is 'The Veiled Prophet of Khorassan'.

Rowland's Kalydor: a brand of face-cream or other cosmetic.

Peruvian bonds: bonds issued by the Peruvian government: presumably a risky but high-yielding investment. On joint-stock banks, see above, p. 40 n.

'surveying mankind from China to Peru': Samuel Johnson, 'The Vanity of Human Wishes': 'Let observation with extensive view | Survey mankind from China to Peru; | Remark each anxious toil, each eager strife, | And watch the busy scenes of crowded life'.

114 *'So near that . . . you might have counted to twelve,' said Miss Pole*: in *HW* 'said Miss Pole' and the inverted commas are omitted, so that the comment appears to come from the narrator.

'Tibbie Fowler': a Scots ballad. The reference is to the lines: 'Be a lassie e'er so black, | An she hae the name o'siller, | Set her up:' Tintock-tap, | The wind will blaw a man till her.'

115 *chloride of lime*: a disinfectant.

116 *merinoes and beavers*: kinds of thick warm woollen cloth.

117 *the Queen of Spain's legs*: this derives from an anecdote in chapter 1 of Madame d'Aulnoy's *Mémoires de la cour d'Espagne* (1690), in which a young Austrian princess, arriving in Spain as its future queen, is given a present of silk stockings. Her major-domo returns them furiously, announcing: 'the Queens of Spain have no legs.'

118 *welly stawed*: almost stopped.

121 *green tea*: unfermented tea, supposed to be bad for the nerves.

126 *the sister who had insisted upon investing their little property in that unlucky bank*: there is a possible parallel in Emily Brontë's insistence on investing her own and her sisters' capital in a railway company which failed; see Gaskell's *Life of Charlotte Brontë*, i. 340; ii. 124.

128 *the Rubric*: in the *Book of Common Prayer* the directions for the conduct of the service used to be printed in red.

129 *serve Mammon*: Matthew 6: 24: 'No man can serve two masters: for either he will hate the one, and love the other; or else he will hold to the one, and despise the other. Ye cannot serve God and mammon.'

130 'Ah! vous dirai-je, maman?': a song from Francis Sands, Les Amours de
    Silvano (c.1780).

131 muslin embroidery ... loyal wool-work: the reference here is to the changing
    fashion in needlework. In Miss Matty's youth embroidery or tambour-
    work on muslin, often in white on white, and eyelet-work, such as is now
    known as broderie anglaise, were fashionable and embellished women's
    clothing. A later fashion was for wool embroidery covering the whole
    ground, used for upholstery or framed. The designs were often of natura-
    listic flowers or birds, and skilled workers could imitate in stitches the
    brush-strokes of paintings. It was common to depict the Royal Family by
    such means: this was the 'loyal' part. Such worsted work had by the 1850s
    been superseded in its turn by 'Berlin wool-work' on canvas, in which the
    stitches were regular, and the design was counted off a chart.

    the use of the globes: the terrestrial and celestial globes were used to teach
    geography and astronomy respectively.

    the signs of the Zodiac ... Black Art: the signs of the Zodiac are used both in
    astronomy and in astrology; Miss Matty is ignorant of their astronomical
    application but associates them with sorcery.

    the chapter every morning ... a genealogical chapter: Miss Matty reads a
    chapter from the Bible every morning. A number of chapters in the Old
    Testament consist entirely of genealogies of people with unpronounceable
    names, for example Genesis 10 and 36, and 1 Chronicles 1–9.

133 quality: a person of the upper class.

141 sell what I can: this is the reading in HW, which is altered, perhaps by
    printing error, in 1853 to 'see what I can'.

143 dropped her title: it was the custom for widows of men of title who
    remarried commoners to retain the precedence and style they had acquired
    during their first marriage. Thus she could have married Mr Hoggins but
    continued to be addressed as Lady Glenmire and to precede Mrs Jamieson
    and Mrs Forrester out of the room.

144 Congou and Souchong ... Gunpowder and Pekoe: types of tea.

146 green tea: see above, p. 121 n.

    train oil: whale oil.

147 Old Hundredth: the tune associated with the metrical version of Psalm 100,
    'All People That On Earth Do Dwell', in Sternhold and Hopkins's Psalter
    (1562).

151 an India muslin gown: enough of the very fine printed Indian muslin to
    make a dress.

152 like Baron Munchausen's: fantastic and exaggerated. The hero of Rudolf
    Erich Raspe's Baron Munchausen's Narrative of his Marvellous Travels and

Campaign in Russia, first published in English in 1785, tells tall stories of his own experiences.

the siege of Rangoon: during the First Burmese War (1824–6).

how to bleed: taking blood from feverish patients was standard medical practice.

154 *Sindbad the Sailor*: a character in the *Arabian Nights*.

the Father of the Faithful: Abraham.

157 *formerly her maid*: this is inconsistent with p. 61 above, where Miss Betty's sister has been Mrs Jamieson's maid.

158 *the Preston Guild*: an association of merchants which has held a festival every five years since the fourteenth century.

Appendix I

162 *Mohawks*: in early eighteenth-century London, a gang of upper-class dare devils who attacked and terrorized people walking in the streets at night.

163 *Mrs. Grundy*: in the play *Speed the Plough* (1798) by Thomas Morton (1764?–1838) a character is always referring to what Mrs Grundy will think. 'Mrs Grundy' thus became a proverbial expression for public opinion, especially on matters of morality and etiquette.

flannel waistcoat and drawers: cf. p. 5, and of para. 2.

calls were never paid: cf. p. 2, para. 3.

the cat lapped it up: cf. pp. 78 (last para.)–79.

164 *another table*: cf. p. 7, lines 17–18.

calling Preference . . . Pref.: cf. p. 103, para. 2.

in bed and asleep: cf. p. 3, para. 3.

an Amazonian town: cf. p. 1, first sentence.

165 *haute volée*: literally, 'high flight', the high society of the place.

dainties . . . purchase: cf. p. 14, last para.

the valances of the couch: cf. p. 3, para. 2.

166 *a General*: see p. 63 n., p. 90.

Appendix II

169 *FitzAdam*: spelt Fitz-Adam in *Cranford*.

170 *a cage*: a crinoline petticoat, made of cotton with concentric strips of metal or whalebone applied in casings.

178 *go-carts*: baby-walkers.

ANTHONY TROLLOPE

An Autobiography

The American Senator

Barchester Towers

Can You Forgive Her?

The Claverings

Cousin Henry

Doctor Thorne

The Duke's Children

The Eustace Diamonds

Framley Parsonage

He Knew He Was Right

Lady Anna

The Last Chronicle of Barset

Orley Farm

Phineas Finn

Phineas Redux

The Prime Minister

Rachel Ray

The Small House at Allington

The Warden

The Way We Live Now

ÉMILE ZOLA

L'Assommoir
The Attack on the Mill
La Bête humaine
La Débâcle
Germinal
The Ladies' Paradise
The Masterpiece
Nana
Pot Luck
Thérèse Raquin

The Oxford World's Classics Website

www.worldsclassics.co.uk

- Information about new titles
- Explore the full range of Oxford World's Classics
- Links to other literary sites and the main OUP webpage
- Imaginative competitions, with bookish prizes
- Peruse the Oxford World's Classics Magazine
- Articles by editors
- Extracts from Introductions
- A forum for discussion and feedback on the series
- Special information for teachers and lecturers

www.worldsclassics.co.uk

American Literature

British and Irish Literature

Children's Literature

Classics and Ancient Literature

Colonial Literature

Eastern Literature

European Literature

History

Medieval Literature

Oxford English Drama

Poetry

Philosophy

Politics

Religion

The Oxford Shakespeare

A complete list of Oxford Paperbacks, including Oxford World's Classics, Oxford Shakespeare, Oxford Drama, and Oxford Paperback Reference, is available in the UK from the Academic Division Publicity Department, Oxford University Press, Great Clarendon Street, Oxford OX2 6DP.

In the USA, complete lists are available from the Paperbacks Marketing Manager, Oxford University Press, 198 Madison Avenue, New York, NY 10016.

Oxford Paperbacks are available from all good bookshops. In case of difficulty, customers in the UK can order direct from Oxford University Press Bookshop, Freepost, 116 High Street, Oxford OX1 4BR, enclosing full payment. Please add 10 per cent of published price for postage and packing.